NEW YORK REVIEW BOOKS
CLASSICS

UNFORGIVING YEARS

VICTOR SERGE (1890–1947) was born Victor Lvovich Kibalchich to Russian anti-Czarist exiles, impoverished intellectuals living "by chance" in Brussels. A precocious anarchist firebrand, young Victor was sentenced to five years in a French penitentiary in 1912. Expelled to Spain in 1917, he participated in an anarcho-syndicalist uprising before leaving for Russia to join the Revolution. Arriving in 1919, after a year in a French concentration camp, Serge joined the Bolsheviks and worked in the press services of the Communist International in Petrograd, Moscow, Berlin, and Vienna. An outspoken critic of Stalin, Serge was expelled from the Party and jailed in 1928. Released and living in Paris, he managed to publish three novels (*Men in Prison, Birth of Our Power,* and *Conquered City*) and a history of Year One of the Russian Revolution. Arrested again in Russia and deported to Central Asia in 1933, he was allowed to leave the USSR in 1936 after international protests by militants and prominent writers like André Gide and Romain Rolland. Using his insider's knowledge, Serge published a stream of impassioned, documented exposés of Stalin's Moscow show trials and machinations in Spain which went largely unheeded. Stateless, penniless, hounded by Stalinist agents, Serge lived in precarious exile in Brussels, Paris, Vichy France, and Mexico City, where he died in 1947. His classic *Memoirs of a Revolutionary* and his great last novels, *Unforgiving Years* and *The Case of Comrade Tulayev* (the latter also published by NYRB Classics), were written "for the desk drawer" and published posthumously.

RICHARD GREEMAN, the translator of four of Victor Serge's novels, has written a doctoral dissertation about Serge along with numerous other studies of his work and life. A collection of Greeman's political essays, *Dangerous Shortcuts and Vegetarian Sharks,* appeared in 2007. More of his work can be found at www.richardgreeman.org.

BY THE SAME AUTHOR

NONFICTION

Memoirs of a Revolutionary
The Year One of the Russian Revolution

FICTION

Birth of Our Power
The Case of Comrade Tulayev
Conquered City
The Long Dusk
Men In Prison
Midnight in the Century

UNFORGIVING YEARS

VICTOR SERGE

Translated and with an introduction by
RICHARD GREEMAN

NEW YORK REVIEW BOOKS

New York

THIS IS A NEW YORK REVIEW BOOK
PUBLISHED BY THE NEW YORK REVIEW OF BOOKS
1755 Broadway, New York, NY 10019
www.nyrb.com

Library of Congress Cataloging-in-Publication Data

Serge, Victor, 1890–1947.
  [Années sans pardon. English]
  Unforgiving years / by Victor Serge ; translated and with an introduction by
Richard Greeman.
      p. cm. — (New York Review Books classics)
  ISBN-13: 978-1-59017-247-6 (alk. paper)
  ISBN-10: 1-59017-247-7 (alk. paper)
  I. Greeman, Richard. II. Title.
PQ2637.E49A813 2007
843'.912—dc22

                                        2007029479

ISBN 978-1-59017-247-6

Printed in the United States of America on acid-free paper.
10 9 8 7 6 5 4 3 2 1

CONTENTS

TRANSLATOR'S INTRODUCTION

UNFORGIVING Years is at once the most bitter, the most cerebral, and the most poetic of Victor Serge's seven novels. It was first published in France in 1971—twenty-five years after the author's death—and has never appeared before in English. The setting is World War II, and Serge pushes realism to the modernist limits of hallucination, presenting extravagant, terrifying, poetic visions of men and women prowling the debris of a self-destructing mechanical civilization. In *Unforgiving Years* Serge captured the surreal "twenty-fifth hour" atmosphere of World War II in a way that, according to the critic of *Le Monde*, "prefigured and preceded post-war German literature."[1] The novel poses—without answering—the questions of political action, art, and human consciousness; or rather "answers" them through mysterious metaphors like "the central fire," "funeral masks [that] lie preserved in the earth," and the impudent, irresistible phallic power of a banana...

Unforgiving Years is divided into four sections, four symphonic "movements," each of which evokes its distinctive time and place through its tone and atmosphere. The first movement, entitled "The Secret Agent," expresses the sinister unreality of a Paris indifferent to the approach of war in a chill minor key. The second, "The Flame Beneath the Snow," is discordant, heroic, and secret like one of Shostakovich's wartime symphonies. It portrays a frozen, starving Leningrad during the "thousand days" of the Nazi siege. The third movement, "Brigitte, Lightning, Lilacs," imagines

1. Paul Morelle, "*Les Années sans pardon de Victor Serge*," *Le Monde*, September 3, 1971, p. 11.

the final days of Berlin under Allied bombardment in mode of Wagnerian Götterdämmerung, while the final movement, "Journey's End," is a tragic requiem set in the stark, volcanic Mexican selva where death and life repeat their endless cycle.

Against this panorama of planetary catastrophe, Serge poses his collective protagonist: a quartet of loyal, idealistic Soviet secret agents, veteran revolutionary fighters from the Russian Civil War period (1918–1921), now disillusioned. Operating in Europe where Hitler is triumphing and war looming, their faith in the Party is shaken by the Moscow Trials and the Stalinist totalitarian nightmare developing back in Russia. Caught in this "labyrinth of madness,"[2] torn between a heroic sense of duty and the recognition of a historical impasse, doomed to be eliminated by the GPU apparatus if the gestapo doesn't get them first, they search for an escape from a "world without possible escape" while trying to make sense of history and of their individual lives.

Serge's authentic depictions of character and place are based on his own experiences as a European Communist in the Russian Civil War and an agent of the Comintern in Central Europe. The locales of the novel—Paris, Leningrad, Berlin, Mexico—were the places where he had lived and struggled. Which leads us to the double question: Who was Victor Serge, and why do we still have to have to ask that question in 2007?[3]

A WRITER'S FATE

During his lifetime, Victor Serge (pseudonym for Victor Lvovich Kibalchich, 1890–1947) was admired (or persecuted) both as a

2. All quotations from Serge's *Memoirs of a Revolutionary* (Oxford University Press, 1963), an indispensable introduction to twentieth-century revolutionary politics for readers who don't want to die asphyxiated by political correctness. With close-up sketches of Lenin, Trotsky, and the Bolsheviks; anarchists like Voline, Bill Haywood, Emma Goldman; and poets like Alexander Blok, Andrei Biely, Sergei Esenin, and Vladimir Mayakovsky.

3. Jim Haberman first asked this question twenty years ago in the title of his *Voice Literary Supplement* article on Serge (November 30, 1984).

French novelist and as a Russian revolutionary.[4] As distinct from many Western writers and intellectuals—for example Koestler, Malraux, Orwell, or Silone—who flirted at one time or another with revolution, Serge-Kibalchich was a revolutionary and an internationalist more or less from birth, and remained one to his death. The stateless son of exiled anti-Czarist Russian parents wandering Europe "in search of good libraries and cheap lodgings," Serge was born "by chance" in Brussels, Belgium. Home-schooled by these penniless, idealistic exiled scholars, young Victor imbibed the heady traditions of the Russian revolutionary intelligentsia while growing up poor on the streets of Brussels. So poor that at age eleven he watched horrified as his younger brother died of malnutrition, while he survived on the pilfered sugar soaked in coffee that little Raoul refused to eat. "Throughout the rest of my life," he recalled, "it has been my fate always to find, in the undernourished urchins of the squares of Paris, Berlin, and Moscow, the same condemned faces of my tribe."

At age fourteen Victor is a militant Socialist Young Guard; at fifteen a member of a rebel gang of Brussels apprentices writing and printing their own radical anarchist sheet, *The Rebel* (pseudonym *Le Rétif*: "The Maverick"). At eighteen he is starving in Paris, devouring the contents of the Sainte-Geneviève library while editing *L'anarchie*, lecturing on anarcho-individualism, giving Russian lessons, and translating Russian novels to survive. At twenty-one Kibalchich is sentenced to five years in a French penitentiary for refusing to rat on his anarchist brothers from Brussels who, unwilling to be master or slaves, became bandits—the first ever to use automobiles to attack banks (the police had bikes). Known as "the tragic bandits," most of them die in shoot-outs with the Paris police or on the guillotine. Released from prison in 1917, Victor is expelled from France and comes back to life in Barcelona, where he works as a printer, participates in a revolutionary

---

4. The name Kibalchich is famous in Russia because of a distant relative of Victor's father, the Narodnik N. I. Kibalchich, who was hanged in 1881 for his participation in the assassination of Czar Alexander II.

workers' uprising, and publishes his first article signed "Victor Serge." The title: "The Fall of a Czar."

Soon Serge is attempting to reach revolutionary Russia via Paris, where he is arrested as a "Bolshevik suspect" and held for more than a year in a typhus-infested camp. There he meets his first Bolshevik. Exchanged for a French officer held by the Soviets, he arrives in St. Petersburg (then called Petrograd, later Leningrad) in January 1919. While crossing the frozen Baltic Sea in a prisoner's convoy he falls in love with Liuba Russakova, the daughter of a Russian anarchist. Victor joins in the defense of the frozen, starving Red capital, besieged by Western-backed White armies. Twenty-odd years later, he will draw on this experience of Petrograd under siege to portray the Germans' World War II siege of Leningrad in *Unforgiving Years*. Serge is drawn to the Bolsheviks' heroic energy and participates in the creation of the Communist International (or Comintern). Despite misgivings about Communist authoritarianism, he joins the Party in May 1919 and writes favorable impressions of the Bolsheviks for the anarchist press back in France.[5]

However, by the spring of 1921 Serge's loyalties were severely torn when anarchist and dissident Communist sailors rebel and seize the island fortress of Cronstadt. Serge joins in the thwarted attempt by the American anarchists Emma Goldman and Alexander Berkman to mediate the conflict and then looks on in horror as the rebels and Communist volunteers massacre each other in a fratricidal combat across the melting ice floes.[6] After withdrawing briefly from politics, Serge accepts a Comintern assignment in Germany where the promise of a new revolution poses a last hope for saving the isolated Russian Soviets from smothering under increasing bureaucratic dictatorship. In Berlin Serge serves

---

5. See Victor Serge, *Revolution in Danger: Writings on Russia 1919–1921*, translated by Ian Birchall (London: Redwords, 1997).

6. Cronstadt later became a bone of contention between Serge and Trotsky in exile.

the Comintern both as a journalist and under various identities, as a militant or "agent" (in those days there was little distinction). Under the signature "R. Albert," he sends reports to the world Communist press on galloping inflation, mass unemployment, mutilated veterans begging, strikes, and abortive putsches.[7] Serge's familiarity with the world of secret agents and with the desperation of the German people living through the post–World War I crisis helped him re-create the atmosphere of Berlin at the end of World War II in the third movement of *Unforgiving Years*.

In March 1923, the German Communists are outlawed after the fiasco of their aborted Hamburg putsch, and Serge flees with his family to Vienna, where he works with Georg Lukács and Antonio Gramsci. In 1925, despairing of a renewal of revolution in the West, Serge makes the insanely idealistic decision to return to Russia and join in the last-ditch fight against Stalin as a member of the doomed Left Opposition led by Trotsky. Expelled from the Party in 1928, Serge turns to writing. In quick succession he produces three novels and a well-documented history (*Year One of the Russian Revolution*) and publishes them in Paris—before being arrested and deported to the Ural in 1933.

In a letter smuggled out of Russia for publication in case of his arrest, Serge defends democratic freedom as essential to workers' socialism and describes Stalinist Communism as "totalitarian." After months of interrogation in the notorious Lubianka prison, Serge is deported to the Ural, where he is joined by his teenage son, the future artist Vlady.[8] Serge's wife, Liuba, driven insane by the Stalinist terror, is confined to an asylum. Protests by French trade unionists and writers (including André Gide and

---

7. I first identified "R. Albert" as Serge's pseudonym in the archives of *Inprokorr* on the basis of his style. These articles have been collected and translated by my colleague/comrade Ian Birchall in *Witness to the German Revolution* (London: Redwords, 1997).

8. I was privileged to know Vlady from 1963 until his death in 2005, and he is the source of much of my information about his father. His 2,000 square meters of murals, which reflect Serge's politics and aesthetics, can be seen in Mexico City and on the Web site www.vlady.org.

Romain Rolland) lead to the release of Serge and his family from Russia in 1936, but the two novels he completed in captivity ("the only ones I had time to polish") are seized by the GPU at the Polish border.[9]

From precarious exile in Brussels and Paris, Serge struggles to support his insane wife and their two children while turning out books and articles furiously to unmask the "big lie" of the Moscow show trials and Stalin's murderous intrigues in Republican Spain. His scrupulously documented, eyewitness books and articles are greeted with silence by complacent intellectuals hypnotized by the "anti-fascism" of Communist-manipulated popular fronts. Serge is obliged to fall back on his old prison trade of proof reader and find work in the print shops of socialist papers that boycott his articles. Meanwhile, Serge and his comrades are living in a "labyrinth of pure madness" as Stalin's agents kidnap and murder Trotsky's supporters in the middle of opulent, indifferent Paris. The first section of *Unforgiving Years*, "The Secret Agent," is Serge's eerie evocation of a doomed world capital paralyzed before the looming threat of war.

The character of Serge's secret agent, known as D or Sacha, reflects Serge's Comintern experiences and his personal acquaintance with three important agents who defected during the 1930s. Serge was distantly related to the Soviet diplomat Alexander Barmin, whose *One Who Survived* Serge ghostwrote in Paris. Serge thought of Barmin, who died in 1988 in Darien, Conneticut, as "a perfect Soviet young American." A more likely model for Sacha/D was Ignace Reiss, a secret agent whose break with Stalin's Communist Party was motivated by sincere revolutionary internationalism and Trotskyist sympathies. Reiss was murdered in Switzerland on his way to a clandestine meeting with Serge, having made two fatal mistakes which Serge will attribute to D: Reiss mailed his letter of resignation *before* making his break, and he confided his inten-

9. The manuscripts have never been recovered, despite diligent searches of recently opened Soviet archives. See Richard Greeman, "The Victor Serge Affair and the French Literary Left," *Revolutionary History* 5, no. 3 (Autumn 1994).

tions to a trusted colleague.[10] However, Sacha/D's character owes more to Walter Krivitsky, the former head of Stalin's Secret Service,[11] whom Serge had known in Russia and with whom he had several rather tense meetings in Paris after his defection. Krivitsky could never quite believe that Serge had been released from the Gulag as a result of a protest campaign, and suspected him of being a double agent. During one walk down a dark street, each time Krivitsky put his hand in his breast pocket, Serge did likewise. Yet according to a note in Serge's FBI file, Serge was "deeply affected" by Krivitsky's mysterious death in a Washington, D.C., hotel room in 1941 about which Serge wrote:

> There had been some fine moments in his life; he had been courageous and devoted. Now, in his soul, he was a defeated man. But these types of struggles are so out of proportion to any man's powers—and to one who was misled during the decisive years of his life, that it didn't astonish me. Rare are those who know how to resist demoralization in defeat.[12]

Perhaps Serge injected something of his own undefeated soul into his fictional Sacha/D, who does manage to resist demoralization.

By 1939, Serge is on the verge of recognition with *Midnight in the Century*, his novel about deported oppositionists, which was nominated for the Prix Goncourt. At the outbreak of the war, however, his books—considered subversive—are withdrawn from publication. When Paris falls to the Nazis, Serge, penniless, joins the exodus on foot—accompanied by his young companion Laurette Séjourné and his son, Vlady. They survive a Luftwaffe strafing attack on the Loire and eventually find refuge in a Marseille villa rented by Varian Fry of the American Refugee Committee and

---

10. See Alfred Rosmer, Victor Serge, and Maurice Wullens, *"L'Assassinat d'Ignace Reiss,"* *Les Humbles* (April 1938).

11. Walter Krivitsky, *In Stalin's Secret Service* (Harper, 1939).

12. FBI Archives, Serge's file for February 13, 1941. Courtesy of Susan Weissman.

shared with André Breton and his family. Aided by Dwight Macdonald in New York and by exiled comrades of the Spanish POUM
who had settled in Mexico, Serge and Vlady board the last refugee
ship out of Vichy France and end up in Mexico City in 1941, a year
after Trotsky's assassination. Here Serge finds himself politically
isolated—cut off from Europe by the war, unable to publish, boy-
cotted, slandered, and physically attacked by Stalinist agents.

Nonetheless, it is in Mexico that Serge completes his most enduring work: *Memoirs of a Revolutionary, The Case of Comrade
Tulayev*, and *Unforgiving Years*. He also studies psychoanalysis,
writes a manuscript on pre-Columbian archaeology, and medi-
tates on consciousness and death. He explores the meaning of the
war not only in theoretical and political "theses" but also in terms
of dreams, earthquakes, volcanoes, and luxuriant vegetation. All
these elements come together in *Unforgiving Years*, which he finishes in 1946. In 1947 his heart gives out, stressed by the altitude
and exhausted by years of prison and privation. Penniless and
stateless as usual, Serge is buried in a pauper's grave and registered
as a "Spanish Republican." His posthumously published *Memoirs
of a Revolutionary* concludes:

> Of this hard childhood, this troubled adolescence, all those
> terrible years, I regret nothing as far as I am myself con-
> cerned. Any regret I have is for energies wasted in struggles
> which were bound to be fruitless. These struggles have
> taught me that in any man the best and the worst live side
> by side and sometimes mingle—and that what is worst
> comes through the corruption of what is best.

A NOVEL'S FATE

Serge's books have had almost as hard a life as their author. At the
end of World War II, when Serge began *Unforgiving Years*, he was
painfully aware of writing "exclusively for the desk drawer"—in

which his classic *Memoirs* and *Comrade Tulayev* were already languishing, unpublished. Little hope in postwar Paris, what with paper shortages and the influence of the Communists in publishing. No luck either in New York and London, even with the help of Dwight Macdonald and George Orwell. With at least one Stalinist and two conservatives in every publishing house, "I'm at the point where I wonder if my very name will not be an obstacle to the novel's publication..."

Tulayev and the *Memoirs* have attained the status of "classics" (albeit neglected ones), but Serge the novelist has remained marginalized. Yet he is arguably as important a novelist in the political genre as Malraux, Orwell, Silone, Koestler, and Solzhenitsyn. On the one hand, Serge's radical socialist politics are seen by many critics as having no place in a novel, while on the other such is his prestige as a revolutionary participant-witness, often quoted by historians and political scientists, that his work as a literary artist is then deemed of secondary importance. For example, political scientist Susan Weissman's recent book on Serge takes the position that "writing, for Serge, was something to do only when one was unable to fight."[13] Another reason for Serge's neglect is his nationality, or lack thereof. As a stateless Russian who wrote in French, he apparently fell through the cracks between academic departments organized around national notions of "French" or "Russian" literature. As a result, there are as yet no Ph.D.s on Serge in any French university, nor will you find "Serge, Victor" listed in French biographical dictionaries and literary manuals.[14]

Serge wrote in French, but his work is best situated in the Russian intelligentsia traditions of his expatriate parents. He inherited his father's scientific culture (physics, geology, sociology)

---

13. *The Course Is Set on Hope* (Verso, 2002), p. 67. The book's main argument is that "Serge's critique of Stalinism was the core of his life and work" (p. 6), and she gives short shift to his anarchist years, his poetry, and his fiction, which she finds "useful" in understanding Stalinism.

14. Serge is better known in US and British French departments, with two Ph.D. theses: my own (Columbia) and Bill Marshall's (Oxford), later published as *Victor Serge: The Uses of Dissent* (New York: Berg, 1992).

while his literary culture came from his mother, who taught him to read in cheap editions of Shakespeare, Hugo, Dostoyevsky, and the Russian social realist Korolenko. His mother's family was apparently connected with Maxim Gorky.[15] By his concept of the writer's mission, Serge saw himself "in the line of the Russian writers."[16] And although he borrowed freely from cosmopolitan influences like Joyce, Dos Passos, and the French unanimists, Serge developed as a writer within the Soviet literary "renaissance" of the relatively liberated period of the free-market New Economic Policy (1921–1928). Indeed, during the 1920s, Serge was the principal transmission belt between the literary worlds of Soviet Russia and France. Through his translations and regular articles on Soviet culture in Henri Barbusse's *Clarté* he introduced French readers to the postrevolutionary poetry of Alexander Blok, Andrei Biely, Sergei Esenin, Osip Mandelstam, Boris Pasternak, and Vladimir Mayakovsky, as well as to fiction writers like Alexis Tolstoy, Babel, Zamiatine, Lebidinsky, Gladkov, Ivanov, Fedin, and Boris Pilniak—his colleagues in the Soviet Writers Union.[17]

By the mid-1930s, many of Serge's colleagues had been reduced to silence (suicide, censorship, the camps). "No PEN-club" wrote Serge in exile, "even those that held banquets for them, asked the least question about their cases. No literary review, to my knowledge, commented on their mysterious end." Only Serge—because he wrote in French and was saved from the Gulag by his reputation in France—managed to survive. Only Serge had the freedom to further develop the revolutionary innovations of Soviet literature and to submit the world of Stalinism to the critical lens of fiction in novels like *Midnight in the Century, The Case of Comrade Tulayev,* and *Unforgiving Years.* As one Russian scholar put it:

15. Serge went to see Gorky as soon as he arrived in Russia in 1919, but declined an offer to join the staff of Gorky's newspaper. During the civil war, Serge depended on Gorky's relationship with Lenin to intercede to save anarchist comrades from being shot by the Cheka.

16. Serge, *Memoirs.*

17. See Victor Serge, *Collected Writings on Literature and Revolution,* translated by Al Richardson (London: Francis Boutle, 2004).

"Although written in French, Serge's novels are perhaps the nearest we have to what Soviet literature of the 30s might have been..."[18]

Thus it was that *Unforgiving Years* remained unread for a quarter of a century. It was first published in Paris in 1971 by François Maspero, who was also bringing out many of Serge's political books as the anti-Stalinist New Left developed in the 1960s. Praised by the critics at the time—*Le Monde* ran "The Secret Agent" as a serial and hailed the novel as Serge's "political and literary testament"[19]—now, sixty years after it was written, it is appearing for the first time both in Russian and in English translation.

"A RATHER TERRIFYING NOVEL..."

Serge began writing *Unforgiving Years* (draft title *Sands, Snows, Fire*) in Mexico in September of 1945. In January 1946 he announced his subject in a letter to Daniel Guérin in newly liberated France: "in progress: a rather terrifying novel on the problems of consciousness in wartime which is giving me actual headaches." And indeed, *Unforgiving Years* is the most pessimistic, the most inward, and the most contemporary of Serge's novels. His 1946 characters are asking twenty-first-century questions: How to live if history no longer has a meaning? What remains of human consciousness if society has indeed entered a regressive era of ideological repression and technological pan-destruction?

These themes are developed through a series of encounters among a quartet of Comintern agents—dedicated, idealistic men and women coming to terms with the transformation of their struggle for historical progress into the nightmare of totalitarianism and mechanized war. The Moscow Trials—the physical and moral destruction of Lenin's 1917 "general staff"—have left them stunned. Yet they also understand the secret logic of these loyal

18. Neil Cornwell, review of *Midnight in the Century*, *Irish Slavonic Studies* 4 (1983).
19. Morelle, p. 12.

old Bolsheviks confessing to the most absurd "crimes." They feel bound by a similar iron loyalty to the Party. Unthinkable to break, much less betray, what with the capitalist democracies coddling Hitler in the hope he will rid them of Red Russia. Where to turn? Trotsky may well speak the truth, but his puny "Fourth International" is riddled with Stalinist agents. "I can believe in nothing now but power," thinks Secret Agent D. "Truth, stripped of its metaphysical poetry, exists only in the brain. Destroy a few brains, quickly done! Then, goodbye truth."

The death of consciousness is the central theme of *Unforgiving Years*, written at a time when Serge was meditating on his own death and on that of the planet—conceivable since the explosion of the "cosmic weapon" of August 4, 1945. "The most tragic thing about death, the most unacceptable thing for the mind," Serge noted on the passing of his friend Fritz Frankel, the cultivated psychoanalyst and fellow Comintern veteran, "is the total disappearance of a spiritual greatness built out of experience, intellectual elaboration, knowledge, and understanding, much of it incommunicable." Serge's *Notebooks* continues: "The individual strives to gain enduring existence for himself by the fame of his activity (accomplishing a mission, pursuit of glory; for the writer and the reformer, the need to capture the moment, to express, to teach; the need to be integrated with history)."[20]

Serge and the protagonists of *Unforgiving Years* live by this ethos, inherited from the nineteenth-century Russian revolutionary intelligentsia and derived from the Hegelian (and Marxist) sense of "Consciousness" as a historically active thing in itself, the world spirit unfolding through time, the self-discovery of human intelligence as the dialectic of freedom, the meaning of life. "The sense of history," noted Serge in 1944, "is the consciousness of participating in the collective destiny, in the constant becoming of men; it implies knowledge, tradition, choice, and finally, conviction, it demands a duty—for, once you know, once you have un-

20. Victor Serge, *Carnets* (Arles: Actes Sud, 1985).

derstood, once you have made out the possible courses, you must live (act) according to that understanding."[21] How then to live outside of history, outside of the purposeful struggle, outside (for agents like D and his comrades) the Party?

Each of Serge's four protagonists tries to answer (or to avoid) that question in his or her own way. In Paris we are first introduced to secret agent D (alias Sacha, alias Bruno Battisti) on the verge of his "resignation" from the Service; then we meet D's lover and protégée Nadine (alias Noémi); both are connected with a young French Communist, a painter named Alain. Finally, we catch a glimpse of Daria—D's female alter ego—a comrade he has known since she was a girl fighter in the Russian Civil War. The plot, which is not easy to follow, is woven through their various encounters in the four sections of the novel.

In the Paris segment, "The Secret Agent," D and Nadine prepare their escape to parts unknown while Daria refuses D's offer to escape with them, preferring to return to Russia and probable arrest. In the second section, "The Flame Beneath the Snow," Daria is called back to wartime intelligence service (after deportation to Kazakhstan) during the siege of Leningrad. In the final pages of the German section, "Brigitte, Lightning, Lilacs," Daria resurfaces (along with Alain) working for the Berlin underground as a nurse under the name of Erna. In the last, tragic movement, "Journey's End," Daria finds her way to Mexico where she is reunited with D and Nadine/Noémi.

Daria is thus the central protagonist connecting the four sections of the novel. She is also the only character in this oddly allusive novel for whom one can construct an actual "biography" (albeit only by patching together allusions and flashbacks scattered throughout the work). If D, the introspective male protagonist, poses the "problems of consciousness" in the first and final chapters of the novel, Daria is Serge's active protagonist. She is the hero who struggles against fate, the warrior who fights for humankind, the traveler whose quest takes her across war-torn Europe from Russia to Mexico. She is also the lover who experiences passion and grief, the great-souled woman who is granted a rich inner life. Daria's diary and soliloquies explore erotic love, grief, and anger from the viewpoint of a distinctly female sensibility. Indeed, Daria represents a creative breakthrough for Serge the novelist, whose previous novel, *The Long Dusk*, was marred by somewhat clichéd female characters generally seen from without and in relation to male heroes (as wife, daughter, sister, lover).

In the opening pages of *Unforgiving Years*, we *sense* rather than understand the futility of prewar Paris. Defeat is in the air. In this sinister atmosphere, everything seems base and livid: the light, the hotels, the streets, the people. Serge's secret agent is ambivalent about the doomed French capital, admiring the freedom, the easy way of life, even the decadence and cynicism. Crossing place de la République, D looks up at the statue: "a solitary, decorative, and disarmed Marianne, stood ignored by the streams of people following their interwoven pathways around her feet. And no one gives a shit! That's one way—perhaps the most genuine way—of being republicans..." This self-absorbed Paris will soon join Serge's other cities—Barcelona, Leningrad, Berlin—as "fissured icebergs drifting toward naked dawns" in the poem that adorns the title page of the second movement.

Readers of Serge's earlier novels will find it surprising that the characters in *Unforgiving Years* rarely discuss politics, and there are few precise allusions to contemporary events. Do we even know the date of the Paris episode? Has Franco already won the Spanish Civil War? Are we before or after the Munich crisis and the Stalin-Hitler Pact? Whereas Serge's earlier novels may be read as witness-chronicles of the revolutionary struggle, this last novel is denuded of political and historical specifics. If Serge seems to have deliberately set aside chronicle to concentrate on symbol and atmosphere, perhaps he is inviting us to read the novel on the level of meta-politics, of the history of consciousness seen from a geological, biological, evolutionary perspective.

Serge hints he is up to something of the kind through the device of a "book within a book." Deported to a tiny Kazakh village, Daria keeps a journal, which she knows will be studied by the local GPU chief. To protect herself and her comrades, she must censor out all compromising names, dates, places, and events, and this "literary constraint" obliges her to focus on her feelings and sense impressions as she relives the memories of her life with physical intensity. The lyrical texts that result express her intimate feelings of erotic love, anger, and grief recollected in tranquillity. The author then slyly pats himself on the back for this fictional tour de force when the cynical GPU chief compliments Daria on the literary qualities of her journal—before advising her to burn it. It is difficult not to see Daria's journal as a metaphor for Serge's self-censored novel. In his *Notebooks* he remarks: "Curious to observe that I am writing at the present moment, in this free country of America, like the Russians were writing around 1930 when the last spiritual freedom was expiring there."

As Serge was writing *Unforgiving Years*, the dark shadows of Hiroshima, Auschwitz, and the Gulag were casting question marks over the future of civilized human society, indeed of the planet itself. Serge, like Gramsci, responded to this radically new historical situation with "pessimism of the intellect, optimism of the will." Serge's willed optimism came to the fore in an argument with Dwight Macdonald, whose belief in socialism had been shaken by the threat of the A-bomb: "It is possible," Serge admits, "that it all must end via atomic destruction of this terrestrial sphere, as Anatole France foresaw in the final chapter of *Penguin Island*. But this is not at all a certainty. And it seems less probable, rationally, than the proper organization of a society in which atomic energy will contribute to ending the last slavery, that of hard work. As long as this possibility-probability continues, isn't it our job to push in that direction?" The same optimism has inspired generations of readers of his *Memoirs of a Revolutionary*, where he sums up:

I have undergone a little over ten years of various forms of captivity, agitated in seven countries, and written twenty books. I own nothing. On several occasions a press with a vast circulation has hurled filth at me because I spoke the truth. Behind us lies a victorious revolution gone astray, several abortive attempts at revolution, and massacres in so great number as to inspire a certain dizziness. And to think that it is not over yet. Let me be done with this digression. Those were the only roads open to us. I have more confidence in humankind and in the future than ever before.

However, Serge's pessimism of the intellect came out in his private journals, letters, and fiction. In a 1946 letter, he opines that the world "after a period of dark struggles and anxieties, may succumb to a terrible conflagration" and compares the "shock" of modern weapons of mass destruction to "cosmic phenomena." "Today, all explosives have attained such power that their effect is no longer on a human scale." In his *Notebooks*, he reflected that "Trotsky correctly foresaw that we might enter a phase of uninterrupted, permanent warfare if humanity does not achieve a social (and psychological) reorganization, the means to which appear, realistically, pitifully weak." There was not much time left either: "For technological reasons, decisions [about society's future] can not be put off indefinitely." Yet such social changes depend on intellectual clarity, on critical thinking, which Serge increasingly saw both as impotent in the face of mass social conditioning and as threatened with outright extinction: "Destroy a few brains, quickly done! " And if they are the few thousand brains that understand Einstein, Freud, or Marx?

These pessimistic visions inspired Serge's "terrifying" novel about "the problem of consciousness in time of war." The imagery of the chapter titles and the poems placed at their heads evokes planetary catastrophe ("the central fire," "lightning," "smoking rains," "naked dawns"). A Russian soldier wonders that "they haven't invented war toys to split open the planet yet." A German soldier reflects: "There are no warriors anymore: only poor bastards facing exploding volcanoes. The cosmos has gone berserk.... He was... alive, living under the cold light of a huge, dark, sulfurous star: the sun of destruction." The Berlin section opens in an underground shelter where the thunder of bombs sends "huge waves through the earth." "Brigitte, Lightning, Lilacs" is full of images of dreams, geological eruptions, and buried civilizations like Pompeii and Atlantis. Serge had to invent a neologism, "pan-destruction," to express the scale of the devastation.

Nowhere was the destruction so total as in Germany. Serge fearlessly depicted Germany's defeat from the point of view of ordinary middle-class Germans seen principally as victims. This viewpoint is only now being legitimized sixty years later with a re-examination of the unparalleled destruction of German civilian cities by the Anglo-American bomber command and the publication in Germany of World War II memoirs and diaries. Serge satirized the cliché of German collective responsibility in the figure of an arrogant, overfed American journalist who drives up to a bombed-out Berlin neighborhood in a jeep and asks the uncomprehending survivors—whom Serge compares to "inhabitants of Chicago's slums"—if they feel guilty.

As distinct from the rich and powerful Germans, whose country estates were largely untouched by the war, Serge portrays ordinary Germans as more or less good people who patriotically believed what the government and the media told them (like many Americans today). As he explained in a letter to Macdonald: "People are caught up in the gears [of the social machine...] Nothing mysterious about it." For Serge, neither the German soldiers killed and mutilated at the front nor their starved, bombed-out, and mass-raped mothers and sisters were "responsible" for the war. Indeed, the Nazis and industrialists who started it needed first to arrest thousands of German trade unionists, socialists, Communists, and conscious-stricken Christians like Brigitte's fiancé. These were the Germans he had lived with and written about twenty years earlier in *Witness to the German Revolution*.

Serge symbolized German innocence in the angelic figure of Brigitte, a gentle, cultivated, middle-class girl, orphaned by the war and driven to Ophelia-like madness by the death at the front of her beloved fiancé (shot by the SS for questioning the war). A midnight bombing raid draws the ecstatic girl to the roof. We see her frail figure silhouetted against the constellations and the "lightning" of explosions: "The whiteness wove a tissue of radiance around the city, around the entire planet: the planet in her wedding dress. A bright cupola rose high above Brigitte's rapt, thrown-back head." When she is found mysteriously strangled, a neighbor picks some lilacs that have miraculously survived the bombings—testimony to "the power of simple vegetative life"—and lays them next to her fragile body. Alain, the artist, sees her as "Botticellian," and her image returns in his delirious meditations on the nature of beauty and art which conclude the German section.

The final movement, "Journey's End," returns to the question "What to live for?" by posing another: "What will endure, when it all blows up, melts down, or grinds to a sulfurous halt?" It opens with an invocation:

And let fall the smoking rains
over the cerebral forest!
So many funeral masks
lie preserved in the earth
that nothing yet is lost.[22]

Serge's "funeral masks" suggest that enduring works of art can preserve the content of human consciousness from oblivion—even after the destruction of whole civilizations. They may point

---

22. The image of "smoking rains" probably came to Serge after witnessing the birth of the volcano Parcutin in 1943 under a rain of hot cinders which ignited and buried the surrounding dwellings and forest. They also refer, of course, to explosives raining from the sky which destroy the "cerebral forest" of human consciousness—seen as if rooted in the earth like a great living brain. Yet the poet's attitude to this destruction is one of consent, for "nothing yet is lost." Not as long as the earth preserves "funeral masks"—artefacts of dead cultures like the Aztecs and Mayas he wrote about in *Tombeau des civilisations.*

as well to works of literature which successfully "capture the moment"—thus winning their author a kind of immortality. But these are forlorn hopes. In *Birth of Our Power*, his 1930 novel about a failed workers' uprising in Barcelona, Serge had confidently written "Nothing is ever lost"—correctly anticipating the coming Spanish revolution of 1936. The 1946 version "nothing yet is lost" signals a change of historical perspective to archaeological time and from social progress to art.

It is in art that Alain, now disillusioned about Russia, finds his solution to the problem of "what to live for." Daria is still seeking a solution of her own as she crosses the Atlantic and makes her way to join Sacha/D/Bruno Battisti at his remote coffee plantation in rural Mexico. However, instead of discoursing on politics and history with her, Sacha tells her about his life in Mexico, about its ancient peoples, who "lived in an unstable cosmos, as we live in an unstable humanity armed with cosmic powers"; about its seasons, the annual death of the sun-parched earth and its irresistible luxuriant rebirth under the violent rains and lightning storms of the spring. In response to her horrifying account of the bombing of Berlin, he leads her to a banana tree and points to its "violet-tinted, powerfully-sexed turgidity." His consciousness, free of the imperative of historical integration, has led him to this final affirmation: "All that exists cries, whispers, or sings that we must never despair, for true death does not exist."

This striking affirmation illustrates what Serge's son, Vlady, used to call his father's "materialist spirituality"—since it was derived from Serge's scientific worldview rather than from any tendency toward mysticism. Serge's notion of materialism is closer to Spinoza's Substance, Bergson's *élan vital*, Hegelian-Marxist dialectics, Verdnatsky's *noosphere*, and Edgar Morin's Complexity than to positivism and vulgar scientism. "The immaterial is not in the least unreal, but on the contrary an essential form of the real (thought) completely unexplainable by yesterday's scientific rules."[23] Indeed,

23. Victor Serge, *Carnets*.

it was after reading two scientific books about recent discoveries and theories in genetics that he noted: "The old materialist schools would wax indignant and yet it is quite evident, however mysterious nature may be, that thought is the product of life, consubstantial with life, and that there would be nothing particularly bold in maintaining that it [thought] is itself life coming to discover and know itself." In consequence, even after a nuclear holocaust, consciousness/life will survive, if only in the form of a virus whose reproduction will, over the eons, evolve toward greater complexity until it reaches the stage of intelligent life in some unimagined form "coming to discover and know itself." Thus while Serge the socialist activist continued to "set his course on hope," Serge the creator of *Unforgiving Years* put hope further off into the long term, to archaeological, geological, and evolutionary time where ultimately "true death does not exist." A writer for our times—which well may be (to quote the title of another Serge novel) *Last Times*.[24]

—RICHARD GREEMAN
Montpellier, November 2007

24. *Les derniers temps* (Monteal: Editions de l'Arbre, 1946), translated into English by Ralph Manheim as *The Long Dusk* (Dial Press, 1946).

UNFORGIVING YEARS

I.

The Secret Agent

Do I still have enough space for an intelligent death?
He who had no idea discovered the central fire.

Around seven in the morning, D personally loaded his two suitcases into the taxi. The street was still slumbering, tinged by the bleak whiteness of a Paris awakening. No one was about except for a milkman. Morning purity of cobbles and asphalt. The garbage cans were empty. D felt no suspicions. He had himself driven to the Gare du Nord, grew irritable at the station buffet because they made him wait for a tasteless cup of coffee, and piled his luggage into another cab which dropped him off in the place d'Iéna. Sure of not being followed, he took in the vast square, a stage set empty of actors, bathed in a dappled light under which one would wish to live for a long while, meditating. Before eight in the morning Paris, in her wealthier neighborhoods, seems delivered from herself; pacified, she is nothing more than a work of human wisdom. D found a chauffeurs' bar where he was served a good, unpretentious coffee and two hot croissants, reminding him of that young condemned man whose sole last request was for croissants, which he could not have, because it was too early. "Just my luck!" said the pale young man, and he was right, for in fact the only thing he ever succeeded in was his own death by decapitation . . . Before boarding a third cab, which he had to call for, D reflected that all these complex precautions, reasonable as they might appear, were actually a semi-lunatic's game. They left the path of danger studded with small markers, perhaps even with milestones. How easily he might have been seen, quite by chance, without realizing, at the Gare du Nord or in the vicinity of the place d'Iéna. Someone could have jotted down a license plate. The business of changing from one taxi to another might attract attention itself. If you took all these possibilities into account, you'd go right over the edge. This time he had himself driven directly to the hotel in the rue de Rochechouart. It was a middle-class establishment of the sort frequented by traveling salesmen, tourists on a modest budget, sedately adulterous couples, and well-behaved musicians with nightclub contracts. "Ah, Monsieur Lamberti," the porter greeted him. D corrected him firmly, the better to steep himself in his new persona: "It's Battisti, Bruno Battisti." "Room 17, wasn't it?" inquired the porter, who knew perfectly well. Inside the room, D checked the locks on the suitcases even though he knew he'd closed them securely. By nine, he was back "home." The concierge met him with a "Morning, Monsieur Malinesco! And me thinking you were gone on a trip!" (So you saw me with my luggage, you old witch!) "Quite so, Madame, I shall be away for six weeks." (For all eternity, Madame!) "Well, it's nice weather for you anyway, Monsieur Malinesco," said the concierge, because you should always say something pleasant.

Mademoiselle Armande turned up promptly at ten, being an odiously punctual person who had been known to loiter in the street with an eye on her wristwatch, or stand for thirty seconds on the landing before knocking. She entered the study through the door left half open and murmured, "Monsieur Malinesco," the words more snuffled than pronounced, accompanied by a deferential bob of the head. She was an insipid woman, rather on the homely side, pink-complexioned and dressed in neutral colors, who wore large shiny spectacles over the face of a wizened, calculating child. D watched her with concealed attention. What did she know about him? That he was rich (he who had never owned anything), and she respected rich people. A philatelist, a bibliophile, a lover of ancient art, liable to jump on a train or into a car and scour Brittany in winter just to bring back an antique dresser... Friendly with artists. Her job was to answer the telephone, write the occasional letter, visit the bank, and receive Monsieur Soga, the embassy attaché, a nervous little man who reeked of cologne; Monsieur Sixte Mougin, the antiques dealer;

Monsieur Kehl from the Philatelist Society; and, more rarely, Monsieur Alain, who didn't much look like a painter. She was becoming a connoisseur of postage stamps and even did a little collecting herself, only the French colonies, not to be extravagant. It's a highly regarded hobby; they say the King of England has built up a remarkable collection. D had Mademoiselle Armande periodically tailed by a detective. She stepped out on Saturday nights with Monsieur Dupois, a civil servant at the Ministry of Education; they went to the pictures; Dupois's concierge referred to Mademoiselle Armande as "the lady engaged to that nice gentleman who has been so unfortunate..." D, who distrusted other people's misfortunes even more than his own, set the detective onto Monsieur Evariste Dupois, age forty-seven, owner of a property at Ivry, divorced...A gentleman who bet judiciously on the horses, bought a weekly lottery ticket, read the right-wing press, and visited a brothel in the rue Saint-Sauveur every Friday evening. An innocent man.

"Are you engaged, then?" inquired D of Mademoiselle Armande.

She did not flinch, being no doubt incapable of such a lively reaction, but her fingers twitched a little.

"Dear me, Monsieur Malinesco...However did you know?"

He saw that her complexion was improved by embarrassment.

"Just a coincidence, Mademoiselle. I happened to see you one Saturday on the arm of your fiancé."

"It has not been completely decided yet," she said reticently.

Innocent, innocent! (But that was not a wholly rational conclusion...)

"I intend to go away for six weeks. You will please pass on the mail to Monsieur Mougin."

If anybody was going to look miserable as a drowned rat in a bucket three days from now, it was definitely Monsieur Sixte Mougin! D regretted the atrophied state of his sense of humor; it would have cheered him up no end to dwell on the troubles of that quavering, servile bastard Monsieur Sixte Mougin.

"When Monsieur Soga calls, tell him I'm in Strasbourg."

Strasbourg was code for "unforeseen complications."

Mademoiselle Armande did not turn a hair. No one suspected anything. Unbelievable that They hadn't moved to place me under internal surveillance months ago! But if the unbelievable were not sometimes a reality, there would be no possibility of struggle. In cramped italics, the secretary was scratching into her diary: "Monsieur Soga. Say Strasbourg..." D, who disliked things to be written down, forced a smile.

"You don't have much faith in your memory, I see!"

"Oh I do, but it's funny, I always mix up the names of towns like Edinburgh, Hamburg, Strasbourg, Mulhouse..."

He hadn't expected that. His throat went instantly dry. In the same code, known to just five people, Mulhouse meant "watch out."

"And why is that?"

"I've no idea, for the life of me! Look, I nearly wrote Mulhouse just now, I can't help it."

"I might go to Mulhouse as well," D said moodily.

He was fixing her with the cold, hard, stony-eyed glare she seldom caught from him—not the look of an art lover. Mademoiselle Armande put on a falsely bright smile, while D rapidly weighed the pros and cons.

"Here's the key to the bottom right-hand drawer of the small cabinet in the hall. Fetch me the Zürich folder, Monsieur Feuvre, you know, the Swiss collection... The files are not in order, you'll have to rummage."

"Yes, Monsieur."

Naturally, she left her handbag sitting next to the typewriter. D opened it with an unhurried dexterity acquired in the mail-interception department of the Secret Service. He scanned a note signed "Your fondly affectionate, Evariste." Leafed through the address book. Saw—sickeningly—a telephone number: X 11-47. The number to fear was 11-74. Numeric inversion! Inside his head suspicion exploded into certainty. The returning Mademoiselle

Armande glanced at her bag—ah, so we understand each other! D selected a letter from Monsieur Feuvre and put it in his pocket. "Will you kindly put the folder back in the file..." But he took back the keys to the cabinet, and she didn't ask for them... Right, then; we thoroughly understand each other, thought D. This changed everything. He remembered finding his first taxicab parked and available only a few steps from the house, and how the driver had leaned toward him in a peculiarly obsequious manner... Soon as I leave here, she'll call 11-74—or another number, just around the corner perhaps, or in this very building... Mademoiselle Armande, clearly flustered, was struggling to surmount some hesitation or inhibition.

"What's the matter?" D demanded unceremoniously.

She explained that in Monsieur Malinesco's absence she would dearly like to take three days off, if that were at all possible, in order to... A matter of an aunt, a small property in the country, Monsieur Dupois. A notary's letter fluttered out of the handbag.

"But of course," he stopped her.

The worst of it was the need to distrust himself, to suspect his own suspicions. D saw the number 11-47 printed on the legal letterhead. Reassured, he stopped fretting over Mulhouse. "In addition, you must allow me to offer you a bonus of 500 francs for the last quarter..." You can assess the degree of corruptibility by the way a person accepts money. The sparkle in the young woman's spectacles was one of innocence.

Just as a magician believes in his little tricks, so D believed in secrets, ciphers, stratagems, silence, masks, and in playing the game impeccably; at the same time he knew very well that secrets are sold, codes deciphered, stratagems outwitted, and silences broken; that masks are easier to read than faces, that the carbon copies of dispatches lie in ministerial wastepaper baskets for the taking, and that the perfect game does not exist. He believed the Organization to be infallible by virtue of its stability, its ramifications, its resources, its power, its single-minded commitment— even by the complicity of its opponents, who feed it, sometimes involuntarily, sometimes as a deliberate ploy. But from the day he had begun to pull away from the Organization, he felt himself rejected by it; and its power behind him, within him, became stifling.

His inner break with the Organization dated back to when the Crime had been revealed. The Crime had burst into view after a long, stealthy approach, like a sinister squadron on the ocean suddenly lighted by searchlights. D had cried out silently to himself, one night, over the newspapers scattered across the rug: "I can't go on! This is the end of everything!" And nothing meant anything to him any longer in this stupidly snug apartment, where the playacting only let up after hours—when he could hunch forward in the armchair with the chessboard set up and solve problems, which he inevitably did, since problems are given away in advance, you just have to keep looking, all problems are hollow in the end. Or at night, cozily in bed under cozy lamplight, a glass of lemon water by his elbow, reading a work of physics, since the structure of the atom is probably the only problem left in the universe and they will solve it; then the age of despair will begin. Such mental exercises calmed him but failed to relax him. There is no real peace for those who understand the mechanics of a world moving toward cataclysms, lurching from one cataclysm to the next.

He bid a discreet farewell to the secretary. "Have a nice trip, Monsieur Malinesco...Count on me...They say Strasbourg is a beautiful city..." The ghost of a smile curled the man's wrinkled face as he teased, circumspect even in laughter, "What's a beautiful city, Mulhouse?" Mademoiselle Armande was mortified. "Oh, you must think me a child..." "Never that!" he said, and meant it. "I trust that when I return, you'll be announcing the publication of the banns." "I might indeed, Monsieur..." she said, with such a glow in her eyes that D felt a twinge of pity. ("When I return— meaning never...")

How many times have I closed a door behind me, never to return! This time...On the landing, he took a deep breath. The salt sea air could not have been more bracing than this first breath on stepping into the unknown, a relief without joy, indeed mixed with foreboding... Once the unendurable burden has been shed, the back straightens. Glad to have proven equal to the task so far, D reckoned he had at least a forty-eight-hour start on his pursuers. The elevator was moving. He ran down a few steps and stopped short, listening. Someone was mounting the stairs with a heavy, spongy tread he thought he recognized...

This someone was in too much of a hurry to wait for the elevator to come back down. D leaned cautiously out over the stairwell and saw, two floors below, Monsieur Sixte Mougin's plump gray hand alighting on the banister. Fugitives have instant reflex. D raced up to the fifth floor on tiptoe while his mind rattled off calculations like a crack marksman. The mind can come alive intensely in a few seconds when it engages life without emotion, while the heart beats calmly on, accustomed to the unexpected. A forty-eight-hour start on danger, eh? Not even one, my friend. You're more like twelve to fourteen hours behind. Old Mougin's here because they sent him. My message, left yesterday, wasn't supposed to be delivered in Amsterdam until the morning of the day after tomorrow. I hadn't foreseen that disinformation could work against me too, that I could forfeit the leadership's confidence, that the special envoy could have been lying about that invitation to a meeting in Holland—or that he could have given someone else leave to open letters in his absence, those letters no one can open on pain of death... Monsieur Mougin was pressing the doorbell one floor below. Such was the silence around the mechanical hiss of the elevator, D could hear the useful rogue wheezing. The door opened, and clicked shut behind him. The street outside might already be one long trip wire, invisibly hooked up to a dozen traps. D moved the Browning from his trouser pocket to that of his coat: a laughable precaution. He entered the elevator. Inside the mahogany cabin, he deliberately turned his back on the mirror, haunted by the image of a double agent he had once escorted in the elevator of the secret prison: a handsome man with a seducer's mustache, undone, who was promptly shot. The image of this banal face, cremated into nothing years ago, gave way to a sardonic but highly disquieting idea. What if the mad finger of suspicion had lit on Krantz, the special envoy? In that case a new man, a super-special envoy, would be opening his mail... We live in lunatic times, I shall cut through the lunacy! With this thought D leaped into the street, taking it in in both directions with one glance.

A gray Citröen stood parked and unoccupied in front of number 15. A young cyclist was starting off slowly, with a small yellow parcel dangling from the handlebars—maybe a signal. If he looks at me, that would mean... He doesn't look, but then perhaps he's already spotted me and he's too well trained... A woman slackened her pace, opposite, fumbling in her handbag for something: a good way to survey the street in a pocket mirror. A green van rounded the corner of the rue de Sèvres and made a three-point turn, as though the driver wished to save himself the bother of a slight detour... Everything seemed at once unremarkable and suspect. D opted to make his way past the empty Citröen.

Nobody followed him down into the Métro. Nobody caught his attention in the first-class carriage. The warren of passages in the Saint-Lazare station lend themselves to dodging and doubling back, to abrupt corrections of deliberate mistakes... D changed direction several times. A brassy blonde wheeled around, flashing a pink-gummed grin in his face. "Do you mind!" D said irritably. It was just afterward that he realized how comical he looked, with his collar up and his overcoat grotesquely buttoned up crooked. He lit a cigarette and strolled into the railway station. Not a good idea: stations make for unexpected encounters. Sure enough here came Alain through the crowd, as though rushing out from behind a newspaper-stall display.

"It's you!" Alain exclaimed, full of joyful surprise.

His face was frank, his eyes more alert than intelligent, his movements vigorous like those of someone used to success; D liked him, to whatever atrophied extent he was still capable of friendship. Alain was an exemplary agent, enterprising, prudent, and selfless, who owed to D his initiation into the job, that is, into the devotion that fills to the brim the cup of existence. So far, D had trusted him with only moderately risky missions, such as meeting minor functionaries or party militants who were embedded in arsenals and shipyards. In the old days, before the nightmare that had made a taciturn man out of him, D used to enjoy inviting Alain and his wife to dinner at a good restaurant. They discussed painting, theory, the news. Alain didn't mind asking questions and D enjoyed teaching him without appearing to do so. It probably did him more good than it did to that cultivated but still rudimentary young mind.

■

"And you?" asked D.

"Swimmingly. In ten days, I'll have some interesting stuff for you. You'll be pleased."

"And me," thought D, "I'm rudimentary, too...It took a whole historical epoch to mold me. At twenty-five I was just like him, minus the handsome face for charming the girls..."

"Walk with me, Alain. I'm so glad I ran into you."

They went up the rue de Rome to the place de l'Europe, the traffic circle suspended high over the railroad tracks. Under the fine drizzle which now began to fall, the great airy intersection, true to its name, drew together arteries named for all the European capitals, arteries inseparable yet foreign to one another... "Here will do fine," said D. Soft explosions of white vapor billowed up from the station. Paris's pallor was serene. They stopped.

"We won't be seeing each other anymore, Alain. Someone will contact you. You'll receive instructions."

D watched a nascent anxiety contract the young brown eyes.

"Yes, that's how it is. I'm saying goodbye."

"I don't get it," said Alain. "Listen... You have confidence in me. You can say a word, just a word. Has something happened? Something dangerous? Are you..."

Fear was pricking Alain, the kind of fear D knew the best (there are so many different kinds!): the fear of guessing right, the fear of confronting, of understanding, the incomprehensible...

"A suspect? No. I am the same person. I'm leaving. It's finished for me, that's all."

"But that's impossible!" the young man said in a very low voice.

Further words appeared to quiver on his lips, but were held back.

"I resigned," said D sharply. "You're to carry on under someone else."

He was conducting an experiment on the boy, while operating alive on himself. Putting friendship to the test by a display of futile bravado. D became aware—odd, for such sentiments ought to have died out in him—of a wish to be understood. After all, he had shaped this youth's very soul; Alain couldn't fail to see that if he, D, was bailing out, if D himself couldn't go along any longer, if even D was giving it up, then serious things must be happening which finally should be condemned. A man's conscience is secondary in the battle for such a great cause—but now it's essential. You cast off your whole life, you "drop" the Secret Service, you say no. I who am alone, disarmed, faithful after twenty years' labor, today I say: No. The situation must be terribly grim for me to have arrived at that conclusion.

D opens his leather cigarette case. Cyclists flit across the square like mosquitoes, human mosquitoes. They know nothing of these problems. An engine puffs below street level. Autumn seeps into the marrow, as needling as the rain. Alain is bareheaded.

"You'll catch cold, Alain," D says affectionately. "Let's go our ways. Goodbye."

But he is watching. The young face has gone pale and looks sick, even nasty. If a woman flung back at him: "Go away, I love someone else!" he might be similarly dumbfounded. Alain sees D through a dull, disfiguring space. He sees a wrinkled old face, flesh wasting away so that the skull shines through. A death's-head pretending to be alive. You don't quit! You run away and you are hunted down and you are finished off, justly, because running away is treason.

"I didn't expect this from you," Alain murmurs.

His tone changes. Rising disappointment verging on contempt, growing almost insulting. Some of the color returns to his cheeks. He blurts out: "You know better than I do that..."

(The old spool unwinds by itself: that every apparently abominable deed perpetrated corresponds to a necessity, since they are perpetrated; that the Party, steered by supremely capable hands, stands above whatever it does; that if we start to doubt we're doomed; that those who are killed are traitors, since they are killed—that YOU YOURSELF taught me all this! D understands the precision of these exact and unalterable formulas that could not be worded any other way, as though a machine were punching them out of metal. Against them he opposes, deep inside, nothing but a stony NO of liberation, a liberation difficult to justify. His shake of the head is barely perceptible; the confident, superior smirk he puts on comes out as a grimace. Isn't this boy going to remember all that I have meant to him, the bits of my past I have shared, the person I am?)

Alain doesn't know what to do with his hands. The right worries a button on his mackintosh. He's stunned. Take him by the arm, look him straight in the eye, no holding back, say: "Take it easy, kid. I haven't changed in any way. I've understood, I've made a judgment, it's because I'll never change that I can no longer bear what is happening. So many corpses, so many lies, so much poison brusquely poured into our souls, into our very souls, do you understand! Forgive me for using such a mystical term..." This is only a fleeting impulse for D. It's not possible, he knows that. It's always rash to be too human...

"You're going to tear off that button, Alain."

The young man's distress spreads across his face in a madman's grin.

"You are a..."

He breaks off and marches jerkily away, as though willing

himself not to run. So, he couldn't quite bring himself to say the word "traitor." Was that because of a regret? A doubt? The smallest sense of what that word's iniquitous, unbelievable implication would be?

"I don't care," D answers himself. "He's a good sort, that boy. Perhaps he'll understand too, when it's too late. More likely he'll be devoured a long time before. He's the kind who believe with their eyes closed, obey, then take the rap and languish for years in the exercise yards of penitentiaries. After that the Service is in a bind about what to do with them, pay them, earn their silence, or eliminate them... In the future they won't be dispatched to Mexico or Argentina, but to the great beyond. Much safer. Alain, just for having known me...

But let's put this at a distance. I didn't want this farewell. Alain is an enemy now. When he gets over the shock, he'll be sorry he didn't act sympathetic—who knows?—his old respectful understanding, just to keep contact. I would have believed in his youth, his concern. He would have led me into a trap. Rule: Trust nobody this side of heaven. Since those who were deserving of all our faith are dead. Defiled and dead. And when all is said and done, we did this to ourselves.

D cast a despairing glance over the place de l'Europe. The rain was falling softly.

■

This was no weather for visiting the Bois, but he had time to kill before his painful three o'clock rendezvous. He wasn't hungry. There must be some direct link between physiology and psychology. But he was thirsty for the sight of trees, water, solitary places; the ideal would be a great sweep of young green saplings and far-off mountains, crisscrossed by birds in flight, scoured by monotonous winds, warmed by a tepid sun, one of those Siberian landscapes that lends a fresh alacrity to sadness (provided you're not in captivity). And you know that a few hours' trek would bring you to the banks of the Irtysh, sluggish river, vision of a vast, purposeless destiny…"To the Bois de Boulogne, driver, and there's no rush."

The ancient taxicab listed to the left. D found himself rocking along inside a grimy, leather-lined compartment. He rolled down both windows so as to breathe in the rain…The Bois was gingery gray, ash-mauve in its feathery depths, strewn with dead leaves. A spectacle of decline, perfect for today. The tar paths, the clearings between the groves of trees, the smooth surface of the lakes like a blend of sky and mud rolled past in a stately neglect that was neither truly alive nor truly lifeless. "Slower, please, driver…"

D rested. A future resembling these paths. Wanting nothing, expecting nothing, fearing nothing. Belonging to nothing, not even to oneself. No longer holding fast to anything. No longer to be that thinking molecule within a formidable, relentless, clear-sighted collectivity, held taut by so much willpower that it no longer knew what it was doing. Am I that discouraged? I'm turning into a character out of a novel for intellectuals…Everything is falling away from me, everything: the commanding ideas, the Party, the State, the new world under construction, the hard struggles of men and women caught (much as in this chilly wood) like soldiers on the front lines under fire, taking shelter in the trenches, stubborn and exhausted, at war despite themselves for the sake of hope. And the hope betrayed! The streets of the one true capital of the world churning beneath scaffoldings and gridded blocks of broad glass panes, each cell of the concrete hive housing undernourished beings imprisoned by a prodigious destiny (and forty percent parasitic paper-shuffling). Capital of torture! The microphotography labs, the special training schools, the dungeons of the secret prison vibrating with the subway trains, the cryptography departments, the central Power. The place of execution, a solidly reinforced cellar no doubt, thoroughly hosed down, rationalized, into which so many men have descended, suddenly realizing the annihilation of everything: faith, reason, life's work, life…The red flags…The red flags, the first raw shoots of socialist humanism

that no amount of dust, filth, and blood could besmirch entirely
... The charm of Western cities, so resistant to analysis, the sensation of a heedless world that knows nothing of hunger, terror,
overwork, or the icy, ascetic exhilaration that alone lends meaning
to the everyday round; the benign live-and-let-live attitude of that
meanly commonsensical, pleasantly hedonistic world, sliding day
by day toward apocalypse... The bitter joy of hand-to-hand combat with catastrophes ready to spring out of invisibility into tomorrow's headlines, that gigantic intrigue snaring countries—
pastel-colored on childhood maps—in its net of information and
disinformation, ignoble acts and heroic achievements, statistics,
petroleum, metals, messages... The conviction that we remain—
however wretched—the most farsighted, the most humane beneath our armor of scientific inhumanity, and for that reason the
most endangered, the most trusting in the future of the world—
and unhinged by suspicion! Ah! With all of that falling away from
me, what will be left for me, what will be left of me? This nearly
old man, so wisely rational, being rattled along by an ailing taxi
through a pointless landscape... Wouldn't he be better off going
home? "Shoot me, comrades, as you shot the rest!" At least such
an end would follow the logic of History (since we have offered
our lives to History... Carrying out our task to the end. If the sun
must be extinguished, then we will extinguish it! "Necessity,"
magic formula...). That would be easy; but what about complicity? What if there were no necessity? What if the great machine
were running off the rails, what if its mental cogs were perverted,
its social cogs corrupted? How did the Old Man put it—"Our
hands have lost control, we have lost control of ourselves..." Here
thought begins to founder, History being perhaps rather harder to
penetrate than we'd imagined, with our three dozen trusty materialist axioms. They will probably kill me quickly. There are three
good reasons for them to do so: 1. I am full of corrosive ideas (a
Japanese cop would say "dangerous ideas"). 2. They are continuing the work. 3. I'm finished... But what work are they continuing, plunging headlong into what abyss?

His days, his nights turned over disjointedly in his mind. He thought of the faces of the persecuted—studied on photographs, for they were under constant surveillance, zealous spies were planted among them, their little apartments were entered unseen, the papers in their drawers rifled, their letters photographed—and they never suspected, they soldiered on at their microscopic activities, mimeographing newsletters, scraping together the contributions for a leaflet, expounding theories—sometimes correct ones —before an audience of thirty people (including three secret agents) upstairs at the Café Voltaire . . . Should I join them? Would they believe in me, when I don't believe in them? I can believe in nothing now but power. Truth, stripped of its metaphysical poetry, exists only in the brain. Destroy a few brains, quickly done! Then, goodbye truth. Power is against them, against me, there's nothing we can do about it. The torrent is washing us away.

D had been expecting to feel, if not the deep joy of deliverance, then at least the relief at the end of a migraine headache. Contrary to all prudence, he talked to himself aloud: "But I'm right, dammit!" The taxi driver half turned: "What was that, sir?"

"Nothing. Keep going. I'm ahead of schedule."

Ahead of nothing. Only negation remains. No, no, no, and no. No to power. I, a nonentity, refuse my consent. I preserve my reason when you are losing yours. I assert that the destruction of the finest is the ultimate crime, the ultimate folly. If power turns against itself and starts savagely destroying itself, then I am right to be against it. But it will survive and I will perish, therefore it is right to be against me . . . Can it survive if it devours itself, if it suffers from so unprecedented an alienation? And surviving this, what if power betrays itself, changes its face and its aims? Then I am the faithful one by betraying it, but that is pure idealism, not practical sense.

He knew so many of the victims—tortured, executed—by their names, their faces, their weaknesses, their eccentricities, their talents, their journeys, their service records, their bookshelves, their greatness, that he had to stop himself remembering them for fear of being overcome by a demoralizing fatigue. Repressed, they massed within him to form the anonymous "cohort," the dark "Number." We fancied ourselves as the "iron cohort," the elite of the elect, that was us! Our hubris has been properly punctured. The dark Number was arrived at by means of scrupulous cross-checks, and varied with the degree of bitterness, rebellion, or pity felt at the moment; in any case, it ran to five figures. So many victims.

What is "conscience"? A residue of beliefs inculcated in us from the time of primitive taboos until today's mass press? Psychologists have come up with an appropriate term for these imprints deep within us: the superego, they say. I have nothing left to invoke but conscience, and I don't even know what it is. I feel an ineffectual protest surging up from a deep and unknown part of me to challenge destructive expediency, power, the whole of material reality, and in the name of what? Inner enlightenment? I'm behaving almost like a believer. I cannot do otherwise: Luther's words. Except that the German visionary who flung his inkwell at the devil went on to add, "God help me!" What will come to help me?

The big newspapers don't have a conscience (he had bribed them often enough, through savvy intermediaries, to know that) and the little ones don't count. The big writers wouldn't believe me. Those who might, wouldn't understand me, and it is not me that must be understood, it's the nightmare of a sick power and the demise of a whole category of thinking men. Writers prefer other subjects anyway, less compromising, more commercial...I won't say anything, not a word. If six months from now finds me quietly in Paraguay or California, I'll order piles of psychology books and settle down to a study of conscience, the superego, the ego, and suspicion, the obsessiveness of suspicion, the sudden urge to liquidate the finest as though to become their equals by replacing them...My notions of all that are probably out-of-date. And there's no such thing yet as social psychology. A day will come when people feel unable to live without such knowledge— more important than the knowledge required to build a machine.

Catastrophes don't need it. A psychology based on drilling men into obedience is quite sufficient for the Education Authority, the Psychiatric Service of the Public Health Secretariat, the Military Morale Office, the Politburo, or the Longevity Institute, devoted to the preservation of State cadres (whom the same State is destroying). Meanwhile these institutions, viewed as a whole, are working to prepare the catastrophes: the circle is closed.

D had the driver stop in front of a small café in Neuilly. Sitting at a white marble table, he ordered some ham and a glass of wine. His depression was lifting. A mysterious ballet where dark thoughts, beams of light, and profound instincts choreographed by an unknown director played out in his mind: physiology plus the spiritual X. The taxi driver, drinking at the bar, was discussing with the patron the finer points of cooking hare in white wine. D felt a rush of friendship toward these two men. Enough of this cerebral debauchery! The noose has been cut. Now to overcome the effects of my overwrought nerves. A little pride, old man, you're one of the strong type. (It's worth telling yourself this from time to time, if only as a means of autosuggestion...) He mentally reread the letter he had addressed the day before to the Special Envoy, twenty lines of calculated platitudes, yet containing this clear and honest passage:

> ...So deeply do I disapprove of what is happening that I find it impossible to carry out duties which are incompatible with doubt and blame. You know of my absolute commitment, repeatedly borne out by my actions. I can only assure you of my definitive retirement into private life, that I vow to say and do nothing that might harm our cause...

A brief memo had followed regarding bank accounts, cases in progress, and liaisons with second-tier agents. It occurred to D that the concepts of disapproval, doubt, and blame (just one would have sufficed) canceled out the "absolute commitment" and the promise. They opened a thousand doors onto problems.

They stood in judgment over the Party, the system, the Organization; any individual who judges the group, by the mere fact of such temerity, places himself outside the law. "After all, I was never afraid of being killed." But now the seriousness of the risk amounted to near-certainty, even as its significance was humiliatingly trivialized. To embrace risk for the sake of the group required no justification. But a risk incurred for oneself? He told himself coarsely: "To live only for oneself is barren—like masturbation."

"...nicely marinated in white wine," the driver was repeating. "The onions browned separate. A clove of garlic, nutmeg..." Another voice, slurred and hearty, finished describing the recipe with an appreciative cluck of the tongue: "That, Monsieur, is what I call fine cooking!" "And hare stew?" D broke in happily. "Let me tell you," said the patron, who was a dab hand with a shotgun. D listened to the instructions without taking them in. How good it would have been to exchange cordial handshakes with these fellows, to meet up for a Sunday's shooting at Suresnes, to drink Beaujolais together! D's gloom returned as he paid the bill. The difficult hour of his rendezvous with Nadine was approaching.

■

"No adulterers in sight today," D said with a smile, when they were alone in the discreetly luxurious tearoom.

There was a lovely fold to her eyelids. Her cheeks were full and dimpled, her mouth richly outlined in scarlet. She had a sidelong way of looking you straight in the eye that was at once demure and forthright, the tough candor of a peasant girl from the steppes who has just stepped out of a smart hairdresser's on the rue Saint-Honoré. Nadine offered her cheek, not her lips: displeased.

"Are you all right, Nadine? No one knows about your return to Paris, do they? Did you follow my instructions without fail—to the letter?"

"Oh, of course I did, what do you think?"

Her voice betrayed irritation.

"It's extremely important, actually."

"Well, not more than usual, is it? Sacha, I really hate it when you treat me like a child."

He insisted: "It's infinitely more important than you think. So, you didn't phone anyone?"

The waitress took their order: tea with lemon and pastries. She was hard put to classify these two. Foreign? Lovers, married? She put her money on a heavy breakup scene, with a sprinkling of sentiment over the top like confectioner's sugar on yesterday's buns, plus a modest check to prevent hard feelings.

At very bad moments, D would feel muscles cramping while a chill crept over his skin, as though his energies were being sucked deep inside, the better to be healed, the better to pounce. His pupils shrank to pinpoints then. Nadine pulled off her gloves. Knowing him through and through—as she thought—she said, "Don't make those eyes at me, Sacha. By now you don't have any lessons to teach me about being careful. And what if I did call Sylvia—surely it doesn't matter?"

"Ah."

The stupid mistake. Like a tightrope walker who trips over a bit of orange peel in the street, when at thirty feet up with the drums rolling, he would never have made a false move. One fractured shin bone and that's the end of the beautiful, brilliant acrobat. Shit!

"You did that?"

Nadine was sincerely bewildered.

"So now I'm to be suspicious of Sylvia, am I? Or perhaps Sylvia's being watched? Sacha you're out of your mind."

He chewed on a slice of lemon. He had traveled, in the past, with a cyanide capsule glued to his scalp. He would have chewed that in the same way under the nose of the detectives. Twice: in China, in Germany…

"How did you get here? By car?"

"I changed taxis at Porte Maillot..."

"Good. Now please try to understand and try not to judge me. We're going to America, it's all fixed. I thought of everything except you calling Sylvia. I've broken with them, Nadine."

Nadine thought in shattered images and disjointed phrases. As soon as an image became too upsetting it vanished, like it was torn up. The sentence trailed off, its gist telegraphed to minimize the disturbance. Everything that concerned her personally remained indelibly printed on a lower register. Departure—America, that's nothing, we've traveled so much already! The word "broken" hit her like a nail bomb. Nadine glimpsed the broad flat nose of old Sémen—shot. She saw the fake but costly pearl necklace on Elsa's white, nervous throat—Elsa, disappeared. The deep bluish hollows around Emmy's eyes, eyes she'd always envied for their bewitching quality, very like hers, except that hers were not so bewitching—disappeared, Emmy who adored confectionery, Paris gowns, gloves, and handsome cads. Stout Kraus, saluting her as former officers do, click heels, bow low, kiss hand—gone, the fat malicious, twice-decorated ex-convict, et cetera, how, we'll never know. The Poluyanovs, a young couple full of promise, thoroughly worldly to all appearances, fluent in four languages, thoroughly Anglicized, and shot, according to an unverifiable rumor. Bald Alexis, the one involved in that dreadful Ploesti business, the tortured hero who got out of prison six months ago—killed himself on being arrested they say, but it's possible he was gunned down like a dog because he shot off his mouth (no noise allowed at night in apartment houses; and if there is noise, a pistol shot does less harm than an indignant voice). Nadine shook off these ghosts. Several others, on the point of appearing, hovered at the edge of memory. A ghastly exhalation steamed from a black pit toward her nostrils.

"How did you dare, Sacha?"

"On strictly rational grounds. If I'd waited, it would have come to the same thing before long. After Kraus, Alexis, Emmy, you know...And those were people with no influence..."

Her phone conversation with Sylvia appeared in a new and disquieting light. "That's right, I'm back from Nice, meeting Sacha later on, off to Les Trois Quartiers tomorrow at eleven ... pure rayon, Sylvette, in two colors, rose and burgundy, what d'you think? With a frightfully low neckline..." Sylvia's husband, the addresses, the passports, the money to be drawn—all the necessary connections fell into place so ominously that she became visibly panic-stricken, and had the shabbiest thoughts in her life. "If they kill him, will they kill me too? I'm only small-fry. And we have so little money..."

"Careful," D was saying. "Remain calm."

Suddenly he broke into an oily, screen-actor's leer, as though playing a roguish but likable bank manager.

"What charming gloves, my dear."

This idiotic pose and change of tone because a couple, a navy officer and a rangy brunette with the profile of a greyhound, had just walked into the tearoom. A true-blue, genuine article of an officer: they don't make 'em like that to order! D feared a hostile reaction from Nadine in view of the enormity of the accident. He had loved this woman for ten years. She was younger than he was, selfish, practical, a skillful operator during missions, superficially romantic when they were alone, gifted at times with a mercurial, inebriated, almost silent laugh and the undefended gaze of a primitive; simple in her loving, and as harmoniously built as a beautiful animal ... For him she reserved her admiration, a flattered, willing sensuality, and a comradely directness of manner. There were no conventional prejudices between them.

An unexpected silence fell. Nadine called the waitress and ordered a liqueur.

"One for you, Sacha?"

"No thanks."

He was held by an expression on her face that he had never seen.

"About Sylvia," she said dreamily, "it's a bore. So silly of me, I'm sorry. If I do what I have to do very quickly, it'll be all right...probably. You can count on me. What you've done is irreparable. I think you've made a mistake, but I understand, it was strangling you. For me, the worst part isn't that."

What lay behind this detachment of hers, this calm as of total disaster? Her hard expression on the verge of tears?

"We're an old couple, Sacha. You know that I love you in a special, profound way. I don't always understand you, but sometimes I understand you completely. For me to take off, to leave now, is a bit...it's a little awful."

"Little and awful don't go together," he said, intent on her.

She brushed her fingers over the man's hand where it lay on the tablecloth.

"I love someone else, quite differently from the way I love you. I was very happy. I wasn't planning to keep it from you or to hurt you unduly. We'll always be what we are—if you want. I can't imagine myself without you, Sacha...But there's this person I love. He doesn't prevent me being yours. You've got to understand...And now, now..."

If a relationship is not free, it's unhealthy. Sexuality can only be mastered through reason, by granting to it the part of us it demands. Thus delivered from its imperious claims, we can live for acts of intelligence and will. The human machine requires a good control mechanism which our physiologists—or moralists—named the brake. Repression diminishes a man as much as promiscuity. Jealousy is a leftover from an obsolete set of customs (among us), based on the subjugation of the female by the male and on private property. Moral hygiene, physical hygiene...The couple is a partnership of free beings, founded on comradeship in struggle...and so on and so forth, in formulas rehashed by Youth Club lecturers until the message had imprinted itself upon the smallest nerve filament. At least that's what D thought up to a few seconds ago. We live on limited notions, dried out like plants pressed in a book. Under the shock, he pretended to stand by those shattered clichés. "Bad timing, in any case..." And four o'clock already. No time to lose.

"Who? Is he one of us?"

He only threw in the second question to provide a spurious justification for the first. What did it matter, when all was said and done? Bad timing for you too, Nadine, it's just your hard luck. Now suffer. (He almost snickered.) We're being tracked down together. The afterthought flashed through him that from now on she might—if push came to shove—betray him. Never expect too much of a woman: she has thousands of years of subjugation behind her.

"Who is he?"

"I can't tell you. Forgive me. It's impossible. I'll take care of everything necessary, and we'll leave whenever you say. But I . . ."

A stubborn violence rose in him. Who? "I need to know so as to take adequate precautions."

"I can't. But I promise, you have no complications to fear from that quarter."

"The quarter of the flesh," he reflected bitterly, with a vision of Nadine's sculpted body, the raised mound of her sex, the thick curls that were lighter than her hair . . . "It's beautiful," he'd said to her once, "it charms me in the same way as your face." Push those images aside. Nadine looked so woefully disconsolate that he was ashamed of feeling dominated by instinct—and of being, as instinct would have it, the stronger of the two.

"Very well, Nadine. Let's assume I don't care, even if I do— more than I would have expected. All I insist on are the precautions. No goodbyes. No letters or signals of any kind, to anyone." (He imagined how many problems this could cause.) "You see, we are in the greatest danger. I've got you a new passport, with visa, and I've reserved a cabin. You have to follow my instructions to the letter. We sail on the seventh. Let's go."

All this pretended calm cost him effort. Oh to send the tea service flying, pick a fight with the naval officer, smash his face in, forbidden pleasures! He accompanied Nadine in a taxi to a point not far from her mid-price pension on the rue d'Amsterdam (it was bound to be staked out by now), which she would be leaving that same evening. "Say you're going abroad, leave everything in order as though you were coming back, and later have a letter posted there from London, so nobody worries about your disappearance. Watch out for anyone taking photos, all right? I'll expect you after nine. Keep in mind you could be tailed, and being tailed could be lethal..." Business over, as they sat side by side, without touching, in a muffled silence like a fog, D was wondering: "Who is he? One of us? A stranger she met on a train, at the beach, at the pension? Our life was wretchedly separate, between hasty meetings...I don't want this obsession. I don't care. Enough. Finished. But who?" Nadine took his hand.

"Have I hurt you terribly? I never thought..."

So convenient, never to think...!

"Oh, I don't know. I'm fine. Worried—especially by your carelessness. It'll work out...See you later."

The cab was driving past the pension. D didn't like the look of the news vendor leaning against the wall. "Is he always there?" "I...I don't think so...If I remember right, he used to stand farther down, by the haberdashery..."

"Bye now, Sacha. Don't be nervous."

Nadine offered her cheek. He placed a cold kiss on it. She got out.

■

It was the day after a hike over the Roof of the World, in a Xinjiang village, if a point on the sterile steppe where a few mud huts cluster around a well can be termed a village. I was dying as I explored the Roof of Life, the environs of death, and they acquired for me the simple features of a continent's bare peak. A diminutive yellow man with an Astrakhan bonnet and a triangular face, his pupils opaque within the fleshy slits of his lids, had fired a slim Japanese bullet at me from his rampart of ruins. I was in love with the ruins. After decoding the dispatches and encoding the reports; after the ceremonious interviews with turbaned elders in striped robes, venerable, devious, and unwashed, and greasy junior notables who were always smiling, homosexual, guarded, and false; after the tea, the salaam, the agreements that neither side would honor; after the hours spent mulling over the probable treacheries, the possible ambushes, and the itinerary of bands on the march along the goat tracks—then, when dusk cooled the air, I would leave the low longhouse of baked clay. First I went to visit N'ga, the keeper of the water. At the center of a blue-white space, jars of cold water stood coated with a sweat of droplets. No one was allowed to approach this water, which N'ga personally drew from the well. The people of this country were adept at poisons that had no taste and that could shrivel a man in a matter of weeks. Your mucus turns blue, your teeth rattle, you become sleepy, incurably sleepy, with a dull ache in your bones...N'ga was devoted to me. He clothed in white his ephebe's body, molded by the lusts of local chiefs, he trilled piercingly on his flute, he played knucklebones all by himself, hooting with girlish laughter when he won. I had healed the sores that were torturing him, swabbed away his pus and his fleas, cleansed him of fear. He loved me with a servile passion, conveyed through his beautiful, blank eyes: it must come as a puzzle that the Powerful White Man from the Country of the Bear felt no hankering for his caresses. We had few words in common. I would ask, "Is the water cold and pure, faithful N'ga?"

His musical voice always made the same reply, gravely reciting, "Water refreshes the wise man, the rose, the beloved..."

This did not bode well for its capacity to refresh me, but I delighted in its taste of melted snow. Wryly, because solitude is a souring experience, I paraphrased the versicle to myself: "The same water refreshes the poisonous plant, the syphilitic woman, the traitor, and the torturer," four classes of being I did my best to avoid.

On a crate within reach of N'ga's tapered fingers lay a curved dagger and a revolver.

I followed a narrow alleyway of a uniform ocher color, reddened as the sun went down. Old low walls punctuated by rare, cramped openings onto other walls. The universe was made of petrified sand, drenched long ago in a deluge of blood. During the hot season, the air was rough and papery; when the wind picked up, the sand whipped the eyeballs, crunched between the teeth, adhered to the skin beneath one's clothing. The alleyway petered out abruptly into a dry streambed. Strange, stunted cacti, robbing the aridity of some vital substance they defended with militant spines, burgeoned between purplish stones, the refuge of scorpions. Some undetectable calamity had recently exterminated the lizards—or they had scampered, sensing the approach of calamity. And this was the Year of the Lizard! Above the line of the horizon rose a marvelous transparency of sky. There were cold days when you could make out every detail of a distant rider's dress with the naked eye, from several miles away...I was going toward the ruins. What ancestor, what descendant of Tamerlane had decided one day to raise a pile of severed heads in the long-gone oasis as a testimony to his greatness? Nomad civilization destroyed the farmers and their crops in order to re-establish the old grazing grounds ...The ruins bristled forlornly in an expanse that had only just ceased to be scorching, and still gave off an insidious heat. A town, a fortress, a graveyard? It is often tombs which stand up best to time, for they have time, and speak to men through time, to tell them of the tomb. Some crumbling stands of blue- and rusty-colored masonry seemed older than the desert. The ruins spoke in a stifled, stifling language to me, like a waking dream. They came alive in my nocturnal dreams, encircled by poplars from Europe, as structures multiplied in eerie slow motion, portals swung open, and a rushing river glistened beyond. Valentine bounding lightly down the black marble staircase, a gaiety soft as shadow floating over her, before the trac-tac-tac of a machine gun mowed down her smile and I came awake. I believe this dream visited me more than once...It was, in psychological terms, a wish-fulfillment dream, and perhaps this impelled me to return to the ruins in search of a precise reminiscence which I could never find. The uncanniness of the space was deepened by a square doorway, half buried in the sand. I wanted to pass through it, but would have had to wriggle, and run a gauntlet of snakes and scorpions; my life was not mine to gamble with, I was being childish. What possible thing could lie beyond this door that I was stumbling my way around? I laughed at myself as one does in delirium or fright, or again, in the presence of some completely meaningless revelation. Were these ruins pre-Turkish, pre-Mongolian, perhaps more recent? What is time, what are ages? If I'd had a work of archaeology handy I would have reveled in tearing it up on the spot, page by page, and scattering the pieces to the wind of the ruins.

Returning from my accustomed stroll, the bullet of a Mongol or Turk grazed my breast. The gunman scurried off down the riverbed, swiveling nervously like a hunted fox. I felt neither pain nor anger. I could have shot back, I didn't care to do so. I pressed down against the scratch with my handkerchief. N'ga dressed it with the pretty hands he then laid, joined together, under the wound to gauge the beating of my heart. "A strong heart!" I told him, for I was proud of it and N'ga's damsel eyes pleased and repelled me in the same second by their meekness. I collapsed with exhaustion. It had been a sweltering day. I fell asleep with two cool hands over my heart.

I must have slept a long time, and did not wake once. In sleep I slid into fever, into visions, into the other delirious reality that had been lying in wait for me. It was magnificent. Heat weighed upon the ancient bricks and insinuated itself into the white room; together sun, desert, and sickness consumed me upon a calm white bonfire; and I felt, at times, bathed in freshness, pure joy, friendship, unselfish love—all the things I had never really known. If I passed my memories in review, scant happiness was there, no serenity, much harshness, steely exaltation, labor, hunger, filth, danger, and moments torn as if slashed by knives; a host of cherished dead whose faces memory averts (because they were often worth more than I was), the women of a night or of a season, the one I thought I loved who betrayed me while I was in prison, and the one who was faithful but died of typhus during a winter of famine, and I arrived too late to see her again, having crossed three hundred miles of snow; there was nothing left for me to keep of her, the neighbors had filched the sheets from the deathbed, the bed boards, the four books we owned, the toothbrush. I called together the taciturn bearded men, the women whose faces were stiff with guilt, the nail-biting children. "Citizens!" I said. "You have stolen nothing from us. You have taken what is yours. The belongings of the dead are for the living, and for the poorest first. And we are scarcely the living! We live for the men of the future..." I was a bad speaker in those days. Some of them came up and shook my hand, saying, "Thanks, Citizen, for your kind words, your human words. What do you want us to give back?" I cried: "NOTHING!" It was then that I understood the grandeur of the word nothing. All words are human, I reflected, even the ugliest of them, and nothing is left. I flew into a hopeless rage against inhuman death. "A biological fact!" I kept telling myself. "Valentine, where are you?" I yearned for church singing, the biology of the void! I was raving. I opened heavy dictionaries at the entry for Death. The Encyclopedia said: "Cessation of the functions of life, disintegration of the organism..." The printed paragraphs were dead themselves. Materialist that I am, I leafed forward, full of guilt, to look up Eternity. A definition as lifeless as the other... This was what I was carrying inside of me, in the neurological crannies where memories endure. And yet the days of fever had a prodigious clarity filled, thanks to a past free of death, with natural resurrection, with clarity, true thoughts, clear streams, comforting shade—all in disorder. Valentine was present whenever I wished for her, we were fused impossibly into a single joyous vibration that was calm, calm! The delirium soothed me for having lived. I don't know how long it lasted; I existed beyond time. There were moments when I recognized the reality around me, but it was suspect, fragile, I felt for the case of secret documents under my pillow, I asked if the water was pure, and listening to the reply—"the wise man, the rose, the beloved" —I realized with no dismay that I was dying. I questioned N'ga:

"Have the planes passed over yet?" "Seven," signed his white fingers. Seven were sufficient for the operation under way. N'ga held a mirror over me and I saw, from my detachment, the chest wound that had blown huge and crimson, like a rose, a beloved, a wise man—a suppurating flower of hideously decomposed flesh, eating into me . . . No, eating into someone else, the rose, the beloved, death, biology, eternity, the encyclopedia! "What mysterious bliss," I thought, and by simply closing my eyes I could summon up the delirium.

I opened my eyes. Or perhaps they were already open, and I merely forced myself to return to the other reality, now ending its useless existence, finite, pointless reality. The low ceiling, veined with green streaks . . . A basin full of bandages. A gangly spider on the wall . . . A stocky serving woman entered, braids coiled over her ears, silver hoops knocking against her cheeks. She moved about the room, I could perceive the attention in her gaze, focused on what? The spider watched her. I wanted to call N'ga, but I could not move or speak. Why was I fretting, about what, since I had nothing more to fear or to desire? The servant was nudging my suitcase, softly, softly toward the door, the suitcase that contained my most precious things, tea, sugar, matches, cigarettes, soap, a scholarly edition of the Manifesto . . . "Thief! Thief! Bitch!" I screamed and the stocky woman heard nothing, I knew that my brain alone was screaming and that its scream was nothing. So then, thought and will were participants in nothingness? The revolver under the pillow—my brain was seizing it, but a brain without hands is nothing, I was a part of *nothing*. Before pushing the suitcase through the doorway, the servant looked shrewdly straight at me. Her little eyes were as sharp and alert as a foraging rodent's. My anger subsided. Take the suitcase, sneaky creature, weasel woman, if you want it to winter more snugly in your den, the spider won't tell. I turned away, toward the places of my childhood: the tall reeds where my father hid his dinghy to wait for wild duck.

Anton emerged from the ruins, clad in gold-embroidered white silk, like a Persian prince in an illuminated manuscript. His horse's hooves gamboled so lightly over the dead city, wasn't it a wingèd charger? Anton on a wingèd charger! I laughed. Ha, you didn't think it was possible? Neither did I, Anton. Then I saw him differently, with his flat face, funny diamond-shaped spectacles, hospital coat, and a syringe between his fingers. N'ga was holding a flaming-red object with both hands, a captive bird—hallo, they've dug my heart from my chest! No, it was a flask. Anton said, "Saved in the nick of time. You've really put me through it, you louse. Bloody hell! Time you came around. The melodrama's over, or d'you want my fist in your face?"

"I don't have a face...What's the matter? Where did you come from?"

"You're the one coming back from a long way off, brother. I got off a plane four days ago. Have some of this iced coffee. I bring you messages from on high. You've got a medal, you skunk."

"I don't care."

"Yes, you do. You're behind with your work."

I was still suspended between two realities. "Behind with my work" brought me to earth with a bump. Clever, Anton. "Tell me about Mania," I said feebly.

"Mania has remarried for the third time since she left you. Getting uglier by the minute. A veritable camel, my brother. More coffee?"

At university, I had adored Anton. We never stopped bickering. He was inventing biological Marxism or Marxist biology or was it dialectical biology...He had no time for old-world romantics who believe in love. "The couple," he would say, in the insufferable tone he adopted to emit verdicts beyond appeal, "is necessarily nothing but a two-bit drama determined by physio-psychological, not to say social, misunderstandings...Most women are garrulous vaginas with the brains of a sparrow...The outcome of a hundred thousand years of domestic exploitation." A textbook case of the believer with a cynical veneer. I wonder what happened to him? Back then he was a favorite of men in high places; he must have followed them to the grave, as he foresaw. "We have built"—it was one of his sarcastic sayings—"a colossal infernal machine of stupendous perfection, and we've settled down for a nice snooze on top of it, wearing shiny red-paper laurel crowns on our heads. There!" Nothing left of him but this memory of mine... (There'll be time to spare for sorting out memories. Anton lecturing about how we should only preserve useful ones: "To forge a living memory, in the service of an active present..." What use is your memory now, dear Anton?)

This unease that recalls you to me, Anton, comes from Nadine. Nadine is straight as a die, mettlesome, instinctual. She's right, I'm wrong: instincts are always right in the end. We all construct elaborate traps for ourselves, and when we walk straight into them, we're stunned...

■

Nadine lit a big fire in the fireplace and the room filled with well-being. She threw in some letters, photos, several passports. Her devastation had attained a calm of utter catastrophe. It was compounded of two disasters, one trivial, the other almost inconceivable, and it was the trivial one that caused the most pain, like an open wound. "Sacha only made up his mind at the end of the twelfth hour, because we were in Hell..." For two years now Nadine had been afraid to open a newspaper, receive a letter, speak a name, think of a person, let slip the least doubt concerning the totally absurd accusations that were universally proclaimed, to seem not to be applauding the unforgivable with all her heart and soul. Conspiracies whirled around like a witches' sabbath... At first she'd believed in them, like everyone; then she'd willed herself to believe the unbelievable; then she'd feigned belief and, lately, she'd been smothering fits of sobbing under her pillow. Sacha, who feared being alone with her—Sacha whom she pictured all alone with his opaque tragedy—packed her off to Mont Saint-Michel, to Nice, Cannes, Antibes, Juan-les-Pins on the least pretext: "Go look after your nerves, darling, I feel better facing all these worries alone..." Nadine at the seaside tried her best to read Proust, such penetrating novels, but what was the goal in life of all those people? She strolled along the beaches in the company of American ladies, an English boxer, flirtatious gentlemen dressed like fashion plates—and these people too had no goal in life, they served no purpose whatsoever, and the sight of them would have been demoralizing had it not been so ridiculous. She was invited to a pigeon shoot. Rigging yourself out in white flannels to perform serial execution on birds—how perverted! It made her sick. Only in small fishing ports, reading Zola, did she feel good.

Sacha withdrew from her so as not to see in her eyes the anguish that tormented him too. "What's going on? Weren't all of these disgraced men trustworthy, intelligent, incorruptible? Where is this leading us? I can't understand it anymore. I'll soon stop believing in anything..." He'd only said that much, but with a look on his face that she would never forget. It was during their dismal night in Juan-les-Pins. Sacha had kept her away from Paris. "Keep as far from the job as you can, we're going through a very bad moment," which clearly meant "I don't want you to die," not that it would prevent anything... From time to time he telegraphed to arrange a meeting: two or three days of fresh air, two or three nights of lovemaking. The news must have been dire, because he was unable to unwind in Juan-les-Pins and when she came to bed beside him, naked, he noticed neither her new perfume nor her white enamel earrings—not even that her breasts were the firmer after a regime of massages and cold showers. Instead of making love, they conducted a frosty, fitful conversation—all in veiled allusions. "No, I'm not in a bad mood, darling..." "Then look at me, Sacha, and stop glowering. Do you love me?" Nadine felt ashamed of the breasts he didn't see. "Yesterday I learned of three disappearances..." He gave three names. "Executed?" "Obviously, ah, you want me to dot the *i*'s..." "But why, why? Is it going to continue?" Nadine yanked the sheet over her shoulders, ashamed of her why's which no longer made sense. He stubbed his cigarette out on the pillow where it made a small black hole, like a bullet's, and stared at the mark with a strange laugh. "Why? You silly girl. Because they were old, well-known, and battle-hardened. Because they were in the way, because they knew as much as I do..." He swigged some whiskey straight from the bottle. Their bodies moved closer without heat, Nadine suppressed a shiver; they did not desire each other. Sacha was ruminating stolidly, eyes on the ceiling. Nadine thought (she was sure she only thought), "What about you? What about us?" and he answered her, "We'll go the way of the others. The avalanche rolls onward, and we're in its path. We count for nothing." Nadine let the shivers overcome her. "Then let's run, Sacha, escape anywhere!" There was an interminable lull before he shot back: "Stop talking drivel! It's treason to run away. Me, a traitor? To save my own miserable skin, or your pretty skin, eh? And then what would we be left with? This old world we execrate? Pass the whiskey." They took pills to be able to sleep... And now she was feeding the postcards from Juan-les-Pins into the fire.

The other disaster, trifling by comparison, sliced into an open wound. No meeting with him tomorrow, no meeting ever again with those boyish clever eyes, that somewhat hard mouth, that wiry athlete's body, those clumsy nimble hands, that lively voice, its flatness rendered abruptly tender under the impulse of a sharp organic impulses... There were so few problems for him, everything was what it seemed, so few backstage machinations in his world constructed out of a succession of planes each of which negates and destroys the previous one! It says in books that it is simple to surrender to a man who attracts you—who needs love?—that the moment's pleasure can be savored like a glass of champagne. And I don't really love him, that overgrown boy who thinks he's a man, I don't love him, I couldn't live with him for a week without finding his naïveté stupid... And so what? It would be a simple kind of love, like a ramble on a heath. But we're not cut out for healthy outdoor rambles, are we, we're better at creeping through tunnels! Tear him out, leaving a throbbing wound behind: the amputated arm still feels pain. Nadine's eyes swam with tears. All she had of him was two notes in his sprawling script, signed with a trenchant *Y*: Yours. She put them to her lips before casting them into the fire. She was packing a small suitcase with what she would take when a knock came at the locked door. Immediately the intrusive rat-tat-tat brought her back to earth. Like a cat she reached the door in two swift bounds, pressing herself against it.

"Yes . . . What is it?"

"If you please, Madame . . . You're wanted on the phone."

The hoops of danger tighten without warning and you can't breathe.

"Tell them I'm not here . . . I've gone out, I'll be back late."

"Yes Madame, very good Madame."

But it was bad, very bad . . . Apprehension made short work of sadness. Nadine slipped on new clothes she had hardly worn, so that she'd be harder to recognize in the street. A green velvet toque pinned to her curls, she applied lipstick almost without checking in the mirror, straining to hear. The room was becoming more oppressive than a prison cell. At the far end of the corridor, the telephone whirred again. Nadine heard the chambermaid say, "Madame's not back yet, Monsieur, no, not before midnight . . ." The word "Monsieur" stood out in black, buzzing letters. Who was it? Who could be calling? If Sacha, then he must have a serious reason. The other man didn't know this number . . . A message from Sylvia? Has the hunt begun? The animal urge to flee coursed through her limbs like a torrent. She caught sight of herself in the mirror, her broad face narrowed into hard lines, a face warped by the magnet of escape. She rang for the maid.

"The gentleman has phoned four times, but I just told him the same thing, Madame, like you told me to."

A good-looking girl from the Midi, the maid, with a hypocritically modest gaze. Wasn't she peering a trifle too intently from under those long straight lashes? Servants are there to be bribed, it's the ABC of the art! Nadine smiled crookedly. Say something natural, aggressive, to break the silence of the telephone and divert the girl's attention . . . Nadine thought she was talking vulgarly, but really her voice sounded deranged.

"Have you had lovers, Céline? No? Well, you will. You'll find out all about it. He's my lover and I'm leaving him, do you understand? I have my reasons."

"Yes, Madame."

"I'm going away on a trip."

"Ooh yes, Madame, it must be painful, Madame."

Nadine opened her bag and pressed a banknote into the maid's hand.

"And not a word. It's nobody's business but my own."

"I'm sure it isn't, Madame."

Air, air, I don't know what I'm doing anymore. The elevator. You never know how far down you're going. Alone in the dark trench of the hall it all vanished: the room, the smoldering papers, the telephone, Céline, their hallucinatory exchange. Nadine stepped to one side and paused to appraise the street. Opposite the doorway, a flower vendor—chrysanthemums—was lowering her basket to the ground. A bus went by, then a couple, a very young couple talking fast and, it seemed, heatedly. The sidewalks were wet, glistening with swiftly alternating reflections of yellow and red from a neon sign. The street was calling: dive in and lose yourself.

Nadine walked quickly, with determination, wary of hailing a taxi straightaway. She needed to check the lay of the land. She stopped before the window of a shoe store: in the glass she could see behind her without turning around. Nobody, apparently, but Paris streets are so crowded at nine in the evening . . . Vaguely reassured all the same, Nadine turned the corner. Someone turned and faced her so quickly that she nearly bumped into the fellow. "Excuse me . . . Oh! You? Alain!"

As he took her arm his fingers squeezed her wrist, hard. His hand was hot.

"Well, what a piece of luck!" the voice sounded false to her. "What a coincidence! Are you in a hurry?"

He wanted to sound tender, but something held him back. Too frank—he couldn't manage one of those intimate phrases that sounded so clear from his lips. Nadine was thinking: think quickly, act innocent, it's logically impossible that he already knows. He's not in touch with Sylvia, but he is with Mougin, with B, with R. Neither B nor R will find out for a while, and they may even be kept in the dark altogether, so as not to terrify the one or demoralize the other. The telephone was still ringing in her ears. She'd just said, "It's my lover," in an echo of her secret obsession. Now she said, "You called me?"

And as he was answering, "No, I don't have your number," she knew he was lying. So he knows. So, concealed not far from my door, he's been watching. Probably with someone else who filled in while he dialed from the bar. The strong hand clamped to her wrist was upsetting Nadine who wished she hadn't blundered into the first side street, with scarcely a light along it, even fewer passersby, and at the end a dark square lined along one side by the decrepit railings of a private mansion that looked abandoned. The hiss of tires made her turn. A black car came up behind them, sliding closer.

"Let's cross," Nadine said. "And let go of me. It makes me nervous. You know we mustn't meet in the street, it's against the rules."

She felt better when he let go of her wrist. Two women and a man were walking toward them. Alain made no objection to crossing the street: since it was a two-way street, the black car could not hug the curb along the other sidewalk. The fear in Nadine's body and soul redoubled: the dark presence of the car triggered her reflexes, the muscles think faster than the brain. Long ago, at the age of thirteen, Nadine had fought among partisans defending the ford across a river, fully aware that if the horsemen on the other bank were to pass over, death and torture would pass over with them. The great scythe, flagellation. Nadine knew in those far-off days that if captured she would be raped, flogged, possibly strung up. She had seen women and children her own age dangling from the trees in their undershirts with glistening, dirty flesh, offering swollen tongues and weirdly purpled breasts to the flies. Prone near the water's edge, shielded by a screen of rushes, her belly pressed against the damp grass, the child Nadine took careful aim at a tall silhouette emerging from the facing bank—a centaur—and when it fell apart like a broken toy, the man tumbling off while the startled horse reared up in the shallows, the child Nadine joyfully cursed the defeated enemy. "You won't be the one to pass over me, you horned devil!" Such schools build strength for the future. She had a jewel of a Browning in her handbag. She casually undid the clasp with the tips of her fingers. (If he notices, too bad!) The appetizing display of a dairy shop shone brightly on the sidewalk. Nadine halted at the edge of that light. The black car overtook them. Past the dairy, a dim bistro belched out loud voices. A ragged chorus in the back room joined in the song's refrain—idiotic but loaded with jollity thick as a heavy wine:

> One little lady in white,
>> In white!
>> In white!
> Oh, oh, oh! Ah, ah, ah!

"Somebody's having a good time," Alain murmured, with a sad little snicker.

Nadine felt utterly remote from him, as though he'd never held her in his arms. The enemy. She was forced to playact, to cloak the hardness in her voice.

"Listen my young friend, you're not behaving seriously! It's not safe. You know we'll see each other tomorrow!"

"And you know we won't, not tomorrow, not ever. Your husband is a traitor."

The rest of their brief exchange was as hackneyed as the lines of a bad play. "Are you crazy? What are you talking about!" "He confessed it to me himself, this morning." "You're crazy. It's impossible, I don't believe you." "Ah, so you don't believe me, you don't believe me...Have you seen him?" "No." This lie revived Nadine's sincerity. "No? Then you don't know yet! Listen, Nadine, listen darling, my head is spinning, I can hardly believe it myself, it's as if the earth and the sky were both quaking at once. Him of all people! If only this were a comedy of errors! I went straight to Mougin, and he knew already. Your husband is a traitor. You can't possibly go with him." The refrain about the little lady in white, in white, in white submerged the young man's unhappy voice. "I shouldn't suffer on his account," thought Nadine. "He really is a big kid who knows nothing, understands nothing, doesn't have an inkling..." To place her hands on Alain's temples, to plant kisses on Alain's eyelids, to say, "My poor love, it's too terrible, calm down, don't judge so fast. Sacha will never become a traitor, he's suffering worse than you, worse than the dead, his conscience is screaming...And that's his only crime." She looks at him with moist eyes.

"Beautiful Alain..."

But she also registers that the black car has come to a halt fifteen steps away. That no one is getting out, that fortunately there are people around and farther off even a policeman, his short cape hanging in stony folds. She pulls herself briskly together, as though to transmit a message learned by heart, and Alain is familiar with that gesture of hers since they used to work together.

"I don't believe you, Alain. You're telling me an incomprehensible story. I'm going to find out about these...these idiotic rumors. Someone may be plotting against Sacha...We'll meet tomorrow. Now go away and simmer down."

Alain, too, looks at the black car for a long moment (though in truth, none of this occurs in a measurable time); he turns his head, sees the police officer, maybe estimating the numbers of passersby, some of whom may be waiting for an agreed-upon signal. The bistro door swings open to disgorge a clutch of raucous couples, still flush with partying. A man's hand cups a heavy female breast swathed in silk the color of wine lees. "In white, in white, in white, a li'l laaa-dy!" Nadine seizes the moment, and almost shouts: "Go away!"

Turning on her heel, she marches off as fast as she can without breaking into a run. Rapid footsteps multiply behind her, she hears the click of stilettos on the paving stones, gropes in her bag for the tiny Browning, not much, better than nothing, at least make a noise...It's only one of the party couples. They stagger against the wall, the man's mouth glued to the woman's neck. Flat pasty faces surge forward under a streetlight, bearing down on Nadine. No question about this bunch! The Browning keeps them at bay. Nadine hovers for a fraction of a second, opposite the policeman. Here they won't dare. The flat faces waver. A laugh of deliverance rises in her throat, just like long ago when the singing bullet toppled the rider at the ford into the green waters of the Ural river. A stone falls into this stifled laughter as into a black puddle. What if the policeman were a fake? Easy enough to arrange. He has the florid, affable face of a wine lover, but what does that prove?

This street is a bit brighter, livelier. A bus is pulling away. Nadine leaps onto the back step, hampered by her carrying case and her bag, and loses her balance as she fumbles to unhook the chain. Someone grabs her elbow, heaves her up, makes room for her. "Easy, Mademoiselle, you could spoil your looks that way ...It would be a pity, you know!" The gentleman's chivalrous smile fades as he sees that it's not a little black purse she's holding in her hand but a little jewel of a revolver and notices wildness in her hard blue eyes. Confidentially he whispers, "I'd put that toy back in my purse if I were you." Nadine, her bag snapped shut, bursts out laughing. "My word! You love him that much, Mademoiselle, and he's a bad lot?" She sees a plump clean-shaven chin, a pair of soft, brown, cynical eyes, a gold-striped tie. "No," she rejoins in a truly detached voice, "still women can be such fools! It's over." The bus irrupts into the vivid lights of the Place du Havre.

■

At the hotel in the rue de Rochechouart, Nadine introduced herself to the porter with aplomb. "Madame Noémi Battisti." The porter was busy with clients, but he inspected her obliquely, with a disagreeably lackluster stare. "Room 17, fourth floor to the left, take the elevator, Madame." Nadine affected the same indifference, but her cagey, alert glance had a furtive charm. "Of all the lying little hussies with knobs on," the porter crooned to himself, "this takes the cake or my name's not Gobfin. Monsieur Battisti sports a fine pair of horns!"

Sacha kept the door locked. He opened it for her.

"Why do we have to stay in this flophouse, Sacha? The porter looks like a tubercular stool pigeon, which he certainly is, or a part-time pimp—which he probably is."

Sacha laughed and took Nadine into his arms, without energy.

"The world is full of small-time scoundrels, why not enjoy them? It's reasonably clean and it's cheap. And the area is crowded with people every night. If they're after me, they'll probably start looking on the Left Bank or around the Étoile."

The symmetry of Nadine's features blurred, as though he was seeing her through running water. "I don't care what you say, that fellow gives me the creeps...And the women, tittering behind every door. A sordid house full of sordid affairs..."

"Women's affairs," he shrugged.

Nadine turned away from him and lobbed her bag onto one of the twin beds, so awkwardly that it fell open and the Browning slid onto the yellow counterpane. As he moved to put it back, Sacha was struck by the fingerprints smudging the blue steel. "So you were playing with that, were you? Anything happen?"

"I was scared. Well, not really scared, but now I am. And the face of that pimp undertaker downstairs, and those threadbare carpets in the corridor..."

"Pimp I grant you," said Sacha, straight-faced, "but undertaker, now, let's not exaggerate..."

Nadine rubbed her hands over her face forcefully to wipe away the sensation of the black street, the black car, the dangerous enemy faces floating up at her. Her eyes reemerged, wider, ominously blue.

"They were singing: One little lady in pink, in pink, no, in white, in white... I thought it was all over... For me, anyway..."

She finished more quietly: "... and that I'd never see you again ... Phew, I feel better..."

The matching lamps on the bedside tables glowed a seedy intimacy surrounded by hostile shadows. Sacha turned on the ceiling fixture: three anemic bulbs nestled in pink glass tulip shades. The room filled not so much with light as with a pinkish-yellow haze. Nadine sat on one of the beds, her head turned away. He saw an artery flutter along her neck and her hair tremble. He could see her from the back too in the mirror, the droop of the shoulders, one arm twisted back, one hand laid flat on the bedspread... He read fear in that neck, those shoulders, that arm, that hand, something worse than fear for all he knew. Overcoming his unfocused anger, he tried to sound as positive as possible. "Come on now, Nadine, we have nothing to be afraid of right now... Did you run into anyone?" (Suspicion, within him.) "Come, you and I, we're old friends, you can tell me anything..."

"I want us to change hotels, I insist we change. Is it too late tonight?"

"Were you followed?"

"No."

"I promise we'll do whatever you want—but tomorrow. Why can't you trust me? When have you ever known me to be reckless?"

What must be feared above all, in the struggle, is panic. Our nerves preserve the imprints of animal fears, of human fears, accumulated over millions of years. A moment comes when they disobey our will. We no longer know what we are.

"Have you had supper, Nadine? I'll order something from room service."

"No. Who could care about supper?"

D went to check the door; an old household lock, a small in-side bolt, the flimsy wood would give way at the first shove... "And you expect us to sleep here?" asked Nadine as if she couldn't believe it. "Could you sleep here?" "Why not?" He drew her to the window and opened it. The empty street below was punctuated by the halos of streetlights; higher up, a vast glow suffused the misty sky, iridescent with flickering light. Nadine leaned out into space with a pleasurable feeling. D upbraided himself: you don't open a window at night without turning the lights off first. Now he did. Fifty feet down, shadowy doorways provided excellent observation posts. The beige carapace of a car crawled by, a puddle of grayish light marked the entrance to the hotel. D put his arm around Nadine's waist. "I had a fright," she said. "I was silly. Look down there. We could fall, and it would all be over in few seconds..."

"Where do you get these notions, Nadine? It isn't like you. We battle on, we persevere, you know we're right. Besides, it wouldn't be over in anything like a few seconds. Just imagine the ambu-lance, the hospital, the blood transfusions, the injections, the in-quest, the hairline crack in your spine that leaves you paralyzed for life... That was a really idiotic thing to say."

"I know. It's hard to end it. Give me a cigarette... You're always so sensible."

She was calmer now, as though returning to reality.

"I met Alain. Mougin knows. They're looking."

She related the encounter in detail. (Alain, Alain, he felt wounded by the name. Who? Alain? Impossible, surely, but why impossible? We are free agents. He sniggered: Now pay the price...)

"We've lost a few days' head start, that's all..." concluded D, his voice steady. "I've sown some clues to make them think we're going to London."

"They won't believe anything you want to make them believe!"

Fair enough.

"Close the window, I'm cold," said Nadine.

Worries thickened inside him: dark waters overflowing their

banks. With the two little bedside lamps back on, the room felt more congenial. And there was something appealing about the maid who brought in their tray of consommé, cold chicken, and weak tea. "You're Italian, aren't you?" Nadine asked with friendly interest. "Yes, Madame. You can see it, no?" "We're from Piedmont," said Madame Noémi Battisti, seriously. "Don't overdo the Piedmonts, what with our garbled Italian," D teased later. "Remember Sorrento?"

"I do," said Nadine, and she looked at him with her beautiful eyes full of wonderment.

"We're starting a different life, Nadine."

(More accurately he might have said: We are ending one whole life.)

"Are you happy with the name I found you—Noémi? A primitive woman's name. I can see you bathing, as in Sorrento . . . It will happen."

(At least admit the possibility. All that remains is to make it happen.)

That they would never again lay eyes on other, more humble places, clothed by winter snows more stirring than the gilded blues of Sorrento. Separately and together they both had this thought—and pushed it away.

"You have a lot of strength left, Sacha . . . " Nadine said sadly.

(Too much to no longer be of any use . . .)

"I've always believed that a man is identical to his will."

She concurred, with her most limpid gaze, wondering whether he could be altogether sincere. Was he saying it to comfort her or to comfort himself? A man's will counts so little these days—and his counted not at all now, not even enough to contrive a shaky salvation for them . . . While he, calm thanks to a courage that might only be a form of discouragement, told himself that will is sometimes no more than a breastplate clapped over a puny torso, stiffening the despair beneath. In order to exist fully, the will demands a goal.

"I almost like this room now," Nadine said. "It's so quiet

outside. And those glimmers there across the boulevard are like flowers reflected in water..."

He refrained from pointing out the inaccuracy of the image. The nocturnal glimmers of Paris are those of a raging commercial furnace: not flowers or lakes, but electric discharges insinuating themselves into the nervous system in order to get people to buy and sell debauched pleasures! The hotel was drowsing off. The whine of the elevator grew fainter, a door closed, the plumbing boomed and gurgled, noises that were a part of silence, a reminder of the many disparate lives winding down their daily cycle. The one certain communion among men is found in exhaustion, in sleep. In the pathos of sleep all faces look alike, resembling the faces of the dead. Under every forehead, dreams play out nearly identical primordial desires in shifting arabesques, but there is no reconciliation there.

"We're free tomorrow, Nadine, we can sleep for ages."

To sleep for ages, a wish that reverberated within him. They got into their parallel beds, then Nadine, her milky arms raised and crossed behind her head, said, "Come here to me, Sacha," because she was touched by a chill of loneliness. Their bodies met without the exaltation of love, letting go to a simple carnal tenderness. Closely entwined, they felt the same warm wave bring them the relief of simple existence. "Don't think, above all, don't think," D repeated to himself. He succeeded, a healthy discipline. Nadine, whose rosy half-moon lids had closed, suddenly froze, her pupils wide and staring. "Listen...that noise behind the door..." Instantly master of himself, D watched the door in a mirror. The revolver within reach. A subterranean crackle came from the hotel doorbell, and stopped; a lethargic footfall grew fainter on the stair... "It's nothing, darling," he said, "don't be afraid." He caught a glimpse in the other mirror of her frantic face. The deep inner wave rocked him anew, a radiant smile erased the expression of apprehension verging on horror in Nadine's features.

The world sank back into an order bereft of excitement, communion, and joy in which one is content merely to have lived, and to be suffering from neither a toothache nor an immediate terror. "Protect your peace of mind, Nadine...I don't like these frightened attacks of nerves. We've run so many risks before!" Many, yes, but minor ones compared to what was in store, poisonous spiderwebs stretched across the final break with all the reasons for living—ideas, cause, motherland, unity in danger, invisible battle for the future, vision of a forward-marching world! Everything was falling apart, only risk itself remained, impoverished, coarsened by the loss of any real justification. "It's awful, though," Nadine said, "I must get used to the idea that..." D followed the curve of her fingers, the sheen of her oval nails, as she wiped the beads of sweat above her eyebrows. Who? This absurd jealousy was humiliating. See how weak the liberated man free of old moral conventions is in you! Nadine sensed that lying motionless beside her, he was slipping away from her. "Don't leave me," she said plaintively.

Mechanically, thinking exactly the opposite, he heard himself say, "Your encounter with Alain doesn't make anything worse."

"Sacha don't mention that name to me ever again if you can help it. I hate him."

He understood, obscurely but totally. "It's really not worth hating him, Nadine..."

Before settling down to sleep, D went out to case the corridor. Two pairs of shoes left for cleaning outside the door next to theirs caught his attention. The male pair was repellently smart: gray snakeskin with crepe soles. The woman's shoes, pushed out of shape by bulging feet, suggested an overweight person always trotting about town. "Miserable creatures," thought D as he listened to the mingled snores of the sleeping couple. Back in their room, he glanced down at the street over which the row of lamps stood watch. Nothing alarming there. Nadine, her profile buried in a pillow under a tangle of hair, was asleep, a big, lovely, pacified child. "There is no sin in you, Nadine...Instinct knows nothing of sin..." He was hurting nonetheless, and reproached himself for thinking in terms of sin. Oh, what did words matter! The two loaded Brownings, each covered by a handkerchief, were luxury playthings, perfectly appropriate for their intended purpose, crafted in noble metal for the grand game of murder and suicide. We've come a long way since the flint dagger, such a cumbersome instrument for killing oneself! Did the primitive Ancestor have any inkling of voluntary death? Or is that an attainment of the higher civilizations, which offer no other means of escape? Let's hope some analyst will one day elucidate this psychological question. As for myself, Mr. Analyst, I can't help believing in an innate drive toward destruction and death. We will only have a true sense of the splendor of living in some distant, still-unimaginable future; perhaps we will have it . . . And that *perhaps* is our greatest justification, it even implies, for now, a sufficient justification of suicide . . . D switched off the lamps. Through the curtains a dim lacework of light patterned the room.

In the depths of slumber, Nadine felt an obscure—colossal—vise tighten impalpably around her. Formless tentacles turned into cold serpents twining around her body, a thick hawser weighed upon her neck. The black car opened to reveal its cramped cells. In each an upright cadaver was propped. Nadine was a little girl walking barefoot through thawing snow, reanimated by the vivifying burn of the icy water. A volley of bells rang out, Christ is risen, risen! There was an onion dome of fiery red peppered with golden stars, swaying horribly over shabby wooden houses, it's going to fall, it's falling! The Black Maria with its cells is leaving; it didn't come for me but for other people, so much the better—not for me! I'm ugly and I have abominable thoughts. Crows flapped from one tree to another, for you, we come for you, they shouted, to pluck out your eyes! "But why must I be hanged?" Nadine demanded of the stern, hairless face that had popped up close to hers. Its lips moved slightly. "Hanged, no." The serpent knots unraveled, vanished, the rope snapped, the gun went off in a violent spurt of night-blue flame within a rainbow cloud of smoke. The horror was in not being able to move—Oh god, it can't be, it's a bad dream, I'm going to wake up . . . Nadine woke up. A motorcycle was backfiring in the street. Her watch said 5:45, the hour of executions, more or less, when executions have an hour. It was still dark. She could only reconstruct the nightmare in incoherent snatches. Her hand shook as it reached for the tumbler of water. She nudged at a fold of batiste with her finger, and found herself intent upon the small Browning. Two squeezes of the trigger, and both of us would be delivered... Her hand shook worse because she was more frightened of this temptation than of all the darkness in the world. Through the fabric, so as not to feel its magnetic touch, she picked up the gun and leaned out of the bed to propel it onto the floor, under the other bed, Sacha's. This move did her good, but now she could see herself in the mirror, a whitish specter looming indistinctly in the ever cold and twilit region where the dead await their turn to be reborn—or not, since resurrection is just another dead superstition... "Resurrection is dead, it's a scientific fact." Without thinking, she switched on the bedside light. Sacha was asleep on his back, broad forehead, thin mouth, protuberant blue-tinged lids, scarily unlike himself. Detached from the universe. Dead. Nadine weighed that certainty. The icy chill from beyond the grave became an all-encompassing peace. I am dead as well. It's good. It's simple.

And Sacha opened his eyes as he did every day of his life, those preoccupied eyes, wise, real, and infuriating.

"What's the matter, Nadine?"

"Oh, nothing, I thought I heard..."

"It's a motorcycle. What a lout, making a racket at this hour! Lie down. Go back to sleep."

He exasperated her. The exasperation melted into tenderness.

"I love you," she said in a childish voice. "I love life, I love death, it's strange..."

His voice echoed hers: "Strange."

■

Monsieur Gobfin, assumed by unobservant clients to be the hotel desk clerk, actually performed much more important tasks. The trust of a proprietor ill with a kidney problem invested him with quasi-managerial status; and if he spent the busiest hours of both day and night behind the little reception counter, distributing the mail, hooking and unhooking the room keys, it was mostly due to his love of the job. An eye on everything! Seven minutes' walk from place d'Anvers, six minutes from the confluence of the rue de Clignancourt and the boulevard de Rochechouart, this hotel was like Lutetia itself, a kind of vessel anchored in the middle of treacherously troubled waters. Fail to count the linen returned by the laundry two days in a row, and you will soon count the cost of your oversight. Neglect to appear in the kitchen two hours before the first sitting for luncheon—and talk about pilferage, my rascals! A reasonable level of theft, let's say around ten percent is par for the course because in this world, or at least here in Paris, everybody's got to eat; but the house has to make a profit too, eh? And Monsieur Gobfin would never stand for "being taken for a fool, what with the price of Normandy butter." "I'm nobody's sucker," he'd say, and people took his word for it.

Monsieur Gobfin's long sparse hair, glued in black strips with brilliantine over his yellowed scalp, along with his hollow cheeks, conveyed such a knowing, indulgent sagacity that his eyes hardly ever strayed below the relatively higher zones. The brown, skittish gaze that never rested, shying away as soon as it encountered another's, shot out simultaneously in several directions, scrutinizing the clients from bottom, sides, and angles, homing in on the glints of soul that show through in the back of a man's hand, the cut of a coat, the timbre of a cough, the manner in which a pen is gripped or a bill examined. A glint of soul, needless to say, is an excessively literary flourish in this context, foreign to Monsieur Gobfin's vocabulary. He would rather have said, "how shall I put it, something like an odor, at times even a bit of a stench." His perusal was apt to begin at the level of the gut, for the belly is infinitely expressive: a pederast's paunch can never be confused with that of a public works engineer who goes for the tarts in the Lune-Qui-Rit bar. The rotundity of the con man is quite unlike, say what they will, that of the stockbroker, who is equally devious but for whom the letter of the law is sacred. The fabric of which garments are made, their quality, their color, their buttons, their wear, tear and care—all are of a revealing eloquence. It is impossible for a sea captain, when in civilian dress, to wear the same three-piece suit in the same way as a fashionable type who specializes in trafficking female slaves—white, black, or other. Their hands, exposed below sleeves or cuffs, the hair on male hands, the bumps and furrows of the joints, the rings on the fingers, say more about someone than identity documents, which are, at least one in ten, expressly designed to say nothing...Monsieur Gobfin was unaware of being a profound psychologist, but practically speaking that's what he was, to the unappreciated extent that it is possible to be one without leaving that vast circle bound by sordidness, cunning, stupidity, and police intrigues. His attention was trained on couples, vices, crimes, expenditures. He could instantly sniff out the legitimate couples, "mousey-spouseys" to him, and these were intriguing only if they hinted at some louche flaw, rare perversion, drama of the wallet or the groin, all of which were easily detected. Illicit couples, for the most part, offered little of interest. (The hotel was too respectable to let rooms by the hour, with some exceptions; but for the night, one couple's money is as good as another's and the gentleman who checks in with a prostitute generally doesn't look too closely at the little extras on the bill...) But hidden crime, now, crime that ripens all by itself behind an innocently harmless exterior, festering beyond the reach of newspapers, prosecutors, and scandal—there lies the common yet rare substance of human relationships worth studying silently from an observation post like his. Of course, the crasser breed of criminal needs to be screened out in short order, to avoid bad publicity. Guided by intuition alone, one night when business was slow and half the rooms were free, Monsieur Gobfin put on his most ingratiating voice to lament, to the giggly young lady in the expensive straw hat and her small-boned gentleman friend with hair dyed the color of flax, that there was nothing available, and sent them

to the competition: "You'll find it very comfortable there, Madame, Monsieur. They're even a bit more modern than we are!"
(Two days later he learned in *Le Petit Parisien* of the sudden and
suspicious demise of this industrialist from the Rhône, whose mistress was being sought by the prosecutor's office . . . It was one of
the supreme satisfactions of his life.) He likewise saw off the obese
individual bursting with commercial probity—a respected notary,
solicitor, company director?—who turned up with a transvestite
playing the part of the young mistress to perfection; the competition found itself the scene of an uproarious farce, kept quiet by a
hefty sum of hush money. Monsieur Gobfin was only half grati-
fied by this outcome; he took pride in his perspicacity, but missing
out on a hefty sum because of it is galling, you have to admit.

Police Inspector Barougeot regularly dropped by around nine
a.m., glanced over the registration forms of the foreign guests,
scribbled down a name or two for the sake of appearances, and re-
paired to the dining room in the company of Monsieur Gobfin,
where the two of them sat over hot black coffee washed down with
a shot of vintage marc. At that hour of the morning, the restaurant
was bathed in pleasant white light. Two Englishmen were wolfing
down their ham and eggs; an old lady was munching croissants,
with a romantic novel by Gabriele d'Annunzio propped open
before her. Inspector Barougeot showed Monsieur Gobfin a batch
of photographs being circulated by the information and investigation services (as well as a few private agencies). Monsieur Gobfin
put two of them aside, not seeming particularly curious about
either. "The reward is two thousand francs," the inspector said.
"Skinflint millionaires . . ." he sighed.

Monsieur Gobfin concealed his nervousness, which turned
him yellower. By twenty past one, the need to talk had grown so
pressing that he went up to the dining room. Madame Noémi
Battisti had just left the table and returned to room 17. Bruno
Battisti was reading foreign newspapers and nibbling on raisins
and nuts. At the other end of the room, the Negro sitting alone at
a table had started his lunch. There were some other, insignificant

people, like the man and woman who had business interests in Dijon, and their pale daughter, sapped by solitary vice. With no apparent hesitation, for his hesitation was inner, Monsieur Gobfin toured the tables making a slight bow beside each one, like a head-waiter.

"Monsieur Battisti, isn't it?" he said. "We trust you find the service to your satisfaction. Today is our day for Burgundian cuisine..."

D had seen him coming. He folded the *Berliner Tageblatt*.

"Er... yes, an excellent meal, thank you very much... Couldn't be better."

Both felt that the emptiness of these words had done nothing to clear the air. Something made each of them hang on to the other. In D's case, the desire to know "what's eating this stool pigeon with the face of a worried bedbug" made him adopt a hypocritically debonair expression that was almost engaging. More complex emotions raged within Monsieur Gobfin as he wrestled with indecision, on the brink of small but unknowable risks.

"Why, you haven't touched your coffee, Monsieur Battistini..." (Was it some kind of a ploy, to mispronounce a name he knew perfectly well?) Have you sampled our vintage marc, Monsieur?"

"Not yet."

Monsieur Gobfin summoned the waitress. "Elodie, some marc for the gentleman... No, not a shot, bring the decanter..." He hovered between the white tables, a yellow smile suspended between his sunken cheeks. A vague sense of embarrassment gathered with each passing second. "Something's up," thought D. "The bedbug's being too friendly by half..." It was a relief when the amber-filled decanter arrived with its retinue of miniature glasses.

"Let's try some, then," said D with composure. "But we must touch glasses together. Please sit down, Monsieur."

Monsieur Gobfin was only too pleased to accept. The hovering stopped. "If I may be so bold..." The opaque marbles that passed for his pupils probed the room; he sat down so as not to present his back to anyone. "No good lunch is complete without some old marc," he said meditatively. "That's what I always say. You be the judge." At three paces he was no more than unpleasant-looking; at a foot and a half, he looked scrawny and tough, a withered skin stretched over a narrow skull. His personality emerged from a sickly, malevolent weakness. D felt himself observed from all angles and broken down by unknown methods. He glanced ostentatiously at his watch. "Oh, but if you're in a hurry, Monsieur Battisti..." "No, not at all." (If I let him go, I'll never figure it out.)

"The fact is, I'm quite perplexed," Monsieur Gobfin began.

D appeared to be astonished.

"And why might that be? It's none of my affair, of course, but since you bring it up..."

"The foreign press is better informed than the Paris papers, I suppose?" asked Monsieur Gobfin, either playing for time or committing a major blunder.

Very significant, that remark. Whenever he scented danger, D became perfectly, sinisterly calm.

"Surely that's not what's perplexing you?"

Mr. Gobfin's wandering gaze locked for a split second onto the eyes of his companion.

"No indeed, Monsieur Battisti, you are an honest man and I don't need to know you to be convinced of it. A man of experience too."

All this is recklessly direct. He's sounding me out. I've been nailed. How did They trace me so quickly...? D advanced a clenched, square fist across the table. A clean and daunting fist.

"I certainly hope we're among honest folk here," he said. "As for experience, I don't mind saying I've had my share. Some rough experiences...the colonies, and I don't mind skipping the niceties sometimes. And too bad for people who are a little too smart for their own good."

Gobfin responded to the veiled threat with rapture.

"Ah, then I made no mistake, Monsieur, in turning to you! I am dreadfully perplexed, and in need of advice."

"Spit it out," D said succinctly—perplexed himself.

"It concerns a murder."

"You know what, I'm not a detective and I don't care a fig about murders. I've seen enough of them. Just forget it. Will that do for advice?"

"No."

Gobfin drew a small photograph from his cuff—or from a secret pocket in his sleeve, or from his tie, or from his long straight nose with a twist at the end—and flicked it with his finger in the direction of Monsieur Battisti's fist. It was the picture of a black man, wreathed in a professional smile—the smile of jazz musicians entranced by their own cacophony.

"The murderer."

This could be a consummately skillful move. D was nonplussed. What could be neater, at the right moment, than to whip out the ace of spades where the ace of clubs was expected?

"So what," he said, his breathing labored. "There are murderers all over Paris. What's it to you?"

(Are They about to have me arrested for murder? To request extradition, after framing me? There's no treaty... but there might be an international police convention I don't know about... hadn't thought of that... This Negro fellow might have accomplices, he's been bribed to accuse me...)

Monsieur Gobfin, having produced his effect—or simply unstoppered by relief—now became garrulous, pouring himself out in breathy tones of irresistible intimacy. "The place de Clichy murder... Come come, Monsieur, you must have read the newspapers, it was exactly a week ago..."

(Exactly a week? I have no alibi, I'll never be able to say who I was with... We were working on the Crime of the Capital of the World...)

"A young sculptor, queer, you know, very good family, millionaire parents, does that ring a bell?"

"No."

"Found in his studio, hands tied, throat cut . . . naked . . . Now do you see?" "Vaguely . . ." D searched his memory, at the same time wondering whether it wasn't a fiction. Adolescence, nakedness, tied hands, he recalled the gist of it or imagined he did. "But between you and me, like I said, I don't give a good goddamn!"

The "get off my back with your sordid gossip," clearly implied in that last retort, could scarcely escape the cloying attention of his host. Either because he had made up his mind to persist or because he was just bursting with it, Monsieur Gobfin became even more confidential.

"Look straight ahead. I believe we have the killer."

The Negro wiped his mouth and inserted a toothpick. His placid stare brushed against the more troubled gaze of Monsieur Battisti. "A trap," thought D. "They're both in it together, the black and this creep . . . To mix me up in some botched arrest—and by mistake—fine jam I'm in." There was an obvious resemblance between this sharply etched, vigorous, shiny black head and the one in the photo. The living head, with its purplish lips and sharply etched eyes, pure white and pure black, appeared to D is if about to be chopped off. He saw the coppery tint, paler at the cheekbones—a sign of previous interbreeding, like the delicate ridge of the nose. "The man in the picture is much blacker, I'd say . . ."

"A trick of the light. The light is behind us. Look at his hand."

Darker than the face, the big hand curled loosely on the white cloth suggested animal strength refined by the exercise of some craft—a hand deft with a mandolin, a trapeze bar, a sharpened razor . . . Why not?

"Hmm. An honest hand, why not?" Monsieur Battisti said. "You're letting your imagination run away with you." Monsieur Gobfin eyed the clenched fist on their own table and felt an unpleasant intimation of anxiety.

"In short, Monsieur Battisti, what do you think?"

"I'm loath to think anything. Except you should err on the side of caution. A mistake could land you in all kinds of trouble . . ."

To stand up with no more ado, to say to this groveling sneak, "I've had enough. Now get my bill, you've thoroughly put me off your grisly fleabag..."—would that be reasonable? D weighed up the unspoken tenors of the conversation. "It needs careful consideration. Do you have any other pictures of the same sort?"

"Not many. The inspector doesn't like to let them go."

Mr. Gobfin opened a scuffed leather wallet. First he pulled out the photo of a frail-looking woman, probably blond, pretty, her eyes round with fright. A series of white numbers barred her chest. "Chronic swindler, I know her... She's awfully nice to me since she learned that I carry this around, if you catch my meaning."

"Say no more."

"Her sort, you just got to know how to handle them," snickered Gobfin, olive-yellow. "Then they're nice as can be... Here, look, one that came in this morning."

D recognized himself straightaway. The picture had been snapped in the street without his knowledge. They were taking no chances! Or had I already been spotted? By whom? It was from six months ago, on his return from Madrid, with sixty frames from the Alcántara file rolled into the handle of a shaving brush... "Who is it?" he asked casually. Taken unseen on the big boulevards, the picture showed a man with tortoiseshell glasses and a broad smile, wearing a felt hat that obscured the upper part of his face, the collar of his coat turned up; he was standing beside a car. Beyond was a pharmacy, and two ladies seen from behind... A male shoulder faced the hatted man. Whose? On the back of the picture, in copperplate hand: X, alias Isoray; Marcien, alias Zondero-Ribas; Juan, alias Steklansky; Bronislaw... (1. The photo unquestionably comes from Them, from our people. 2. They haven't got a more recent one, good. Or They don't choose to release a clearer one... Good. 3. They haven't listed my alias as Malinesco, Clément, in order to comb through the flat in peace ... Therefore I'm being denounced as an agent of the others... Which others? 4. A useless photo. Only the lower half of the face is at all recognizable.)

"An embezzler?" ventured Monsieur Battisti.

"A suspicious foreigner, suspected spy...You think one of those birds would ever come to a decent unassuming place like this? They stay at palatial hotels."

Monsieur Gobfin looked Monsieur Battisti straight in the eye for the first time.

"At any rate," said Battisti lightly, "I think you're after the wrong Negro."

"And I," Gobfin responded, "am almost certain I am not—especially since our little chat. If you'll excuse me..." The marionette withdrew, leaving after him the image of his politest smile—the smile of a stool pigeon in a dull black suit.

■

D did not wish to show any sign of alarm: the Battistis remained at the hotel. Past the reception desk, the hallway expanded into a very modest lounge, furnished with a rattan couch and armchairs. A round table was littered with tourist magazines. This inhospitable setting was a good place to observe the outlines of people passing in the street, note the comings and goings on the stairs and elevator, and keep an eye on Monsieur Gobfin. The lounge was rarely vacant. Sometimes there was an ordinary-looking fat gentleman smoking and lolling drowsily over his paper. Sometimes a younger man, pencil in hand, attempting the crossword. Neither was interested in this corner of the world—the bottom of a jar where they were waiting to shrivel dry for all eternity. D settled into an armchair opposite the stout reader. The man blew his nose. Monsieur Gobfin, at his post, unhooked the telephone receiver. "Allo, Félix? Gobfin here. Send us a taxi on the dot of five twenty-five." An ordinary request to all appearances but which, D noted, contained the figure 525. A female voice rang out shrilly, accompanied by muted trumpets of deliverance: "And you didn't forget to order me a cab for five thirty?" "Not to worry, Madam, it'll be here." Still, five thirty was not 525 and this woman's car might have been ordered beforehand... The trumpets faded away. The fat man folded his paper and moved off, with a heavy stare at D. He didn't leave his key at the desk on the way out, passing Monsieur Gobfin without so much as a nod. Rude of him. Should I follow? As D tried to make up his mind, the appearance of Nadine rescued him from a budding obsession, but now Gobfin had picked up the phone again... "Well then," Nadine said, "are you coming?" D blinked a signal; idly he toyed with his lighter before touching it to the cigarette. Gobfin was calling a Monsieur Stevenson on the line. A novelist's name that had passed into the public domain, *Treasure Island*, and this Stevenson in turn will be communicating with a Mr. Milton on the subject of *Paradise Lost*, you can bet your life. "Yes, sir, I received a wire for you at three forty... Yes, sir..." One hour and forty minutes' delay in reporting the arrival of a telegram? Fishy, that. And what's three forty, 340, in code? I'm going crazy, D thought. He went outside. So many people, hard to tell anyone apart. The stout reader was returning to the hotel with a Spanish-looking woman on his arm. "They're going to bed, that's all, that's why he kept his key... Unless he went to fetch her in order to finger me..." The couple, bent forward, dived through the doorway as though headlong into a hole.

It's not in their interest to have me arrested. After all, I could claim the protection of the French authorities. They're only trying to locate me, which is worse. And have they? The question mark revolved around Monsieur Gobfin. The pros and cons oscillated evenly, like a pendulum. "Nadine, I need to check the back issues of *Le Matin*." The hubbub of the city always comforted D, even if it's a mistake to feel any safer, any more alone, any more lost on a pavement teeming with lives than behind walls protected by secrecy. It must be that mingling with other men and women restores our means of contact, of direct hand-to-hand combat. A host of random factors can work against the lone figure in the melee. Some of the odds are with him; but when he is pitted against huge, well-equipped organizations, the grim probabilities outweigh the lucky chances. All the same, big-city streets—sown with traps though they might be—appeared to give D the initiative. The city dweller, even when invisibly surrounded, relies upon himself at every turn. He reacts to encounters with the life-preserving ingenuity of a beast in its native forest, that sees a bolt-hole in every bush—a cruel illusion, if the beaters have done their job. But the hunters are also sure to make mistakes, and if their quarry doesn't panic, there's always a chance of salvation. What sets man apart from beasts is that humans have the option not to panic.

The presses were humming quietly in the *Matin* offices, a glass-walled building painted a dirty red. Bruno Battisti quickly tracked down what he was looking for in the volumes of recent issues—the crime, not on place de Clichy but on a street off place Blanche, a murder needlessly illustrated with a picture that suggested a big cockroach squashed onto the page. A teenager's body stretched prone, arms flung forward, lashed together at the wrists. Beneath the throat the sheets were stained black. The reporter, a pseudo-cultured hack, described the victim as "a disciple of the British aesthete Oscar Wilde, whose scabrous misdoings were the talk of the town in his day..." Stupid! Stupid! The reference to a "mysterious black dancer" cleared Monsieur Gobfin of the mists of suspicion.

"All's well, Nadine. Do you want to go out and find some distraction tonight?"

"It won't be easy," replied the young woman, smiling gamely. "If you wish."

Out of habit he turned to the classified ads, which he hadn't checked since making the break. And the appeal he found there hit him like a blow in the chest. "JOSSELINE begs Yves to write. Urgent. Overwhelmed grief. Faithful."

"Nadine, there's a message from Daria..."

"I think we can trust her, Sacha..."

We can trust no one any longer. No one will trust us, ever again. That terrible bond, that most salutary of human bonds, those invisible threads of gold and light and blood attaching men sworn to a common endeavor—those bonds, we've broken them, and suspicion had already broken them before, we never knew how... "You've no idea. There's no trust left in the world. Everything has collapsed. We were trust. We thought we understood the ways of history and were participants in it...And what are we? Wake up to the reality..."

But D stopped himself from saying this aloud. The Porte Saint-Martin, a shabby looming shape, resembled a triumphal arch dedicated to forgotten victories. Its old stone flanks were corroded up to arm's reach by a whitish mold made of soggy old handbills and ads. That's as high as the bill-posters could reach in their search for a pittance—or a steak—ready to pick it out of the gutter if necessary. Let's not be fastidious! A third of the dressmakers, florists, and seamstresses who advertise for apprentices and part-time female employees have connections to a brothel, or at least to prime stretches of asphalt. Cabinetmakers' notices are honest, as are cycle-repair signs (though these are a lure to bicycle thieves); but why can't a pretty girl set herself up as a cabinetmaker? Nearing place de la République, the first lamps of dusk gleamed through a drifting grisaille that was sweet to see and breathe. Like a coward, D reproached himself with having—out of a moral reflex—revived a broken contact....Daria's call rose through him from the richest, purest, most distant sediment of the past. Yes, there are sediments that are pure, even beneath cruelty.

"I won't have time to see her," he told Nadine, rehearsing an excuse for himself. "We're off in five days."

"Do whatever it takes, Sacha, you can't abandon her like that! She's no threat."

Five days, and the page will be turned. The neon signs of Paris bursting magically into life—all of them advertising businesses, many of them dirty, deadly businesses—merged together into a great fantastical poem. The little café bars and their friendly clientele, the metal cubicles on the sidewalk showing the trouser hems of pissing men (drink, citizens, piss, citizens, there are good things

in life, why hold back? It's fine to proclaim this along the boulevards!), the windows of clockmakers, cobblers, and booksellers,
the elaborate foodstuffs, the color postcards full of gross jokes and
sexual innuendo, all this bespeaks a vulgar, proud civilization, an
extremely comfortable one too, in which human beings have attained the maximum possible degree of self-indulgence, and thus
the height of freedom, of relaxation...A dangerous thing, relaxation...One of the charms of Paris, unique in the world, is that
people here neglect ferociousness—that power—and the organized brutality that drives great empires. A grandeur of another order is germinating here in the very rottenness (all social grandeurs
are rooted in a compost of decay), ahead of its time. We may pay
dearly for this clumsy attempt at a human life, more human than
ever...The six-story apartment houses were conglomerations of
walled-off lives: dramatic, well-fed, grossly carnal yet exquisitely
sentimental at times, curiously spiritual; in the vast place de la
République, with its dingy affluence and bad lighting, Yiddish
was heard as often as French and the floozies parading under terrace awnings were plebeians, servants gone over to the love trade,
to another form of service...The blackened statue, stone and
bronze, bronze blossoming from stone, of a solitary, decorative,
and disarmed Marianne, stood ignored by the streams of people
following their interwoven pathways around her feet. And no one
gives a shit! That's one way—perhaps the most genuine way—of
being republicans...

In a few days' time this will be the past, superimposed upon
other poignant images more irrevocably gone. The Tower of the
Savior and the Tower of the Dog...The delicate gray monastery,
the flat colonnade of Smolny...What will become of Paris, what
will become of our towers?

"I'll take you to the Left Bank, Nadine, how about it? Don't be
depressed...The champagne's on me."

But it was he who felt depressed. Daria's appeal reopened severed veins, poorly sutured. The veins of memory which no mental
surgery can close.

∎

In the beginning was surprise that enthusiasm could exist, that the new faith could be stronger than all else, action more desirable than happiness and ideas more real than old facts; that the world could be more alive than the self. The commissariat of an army in rags demanded uniforms—or any kind of clothing—for the worker and peasant battalions. (And let's not forget the battalions of pickpockets, con men, burglars, convicts, and pimps, no worse than the rest...) The regional commissar rolled his *r*'s, the marbles of his eyes, his shoulders, his hips, whatever moved in that fleshy ex-acrobat's body, and he would say, "With six weeks' training I'll shape you the dregs of the dregs into near-palatable machine-gun fodder, with a few heroes left over... I've got four decent noncoms and a captain of the old regime trained up like circus poodles. But I need britches! You can fight gloriously for the Revolution with no courage, no officers, no maps, and close to no ammo. The enemy's got all of that, you just go and take it from him. But you can't fight with nothing to cover your ass. Britches, that's the first condition of victory!" An erudite listener objected, through an interpreter: "What about the sansculottes of the French Revolution...?" "They wore long pants!" I was put in charge of supplying local manufacturers with material. I intervened forcefully, because pants would require more cloth than reasonably short breeches. I went to the socialized factory. A broad country road, lined with pastel-painted cottages enclosed by fences and trees, led to the bleak edge of town. Here the steppe began, the sky resting flat on the featureless land. The redbrick factory breathed neglect through shattered windowpanes; the holes in the picket fence gaped brokenly onto yards turned to waste grounds and on the black forests of the horizon. This palisade shrank a little every night, as the townsfolk scavenged the planks to restock their woodpiles. The half-dead factory filled me with a kind of revulsion. I knew that a tiny but invincible fungus was devouring the floorboards; that of the four hundred women

in the workforce, fewer than half spun out days of hunger and bitter inactivity on the premises. Old women with no ties to life, war
widows, mothers of vanished soldiers who might at this moment
be roaming the highways of a world in thrall to the Antichrist.
Their cow once bartered away, their dog stolen, their cat strangled
by some Kalmuck, I could imagine how such women might have
lost their last apparent reason for living had they not come here,
propelled by a kind of somnambulism, to sit before the work-
benches and sewing machines with their hands clasped on their
laps as they told each other their troubles. More inexplicable were
the emaciated, sly young women who came in to steal the last reels
of cotton, odd needles, and pieces of drive belt, a booty they
squirreled away between their thighs for fear of being frisked...
The winters of this town were arctic, the rations meaner than anywhere else (every town claimed this distinction, and perhaps every
town was right, contrary to common sense), and the social consciousness matched the conditions. I entered, as one enters a deserted windmill. A phantom opulence clung to the director's
office; the green desktop baize was torn, the couch broken, the
dwarf palm dead in its pot since last winter. A slip of a girl met me
with a brusque: "What do you want, Citizen? I'm busy." In those
days I always looked closely at women... This one wore a brown
woolen skirt, a leather jacket, a fine wool shawl around her head
and neck, and oversize boots. Monastic. Beneath her heavy garb I
guessed her to be small-boned and neat, I sensed her chastity. Her
pale oval face was drawn and yet charming. Blue lids, long lashes,
strictness. Plain or pretty, I couldn't decide. "The committee secretary?" I hazarded. "That's me," said Daria. "I am the committee.
The others are half-wits and loafers." I explained my mission.
Checks, controls, imperative requirements on behalf of the
Regional Economic Committee by virtue of the powers conferred
by the central authority, military supply requirements; compulsory duty to inform the People's Tribunals about any acts of sabotage, even if involuntary, and to report the least lapses to the
Special Repression Commission... "Fine," Daria said, without

troubling to conceal her irritation, "but all your orders, threats, red tape, and tribunals won't get you one blessed breeches leg stitched. And I warn you, in case you're the arresting sort: you won't take a single one of my people away unless you throw me in jail first. Even though they're all thieves except me. Now let's be clear: production is getting off the ground. The factory is working, insofar as a factory that's four-fifths wrecked can be said to work. Come on, I'll show you." One hundred and fifty workers were apparently engaged in doing something... Indeed I heard, with a strange rush of delight, the purring of the machines. Stoves crackled hotly in some of the workshops, fed with doors and floorboards from the others. Four hundred breeches, and the same number of smocks and tunics, were pledged for the following week. Daria's young voice was hoarse with a mixture of apology and defiance. "We can go on like this for three or four months. I burn moldy floorboards from the disused workshops. That's illegal, I don't have the permit from the Nationalized Companies Conservation Commission. I sell one-fifth of the output to the peasants, plus defective items, which means I can provide potatoes for the workforce. That's illegal too, Comrade. I pay for sixty percent of my raw-materials allowance in kind—illegal. I provide a weekly ration of red or white wine to pregnant women, convalescents, over forty-fives, and anyone who's clocked in ten days running, to everyone, really. That's probably illegal... And I send cases of cognac to the president of the Special Repression Commission, to keep myself out of jail." "That's certainly illegal," I said. "Requisitioned wines and spirits are to be placed at the disposal of the Public Health Bureau... So what's your source for all this liquid fuel?" "My father's bourgeois cellars," she said, reddening slightly. "My father is a worthy liberal who can't make head or tail of anything; he fled..." Thus Daria at nineteen—with the eyes of seventeen—in the year 1919, during the time of famine and terror. We walked through workshops buzzing with activity, and others where we could see the flagstones of the ground floor through the holes... And I sent her, both in the same envelope, a pile of proletarian denunciations directed against "the pernicious counter-revolutionary sabotage and waste carried out by the daughter of the former capitalist exploiter of the masses, et cetera" and a Certificate of Constructive Illegality.

In the year '22, after a good deal of throat cutting, I ran into her again at Feodossia, tending to her lungs which she said were "as wrecked as the floors of that factory, do you remember?" and striving to keep a glimmer of life going in the body of a scrawny baby girl, ten months old, who was soon to die. Daria was a director of schools, "no paper, no books, twice the children, half the teachers" and those at their wits' end. Hunger; two successive waves of terror. Premature aging had spoiled the childish charm of her youthful looks; her nose was pinched, her lips drained of color, her mouth twisted slightly out of line. I found her obtuse, almost stupid, with an edge of hysteria, one cool night on a pebbly strand bewitched by the most sparkling stars, when I tried to dispel the bitterness I perceived in her by defending the Party's behavior... Forehead banded by a black lace scarf, hands on knees, squatting on her heels like a sulky tomboy, Daria answered me curtly, clipping her phrases as she would have coldly ripped up the beliefs without which we could not have lived: "Spare me the theoretical considerations. And the lofty quotations out of books! I've seen the massacres. Theirs and ours. Them, they're made for that, the rubbish of history, the debased humanity of drunken officers... But us, if we're no different, then it's a betrayal. We've betrayed plenty, I can tell you. See that rock out there? Officers trussed together, driven with sabers to the edge of the cliff. I saw men falling in bunches, like big crabs... There are too many psychopaths on our side... Our side? What do I have in common with them? And you? Don't answer. What do they have in common with socialism? Keep your mouth shut, or I'll leave."

I kept my mouth closed. Then she let me put an arm around her shoulders, I felt her thinness, I squeezed her to me in a rush of affection, I only wanted to make her warmer, she froze. "Leave off, I'm not a woman anymore..." "A great big child is what you are

and always have been, Daria," I told her, "a wonderful child..."
She shoved me so violently, I almost lost my balance. "Be a man,
then! And keep your platitudes for a more appropriate time." We
remained good friends. We took long hikes over the parched
Greek hills of Feodossia. A kindly sun warmed the curves of the
rock, the sea was incredibly blue, the horizons of the parched land
were turning green. Great birds with azure plumage more shim-
mering than the sea alighted close to us from time to time, inquis-
itively. "Not a hunter, are you?" Daria asked. "Don't you want to
shoot at it?" She buried her baby, cured her lungs, rebuilt her
morale.

At a Trade Mission soiree in Berlin, there she was, looking elegant and youthful, her health restored. She was attached to a clandestine branch that took care of certain prisoners; having grown
up with French and German governesses, she was able to pose as
the wife of the political prisoners she visited. The jails of the
Weimar Republic were tolerably good, in keeping with a judicious
liberalism comfortably greased by dollars. "What do you think of
those men, Daria?" "I think they're admirable and mediocre. I like
them. Nothing great will be achieved through the likes of them."
Her white teeth were laughing. We were of one mind about the
frailties of the West: its deep-seated habits of selfishness, its total
oblivion to the implacable rigors of History, its fetishization of
money, its craven slippage toward disaster due to the fear of taking
risks...Its absurd belief that things will always die down so that
people can go on living. "Whereas we," Daria said, "we know how
inhuman the dying-down can be...That's what makes us superior." A year's prison sentence, served in Central Europe, spared
her the heartache of our first internal crises.

And years later, we were walking along Kurfürstendamm toward
Am Zoo, through the flurry, the luxury, the bright lights and
ready pleasures of Berlin at midnight. Here and there a jobless
man slunk through the cosseted throng of men with porcine rolls
for necks and she-grenadiers covered in furs. Girls with painted
faces—the only attractive creatures in sight—mimicked the airs of

perverse young men. Daria burst out: "Our unemployed are going over to the Nazis, who buy them bread and boots... How do you think it's going to end?" "In apocalyptic slaughter..." We saw each other in Paris, Brussels, Liège, Stuttgart, Barcelona... Daria married a construction engineer who got caught up in a purge of technicians; she divorced. "He's honest, but stubborn. We don't build as others do, we build the way you put up concrete bunkers on the front line... He'll never grasp that reason and justice take second place to efficiency, and as we're sacrificing millions of peasants, we can't appear to be letting the technicians off..." I was glad to hear her being so sensible. As the dark years wore on, those of us working with the secret services abroad were in no position to know or sense everything that was going on. We heard of new towns rising on lands which only yesterday lay fallow, of automobile, aluminum, aviation, and chemical industries developed in less than five years... On the banks of a Meuse river clad in gray silk, outside the stern old Maison Curtius washed up there like a stone coffer full of the wealth of an artisan people, Daria lectured me on the by-products of the tinplate industry. "Production will bring about justice. The rational exploitation of by-products is more important, in the short term, than ideological errors or judicial excesses. All those faults can be rectified over time, so long as there are enough little medicine tins being made... And if political reputations are unjustly damaged along the way, well, that's secondary, don't you think?" I was the one nagged by doubt. Should one not, while attending to all those pillboxes and blast furnaces, have a thought for man? A thought for the poor devil of today, for the occasionally great poor devil, who cannot content himself with straining under the yoke while waiting for tomorrow's medicines and railway lines?—The end justifies the means, what a swindle. No end can be achieved by anything but appropriate means. If we trample on the man of today, will we do anything worthwhile for the man of tomorrow? And what will we do to ourselves? But I was grateful to Daria for not doubting, at least not overtly.

When our blood began splattering the front page of every newspaper and flowing down every sewer, Daria seemed to me to get older; she put on the expression of an embittered nun with that pursed, slightly skewed mouth, and we avoided all talk of what would have made us lie and dissemble for safety's sake, or question everything and feel helpless, and admit that our very horror of treachery was tempting us to flee, to betray... We chatted about films and music. But once, in a cinema on the Champs-Élysées, Daria had a nervous breakdown. She seemed to be sobbing over the tragedy of Mayerling... It was right after the secret execution of the twenty-seven.

■

The beat of the tom-tom filled the cellar with a hectic panting. It projected an anxious din of constant celebration against the empty night; a clamor reverberating under the low vaults of the ceiling. Brown-skinned men dressed in white whipped their African instruments into an exultant frenzy. The glare of a naked lightbulb exposed sinewy arms, gleaming teeth, and the animal sadness beneath their impudent laughter. This group blocked the entrance to a private room, where a party was in full swing. A sallow boy in pantaloons and fez was carrying in a tray of liqueurs. The youngest of the musicians plunged into this secret redoubt in one effete, athletic bound... The club's public section, linked to the street by a narrow flight of steps which one could only descend bent double, feeling along the lime-washed walls, imitated a rather dingy Algerian café, partitioned by the cellar structure into a dim maze of booths where groups and couples sat on benches covered with old carpets. The torrent of barbaric rhythms, slamming from wall to wall in brutal waves, invaded brains, throats, nerves, and eyeballs like an elementary toxin.

"I've been thinking about Daria and you're right, Nadine, I have to see her."

They were coming to the end of a depressing evening during

which they had steered clear of bright plazas, cinemas, cafés, and boulevards so as not to tempt the fate that presides over chance encounters. Here they felt secure, protected by darkness as they huddled close together under a low arch; all they could see clearly of the booth next door was a pair of long legs sheathed in black silk fishnets. A woman with a mane of orange hair lay flung back against the indistinct body of a man. The reddish tip of her cigarette traveled slowly from fingers to lips. Curlicues of smoke rose and mingled under the vault. Whenever the drumming was interrupted, silence burst like a breaker exploding into countless droplets of spray; the head filled with throbbing emptiness like an undersea cave... Fortunately, this emptiness never lasted long before the trance returned.

Nadine turned an imploring face toward Sacha's shoulder.

"Do we have to go back to that horrid hotel? It spooks me. As late as possible, Sacha."

"But it's a perfectly nice hotel! What more could you ask?"

"Tell me about that murder in the newspaper which interested you so much."

"Which didn't interest me at all, you mean. I was trying to put together a few dates"

Nadine hugged up against him. "I can't tell you how fed up I am with murders. I see their shadow everywhere. I fancy the passengers in the Métro are thinking about murder. Some are afraid, watchful, agitated, everyone's caught in a huge dragnet... Will it ever end?"

The stifled, stifling din of the tom-toms bore down on them with all its beneficial weight. D sniffed the air saturated with noise, smoke, breath, mold, and perspiration. The Berbers or Arabs who were making this music, the music of an oasis in heat, exuded a muscular joy... Here's something that cerebral people have lost: the elation of leaping around a bonfire to the cadence of drums, the intoxication of feeling alive, simply. This loss must result in many strangely disastrous crimes...

"Nadine, for us it'll be finished in just a few days."

D was thinking: "Unless it is we who are finished...Anyway we remain on the level of victims...A semi-deliverance already...I hate the role of victim—only the opposite is worse. A necessity that resembles complicity often binds a victim to his torturer, the man on the scaffold to his executioner...It's an unhealthy notion...Nemesis..." During the days when we were performing so many terrible deeds in order to lay the foundations of a different future, we regarded ourselves as righteous. For it was we who sought to break the vicious circle of warfare and man's dehumanization at the hands of man. And yet we had sporadic intimations, without admitting the idea, that we deserved to be punished...That our attempts to outwit the logic of blood were merely dragging us more deeply into it. Should we have opted, then, for nonviolence? If only it were possible! (The shape of a long-dead comrade, fallen at the Far Eastern front and buried beneath the snow with what humble military honors we could provide, derisory materialist speeches of "Eternal in our memory, brother!"—this outline appeared on the inner screen. A fine, leonine figure of a man, who emerged from a victory followed by mass executions, bellowing like a drunken prophet: "Just wait and see, my friends! Winners or losers, ten months, ten years from now, we'll all wind up shot! Necessarily." We flung a bucket of cold water over him. The eldest of our company, reputed to be a sage, was muttering: "Nemesis." I flew into a rage. "What does old Greek mythology—the devil take it—have to do with our Marxist revolution?" This old comrade cursed me for a fool. He was the author of long, remarkable books on the problem of culture. The books were banned. The author died of scurvy in sub-Arctic latitudes where neither knowledge nor ideas, nor culture, nor authentic stoicism are worth a warm reindeer skin.)

A dancing girl from south of Oran came in. (The reindeer civilization knew Greek dances from the Black Sea region...Finno-Ugrian, Mongol, and Scythian women re-created the magic dances of the Ionian Isles...And what of the continuity, the human constant that is dance...Something to think about.) She was a vigorous dark girl, almost black, but amber-black, high-waisted, and wide-hipped, whose muscles in repose played softly beneath the skin. A saffron turban wound about her head, her full breasts held by a band of raw silk, a low-slung skirt falling to her bare toes, she began by sending out slow currents with the undulations of her cool, strong arms. Her navel quivered, and the smooth dark stomach became a concentrated vortex of female vitality. The heavy face, set into an inert smile, conveyed nothing but the blankness of animal beatitude. D observed her from a distance at first—from a different bend of the single spiral along which we all move. Gorgeous creature sold to our gazes, help me banish the troubles, the memories, the worry, and the bitterness that rise from my belly, just as the oldest temptation rises from yours! I thank you. The dancer, standing stretched like invisible palm fronds, let herself be borne upward by a lascivious violence. Belly, hips, and eyes quickened into rapture, agleam with sweat. Her arms flew up to undo the turban which now she tied around her haunches like a sash, forming a big rose of saffron silk that flicked between her thighs. She fell to her knees and arched her back, miming the swoon of passion.

"Has this splendid escapade lightened your mood, Nadine? Shall we go?"

They left the cellar. The street was deep in its midnight reverie. They paused at the gates of the Luxembourg to look in at the sleeping garden, utterly different from its luminous or hazy daytime self. A whiff of decay drifted from piles of dead leaves. Bare boughs peopled the darkness, striking motionless poses without shadow or duration.

"The future," Nadine said.

D seized her brusquely by the wrists.

"I didn't know you were so weak. I forbid you to be like this. What are you afraid of? Being killed, like so many others? It would only be a relief. I tell you we're starting our life over again—blindly. All we ever worked for was life, in the end, we've got a right to it."

Emerging out of the asphalt and the shadows a shuffling form approached: it was an old man in a dented felt hat, leaning on a cane. A hoarse voice spoke to them softly from the depths of weariness: "Ya' shounna make a scene 'frunna the little lady, M'sieur. What can she do about it? Don't you agree?"

"Hear that?" D exclaimed, "the night itself is speaking to us... What can you do about it?"

The limping form passed on, leaving a trail of words waning behind. "Course night shpeaks sometimes, why shounna it shpeak, night? Gotta be..."

Nadine and D burst into laughter together. Let's go home. The cafés threw their cozy glow across the intersection. At the end of rue Soufflot, the peristyle of the Panthéon guarded a necropolis eerily blanketed in mists, but life, simple and unadorned, retained its usual charm along the boulevard Saint-Michel.

■

Precaution might be regarded as an abstract, practical science, analogous to geometry (the non-Euclidean kind, needless to say). Given irregular surface A, bounded by mobile straight and curved lines D (for danger), insert point Z, likewise mobile, into one or more zones W (work) at the greatest possible distance from lines D... Bear in mind as you perform this exercise that the dynamics of the problem include unknown quantities O and I, pertaining to a fourth dimension that corresponds to enemy levels of organization and intelligence. Further bear in mind the fifth dimension P, for psychology: nerves, fear, betrayal; and, lastly, random elements X. To all these oppose dimension U (us), comprised of our own organization, our own intelligence, our own nerve. From now on, as far as D was concerned, the seventh dimension U was coterminous with the fourth, fifth, and sixth! Point Z was left with nothing to guide his movements but a demagnetized compass. No support from any quarter, and everything to fear from the services to which he so recently belonged. As days went by they were regrouping, positioning their guns, spreading their nets. It was impossible to guess what they knew, what orders they would receive, how they would plan to strike. The hypothesis of calculated inaction, however implausible, could not be ruled out. In formal terms, D's resignation infringed none of the articles of the special law that entailed the death penalty; but resignation was not envisaged by any of them. An unwritten law dictated the elimination of agents who were guilty of grave disobedience, and disapproval of the regime was the worse disobedience of all, implying the revolt of that metaphysical X—personal conscience—whose mere existence could not be brooked, for it would pull down the whole edifice of what we called "iron discipline" and others called, "corpse's discipline." As a citizen, D came within the scope of legal provisions for the punishment (death, without trial, on simple proof of identity) of soldiers deserting abroad, even in peacetime. He knew all about the ruling psychoses, for he was standing up against them. The notion that a man might bow out without betraying, as faithfully as it were humanly possible (the vagueness of that formula!), faithful to the extreme of objecting to the intolerable, and its destruction of us; that a man might withdraw only to vanish into insignificance, well, any of his chiefs willing to believe that would be deemed a lunatic, or an accomplice to be liquidated without delay.

He discovered that the absolute of trust no longer existed for him. Without that unshakable feeling, clandestine work would be impossible. Trust that the Organization would never let you down; that no matter what the crisis, no matter how acute, the Organization would never cease to weave its tight defensive web around you; that each and every member of the Organization, regardless of personal feelings, would accomplish his anonymous duty toward you; that the top of the hierarchy was staffed by leaders wielding infinite powers of secrecy and authority to ensure that no one came to grief, save at the behest of the most supreme necessity; the confident knowledge of these things endowed one, amid all the risks of the profession, with a victorious sense of security. ("None of us will perish, except by his own fault or at our hands!" one chief had proclaimed. "There is no such thing as an insurmountable obstacle!") And D had served some fifteen years in a dozen countries, including that terrifying wasps' nest, the Third Reich, where all the sappers were themselves sapped with diabolical meticulousness...

Now his rendezvous with Daria was causing him small but insoluble problems. He had no doubt that she could be trusted, that she must be going through a phase of deep distress, that she was bound to him by a friendship more definitive than love. But, for those very reasons, she might herself be caught in an invisible net. Behind a front of desperate hypocrisy she too had begun to break away. They suspected it, because no serious assignments had been entrusted to her for six months. "Take some time off," they said, "you deserve it after all you went through in Spain..." Eventually he settled on a plan. He would telephone Daria and give her fifteen minutes to get to an address on the reliably uncrowded rue des Saints-Pères. We'll synchronize our watches and I'll pick her up in a taxi and take her...where? The most convenient place would be a room in a discreet hotel. But though she's no prude, Daria might well feel offended by the awkward pretense of a lovers' tryst. And chambermaids have been known to eavesdrop, and walls have peepholes, cleverly drilled by silent voyeurs... We'd look like the most suspicious old couple, drawn by neither pleasure nor vice, brother and sister, ravaged by mutual confessions... Paris, for all its bottomless resources, had no haven to offer to a farewell meeting that boded nothing but desolate frankness.

D ruled out museums, churches, railway stations, squares, parks, both the Buttes-Chaumont and Monceau, tempting though they were; it might rain and the November cold was biting; it would be so melodramatically glum that they might just as well go to Père-Lachaise, or make one last pilgrimage to the Mur des Fédérés—fortunate Communards, to die with all the future before them! Hang the weather and what it might do. He wanted the open air. We'll go to the Jardin des Plantes. The small cafés around the botanical gardens have quiet back rooms that are often sought by troubled couples. The most dramatic marital scenes, played out in low voices, shock neither the waitress nor the patronne who keep a sly watch on the proceedings, hoping for another banal tragedy to be splashed over next day's paper: STAR-CROSSED LOVERS SINK IN SEINE or AFTER SHOOTING FAITHLESS LOVER, WOMAN TURNS GUN ON SELF. The headlines come to life when you recognize the photos. That's them, they were at the far table, remember? The dark-haired girl, with the cruel lips, "I said to myself at the time..." Such strokes of luck are rare. Most couples make up, or annihilate each other in ways that provide no pickings for crime reporters.

Narrow walks sprinkled with clean gravel stretched through the Ornamental Shrub Nursery, the Pod-Bearing Trees Nursery... The rusted shrubs, white sky, and rectilinear lines enclosed a shrunken landscape. Daria said, "I've brought you a message from Krantz."

Unexpected. Terrible. Had Daria appealed to him on orders, rather than in distress? Was he walking into a trap?

"Krantz? He's in Paris?"

"Don't worry, just a tour of inspection. It was him who got your letter."

("He had no right to open it... Or every right, perhaps...")

"I work with him. He knows we're friends. He was so understanding about it... I didn't know there was such kindness in him. He said to me, 'Poor fellow! His service record is outstanding, we'll fix him up with a special posting in the Far East. The war is coming, and we lack men of his caliber. Find him if it's the last thing you do... Tell him he has nothing to fear for the moment, I have a lot of pull and I'll stand up for him. His nerves have given way. Do you think mine are in good shape? And I won't inquire after the state of yours... These are terrible times we're living in, rife with wickedness, we need blind faith and boundless energy or else we're lost, I mean all is lost, because him or you or me, we hardly matter! I can still burn his letter and persuade them to be lenient. He can't remain abroad of course, but I promise him a challenging job in strategic economics, good hard work a long way away. They'll forget all about him, and then they'll reward him, and one day he'll thank me for having saved him from himself...' So there you are. Krantz begs you to meet him, just for an hour. I believe he means it..."

"You do...?"

D's blood ran cold. He shouldn't have met with her! Pure sentimentality—idiotic—the memories, the heroic years, and the rest, a quagmire. How many times has Krantz delivered himself of similar speeches? And how many dupes and dead men does that make? And if he does mean it, which he might, is the system equally sincere? The system doesn't give a hoot for the sincerity of a Krantz, it goes its own way. Good job I only gave Daria twenty minutes to get dressed and meet me, or she could have alerted the whole pack for all I know. She did have time to phone... A stooped figure turning the corner into their path riveted D's attention, until he saw the small boy who caught up and clung to his grandfather's hand. D's ideas went off on a new tack. Informed by Krantz, Daria is now hopelessly compromised and she knows it. What fate can she expect? Unless she moves against me, no-holdsbarred. That would be her only lifeline, and a precarious one at that. D feigned assent.

"Krantz is a very fine comrade." (To himself: How has he survived so long?) "I don't have to tell you, Dacha, how hard these last days have been..."

He turned toward her with a wry smile on his face. "You know, I was in a cabaret the other night, and there was this big girl singing a soppy love song:

> It hurt me so bad
> My heart's going mad...

"Somehow it stuck with me—though I'm not the sentimental type—and I sent her a bouquet, with a card from my next-to-last alias. Red roses, naturally."

He couldn't meet her steady gray eyes.

"I'll see Krantz, he'll burn my letter, and I'll go home. If I'm brought before the disciplinary council, I can bank on ten years—without the letter. Rehabilitation through labor, that's what I'd like. If Krantz is as influential as he claims, I'll put in for a navigational job on some great Arctic shipping route..."

"Are you serious?"

"Yes. This garden's like a cemetery. Let's go a café downtown. No need to hide anymore. You're my salvation, Dacha, and I'm glad it was you. You, the same as in Feodossia...I'm very tired, you know..."

"Don't do it," said Daria sharply.

The same, indeed, as in the old days. Her child-nun face scarcely marked around the eyes and the corners of the lips by the hardship of living. Hardening.

"Krantz can't help you—no one can. If you go home you're lost...You'd be lost even if you'd done nothing. And I'm probably as doomed as you are."

They were face-to-face and he impulsively moved closer.

"Then let me be the one to save you. Come to us. Wherever we find a safe haven, I'll call you."

"You do me so much good," she said, enlightened.

D was already regretting his impulse. His apprehensions had been turned around too simply. How to see into the true depths of another person? He had flipped from humiliating mistrust into effusive fondness.

Boulevard de l'Hôpital has little character. One trudges past drab buildings, factories, the Salpêtrière, to the noise of locomotive whistles from the nearby station. There are brewery trucks, cement mixers, Maggi dairy vans, railroad trucks; a Cadillac, here, would stand out like a lady in a haute couture outfit from the place Vendôme. The space is vast and colorless. Events there must be commonplace, like registered trademarks, without the pathos of luxury. There Daria and D found a secluded café with tan leather upholstery, brightened by blue piping. "When, if ever,"

Daria wondered, "will there be bars like this at home, so cozy and unpretentious that you don't even notice?"

"When we're dead. We had not the faintest inkling of the sweat, blood, and shit that go into forging a people's well-being..."

"Careful. You're sounding like a big capitalist. Don't you think what's needed is a greater effort of generosity and intelligence? The days of primitive accumulation are behind us."

"Not in our country. And the days of destruction lie ahead."

Thus they embarked on the double monologue around a common obsession they share with other troubled minds. "For two years now, I've been living in a kind of dark hallucination," Daria said. "Me too..." "You know that business of the embezzlement of Forest Trust funds, part of some dirty scheme, I forget which? Well, I happened to be involved, I carried a part of the funds, I know where they were going and on whose orders! And there was the Fat Man confessing his head off, spewing his poisonous drivel left, right, and center, poor fellow, what they reduced him to! I read the papers, listened to the radio, heard his voice, plausibly delirious, began to doubt reality, I couldn't look people in the face, I went through the streets covered in shame...I tried so hard to understand. Is it possible to understand? Please, Sacha, don't put on that hangdog suicidal look."

"Suicidal, did you say? On the contrary, I'm fighting to stay alive in order to understand, to witness the next chapter and the epilogue...Could we have got it horribly wrong on some hidden point? I don't think so. The planned, centralized, rationally administered economy is still superior to any other model. Thanks to that, we survived in circumstances that would have made short work of any other regime...But a rational administration must be humane. Can inhumanity be rational?"

"Sacha, I'm going to ask you a question that might seem thoughtless or infantile, but listen to it anyway. Didn't we forget man and the soul? Which are perhaps the same thing..."

"We did, because first we forgot our own selves. Individualism—once you get beyond the crude Darwinian law of the war of all against all—is no more than a sorry delusion. And by over-coming it, we were able to raise up a heavy piece of the world, able to become better, more energetic people. That's why my heart is with those who have forgotten their very names and won't appear in the history books, either, after serving as the catalyst for events that will never be fully understood, since the people who brought them about will remain unknown ... Our unpardonable error was to believe that what they call soul—I prefer to call it conscience—was no more than a projection of the old superseded egoism. If I'm still alive, it's because I realized that we misrepresented the grandeur of conscience. You don't have to tell me about the de-formed or rotten or spineless consciences, the blind consciences, the half-blind consciences, the intermittent, flickering, comatose consciences! And spare me the conditioned reflexes, glandular se-cretions, and assorted complexes of psychoanalysis: I'm all too aware of the monsters swarming in the primeval slime, deep inside me, deep inside you. There's a stubborn little glimmer all the same, an incorruptible light that can, at times, shine through the granite that prison walls and tombstones are made of; an imper-sonal little light that flares up inside to illuminate, judge, refute, or wholly condemn. It is no one's property and no machine can take the measure of it; it often wavers uncertainly because it feels alone—what brutes we've been, to let it die in its solitude!"

"This little light of yours has been around a long time, in liter-ature. Tolstoy says something about 'the light shining through the darkness ...'"

"Wrong, Dacha. the Apostle John said it before him, and he can't have been the first ... I'm going off the rails into metaphysics and mysticism, aren't I? Go on, say it, your eyes are laughing at me ... We committed a mortal error, materially mortal I mean, leading to countless heads blown apart by executioners' bullets, when we forgot that only this form of conscience can accomplish the reconciliation of man with himself and with others, and keep a watch on the old beast that's ever ready to be reborn, equipped with the latest political machinery...Our language has separate words to denote objective consciousness and moral conscience—as though the one could subsist without the other! I've boned up on the relevant literature. Some scholarly authors define such phenomena as a superego that precedes the individual. Let's not be afraid of psychological definitions, anymore than we are of ghosts. We successfully blasted the social superego with the existing artillery; empire, property, money, dogma, oppression, all were blown away. It should have meant the release of what is best in man, but that got smashed along with everything else, I fear. And we've become the captives of a new prison, more rationally conceived in appearance but more crushing in reality, because its foundations are firmer...Empire, dogmas, and all the rest were soon reconstructed on planned machinery, while conscience died out...I'm getting out. I'm escaping. You must escape too."

"Be still for a moment, I beg you," Daria whispered, "people are looking."

D was speaking this way for the first time in his life, and it helped him to see more clearly; he felt new strength surging through him. But anxiety transmits itself in subtle ways, and he was as quickly overtaken by despondency. "What are we escaping to? I'm talking as though one could escape into space. The whole edifice is collapsing, and the only certainty is the coming war which will be continental, intercontinental, chemical, satanic. We'll be left to ruminate sullenly in our corner, isolated, unknown, and useless, muzzled by what cannot be told, as the catastrophes move closer..."

Daria said, "I'm sorry. You're right, and it makes me indignant to hear you. You talk like a symbolist poet:

> Hearts once full of enthusiasm
> Have nothing left but fatal nothingness ...*

*Alexander Blok, 1914

"And there's another poet, a Frenchman who betrayed every one of his promises, who wrote:

> Traitors are saints
> And the purest hearts are those of murderers...*

"He was onto something there. I wonder if literature notwithstanding, we don't deserve to be ostracized or shot as much as anyone. Are you sure the Master doesn't have good reason for the killing, some higher reason we don't know of?"

He watched her twist her gloved fingers as though twisting her own arm. His answer was blunt.

"You're ten years younger than I am, Dacha, and so the Master means more to you. We of the old guard, we were trained to depend upon ourselves, we had no use for masters, except those anointed by trust... But to the snot-nose brats of the next generation, intoxicated by the loudspeakers, no doubt he seemed a kind of god. Those youngsters will only sober up inside the grave he's digging for them, or on the very edge of it, like us for that matter...I met him twenty years ago. There was no genius about him, there was no more to him than to any of us—something less, in fact. This deficiency served him well, as scruples and high-flown ideas can only interfere with the practice of tyranny, while a sense of the ridiculous might have prevented him from deifying himself. Remember how he rose to the top: it wasn't particularly forceful or successful, and, above all, not even all that cunning. Historians fabricate greatness, as they call it, because they are mediocrities with lame imaginations who can only plod along the beaten track, and they're cowed by the cudgel and their own mediocrity into shoring up the cult of established power... Power has the same hold over the tyrant as over anybody, because he has seized the levers of power just like a burglar making off with the Grand Seal of State. The burglar must lie low, the tyrant must de-

*André Salmon, 1919.

fend himself even before he's attacked, because he feels the re-proof... Oh, the Master has his reasons all right—the worst!"

Behind Daria's chilly hostility her panic was discernible, much like Nadine's. (Women are more damaged than we are. This world is crueler to women...)

"How profoundly you've detached yourself," she said slowly. "You speak like the enemy."

"Whose enemy, Dacha? The enemy of all that we longed for, that we built, that we served? Of everything I still want? Of everything we were? Of the Party? But what has the Party turned into?

"The worst of reasons can never completely escape reason... I'll suggest several. Treachery, ensconced somewhere among us at the top of the structure. You see, I'm quite capable of reasoning like him, because I share his concern. But I'll discard that hypothesis as too far-fetched. What remains is a kind of madness of suspicion and fear, born of the sense of a crushing mission that is too heavy for those unexceptional shoulders... There is some of that within us too, a vast psychosis of the threat that has hung over us ever since we began to exist... A psychosis that battened on the stifling atmosphere of dictatorship... Salvation lay in opening the windows and letting in the air. Lastly, a reasonable reason, by which I mean an intelligible one, as in certain straightforward cases of insanity: war. This well-fed Europe, smugly wallowing in its pleasures, is so astoundingly mindless that the only people who have half a notion of what they are doing—and half is enough in the circumstances—are a handful of methodical lunatics like the addled visionary Hitler, or the fat beribboned Göring. And what they're doing is driving their machinery over the brink. For me, the war never ended, I'm a soldier of the invisible war, the war of transition; I see the sappers' tunnels ramifying with my own eyes, I see them packed with explosives while parliaments babble on above in blissful ignorance; give me my statistics sheets and a pencil and I'll tell you how long we've got before the fireworks begin. Because mines are designed to blow up, and the fuses have been lit. There's no other way out for this aberrant world. The Master knows it better than anyone. All the cards of the fiendish poker game are on the table, and they rear up, huge, in colors of fire, to taunt him in dreams every night. And he's losing his head. We'll be dragged into the war whatever we do, we'll be stormed, grabbed by the throat, stabbed. So he wants to stand alone over the abyss; he can't tolerate the presence of more talented rivals, because they too might lose their heads (less than him, mind you) ... He doesn't want to feel another precipice behind him, the little personal abyss into which he would assuredly be pushed by greater men ... His true madness is to believe in his mission."

Daria wondered: "Don't you have the feeling of deserting?"

"Deserting what, the secret execution cellar? If I thought I had five chances in a hundred of surviving until the war, I'd swallow the disgust, the horror, the remorse, and I'd stay, I would! Can you honestly give me those five chances?"

"No."

Her tension had subsided.

"What about me, Sacha, what do you think will happen to me?"

"Let me ponder that a moment. Would you like some port, a vermouth?"

They were two peaceful customers in a small brown café, a reconciled couple preparing to go home and resume everyday life. Madame Lambertier, who couldn't abide histrionics, glanced over from behind the till and felt reassured. You see, when you truly care for each other all it takes sometimes is to have things out, candidly, in good faith ... Madame Lambertier also maintained that a decent, well-kept establishment with a family atmosphere, so to speak, encourages marital reconciliation (at least at the times when ponces, tarts, cops, spivs, and other lowlifes who bring in the serious money are not around ...). "Marie," she hissed, "give them the good vermouth, for heaven's sakes!" Meanwhile D was not pondering so much as letting the problem resolve itself in his mind.

"You're compromised, Daria, by your long-standing relationship with me and a few others ... But who isn't, these days. Krantz more than you. Fifty-fifty, I'll give you that much."

"Then I'm staying. I wasn't sure before, I was going to beg you to take me away no matter where. Because I also run out of strength sometimes. I cry, I smoke, I've tried to drink. I tried picking up a lover in a nightclub: it was gruesome enough to keep me chaste for a long time . . . I take tranquilizers and sleeping pills. I have this elderly doctor, a very good man for whom I've had to make up the most hair-raising love affairs, with constant twists worthy of a film . . . He must think I'm deranged. His advice is hopeless, but his pills do the trick. But you've steadied me. You've convinced me I must stay."

D felt a pang of joy, as though this proved that he himself was no traitor . . . He listened to Daria's affectionate voice ". . . and let's keep a possibility of contact, I have no right to know where you're going, but please make sure that if I feel frantic and lost, if I'm all alone in the world, I can come and find you both . . ."

"I will, Dacha."

(It's dangerous, but I will . . .)

They parted with a brief, friendly hug, in the midst of the racket made by an incoming brewer's truck. The boulevard stretched before them, stark and bright under the milky sky.

■

On reaching the hotel desk, Monsieur Bruno Battisti felt a sickening jolt. There was a letter in the pigeonhole of room 17. IMPOSSIBLE since the addressee had no existence for anyone! A summons from the French Sûreté? A message from Krantz, meaning they've got me? Monsieur Battisti took the letter from Gobfin's fingers, affected to barely glance at it, laid it on the desk, and said, with some exaggeration of his courteous manner so as to gain a little time with himself, "Please be so kind, Monsieur, as to prepare my bill, we're leaving in an hour."

At this, Monsieur Gobfin showed such surprise that he instantly appeared even sallower, knobbier, and more shifty-eyed than before.

"You don't say, Monsieur Battisti!"

"I've just said so. We're catching the fast train to Nice."

"Ah, what a pity," Monsieur Gobfin sighed, looking deeply put out. He half bowed, for a lady was coming down the stairs. Confidentially: "Could you not delay your departure—only till tomorrow morning, Monsieur Battisti?"

Monsieur Battisti, who would gladly have driven his heavy fist right between Quince-Face's turbid eyes, merely muttered, "Whatever for?" in a low growling that said "bugger off." Even more intimately now, Monsieur Gobfin filtered "serious accident" words through his clenched teeth: "The police were here . . ." There's no mistaking that voice. Monsieur Battisti took it without blanching, taut as a bow already (and with the envelope of the IMPOSSIBLE letter under his palm). Play close to your chest—for what it's worth!

"What of it?"

"You'll miss the arrest."

To double up with full-throated laughter, if that were allowed, what a relief! A madman! In this mad world, madmen pretend to be calm even at the reception desks of small hotels! So yesterday's fat man really was there for me. The dame in the tit-crushing corset, whom he brought, was there for a sight of me. A brilliant piece of tailing, a prodigious feat! And now this crackpot lamenting my absence at the arrest—or pulling my leg! No future, a dark hole. Upstairs Nadine, suspecting nothing, poor Nadine . . . Now that the game was as good as up, Monsieur Battisti switched to puzzlement, so awkwardly that Gobfin, who had been scrutinizing his client's tie, was taken aback.

"Arrest, what arrest?"

The burly ginger-haired Englishman from room 6, wearing a narrow-brimmed felt hat and a gray shiny overcoat—the kind popular with sailors on leave—was handing in his key.

"No letters?"

"No, sir. Will you take your evening meal in your room like yesterday, Monsieur Blackbridge?"

Monsieur Blackbridge's gullet emitted a sound like chains screeching over a rusty pulley...A scene out of a third-rate melodrama with a noir ending, Blackbridge, Black Bridge, just the name to slug me from behind precisely in the next instant. The chain over the pulley—the chain, the cell—how easily we're scuppered! Frau Lorelei Hexenkrantz, Madame Lorelei "the Witch" Krantz will step out of the lift...The world's lunacy is artistically organized down to the smallest detail.

"No." (The Englishman swallowed back a half laugh, like a chain rattling down a well.) "I'm going to Tabarin."

"A wonderful show, Monsieur Blackbridge," uttered Gobfin suavely.

The narrow-brimmed hat, the iron-gray overcoat were sucked out into the street. The witches carried off this ruddy man who imagined he was sauntering down rue de Rochechouart toward a sabbath of naked thighs...Battisti unclenched his jaws to repeat, as though landing a punch, "What arrest?"

And Monsieur Gobfin lit up, with a drowned man's smile: "The Negro's, of course!"

What Negro? Surely you're not about to tell me I'm black? Anything is possible when madmen start to babble.

"It'll be most discreetly done, in his room or in the corridor. We don't expect any trouble. Two inspectors are already standing by in the dining room."

Things slide mysteriously back into place; what was spinning out of control returns to equilibrium; you thought the plane was nose-diving right into the hard rim of the mountains, but the wings level off, the journey continues...

"Oh, quite right," said Monsieur Battisti, "a great pity as you say. But time is money, my friend. Won't this mean unwelcome publicity for the hotel?"

"Far from it!" Monsieur Gobfin said. "The crime was not committed on our premises, you understand."

I'd like to know what crimes haven't been committed here, you smarmy rat, was what Monsieur Battisti almost replied—but now the plane was diving down again toward a carpet of Paleozoic rocks: Monsieur Battisti picked up the IMPOSSIBLE letter. Curtly: "The bill, please, and fast. We're off in half an hour."

We'll soon see whether that creep doesn't grab the telephone! Battisti withdrew to the rattan sofa; Gobfin, on cue, unhooked the ear trumpet. Battisti kept an eye on him while dazedly reading the envelope again. Interior Ministry...No, what? Vatella and Misurini, Pasta Wholesalers..."Monsieur César Battistini..." Triple blockhead! Or is it a deliberate put-on, the better to gauge my reactions? Gobfin was talking through the receiver to a laundrywoman: "...and a mistake, Madame, in the linen count...We make it twenty pairs of double sheets, sixteen pairs of single sheets, forty-four pillowcases, six dozen napkins..." Monsieur Battisti's ear listened for figures that might be a code...A news vendor pitched his falsetto into the lobby, "Speeee-cial edition! Ministerial criii-sis..." The Negro gentleman ambled in, stylish in his way, with the smooth suppleness of a dancer, the murderer nearing the scaffold, awaited on the first floor by two inspectors drinking red wine, what else. Monsieur Gobfin murmured, "Just a moment, don't hang up..." and handed the Negro his room key, his key to the other world where you might arrive pulling a basket on a string containing your head which is no longer attached to your shoulders. "For pity's sake, porter, put it back on now that I've paid for my sins." You'd have to be a ventriloquist to say it, waving your distracted hands about...Gobfin was beaming with an air of pleased obsequiousness—at the counter of the imagined other world. "Thank you," the Negro said without moving his lips, a ventriloquist already! Ready for his fate. Monsieur Battisti pushed his brief reverie aside.

"This letter, it's not for me..." He couldn't refrain from adding, absurdly, "It's for the black man..."

"Really?" started Gobfin. "Did you see him? He's done for now! But no, the letter's not for him."

An ingratiating, ghoulish grin split his face.

"Not for him nor for you either... My mistake, Monsieur Battistini, begging your pardon."

"Ba-ttis-ti," D stressed. "No 'ni.' Battistini chopped short."

"Chopped short," echoed Gobfin, coming down sharp with the side of his hand, and winking at the thought of the Negro.

In the marketplace of Samarkand, white-haired storytellers still chant the tales of the Thousand and One Nights as they jerk the strings of a puppet theater. Fingers move in the mystery box and out pops the Wicked Black Prince from the subterranean depths of Evil. Another movement, and the scimitar of Righteousness is brandished... The third plainclothes inspector appeared in just such a fashion. Monsieur Battisti immediately identified him by his boar-like neck and shriveled face. "Going up?" Gobfin inquired, with hidden passion. The shriveled face answered with a sinister "Not yet" as it turned to take in Monsieur Battisti. "The main thing is to get out of here," thought D.

"Quick, Nadine! We're off in ten minutes..." "This place is awful," Nadine answered in a low voice. "But do we really have to leave?"

■

We are made in such a way that our fears subside and our obsessions vanish by virtue of a rhythm we don't understand: often a change of scene is enough. The Battistis felt good in Le Havre. The air was salty and damp; light mists blew in from the Channel and floated over the avenues of the prosperous, peaceful city. The trees themselves, though bare of leaves, looked nourished by a richer sap, a healthier breeze, than those of Paris. The big cafés displayed a prosperous dignity. Bruno Battisti was unconcerned to find no reference to the Negro's arrest in the papers. "They might very well keep it quiet for days," he said to Noémi. ("Let's get used to our new names.") The green, foam-flecked, heavily churning sea instilled in them the carefree sense of having completed their escape, as though their connection to insoluble problems would be broken by crossing the ocean.

We live by memories accumulated within the unconscious, thought Bruno. We breathe more freely among mountains, because they arouse a quivering reminder of the primeval forest; caverns oppress us, echoing the age of fear and primitive magic— while oceans promise escape, adventure, discovery. For as long as humans have been persecuting and killing one another, hunted men have sought salvation on the seas, in such numbers that their flight must have contributed to the peopling of the earth; and it is surely fugitives, rather than conquerors, who led the way to new worlds... Even the legend of the Argonauts is that of Jason's banishment and flight, the Golden Fleece perhaps no more than a symbol of escape. Modern man could usefully return to the study of ancient myths in the light of his recent experience... And what of our feeling that the sea is beautiful, when it is actually an inhuman, featureless mass of an enormity to appall the thinking insect standing on the beach? The expanse of it, the aimless movement, the elementary power... shattering concepts! And yet the promise of an imagined safety is stronger still.

Now that cablegrams, police descriptions, secret orders, lies can circle the globe in a matter of hours and there are no more islands to discover, no more hideaways in which to slip the net of the special services, the urban labyrinth is a safer bet than any distant archipelago; which means we are the dupes of a memory wired to our instincts, when we listen to the millenarian song that hums in our breast in communion with the ancestors, paddling out to sea in their canoes... The city is our admirable prison, outside which we now find it almost impossible to live. We long to escape it, just as we involuntarily wish—in horror—for the deaths of our nearest and dearest, no doubt because through their extinction we aspire to our own...

"Nadine-Noémi, I've worked out beautiful plans, like an engineer applying himself to a construction problem. We have very little money, and that merely by chance. They controlled us through that as well, it hadn't occurred to me. (Disregard for money was one of our strengths and it's turned against us.) "We still have our hands, and our heads, useless now... I've decided on definitive liberation, goodbye to Europe, Asia, cities, the coming war... Tolstoy was on the right track in some ways. How much earth does a man need? Enough to feed him and to bury him... We'll have that much in a country that's hot and violently alive. Because in losing everything, we should at least recover the primordial sensation of life."

Noémi rejoined lightheartedly, "The great mystical count professed the philosophy of a petty vegetarian rentier. At least that's what they taught me. Don't sulk, my last-minute Tolstoyan, I love to hear you talk like that."

It was their last morning in Europe. They spent it walking on a wet stony beach at the edge of the cold sea, making fun of the ugly villas that dotted the shoreline, houses as tawdry and pretentious as the stunted lives within. And oddly touching, all the same, for even this second-rate architecture had something to say about man's resistance to the destruction of the best in him. An aspiration to adventure, to aesthetics, translated as plaster busts of Second Empire demimondaines protruding from the rocaille of gardens no bigger than the exercise yard of a prison cell; the love of light, of the purity of the heavenly spheres, was expressed in arrangements of tinted glass balls over fountains kept dry out of thrift. There were villas trying to look like Scottish castles, Bavarian chalets, Turkish pavilions, or Gothic piles; they looked like toys for overgrown children whose imaginations were waging a losing battle against extinction.

Beyond loomed the noble form, gray and tormented, of the cliffs. All the forms of the earth are great and noble. Have you noticed how no terrestrial thing is ridiculous? Ridicule and meanness appear in the works of men. They are defeats... We are all limited and ridiculous... Yellow grasses tousled the cliff top; below, birds nested in the holes and there was a great palaver of beating wings to deter nest-robbers. The toylike cannons of a fort poked over the

summit; its blue-white-red flag waved innocently in the wind...
The Battistis were forced to skirt a recent cave-in. As they contemplated this display of ruined might, they were accosted by a woman with a shopping basket on her arm, returning to some isolated cottage on the beach, curious about this pair of bad-weather walkers.

"It came crashing down a month ago," she said. "Quite a fall!"

"No one killed, I hope?" Bruno asked out of politeness, naturally assuming that no one would be killed out in this lonely place.

"No, no! People only come here on Sundays, during the good weather. It was a weekday and out of season... Just a dog trainer who lived in a hut."

"Of course," said Nadine, as if in agreement. "That doesn't count. Good day, Madame."

They retraced their steps, feeling sobered and yet amused. A cliff battered by the tides cracks open, starts to shift, becomes treacherous moving earth of unstable times, begins to slide; a distant rumbling gathers force, a keening, a subterranean chant, a song! A hunk of chalk and clay, long accustomed to the blistering winds, breaks off and pitches forward slowly like an instantaneous murder. Insignificant catastrophes are prepared and consummated much like those of whole societies, heralded by a mounting murmur that can be heard, provided one has one's ear to the ground rather than listening to jazz. "Nothing to worry about," is the complacent response, "we've heard such noises before, the world is perfectly stable, the proof, look how healthy we are..."

"I can still hear that stupid lady saying 'Oh no, no one was killed...'" began Noémi. "'Nobody but a dog trainer.' Think of him, patiently building his shack out of bits of wreckage, sleeping alone under the fissured cliff to the sound of the tides, waking up to this bleak landscape...I wonder what he trained his dogs to do? Fetch starfish? Beg on their hind legs for a lump of sugar? How many contingencies had to come together for him to die here with his dogs!"

She sized up the cliff face with a glance.

"Do you know, I wouldn't mind living here myself. It looks solid enough. I'd happily run the risk... Then if one night we were buried under tons of rock, so what? It'd be natural. No one else, just us..."

Bruno said, "Soon they'll be writing, 'just' a town, 'just' an army, 'just' a people, 'just' a country... A little country under a collapsing cliff... In a time of wholesale collapse. Professionally trained military staffs are this minute working out the figures for the whole of Europe, in accordance with various scenarios. The first year of the war will cost X million young lives, resulting in an X percent fall in the birthrate and having X impact upon production. Not unlike planning for the annihilation of, say, Belgium— machines, bodies, and souls under a toppling Himalaya... It's only a matter of time. Our calculations are as precise about the initial time frame as in predicting an eclipse... The latest possible date is already settled, though events may well jump the gun. The madman-god of history is in a hurry..."

A nippy salt-sea wind had risen against them. Noémi turned around, the better to be enfolded by it. She saw Bruno trudging toward her, hunched, bareheaded, his hands stuffed into his pockets. His determined tread over the slippery stones, his wrinkled brow, the bitter set of his mouth, made her shout, "What did you say? I could hardly hear... the wind... Sacha..."

"Nothing... nothing."

With all his strength, he wanted to shout, "Nothing... I announce Nothing! Cruelty, destruction, madness, nothingness... Nothing!" For this long-ripened vision burst within him with the impersonal clarity of a mathematical formula explaining the past, the murders, the future. "I have to stay... To defend... What? You'd defend nothing, you'd disappear before you could move. Nothing is possible... The magic word, the keyword of our time: Nothing.

"If only I could be one of those industrious ants who will soon be trying absurdly to rescue a child, an injured man, a tool, a book from the rubble of some flattened city... One of the infinitesimal brains working underground in enemy strongholds, tirelessly sapping the bureaus of the planners of destruction . . . The final justification of life: to destroy the destroyers without knowing whether one is not, in reality, finishing the job for them."

He cried out into the wind, with a bitter joy, "Nadine-Noémi, I've found the formula . . ." (A gulp of salt air made him cough and spit, touched by the thought of poison gas attacks.) "Here's the formula: the destroyers . . . will be destroyed . . . destroyed!"

The wind suddenly dropped. Noémi let him catch up, and he put his arms around her.

"What were you shouting, Sacha? You looked half insane. It suited you, actually."

"Nothing." (Is that word to come up again and again of its own accord, is it my answer to everything?) "I was thinking we should stay, whatever happens. I'm fond of this world, and we should stand up for it. I'm ashamed to be running away . . ."

"Stay, where, old friend? Doing what? You know what would happen . . . It hurts me as much as you."

Disheveled, he shook his head, losing his excited grip on the vision, annoyed to be showing his weakness.

"Don't worry, we'll be boarding ship in a little while. I'm tense and I'm depressed, that's all. I need rest. It's nothing."

Nothing. Another discovery of lucidity. If you were fully conscious of it, could you go on living? You always return, without knowing how, to your own reasonable normality. That's better.

They boarded the liner quietly in the afternoon. Unimpeachable passports, the real thing at last, and the right nationality—Blackshirt Italy inspires such confidence, not like the travel passes of stateless aliens or Spanish Republicans! There were no obviously suspicious characters among the groups lining the quay (or there were nothing but). D felt almost disappointed at things proceeding so smoothly. They took possession of their cabin which was decorated in two colors, cream and blue. D asked the purser about their neighbors and any notables among the passengers: there was Herr Schwalbe, the diamond magnate, and his lady wife; Pastor and Mrs. Hooghe and their small son; Monsieur Gilles Gurie, French vice-consul at...; Miss Gloria Pearling, the dancer, and her secretary. "Excellent," said Mr. Battisti, "I see we shall be traveling in good company..." "Most emphatically, Monsieur. We also have Crown Prince Ouad and his court, and the American philanthropist, Mrs. Calvin H. W. Flatt..."

"Oh là là!" commented D, in a vulgar voice that contrasted with his manner and diction.

The purser disappeared down a staircase leading to the bowels of the ship. So one is saving his diamonds in time; another has religiously wound up his European tour with its museum visits, evangelical dinners, and surreptitious, burning glances at the perdition of Paris; the third is off to his pleasant sinecure overseas, congratulating himself on dodging the prospective mobilization, at least for the moment; while the platinum-haired dancer drawls to her copper-haired secretary—chosen for contrast. "Alone at last, darling!" crude as the hand she claps on a dusky breast. And who's this prince? An Egyptian? An Iraqi? Awash in dollars stained by the sweat of Bedouins and fellahin? Does he go around in a burnoose, for photogenic effect, or as an habitué of Monte Carlo? Is he interested in oil? Will he seduce the philanthropist from Chicago or be seduced by the dancer? Our purser seems to have taken his cast from a penny novelette. So it goes. To each his checkbook, and may the world go to hell! The joke is that in all probability these are people—possibly excepting the prince—who are innocent of the least villainy and who would be amazed to learn that they have no more notion of what's happening in the world than do moths crackling blindly into lanterns in a garden...At the end of a chic garden party, of course. The only counterfeit in this company is myself, for I am fully authentic. The only one who knows what he is running from, and wishes he were not fleeing...Or else I have too much trite imagination.

"Wait here for me," Bruno said to Noémi. He prowled the ship, scrutinizing forms and faces, and returned from his inspection content—which proved nothing. Nothing at all.

The last scattered points of light on the coast of Europe disappeared over the horizon. The ship's hull was plowing through a resisting mineral sea at the end of which, perhaps, lay nothing.

II.

The Flame Beneath the Snow

All the cities I have known, all the cities unknown
Adrift, sheared glaciers, fissured icebergs drifting toward naked
dawns...

THE ANTIQUATED bomber banked ponderously through the freezing mist. "Difficult zone... Tara-ta-ta..." breathed Klimentii. The cold cut through his furs because the cold was already in his bones. To make a joke of it, he joyfully exaggerated the chattering of his teeth. He said, "I've gone through it so often, nothing can happen to me now. Only trouble is, Comrade, I know that's a superstitious idea... so it bothers me just a bit. What if luck were a superstition, when luck is all a man has left?" Daria said, "You're not superstitious, you're healthy as a wolf... You look like a wolf... True luck is courage, when it comes down to it. Nothing more real."

"But I'm permanently scared stiff!"

"Well, that's real courage, to be always scared and still do what has to be done..."

Klimentii glanced around the inside of the plane. It was cluttered but comfy, like a sturdy tent in the snow, where in spite of the cold you feel good. "It would take so little," he murmured, "and then..." Daria understood, she shrugged her shoulders, said, "And then what?" She tucked the bearskin she'd slept in more snugly around her. The plane's hold made her think of a metal tunnel crammed with parcels and people. The glacial air stank of the excretions of one desperately wounded man. Daria rubbed her face with her fingers, as she often did on waking. "Want to see the earth?" Klimentii offered. The metal body, punctured by shrapnel, had been hurriedly and badly patched up. The soldier shifted a metal plate that was blocking a crescent-shaped hole next to his knee. Daria gasped with pleasure as a jet of damp, cold, but fresh air hit her full in the face. "See the front line? They always take potshots at us around here." But the fog was milky and opaque. "It'll be touch and go landing..." In a low, amused voice he told the story of the luckless VIPs whose plane had strayed off course in this cursed Baltic fog, and landed smoothly, obeying all the usual signals... behind Finno-German lines. All of them shot after a week's interrogation. "Tara-ta-ta, one day the happy life will come, Comrade!"

"Are you trying to scare me, you moron?" said the woman, her eyes pale as the fog.

"Whoa, don't get mad, Daria Nikiforovna! I'll never be cured of fear, no one will, but I don't care, it hardly bothers me anymore. I put up with it like a chronic bellyache, that's all. Man is such a small thing... We don't matter, you, me, whoever, it's the country that counts... I really did mean the happy life, the one in which man will count, will be built one day over our graves. This city is one big graveyard. And I love it. You can't help but love it. I promise you a glass of firewater, you'll see..."

"Is your wife waiting for you?"

"Faithfully, below ground. No carbohydrates, no vitamins, thirteen-hour days at the plant, she went out in six months like a lamp starved of oil... I applied to have her evacuated, but the wives of technicians, officers, and heroes come first. As they should. By the time I got my medal, it was too late. I'm cold to the marrow, no one's waiting for me, I'm the one waiting—waiting for what luck will bring. The epilogue, or another attachment... It's always the same warm rush between two people, isn't it? The warmth of the past is never completely dead, while I'm alive... I won't remarry until after our victory, though. 'Togetherness without tears,' that's my motto."

"And quite right too, Klim," Daria said.

He concluded, proudly or mockingly, it was hard to tell with him: "I've learned."

The whitish mist was thinning under the bomber's belly, allowing glimpses of flat black country marbled with white veins. A wide dark loop sliced through it, like a fissure in the earth's crust. They haven't invented war toys to split open the planet yet, but they will at the rate we're going... "The Neva!" Klimentii cried.

Stupidly, like a schoolchild, Daria found herself imagining that intelligent sadistic brute Czar Peter, pacing the moors on the banks of this river and suddenly pulling his sickly-soft, wrinkled, feline face into a mask of will, saying, "On this spot I will build a city!" Asia will open a window on the West here, we will no longer be Asia... His inspired folly aimed at our escape from Asia. Then he had the severed head of his wife's young lover preserved in a jar which he put on the mantelpiece under the great mirror so his wife, Empress Catherine, could join the three-headed tête-à-tête supper... We have good examples to follow.

■

When I came through this city four years ago, Daria was thinking, we were coming back to life. The passably well-dressed crowd of the privilegentia ambled down the central prospect in soft spring sunshine. Our dead shivered within me, but the crowd was indifferent to them. It only wanted to live its own life; there was a lot of dancing... I was aghast at the nightmare of the coming war, of which the crowd knew nothing because the papers were full of the peace policy and how it would prevail, if it meant a pact with the Devil himself. Let the Devil take his hellfire elsewhere, we just want to live in peace and quiet, and we've earned the right having suffered so much more than the egotistical, degenerate bourgeois West... It's the West's turn to pay for a change: let it learn that life's not just about a good meal, a good roll in the hay, and a good night's sleep but something ferocious, so ferocious there's no name for it. We know that, don't we—for having tried to change the world (and no doubt too for failing to put a more human world in its place, or to prevent the return of the cruel ones...). On the broad sidewalk with its leisurely succession of palaces, where bronze horse trainers rear over the four entrances to a bridge, I met corps-de-ballet starlets who were more or less the mistresses of influential men; writers doing their best to produce a felicitous page in spite of the censor, and spending more time censoring themselves than writing; engineers released from concentration camps with medals; historians fresh from prison who were busy tracing the glorious continuity between Ivan the Terrible, Peter the Great, and socialism with all the rigor they once applied to demonstrating the same thing between Gracchus Babeuf, the Paris Commune, Karl Marx, and ourselves... "But, you see," a fat academician assured me, "it's all true, we're just widening the scope of historical continuity..." He may have been right. Dramatists were writing plays about betrayal, and I met one who had hastily adapted his epic for the treason market so that in Act Five, the hero is unmasked as an enemy agent. It was the hit of the season.

They flirted, they talked books, they led silky hounds on leashes. The cathedral colonnade of Our Lady of Kazan seemed svelte, white clouds were reflected in the dark water of the canal, the church of the Holy Savior on the Blood (an emperor's blood) was as vividly colored as an illuminated manuscript, for blood causes color to blossom from stone... A group of us went to look at the gilded, winged lions of a small Chinese bridge, and I was pestered for news about Paris fashions and the bombing of Madrid, rather more about the fashions than about the bombing (though it was good form to seem concerned about the demise of Spain). There were finely bound books for us to leaf through. I went to admire the vertical waves of pink granite of the security building, erected on the site of the small old law court burned down in 1917... Fifteen stories high, how many offices! A towering proof of progress. The prison next door looked unchanged ... Painful topics were never broached, out of understandable caution or as a kindness to me. No one seemed to doubt the future... I listened politely to the views of a man of letters. "Tragedy is just one of history's overhead costs... Paris frolicked while Robespierre's men were being killed. Paris was right. The true, the lasting revolution was never about extreme issues, the justice or otherwise of the guillotine, the victories in rags. It was all about vitality, the Parisian flair for *l'amour*, its lust for life in spite of everything, its rich exuberance... I'm going to write a novel about Madame Récamier. Marvelous character!" "What about Madame Rolland?" I demanded. "Wasn't she quite a character too?" "Dear me no, she's a bore. So pedantic, up to the very last minute! And a Girondist. I can't bear the Girondists." This scribbler was installing his porcelain collection in a villa on the gulf, and pressed me to visit: "I have some extraordinary Meissen!" I promised, cravenly, without mentioning that at least the Girondists had given up fine china... His gaze was keen and melancholy. I nearly asked him, Why do you always lie? But that would have sent him off drinking for a week. He was killed at the front. His last war dispatches were completely worthless... He had a sentimental kindness. He cried like a child over calves killed in the fields, so whenever he had to interview some optimistic general, his attempts at valiant patriotism gave off a hollow ring...

"Has the city suffered very much, Klimentii?"

"Not as much as you'd expect... At least not the stones. It's architecture that ensures permanence, after all. We suffered a little less than a million dead last winter, or perhaps more than a million, who knows? One in three, let's say. In some areas, one in two..."

"What are you saying!"

"Don't get upset, Daria Nikiforovna. In a country like ours, a million is one hundred and eightieth... In a war like this... Anyway, isn't the earth already overpopulated, in relation to the means of production?"

Again Daria had to wonder whether he was being simply honest or unpleasantly scathing; she inclined toward the first. Dexterously he closed up the horrible gash in the plane's belly. The badly wounded man had fallen into a fitful, whistling sleep. A cockpit voice intoned "Prepare for landing..." Klimentii's pallid thinness concealed no irony. It seemed to say: This is how we are, the young generation, what's left of us: resigned, aware, steadfast, no more bitter than the statistics, no more discouraged than the course of history. The river believes in itself. Ferrying blocks of ice, bits of straw, dead bodies, or fecund silt, the river passes—and remains—with no regret for the drops left behind among wild bulrushes, or dashed against the granite quays. Klimentii was fitting the straps of a knapsack over his shoulders. Daria thought suddenly about herself.

The release she had been waiting four years for brought her no joy, probably because there was no joy left in the world. The bitter years fell away in one go, without regret or longing, with barely a dull wonder at this unexpected new start. A message had arrived from district command with her marching orders, the next combat mission, as though nothing had happened since Paris: "...to report to Service X, Army X..." "When can you be ready to leave?" the district commander asked. "Oh...by tomorrow," Daria replied unthinkingly. I could just as well leave tonight, there's nothing to keep me in your desiccated wastes, your sordid tedium, my useless life...

■

All she needed was the time it took to collect some linen and a few clothes, the time to burn the journal she had kept to ward off the fear of sinking into obsession. A curious document, this journal, whose carefully chosen words sketched out only the outer shapes of people, events, and ideas: a poem constructed of gaps cut from the lived material, because—since it could be seized—it could not contain a single name, a single recognizable face, a single unmistakable strand of the past, a single allusion to assignments accomplished (about which it is forbidden to write without prior permission). No expression of torment or sorrow (this for the sake of pride), no expression of doubt or calculation (for the sake of prudence), and nothing ideological, naturally, for ideology is the sludge at the bottom of the pitfall...

The construction of this featureless record, similar to a thought puzzle in three dimensions turned entirely toward some undefinable and secret fourth dimension, had furnished her with an exhilarating occupation. In it, Daria could not evoke either Barcelona or the Caproni bombers, or the efforts to save a republic in its death throes, or even the ravishing interludes of those times: her nights with a man of artless energy for whom the slaking of passion was such a feast that afterward he would talk on and on, with a touch of genius, about the war, the future, the sense of the human, the whole world which he loved...Of these discussions punctuated by embraces nothing, nothing! Every sentence, read by a professional third party, would have prompted an unjust condemnation, and this man might still be living (with another woman—fortunate woman!—I only hope she understands him). Daria wrote of the colors of the sea, the heave of the swell contemplated from the top of the nameless mountain they had picked for their meetings. And it did help to refresh her at times when the hot sand rolling in swirling waves of suffocation across the desert clouded the village, penetrated the low clay hovel, and made the flame of the lamp tremble. Daria described the man's breathing without saying it was the lover's breathing, and the enchanted tremor of his muscles without saying it was during the communion of love. Waves, swells, exhalations, movements, tightenings, releases, surrenders of the flesh, phosphorescences of the spirit transmuted into inner riches she'd had no inkling of before, an inexhaustible treasure that she could draw up from a well of darkness and carry into the light! No wave, no contoured shoulder, no quiver of lashes can ever be wholly expressed...We live almost without seeing, and now it turns out we see what is no more, but once was, through a prodigious magnifying lens, so that the rough grain of a skin or the carved planes of a torso gain an intensity of pathos whose pale echoes we recognize in a fragment of Greek sculpture. The broken piece of statue arrays itself in mystery, stirs the imagination, and should it happen to be a breast swollen with life, that breast, alone and unique on earth, asserts its own human density and the whole of woman.

The man's face would have filled a book in itself, if overwhelming feelings had not often interrupted her as she worked on those pages. All faces are illuminated in a single one; yet his appeared incomparable, its radiance lighting up souls without number. Daria didn't feel strong enough to confront so great, so stabbing a vision on her own. The face stirred the totality of life, internal and external simultaneously, communicating through the natural marvel of the eyes, of expression ... The dizziness of looking, the dizziness of standing on the edge of a sovereign understanding ... Daria fell back to the world, that is, to the sensation of a storm in calm weather, in the middle of a blessedly fine spring day when several modern reinforced-concrete buildings suddenly blew up, expelling all of their human contents from their carcasses; but there was no description of falling rubble, of a city gone mad beneath the planes, of planes in the fulminating noonday sky; the writing created only a naked feeling of storm and terror, of revulsion and murder, of a fragile universe; it was a sensation born for no apparent reason out of the gilded blue zenith.

How to express, in this tangential language embroidered with arabesques around essential blanks, the anguish of thought? Present and absent, it was everywhere at once, and everywhere elusive. How to refine a set of contradictory yet blinding clarities into nuances of shadow? Daria believed she had done it. That first rendezvous with Sacha at the Jardin des Plantes, then in the back room of a Parisian bar on boulevard de l'Hôpital, translated into the play of light on the streets, a drab scent of autumnal decay floating among pruned shrubs, a blue sheen of greenhouses in the distance, an unease of footsteps on the path, a tan-upholstered interior in all its tense, hospitable, anonymous, shattering banality. Sacha himself was associated with images of tropical landscapes that she was wary of developing. (Because they knew she had never been to the tropics and might ask: Who do you know in those countries? They might even guess.) Instead she painted—in words—a little bamboo wood in an Adjari botanical garden near Tsikhes-Dziri, those names unspoken though, no names, no names! Thin green shoots after rainfall, the pungency of red earth, the graceful thrust of ferns . . . She also wrote a gloss on Lermontov's classic poem "Three Palms," in which the sensations of her childhood were ramified.

The worst questionings, the ones born of devastating bereavements, had her filling a notebook on the death of the musician, the death of the gold-seeker, the death of the inventor, the death of the great atheist believer, the death of the devout but limited believer, the death of the cynic, the surprise at death of the intelligent utopian, the indignation at death of the misled fighter, and how each of them faced up to the end with scruple, astonishment, courage, consciousness of the void, furious disappointment, desolate faith, quailing flesh . . . This was the most imprudent of the notebooks—and the one it would have been impossible not to write. She did not, however, write about the simple death of the militant, and most often when she talked about death, she was really only talking to herself about the higher life of the mind. Not good enough! The abyss, the plunge into the abyss were unequaled . . . Those pages she burned quickly, well before her departure, and none too soon, because when Major Ipatov of the Special Troops showed up on a tour of inspection, he was affable and comradely, left some quality cigarettes and a flask of Armenian cognac—"more aromatic than Hennessy, you know"—while inquiring in a familiar way about just what this deportee could possibly be writing through the long and lonely evenings in her hut. "I know how many copybooks you order, I know you write and write, I know everything!" Daria slapped her notebooks onto the table. "May I?" He thumbed through them, paying careful attention to some passages, and wanting to know the reason for certain crossings-out. "Good gracious, you're turning into a regular prose stylist, Daria Nikiforovna! Are these the preparations for a book?" "Yes." "I sincerely hope they'll let you publish . . . You could make twenty thousand rubles out of it one day. Very fine, this paragraph on the rain. Of course, it might be a bit too disjointed for the average reader . . . But here, this piece about the hands, deeply moving I think..." It was too dark for Major Ipatov to see the exile's face redden. "I see male and female hands, I sense a complexity of relation between them... In such a refined form, I wonder if it's really publishable... You have talent!" Since he was not untalented himself as a lettered-bloodhound-reader, Daria congratulated herself for having destroyed the death notebook two days earlier. Major Ipatov might actually have understood it.

She burned all the books without a twinge of regret. (There was not one line in them about regret.)

■

The little village, made up of some fifty Kazak families, lay along the edge of a streambed blessed with a muddy trickle for a few weeks only, during the spring in the mountains. Its fifty-odd uneven shacks leaned at angles, like outcroppings of the earth, that is, of hardened sand; the tallest, reaching twelve feet to the top of its crumbling turret, was surely the most godforsaken of all the Prophet's mosques, though an ardent faith still burned among its faithful. Flat roofs shone dustily red at this sunset hour. Timeless women seemed fixed motionless around the well, thick silhouettes becoming graceful as one drew near: the young ones had slender bodies, angular features, and eyes like fawns; the old ones, worn down at thirty by the privations of this lonely spot, had been drained to the bottom of their black gaze by the unvarying spectacle of the desert and relentless worrying about food and water—since the fitful stream of the Ak-Aul dried up even quicker than maternal breasts... Beside them crouched the freakish outline of a camel with flaccid humps.

The peaceful fire of the horizon set interiors ablaze with gold reflections. Daria had to visit almost every house in order to say goodbye to the schoolchildren. "I won't be able to tell you any more stories about the Golden Cockerel and the Cat That Purred. Work hard on the alphabet and love our great country, which is destined for a happiness you'll know when you're grown up..."

(Those of you who do grow up, if the enemy universe doesn't slaughter us, if our own young egotism doesn't drag us down to the abyss...) "Your elder brothers are fighting as bravely as the warriors of Timur-Lenk..." That at least was something they understood: Tamerlane! A historic figure who now seemed distinctly modern... The ironwork glinted on ancient chests; old people rose to receive her, tiny women hung with necklaces of antique silver coins and their bronzed, wizened menfolk, stern, morose, wearing robes of brightly striped cloth eaten away by filth. Grave, parchmenty faces inclined before her, thin dark lips shaped words of good wishes for the future in formulas prescribed by the Koran to attend the departure on a journey of a friendly traveler, be he an infidel...

Daria distributed her riches: a kilo of dried black bread, a pound of sugar, some boiled sweets, and a bar of perfumed soap which she cut into slices to go around to the new brides and young mothers, kindling sparks of delight in the glossy sable pupils, for "you'd think it was a cake of roses," even if nobody here could have the least idea of what roses were. Daria left some borax to treat the children's eyes, inflamed by the mineral dust and often eaten away by conjunctivitis resulting from venereal disease. She urged the Polish woman to take over the school, assuring her of official backing to come. "The intelligence of those children, it's so alive! Their minds are as thirsty as the earth..." Then, a knapsack on her back, she walked away alone into the flat distance, the tragic, darkening horizon where the quenched fires of evening had left only violet dunes, a yellow-blue sky, the sense of a vast cicatrization covering vast mute sorrows...

"Congratulations," said the chief of the region, "I'm going to drive you to the aerodrome myself." He was smoking coarse seedy tobacco rolled in newspaper. Outside, the petrified sand sparkled. Seeing this officer in this abandoned office—scrawny, his right eye covered with a black patch, his hands dirty—Daria realized for the first time that his feeble persecution of the deportees was merely a way to escape the suffocation of total boredom. "What news from the front, Akim Akimich? The second front?" "Oh yes, the second front of those imperialist scum, you believe in that, do you?" sneered the one-eyed man. "They're all in it together, they intend to wipe us out, you mark my words. We're on our own." And the fire went out of him; he seemed exhausted by this small fit of verve. Daria told him about the school, sixty-seven eager children, two hour-long lessons every day, reading, writing, arithmetic, I'd recommend the Polish woman, she's very keen...The regional boss, Akim Akimich, whose eye had been put out by a Polish bullet, replied sharply, "She's a landowner's daughter, she's the widow of an insurance company tycoon, a capitalist, and a Catholic to boot! How can you answer to me for her where the education of our children is at stake?"

"I'm not answerable for anyone, in any shape or form, I wouldn't even answer for you, if they asked me! But the school happens to be under your jurisdiction, Akim Akimich. If you could arrange to have a professional teacher sent here, I should be delighted to hear it..."

That deflated him, for he was both leery of responsibility and flattered to have some degree of it in the midst of all this hateful sand which makes you want to drink yourself into oblivion. Mentally, he considered the pleasure of ordering in the Polish woman for an interview laced with implicit threats, at the end of which might lie the belly of a white woman...

"I'll think about it...It's true that we should make the most of the human material we've got...How's morale among the Kazaks?"

"They're hungry, Akim Akimich."

"And you think I'm not hungry too?"

"Much less than they are, Akim Akimich."

He spat into the inkwell and scraped at it with a classroom quill.

"I'm even starved of ink. The newspapers I read are a month old. I haven't seen a blade of grass for two years."

"The Kazaks of Aul-Ata have never seen one," Daria reflected, and they never will...But she was beginning to warm to this embittered lonely officer who probably doesn't trust his trio of Uzbek soldiers. "Will you permit me to send you some books about the war?" "Not about the war. I know all there is to know about that. What it does to men! No book can do it justice...You can send me things on plants. With pictures of trees, if possible. A botanical treatise."

"Or the tale of the Sleeping Forest?"

"And of the whispering reeds, Comrade!"

They regarded each other amicably. And yet how he had plagued her, this wrinkled, red-haired, crafty Akim, delaying the mail and spreading ridiculous rumors about her with the wiles of a village sorcerer—just to enliven the tedium of the desert days and give himself the illusion of existing as a human!

■

A blizzard of thickly falling snowflakes, more opaque than white, held nightfall back over the airfield and gave Daria her first deep thrill. Snow, I salute you, dear whirling snow, you that soften the cold and fill the darkest of nights with intimations of lightness, blotting the pathways, making space huge, and setting the wolves to howling! You deliver me from the sands, no more desert, yesterday is simply the past. You deliver me from the rot of inaction. We never feel ourselves dying in life except through such contrasts, when one present suddenly splits apart to let another in, and we come back to life as yesterday's being dies. When the slaughter is over, perhaps man will find that by transcending erstwhile distances, by flying over continents and climates, he has grown and conquered the possibility of self-renewal. Who knows, one day neuroses may be treated with airplane travel.

"Military ID check. Are you dreaming, Citizen?"

"Yes, I am," said Daria joyfully.

The small snow-covered shack was glacial; a single bulb struggled fearfully against the piercing night. Haggard NCOs, their boney faces framed in fur, were working noiselessly. One murmured numbers into the telephone. Another was changing the dressing on his right wrist. The one who had just spoken was going over some papers. He sniffed as he heard the crump of an explosion reverberating into the emptiness beyond, like the dying sigh of some colossal monster.

"They've got ammunition to spare, the bastards! It's the same thing night after night."

Her three documents were in order, unambiguously so, yet tainted by a whiff of mystery and prison. The man looked her coldly up and down, not without sympathy. People so rarely emerge from mysteries and prisons these days...Then again, it seems it's possible to survive and that nearly everyone will have his turn...

"You won't be able to report to military headquarters until tomorrow...Do you want to spend the night here in the barracks? You're welcome to my bunk, Citizen. It's all right as shelters go. I'm on duty till dawn."

Klimentii stepped in and Daria realized that he was waiting for her. "The citizen can easily spend the night at my place..." The checkpoint corporal stared at them. He was around twenty years old, extremely skinny, with scarcely more than a glimmer, an indomitable spark, of vitality left in him.

"Been at the front long?"

"Oh, about a hundred years."

"Is that all?"

"Not enough in your opinion? Try it."

Embarrassed at seeming to rebuff a kindness, Daria said, "Thanks all the same, Comrade." He threw a black look at before resuming his businesslike manner. "Four hundred yards to the truck. Compulsory wearing of shrouds. And no smoking!" One swoops down from the sky, having vanquished distance and danger, and then one puts on a shroud to go into the city at night...The conceit pleased Daria as she got into the loose, hooded overgarment of white canvas. The twenty-year-old NCO sang under his breath:

"For whom the cups, the cups, the cups,
The cups drained of wine?"

He walked ahead of the new arrivals through the swarm of gray flakes that softly buried everything around. Their shrouded forms, resembling dim cutouts of fog, were invisible at more than three paces. Klimentii was silent. Daria continued the poem in her mind, lines once written by a poet (who had recently died or been killed at the front) for another poet, who had killed himself.* So it goes with our poets, Old Russia, Young Russia!

The terror of pathless plains
Where horses lose their way!
Brother, I accuse you not,
I accuse you of nothing!

Frustrated at being unable to recall more than that one quatrain, she racked her brain for other important lines, those two lines that say it all—how do they go? She stumbled in the pathless snow, dark as cinders. Klim's arm held her up firmly as she was about to fall, and Daria regained her balance like a dancer on her partner's arm. "What did you say?" he asked softly. "Nothing, I was remembering two lines of poetry..." But he had already let go, and the two meaningful lines shone for her alone, unspoken:

There is the right to live
And the right to die.

She almost bumped into the ghostly truck. The journey was slow, guided by phosphorescent signals that moved along the ground. The invisible convoy traveled through a shifting, milky gloom of formless shadows. A desperate cold penetrated the flesh. The suffering was one of organic extinction and it effectively

*Written by Josef Utkin (1903–1944) for Sergei Esenin (1895–1925).

extinguished all thoughts apart from the craving for deliverance, the craving for warmth. Klim, Daria, and three shapeless, faceless soldiers squeezed together into a human heap at the back of the truck so as to conserve their meager supply of warmth. At times all that Daria could see were a pair of slanted eyes, green as a cat's, seemingly full of quiet anger. It went on forever. Toward the end, a hand crawled between the compacted furs and bodies to find Daria's gloved hand as though by instinct, squeezed it, and she returned the friendly pressure. Klim said, "We're entering the city..." How did he know? They couldn't see a thing. But through the gash in the mica window black walls slid by. The truck was weaving slowly, no doubt to avoid the potholes. Melodious night-watchmen's whistles rang out. Klim extracted himself from the huddle. "Ahoy, comrade chauffeur! Stop your dreadnought. I've reached port." The driver was clearly in no hurry to oblige, either because he was hanging on to the wheel half asleep or because he had no sympathy for someone who thought he'd reached port: you're never home safe in this bloody life, or when you are, it blows up in your face. No such thing as a port! Not even a berth in the cemetery, unless you can produce half a loaf for the grave-digger! Barely raising his voice, Klim displayed his cursing abilities with contained fury in a barrage of the filthiest army swearwords combined with imperious supplication. The truck hiccupped to a halt, like a drunken mastodon. Klim helped Daria to get down. All that could be seen of the driver was his bearish bulk as he hopped up and down on the ground to get his circulation going and to shake off the cold. (The dancing bear, the fossil masto-don...) It was no longer snowing; there was not a spark of life in the night.

"I couldn't stop before, idiot, it's not a good place. Bombs fall on it. I don't give a fart for your skin, but I'm responsible for the vehicle, you jackass."

"My skin, your skin, and your rolling rat-trap, add 'em all up and the price is still cheap," observed Klim sagely. "Here, take a swig."

He passed his canteen to the dancing-bear man.

"That's better," the driver said, after drinking. "Thanks, brother. Six months I've been driving this piece of shit over this goddamn road, and still not a scratch! Can't last, can it?"

"Sure it can, brother. The road can last."

"Wiseass!" said the other, chuckling.

"There is no right to live and no right to die," thought Daria, who had grown so stiff with cold and immobility that she found it hard to walk. "Klim, where are we?" "Near the Tauride Palace." A handsome, wealthy district in its time, built around a little palace with a cupola and white peristyle; a poem of a park with pond, willows, silver birches; the history of the heady days of 1917. And now there was nothing left but the towering cliffs of a dead city. Yet there were watchful souls in this necropolis, since suddenly, inexplicably, one was beside them, and a ragged voice was saying, "Your papers, please, Citizens." The watchful soul played its torch beam over the frame of a door where the wind gusted malignantly through two gaping holes. "These are not permits to circulate at night, Citizens." Now it was a woman's voice, cracked and hoarse. "Orders to complete mission. Valid twenty-four hours," explained Klim. Swaddled in sheepskin to the eyes, to the mouth, the woman leveled her short carbine at them. "Drink," said Klim, proffering the canteen. Before accepting she shone her light into their two faces and was reassured. "Show us your face too," Daria said gently. The woman with the carbine turned a furtive beam onto herself. Her hard features seemed molded out of gray clay, nostrils like flared dark holes, tiny penetrating black eyes. "Look at me," she cackled, comforted by a draft of alcohol, "a beauty, right?" Her laugh was bitter, cut off abruptly. "Now don't take that street, you'd be stopped by the artillery gang, real pains in the ass . . . Go around by the demolition site, and watch out for the crater, it's a nasty one . . ." One arm pointing the way through nothingness, she guided them on for a while. "I know my way around here, thanks," Klim began to say; at that moment he tripped and nearly fell over something like a flabby stone. Stooping, he whispered, "It's someone," having bitten back the words "a corpse." All three knelt down to touch the elongated human form. "Wasn't there when I made my rounds," grumbled the militiawoman. "Always the same thing…" The flashlight revealed the supine body of a woman in a cavalry greatcoat, whose open eyes inertly reflected the light playing over them. "Dropped dead," said the militiawoman. "No mistaking those eyes… They go out without a permit and drop dead in a vacant lot." "Dropping dead without a permit," commented Klim. The pocket lamp threw the dead woman's hands into momentary relief. The right was still clasped around an end of twine, leading to a small sled piled with broken boards and a saucepan full of ice. "She's from the neighborhood, for sure…" the woman said ruminatively. "Was it hunger?" Daria asked. "What d'you think? Ah, well. I'll take care of it tomorrow. Our daily bread, as you might say."

And the right to die… "Klim," asked Daria, pressing into the young soldier's side as they walked, "is suicide punished, in the army?" "Obviously, if you bungle it… And it should be. Selfishness must be punished—so must incompetence." They circled the massive crater: at the bottom, under fissured ice, they half glimpsed the murkiness of water with eyes that had grown accustomed to unrelieved night. A street welcomed them, petrified but intact. "Home!" Klim announced. "Be the welcome guest, Daria Nikiforovna, I offer thee bread and salt." She looked up at the strangely smooth wall, four stories high, which seemed to be—no, was—swaying with a faraway deadened crackle, as of winds in sails. "Unusual architecture, hmm? You can admire it in the morning. Canvas, light wood frames, some paint, and you'd be fooled at a hundred yards. Well, no one is fooled anymore… The wall collapsed six months ago under a bomb. Four picturesque and habitable apartments survived…" He knocked on a rickety door, sending waves up the façade. "Who's there?" Klim spoke his name, a small grill half opened, and someone could be heard dislodging the timbers that braced the entrance. It was a grizzled old man whom nothing could surprise, of that race of solitary hunters from the forests of the north who have preserved the same beard, the same eyes, the same attire, the same gait since Scythian times. "Still alive and kicking, then, Frol!" "Yes, God forgive me," quavered Frol into his beard with unexpected meekness. "How about the tenants?" The reply came vaguely: "To each his fate..." "When's this filthy war going to end, Uncle?" They had begun speaking by the light of a match, now they could not see one another. Idly the old Scythian cracked his joints. "Never, my boy, never. Good night." He began to re-barricade the entrance.

The staircase mounted steeply toward the sky whose cloudy vastness was visible. To the right, on the very edge of the drop, Klim unlatched a door which he closed behind Daria. The air, though it felt less icy cold in this obscurity, was rank and stagnant, clammy with slumber: a glow between his fingers revealed two blond infants, packed side by side into a sort of basket. The skin lay so gray over their bones that they might have been dead. At last he undid the padlock to his room. He lit a church candle which yielded but a tiny flame, joyful after so much night. He rubbed his hands, dropping satchels, muster bag, and parcels to the floor. "Make yourself at home, Daria Nikiforovna, we're going to make a fire..." They were in a storage closet measuring some six feet square. It contained only a mattress covered by a knot of grubby blankets, a small brick stove whose pipe vanished through a clumsily hacked hole in the wall, and a splendid armchair with green velvet upholstery. Designed for the soft white ass of some high-ranking functionary, preserved through wars, revolutions, industrializations, and bombardments, this old-fashioned armchair provoked a half-crazed squeal of laughter in Daria. In a corner lay some gas masks and a German helmet. The fire, already built up with splintered parquet for kindling, burst into life at once. Klim went to wake the neighbors and scrounge a little water; he put the kettle on. "Whenever I go away," he explained, "I build a fire. It's my love of comfort. And if one day I don't return, the citizen who takes over the room will know I was someone who thought ahead. That's all he'll know of me..." He looked frail with his sheepskin off, "almost an adolescent," Daria thought, but he was wearing the epaulettes of an NCO and two medals. "How old are you, Klim?" He clicked his heels, snapped to attention, and introduced himself. "Sublieutenant Gavrilovich Rybakov, twenty-three years of age, eighteen months at the front, three times wounded, three citations, ex-would-be teacher, bedrock optimist, some reservations about human nature." "Me," Daria said, "I'm an optimist about human nature, but over the very long term..." The young man was applying his army knife to a can of American corned beef. "Would a thousand years do for you, dear Comrade?"

"Perhaps, but I can't guarantee it."

"With good psychological techniques, in well-planned societies... Help yourself."

Daria contentedly unwrapped a piece of slightly moldy black bread. Klim was a young athlete without a trace of fat. His nose made a straight line down the middle of his face and his slash of a mouth drew a horizontal line below, as if nature were experimenting with a diagram; but nature's plan had been foiled by large deep-socketed eyes, resembling the eyes of visionary saints drawn by the ancient icon painters... The soul trumps the diagram. No doubt Klim didn't believe in the soul... The soul has every right to deny itself.

"Your name should be Cyril or Glaebius or Dimitri—" Daria said, interrupting herself because she had just thought of Saint Dimitri the Assassinated.

"Why, don't you like Klim?"

"Oh yes, I do!" she exclaimed, conscious of blushing like a fifteen-year-old.

"Names don't matter, anyway. We're all nameless. Incomplete."

This was so true that they fell into a pensive, companionable silence. The smoking stove made the room feel like a nomad's yurt. "Well then," Klim said at last, "how shall we sleep, Daria Nikiforovna? We can make another mattress with our fleeces..."

"Together," she said softly.

He answered without looking at her, "We'll be warmer."

They suddenly became aware of such overwhelming fatigue

that their movements were slowed by it, the candlelight was dimmed, and nothing was able any longer to be thought or uttered, as though fatigue itself had taken over; and it was not the fatigue of the journey but a different kind, vaster, more penetrating, more irrevocable. The black bread, the knife, the tin of corned beef, the white cup in which they had taken turns drinking their murky brew of tea leaves were pitiful. Klim went out to shake the dusty blankets over the sheer drop, then spread them to form a bedding the color of earth. Lumpy pillows were improvised by stuffing bags and haversacks under the mattress. "Like sleeping on the bare ground," Daria thought. My first night in the city of a million dead, our lovely victorious city! (So is victory the same as death?) She took her clothes off unselfconsciously, tingling with the cold, unable to see Klim but trying to picture him: the face that floated at the back of her brain was clean-cut, impersonal, and compelling, detached from everything, as singular as a new abstract sign. "We're going to make love," she thought, frozen. She tried to arouse something in herself. A man over a woman, the great shared upsurge of heat, both exhilarating and soothing . . . so many lackluster notions, devoid of desire. "Am I half dead already? Just us, joined together, the only reality in the universe for a moment, ourselves alone, in our intensity of life . . . And the rest, the fighting and the dying, those things will be as real as ever . . . But the dead aren't real anymore . . . There will only be us . . ."

Notwithstanding the cold, playing for time, she tidied her clothes, casting about for an idea that would warm her. "Men at war are hungry for a woman, one has to give oneself, one must, so they can have at least that cry of joy . . ." But what if the cry contained no joy? The stove had gone out, but Daria naked did not feel the cold. She was not ashamed of her sagging breasts. She felt herself. A statue of flesh, straight-backed, resilient, nervous, nurturing, pale-faced, dry-eyed. The eyes that watched her from under the covers shone with dark brilliance.

"Put out the candle," Klim said. "Light's a limited commodity."

"No, I'll give you one, I've got some. I don't like the dark."

First she knelt on the bed, and as she did so uncovered, in one pull, the whole of Klim's face; she was smiling, and the brightness of her smile seemed to reach to her shoulders because of the idea that was dawning on her. He's a big child, a man-child from the dark of the war. How desperately they need to be enfolded between soft arms, soft legs, to be bathed in tenderness! They are chilled to the bone. How many youngsters just like this boy have fallen, never to know another second of tenderness! How many? Klim's eyebrows rose into arcs of quizzical amusement. "You said how many, Dacha, how many what, or who? What are you counting now?"

"How many dead," said Daria, still bending over him. He lost his temper.

"Strange woman! Don't bother me with the dead. We'll never finish counting them. We happen to be alive. Come to bed. I'm not one of your mystics."

Her arms at her sides, eyelids half closed, Daria made no move to touch him; but listening to his breathing, she was aware through and through of Klim's presence, like an inconceivable warmth about to break over her, a lulling that would bring her to rest. "I've been alone so long," she whispered, "and now I'm cold..." The hard bar of an arm pinioned her neck, a scorching body pressed against hers. And the narrow boyish virile face dominated her from a great height; thus does the hawk dive from the heavens onto its earthbound prey... His lips tasted sour, his teeth were dry. Rapture is like that, bitter and violent, it hurtles out of a black sky onto the helpless creature and spears it... "Beautiful Daria, dear one," Klim was mumbling, grateful and sloe-eyed. She started—"Don't lie..."—but shaken as she was by the carnal storm, and full, so full of happiness, she might in truth have been beautiful...

Later, relaxed, hugging her close and stroking her—those calloused palms—he said, "You are good...Who are you? Tell me something about yourself...Me, I'm just another fighter, one of the lost generation; one who's been lucky. I haven't seen or done anything the others haven't . . . Nothing interesting. I'm not at all interesting."

"And I'm not anything, Klim. Nothing, do you hear? No one. A being, for work. A woman, for you . . . I'm not interesting either."

That "for you" was subtly hurtful to both of them, because it could mean "for you just now" or "for you, or any other man." Either way they couldn't change it, whatever they might wish. War is a time for submission, for being rational; one can't want anything for oneself beyond the fleeting moment. Klim spoke reasonably.

"I'll be stopping here a week or so. I want you with me during that time."

"If it's possible, Klim. That'll depend on the service."

■

Daria was discovering a fantastic city, although the objects and beings it contained were of heartbreaking ordinariness. The Baltic sky covered it with a low ceiling of gray snows. The diminished light seemed to be on the verge of exhaustion. The broad straight avenues lay crushed by whiteness. The snow was banked into little odd-shaped mountains, around which a few rare pedestrians made their painful way along cleared paths. The buildings had aged by a couple of centuries in a few short seasons, just as men and women looked decades older in only a few months; the children had aged a lifetime before knowing what life was. People wrapped up in rags and tatters over furs showed plastery faces. The first glances Daria met disturbed her. Nowhere in the world had she come across this precise variety of human gaze. She clearly remembered the famine of her adolescent years, during the revolution, and yet this look was inexpressibly different from the looks of the past. She hadn't known that eyes could change so, and cry out so loudly in silence something intolerable. It was neither pain nor hallucination. What, then? Daria plumbed each gaze, feeling guilty about her own well-being, because it must be plain to everyone that she'd just breakfasted on a can of pork and beans, and massaged her body with a flannel soaked in spirits and ice water. Her flesh still bore the imprint of love, she was heading for her work, and she was proud of this city, our invincible city, our granite stronghold! But neither the gladness to be alive nor the pathos of history and fine-sounding slogans could withstand the tiny blows dealt by the looks in those eyes. To be in good health, walking around in a clean, hale, supple body under the unforgiving sky, wearing a thick reindeer coat and new felt boots among so many rags brought a discomfort that shaded into guilt. The sullenness of the women and children planted motionless before a boarded-up cooperative, was that it? What were all these eyes saying? That they had weathered, day and night, indefinitely, the storms of snow and terror, of filth, exhaustion, cold, hunger, fright, sickness, with no hope of escape, no hope of healing... That they were watching life die away within themselves. One neighbor eyeing another: She won't last three weeks. And I... The neighbor shiftily looking back: He'll hold on longer than me, he's a tough old bird! A small girl reckoning how long her mother and aunt were good for— maybe a month? The librarian on the third floor had those very same yellowish blotches around her mouth when she dropped on the stairs without a word and never moved again. The small girl's name was Tonya and she was scared, she loved her mother and aunt, of course she did, but she also knew that by selling their clothes she could buy a few more weeks for herself. She'd heard the sisters whispering: "Much better for the little one if we can both die at the same time, so there's only one funeral..." The mother added, "I've left instructions. I don't want Tonya going hungry just to pay the gravedigger... Let's be put out on the snow with the others, what's it to us, eh, Nissia?"

There were ways and ways of dying slowly while remaining partly alive, getting dressed, walking down the street, doing the day's work, eating tasteless food, submitting to the ceaseless assaults of the belly and its deliriums during sleep. Some shrank till they were nothing but insubstantial bags of skin over the knobs of their bones, with dreadful ball-like eyes . . . Others swelled up. Others became hollowed from within, pretending to be fit until the day they collapsed against the wall, saying, like Valentinov the schoolmaster: "Here we go, I'm dying . . . Twenty-three years in the teaching profession . . . Please doctor, put a little piece of sugar on my tongue. Ah, so good, thank you . . . And tell the principal from me that . . ." This man expired in a sigh of euphoria, but was it really wise to lavish sugar upon the dying? Doctor and nurse shook their heads uncertainly, one cube the poorer. You can't be rational to the bitter end. The doctor could always tell the ones who were faking it, both men and women, even military officers, even technicians! They had themselves brought in on a toboggan dragged by a woman, feigning to be at death's door, all to obtain a drop of glucose. Once he found an old friend reduced to this ploy, a professor of mathematics named Aristi Petrovich. "You, my dear friend, and in such a state!" The doctor was playacting too, as though he had been taken in. He rummaged in his precious store cupboard for an onion (but not the largest, to be fair): "Here, Aristi Petrovich, it'll do you good, you must eat it in three stages to avoid a stomach upset . . ." (That old Aristi, he got around me!)

Each corpse was firmly tied to a sled pulled on a string by its next of kin; a new breed of resourceful specialists earned their food by sewing discarded sheets or squares of sackcloth around the remains: There, look, isn't that nice, almost as snug as a coffin! Daria passed several such mummies on the street, rigid pods floating just above the trodden snow. A living man or woman to pull the string and sometimes a child behind, steering the mummy so as to spare it too many knocks and jolts—a somewhat superfluous solicitude . . . Inclined like a figurehead, a solitary form was plowing toward you, in a fading halo of snow. Her shawl framed the slightly scary face of a wizened child, and what she was pulling could not have weighed much—a small form neatly parceled in tar paper and string, with some naïvely cut-out cloth flowers pinned to its breast. Daria greeted her. "Going far, Citizen?" "Too far by half! The Smolenskoe cemetery . . ." "That's on my way,"

Daria said, "give me the string for a bit." No, not heavy at all, not even with the weight of a question . . . The young woman was explaining nonetheless. "There used to be four of us and now I'm all alone in the world. It's probably for the best, don't you think? . . . If I can hang on for another three months, the factory's promised me an evacuation permit. I'm still meeting my production quotas, though!" "I'm going too fast, sorry," Daria said, "you're out of breath." "Oh, don't mind me, I'm always out of breath!" The young survivor halted, with a brief smile of distress. The cold was gentle . . .

There were caved-in roofs, whole stories exposed to the air and clogged with snow, gaping bays, stage-set façades of wood and sailcloth with rows of windows painted sketchily across them. A faded inscription read INTREPID CITY! TOMB OF ———. As the banner was torn, its last words missing, the city could be the tomb of whoever you liked . . . Daria noticed the absence of huge pictures of the Chief, and indeed it was hard to imagine one. How would he look? Standard confident smile, full cheeks, bushy mustache? No portraitist would dare to give him the only face appropriate for this city—hollow as a death's-head, wet with tears. The only things that must remain officially foreign to a nation's Leader are tears, desperate suffering, the most human of human things . . . So how is it that leaders do not go mad? "Perhaps they are mad," Daria answered herself.

A tram, looking out of place on these streets, clanged slowly past a rubble of white armor platings, snow-caked sandbags, the burned-out carcass of another tram. "Their artillery often targets this crossroads, once they got sixty people in one hit, a whole tramload . . ." It was by the public library that used to house the books of Voltaire. The streets were punctured with what looked like wells dug into the cemented snow, boreholes over burst pipes, where women and children and people recovering from their wounds lined up with listless discipline to lower a saucepan, a jug, a can on the end of a wire hook, down into the greenish sludge. An icing of snow lay over the mountains of human waste scraped together in the center of vast square courtyards; what a festering would be released by the thaw, what epidemics would steam from the ground poisoned by rotting shit! But that's the least of our worries, for spring is an age away, and who knows which of us will live to see it! The squares stood triumphant as ever, lined with colonnaded palaces, dominated by golden spires, gigantic and deserted. The empire of cold whiteness. To cross them was to plunge into implacable solitude; and should some bomb land just then, its nearby explosion was endowed with a natural solemnity that in no way disturbed the dignity of these spaces and architectures. A cupola that once had shone pale gold, now dull, reigned over the iceberg city.

Daria walked into a nondescript house where she found a guardroom scrupulously swept of dust, but brown with ingrained dirt from floor to ceiling. She showed her papers and was given a pass for the second floor. A man with a bayonet opened a door onto an expanse of freezing corridors, there was a marble staircase, a warm whiff of cabbage soup, and an anteroom full of captains having a smoke; then the astounding office of Major Makhmudov. Astounding in that it was spacious, heated, with green filing cabinets and leather armchairs, tastefully adorned with drapery and plants; in short, a proper office in a city whose apartments were now little more than lairs for beasts. Telephones, the Leader's picture (he was looking well), maps, calendar—this was no painted scenery, the presence of Major Makhmudov testified to that. At first all she saw was a razored, greeny-pink scalp. "Sit," he said, without looking up. Burly, almost fat, how strange. His blue pencil was underlining words on an arcane mottled document. "Well, what?" he said. "Your report?" The voice was neutral, too low for that polished-stone dome. Daria pushed her papers across. He went "Ah!" A round face, two yellowish chins, a blob of a nose, puffy eyelids, no neck; he lacked the infernal eyes of the street people, but the erratic gaze was animal in its own way... The upper lip peeled back, presumably in lieu of a smile. "Four years in Kazakhstan... Cured of a few errors, are we, Comrade? Serious medicine. Well, you come recommended by Krantz, that's good enough for me. Speak German? *Sehr gut.* You're assigned to office 5 downstairs, room 12, under Captain Potapov. On the front line. Here the front line is everywhere, I warn you..." (As though to confirm this, an emphatic explosion resounded some hundred yards away...A blinding idea: that it was supposed to land here, between the telephone and the winged chair, no it couldn't land here...) "Dismissed." He called her back with a short cluck of the tongue. "The rule is discipline and silence, understood?" "Understood, Comrade Major." He dialed a number, pressing his foot on a bell button hidden beneath the carpet, and a door swung open to the right. Through it came a young soldier in green, pistol in hand, followed by a bespectacled man with a beard, clad in the tunic of a Wehrmacht officer. Makhmudov began shouting, "So, Herr Dingel, you lied to me!" Daria caught the German's muffled, shaky reply: "It was my duty..."

In room 12, Captain Potapov asked his secretary, a small ugly woman in uniform, to leave them. Daria guessed that this old officer had not had an easy time of it; he seemed browbeaten, chastened, secretly discouraged despite his ramrod figure, buttoned into a relatively neat uniform made from cheap material. His epaulettes did not shine. Aged about fifty, he had spare features and excessively shiny glasses covering the opacity of his eyes. Nothing alive in this tiny office except the ferns of crystalline frost that curled over the panes of a double window. Potapov questioned her laconically, with an absent air. Then: "Quite right. Our work consists in deciphering enemy intentions, through enemies who are often themselves ignorant of them...Let me put it this way: the average prisoner is in possession of, at best, one letter of the coded alphabet. Are you with me?" The old officer was not as insignificant as he looked.

"War is a great game of psychology. The enemy calculates and so do we. Strength only enters as a function of these calculations. An error is sometimes the product of a flawless but excessively linear calculation which fails to allow for the unstable, the unknowable, the irrational, call it energetic or mindless folly... Hence reverses and defeat are the penalty of error. This enemy is conducting a technicians' war. He is convinced of his superiority, and with good cause. His machines are better and more numerous, his special forces are better trained, more numerous and organized than ours, its officer class more highly educated. I would even grant that its winter equipment makes a mockery of ours... But winter is on our side. We are winter men..."

Daria took pleasure in listening to the veteran captain, who must have few opportunities to hold forth; strange of him to open up so on their first meeting. (Was he aware of her history as a deportee? Or perhaps he was steeling her for the task ahead?) She asked with concern, "Do you think, then, they might take Leningrad and win the war?"

"I do not. Beware of false deductions, they lie at the end of the shortest line of reasoning. The world is only logical in appearance, on the lower scale of perception; in reality, it is rather mad... I am persuaded that, for precisely the reasons I have listed—and several more besides—the Germans will never take Leningrad, and the Germans will lose the war."

"A brilliant paradox, Captain. Perhaps you're counting on the Allies?"

He looked bored and dull for a few seconds, before rousing himself to pick up the thread of his ideas.

"The art of war, as I understand it, excludes paradox, the better to comprehend facts that are hidden or contradictory. Although it cannot exclude what the Americans call wishful thinking, passionate thought that wills itself into truth... How can any side prevail without passionate thinking? I am not interested in the Allies. Above all they need the blood of our muzhiks, as we used to call them, for they are economical with their own; they loathe us, and would perhaps be only too pleased to postpone victory until five minutes after we were crushed. They're mistaken on that score, and will be thwarted. I understand Russia. I know Russia's wars, this being my fourth..."

"Your fourth? How is that?"

"Carpathian campaign in '17; two civil wars, Comrade: a year with Denikin's Volunteer Army, against the revolution, and that's where I came to understand Russia, because the revolution was Russia, apparently senseless and beyond that highly reasonable, exceedingly logical in order to master and exploit her deep incoherence... Then three years with the Red Armies, Volga, Urals, Baikal, Crimea... Remember: we never wage anybody's war but our own, which is selfish and messianic—messianic in the service of a boundless selfishness, the selfishness we need to survive. We have plenty of wombs in production—God bless the women!— plenty of men, and so much space that we can afford to lose territory and troops in the interests of gaining time; we can inflict on our foes the weariness and despair of expanses without roads, victories without solutions... Indeed that's all we can do—at first: suffer more than they do. But before overpowering us, the Germans would have to reach Tobolsk, Novosibirsk, the Yenisey; and by then they would be falling prey to our distances and our winters, and still wondering how to reach Vladivostok, how to take the Arctic... And since we should be incapable of capitulating in good faith, their task would be interminable. You see, this old Mother Russia of ours is providentially blessed with a most rudimentary organism. Cut her into six pieces, and the six will live on... We cannot be invaded, and this is something intuited by the rudest yokel of the Irtysh, confusedly and then with sudden clarity while defending a wood with his trusty automatic rifle and nimble legs, always quick to run away, but only so as to turn and charge again. His tactics are all in his nerves, without quixotism or panache: only by killing the enemy can he lay hands on enemy boots and vitamin pills, and thus our very deprivation becomes a source of strength, a primordial strength as irrational as life, and imperfectly understood by the strategists of the old industrial empires... If the enemy high command were staffed by genuine Nazis, that is, by a gang of déclassé adventurers, it would be far more deadly, for those are people who know how to unleash instinct along with tanks, shrewd calculation, and a hefty pinch of absurdity...But it is made up of generals of my generation or older, formed in the days of bourgeois reason and the equations of profit; thrifty, sober, cautious planners for whom each operation must yield at the very least a tactical benefit, just as each commercial transaction must be seen to pay off at least in terms of publicity. It is only the primitive energies of man that are invincible, and they are indifferent to waste; material gain counts, certainly, but in a peculiar, non-mercantile way; it may be more important to capture a stockpile of potatoes than an oil field...Our Field Marshal Mikhail Illarionovich Golenischev-Kutuzov was one of the first to grasp this, precisely because he was somewhat stupid. He pitted our instinctive, sometimes blockheaded, common sense against the genius of Napoleon, and Napoleon paid dearly for the superfluity of his genius. Go back to Tolstoy, who knew nothing about war but understood the Russian land and its people..."

He had pronounced Kutuzov's name with dry gravity, as though from a lectern; professorially.

"Have you ever taught, Comrade Captain?"

"I have. Even in the concentration camp...But please refrain from interrupting. I am speaking to you because I must..." (Here he managed a faint smile). "I do so with pleasure. I have faith, and you must have it also. Without faith, it's the end of Leningrad, the end of Russia, do you understand? A reasoned faith, no more farfetched than that of the baby which never doubts its mother's breast. Axiom: Russia will only lose a war when she loses faith in herself, or when she feels at odds with her faith, God forbid..."

Why did he speak in the future tense rather than the conditional? Daria thought she heard a bitter undertone of menace in his voice. She shivered. Captain Potapov went on.

"So we find ourselves at a disadvantage, half beaten, yet doubly invincible since we cannot be beaten further without succumbing, and it is absolutely impossible for us to succumb. Concretely speaking, however, we do find ourselves in a fairly desperate predicament. Any technician worth his salt, steeped in Clausewitz,

Moltke, Schlieffen, Ludendorff, and Foch, would come up with twenty-seven irrefutable reasons for concluding that the war is lost. But from our point of view, the only conclusion is to go on the offensive, beginning with retreat, if necessary. Usually it is. I give you a principle of our military art: retreat is the preparation for a counterattack, flight is the opportunity to regroup, and defeat is fundamentally a maneuver. Another principle: strategy is not a game of chess played with a quantity of machines, it is above all a duel of wills. The enemy is so technically ferocious that we must humanly outdo him, be harder and more ruthless, toward ourselves in the first instance. Okay?"*

"Okay."

"We are poorly fed and poorly dressed compared to them, and more harshly disciplined. Our officers have the right, indeed the duty, to shoot any combatant who falters under fire, without trial or delay—an excellent provision, though no civilized country would have the nerve to adopt such a law. The war leader is essentially the man with a license to kill beyond the reach of law. We are freer in battle than the enemy, more enthusiastic, first because we are defending the motherland, second, because we rely upon ourselves rather than upon technique. And so technique, which we do not neglect, becomes a part of man unleashed, rather than the controller of a motorized soldiery... If one day this relation is reversed, we are doomed...

"My guess is that the enemy deliberately put off the conquest of this position, here, when he could quite easily have taken it. He wanted to choose his moment, ensure his dominance over a hinterland, seize a great and serviceable port and not an isolated city, requiring to be fed, however little... It was a sensible decision but the moment has passed, never to return. In strategy as in life, lost opportunities are lost for good. The single factor of action with an overwhelming probability of disobedience is time, which is an admirable factor of inaction..."

---

*"Okay" is spoken in English in the original French text.

"That sounds a bit confused."

"Not at all, not to me . . . Inaction is never total, in that it stores up the givens for action . . . We are experts at the war of inaction, allowing opportunities and forces to ripen, rather than throwing them away . . . Another of the enemy's disadvantages: its integrity. Their men march all of a piece, like clockwork. If one division breaks up, two rational units emerge to cancel each other out. We, by contrast, never lose sight of our instinctive cohesion even in the depths of incoherence . . . We are the richer in internal contradictions. Our men are prone to fury, to panic, to flight, to turning in on themselves, and then the cowards become the bravest fighters on earth. We possess limitless resignation, steeped in limitless strength. I doubt whether the average German can ever feel completely resigned to this war, which only brings him intolerable privations likely to terminate in a stupid death. We don't tend to ask ourselves such questions, we believe in neither comfort nor death, the individual or . . ."

The old officer's voice tailed off in mid-sentence. Daria pretended not to notice.

"Because we retain a primitive belief in ourselves, because our ideas are the reflection of ourselves, an obscure, communal we, advancing toward consciousness . . . There's nowhere that ideas, even unsustainable ones, are more alive than here. Over and above our contradictions, we have an ultimate unity which harmonizes the feeling for death, murder, and pillage—indispensable to war— with our love of a peaceful world and of mankind; with our slavish submissiveness and our revolutionary sense of justice . . . We redress error through terror . . ."

"Are you a Party member, Comrade Captain?"

"A sympathizer. A professional. I am drawn to war as an art. Pure thought, dialectics, mathematics, surgery, patriotism, the rampage of the unconscious, paranoia . . . Do you follow?

"One last point. In this service we are the eyes, the ears, the antennae, the calculating machine and the imagination of the army. We decipher the undecipherable, almost without fail. In cases of serious misjudgment do not expect leniency. Now get yourself into uniform, I'm busy."

Daria's initial job was writing analyses of prisoners' letters. Half a dozen people combed through the packets that were brought in from the front line, revealing, in the form of soiled bits of paper, the very substance of sacrificed lives. Photographs: a beaming young woman at a garden gate, a baby, a gentleman with a walrus mustache beside a sad, stout lady; a basset hound with human eyes; naked Fraüleins; a village high street... Sublieutenant Effros gathered the whole team around his desk to apply a magnifying glass to some tiny, wildly salacious snapshots found in the notebook of Hauptman Lazarus Meister. "The dirty dog!" hooted Effros. Ostentatiously he dropped the pictures into an envelope marked "For the Captain's Attention"; the others felt sure that he would contrive to keep a few back... Daria took a closer look at Hauptman Meister's book. Apart from addresses, there were quotations from Schopenhauer and the Führer. She read: "'In defending myself against the Jews, I am fighting to defend the work of the Lord' (*Mein Kampf*, page 72)." In the margin was scrawled "Jewesses." Didn't he know that the Lord was a child of Israel, born to a woman of Israel? "What happened to that swine," Daria demanded, "is he dead?" She must have been assuming he was, because it was a surprise to be told, "No, it's from a POW camp." A certain sadness mingled with her disgust, but she found herself glad to know the fellow was alive.

Back at her own desk beside the stove, she read the letters written by a peasant woman to her husband from Württemburg. "My dearest Albrecht..." The children were in good health, two cows had calved, Hermann was sending some cloth from Paris, the Polish prisoners were better workers than the French but one of them had just been thrown into jail, likely to be executed for sleeping with the widow G: "what a trollop, can you imagine, when she was questioned in public she said a man was a man, they gave her a good flogging, but we send her milk and preserves all the same..." Nothing of interest here. A man is a man. "I am the Way, the Truth, and the Life..." Daria stared at the yellowed ceiling. In a bundle of unsent letters from First Sergeant Wilhelm-Hans Guterman, she found a story which she was able to summarize by collating extracts and rounding them out with notes.

The story haunted her for days... Garrisoned in a small Ukrainian town, Sergeant Guterman met a flaxen-haired girl in the marketplace, "just like our girls at home," named Svetlana, Clara. She was "strong and quiet," again "just like our girls" and they probably took strolls around the ponds together. "A handsome people, the Ukrainians," he mused, "very similar to our Teutonic ancestors..." When Svetlana fell pregnant, Guterman "hatched a plan" to send her to his family in Thuringia as a work volunteer, but she suddenly refused to leave the country and he expected to be moved on with his division to some new destination at any minute, for the inscrutable purposes of strategy. He promised Svetlana he'd come back for her "after the war"; he got a friend, whose strong suit was mathematics, to compute his chances of surviving, mutilated or whole, in captivity or otherwise, assuming the war lasted for eighteen months from such-and-such a date... Guterman was popular with the locals, since he performed all sorts of small favors for them. This was how matters stood when a band of partisans ambushed a supply train, to the spitting fury of the commander. Guterman indirectly conveyed his relief at being passed over for the reprisals detachment. (Not a bad sort, this boy, Daria thought; Klim in Germany would behave the same way...) "Twelve arrests in the Little Woods quarter," noted Guterman. Svetlana was scared, "she looked so adorable with those great frightened eyes in the moonlight, my God, why must they..." Piecing together the rambling chitchat of the letters, Daria glimpsed Svetlana's arrest and the terrible time that began for the sergeant, not daring to speak up to anyone, haunted by those great frightened eyes... His letters to his sister turned into a journal that would never be mailed. "She's at the Grange, guarded by the special detachment..." He manages to smuggle some biscuits through to her. First Lieutenant F summons him for questioning on the subject of this girl—a partisan's niece, convicted of having run missions to the forest. "You're aware, Guterman, that you could have got yourself into very serious trouble indeed? You have a good record. I'll simply note the facts on a file card. The girl will be hanged." Guterman cried over her in dry lines, not daring to reveal himself on paper, ignorant of any but stock phrases from popular novels. Out of prudence, perhaps, he went so far as to justify martial law, whilst pleading to the Captain on behalf of a misguided creature "who bears in her womb a future soldier of the Great Reich" (a clever touch, that!). But the captain, good fellow, retorted: "In the first place, who's to say it won't be a girl, or maybe two? Second, there's been no official pronouncement as yet on the legal status of minors in this category. And lastly, I'll only mention it to the chief if I find him in a good mood, otherwise it'll just be another black mark against you..." And one against himself too, for sure. The garrison commander was not in a good mood: the partisans were wreaking havoc on the railway. Guterman polished his uniform buttons and shined his boots in preparation for the parade of October 18, to be held on the town square in front of the small blue-domed white church. From his place in the rank he saw the scaffold made ready for seven hostages and criminals. He could still hope, there were more than twenty prisoners—oh, let her be spared! He is in the front row, thirty yards from the scaffold, hearing the sobbing murmur of the people, a chatter of prayer and malediction. He recognized Svetlana, she'd lost weight, her eyes seemed to be searching for him, he felt a trembling rising in his muscles, discipline kept him rigid, he fastened his gaze on the blue onion over the church while a mechanical voice in his head repeated "My God my God my God..." Then the mass shudder of the crowd broke over him and he saw Svetlana's body dangling, oddly twisted, next to the long frame of an old man with his tongue hanging out.

Daria suggested to Captain Potapov that this narrative, revised by a writer (for it was poorly expressed, marred by clumsy attempts to dissemble), could usefully be published. "I've read few that are so moving," she said. Her superior listened, doodling stars onto his blotter.

"Moving? War is not moving. Human testimonies, if authentic, are more apt to be demoralizing... Let our unionized pencil pushers do their own writing, they know their business. I shall want those papers for the psychology department. You must focus your attention on information with some practical use. Have you made a note of the movements of this Gutman, dates, unit numbers, and so forth?"

"Yes, Comrade Captain."

"That's what we need."

There was a touch of pained reprimand in his tone, as though he had been about to say: What are you so bothered by? One atom of cruelty in the bloody nebula we inhabit? It doesn't mean a thing, nothing counts now except pitiless efficiency, get that into your head and start being a tiny cog in the machine... At least, that was how Daria took it.

■

The shelter with its log ceiling provided a deceptive impression of security... You scrambled down an embankment and entered an underground passageway, at the end of which the command post opened out like a roomy cave, lit by oil lamps. It had bunks, telephones, a stove; the pungent scents of leather, tinned food, and urine hung in a dank chill of cellars. The liaison officer, Ivanchuk, sat permanently glued to the receiver: his dimpled, rosy cheeks were a welcome sight. He was just in from Siberia, and still radiated the plenitude of life. Everyone who met him must have said to himself: "If you only knew what you were in for..."

Colonel Fontov, by contrast, was a greenish individual with a visionary glare, ravaged face, too-long neck, and jutting, prickly beard; he usually leaned on a thick wooden stick and seemed not to have slept for weeks; he stared at you with the eyes of a nocturnal bird capable of strange divinations. That night he was there only for some raids that had been put off by a shower of torpedoes and a blizzard of snow. His glance frequently alighted, with pleasure, on Daria. A woman in the midst of all this, a real woman, recalling to mind the lost world out there; it was better than a big glass of alcohol in the belly, for it sharpened the faculties. As heavy crashes shook the earth around them, Fontov rose from his table and paced up and down, smoking (he limped without his stick; his beard poked irascibly sideways). "Everything all right?" he asked the telephonist. "Yes, Comrade Colonel." "Check on post 4." The younger man was trying not to look rattled while bits of earth sprinkled down from the quivering ceiling, like the sly patter of hail: it was thoroughly unnerving.

Fontov sent some lieutenants up to reconnoiter what was happening outside. It's best to keep the men busy under bombardment, especially the younger combatants. So they won't have time to think, so they'll only follow orders. "Quite a hailstorm," said the colonel to Daria. (If he addressed her, it was as an excuse to look at her without embarrassment.) "Can't think why the sons of bitches are squandering so much ammunition, they'd be insane to attack in this sector... But insane is what they are, sometimes." A troubling thought shifted his gaze, and Daria was forgotten: of course, there was always the possibility of treachery. A soldier strides over pack ice, sure of himself and of the awesome cold; but the ice is cracked, the trap powdered with new-fallen snow, the somber waters beneath suck you into their bubbling vortex, goodbye to the man, the darkness carries away what they call a drowned man... The shelling having tapered off, the Colonel assembled his officers for going out. Daria volunteered to go along. "No," he said, "it's not advisable, that hail can fall again at any moment..." He was a man without nerves, who spoke in a penetrating voice, managed never to lose his temper, and mastered himself with unanswerable firmness. Daria was amazed that the human animal could be brought so firmly to heel. She saw that he had been worn down to the last fiber—the last, steely fiber that held him together. The only puzzle, thought Daria, is whether he will be wounded again before his nerves break down, or whether he will crack up before his next wound . . . In the first case, he will be decorated and nominated for promotion; in the second, he could wind up in front of a firing squad—for raving in the middle of a division chiefs of staff meeting, or declaiming a speech during the launch of an attack, or howling at the moon all alone in the snow!

Daria could not know that Colonel Fontov had already been through those stages; that he kept his crises in check by smoking, that he no longer expected anything either for or from himself, and that he adored a callous man-made deity which may be no realer than other gods but which you have to believe in to impose perfect discipline on soldiers, whether on the production line or the line of fire: the god Labor, brother of Death since its ultimate effect is to destroy the laborer. The machine invisibly devours the mechanic's very substance, which is time. Production, you say? Production feeds and prepares war, which is a destruction of production and of man. Expanded production of the means of production is expanded destruction of human substance; the production of consumer goods has as its object maintaining the workforce in a fit state for labor, that is for wearing itself out, and this is the ring that closes the chain of pan-destruction . . . Idle for a few minutes (it was never more than four), he had spoken again to Daria. "I'm more of an economist myself. Political economy is worse than war . . ."

If he had begun to speechify—but before whom?—he would have said: "Our beautiful language, forged by serfs and by sages, employs the same word to denote two concepts: will and freedom . . . One word for an absolute antinomy, of a nature to delight the philosophers, who are for the most part mystifiers. What we mean by the will only acts to suppress freedom; what we mean by freedom is nothing but an illusory flight from the will . . . The living writhe between these two poles of incomprehensibility. I admire the determinists who think they've understood. I'd like to show them a bit of introspection five minutes before the signal to attack! The soldier obeys: neither will nor freedom, is that clear?

The leader needs no more, and the leader himself obeys. It's all anybody needs! The soldier is trapped between several formidable fears: fear of being killed while obeying orders, fear of being executed for disobeying them, fear of being a coward or appearing to be one, fear of despising himself, and many other fears all churning in his belly, causing him to piss and shit abundantly. What we mean by courage is decanted through this physio-psychological process which answers to profound natural causes: wounds to an emptied bowel are much less dangerous than wounds to a full one ... Savages have magic formulas. In war, we are savages furnished with technical know-how. My magic formula comes down to this: work! Labor operates a practical synthesis of obscure imperatives, more potential than actual, more imaginary than real: will, liberty, necessity, finality. Labor destroys men, objects, and time, but it is a destruction which provides itself with aspects of creation. That may be the last myth. In war it's clear and even yields an instant gain in accord with brute instinct. I work to destroy the enemy, a breed of men which must be destroyed so that our own breed may be able work in peace ... I work to defend four kilometers of threatened road, whose loss would translate into twenty thousand deaths inside the city within a week ... So, to work! Since the work consists of killing, it is only natural that we shall eventually be killed ourselves ... To work!" Earlier, Fontov had exchanged only a few elliptical remarks with Daria while he was soaking his feet in a bucket of warm water; but Daria reconstituted what he would have said if he had expressed himself at leisure; which he never did, lacking leisure but also disdaining words, and out of prudence. The worker must be prudent and fear nothing so much as expressing truth or sincerity.

This night's mission was to obtain information by capturing enemy troops—but not men out on patrol, who don't carry anything on them. Battalion commanders would send raiding parties out into the enemy lines or against advanced outposts. Vosskov designated six men and a lieutenant. He seemed to know them personally, to be assessing the fortitude and destiny of each man as he considered him. Daria wished she could see into their souls. They were an ordinary bunch, with ordinary names. The inevitable Ivanov plus a Sidorov, to refine the banality, both unremarkable, stumpy, and gray-skinned; a Tziulik from the Ukraine whose name made the others laugh and who indeed had a tiny head on the body of an extremely wiry Punchinello; a moon-faced Tartar oozing deceptive sweetness named Maymedov-Oglu; Dzilichvili, a wiry Caucasian highlander; and Leifert, who was of German ancestry. Finally there was Lieutenant Patkin, who sported black tufts of eyebrows over a snub nose, and resembled the kind of small-time hood that prowls around marketplaces—clever brutes with a knack for counterfeiting and bootlegging, slipping home a blade under cover of a brawl, hopping over fences and bamboozling the girls with fine-sounding words (not one of which they mean). "Quite the charming rogue," whispered Daria into Major Vosskov's ear. "You've got it. He started off as a child of the road and the wastelands, spent two years in a penal colony, recently graduated as a cadre, with several commendations . . . He's both astute and extremely brave. After the war, I can see him making a first-rate gangster . . ." Patkin was memorizing the map of the operation. Here the ice is cracked; but over here, right in the middle of the impassable section—as they believe it to be—the ice has resealed itself, the planks are laid, you can wriggle across one behind the other. There are forty yards between the two machine-gun nests on the opposite bank. Their trenches are damaged, and badly guarded ever since they pulverized ours; we've ostensibly moved our earthworks a little farther back . . . This is where their shelters begin . . . "Only shoot as a last resort, bring two or three prisoners back, whatever the cost. Whatever the cost," repeated Patkin, frowning as he measured this authorization to sacrifice his companions if need be. "It'll be done, Comrade Commander." He spoke the words unemphatically, in an unwilling, almost bitter voice.

The six men waiting in the shelter formed an obscure mass, huddled within its silence. How many would return? They were a broad sample of the people of the Union. Each had turned over his documents—penciled letters and few personal belongings; the commander was now arranging these in little piles on the table, like the possessions of the dead. What a gap is left inside a man, when he has to part with his letter from home! They were trying on the white shrouds, lowering hoods over eyes, experimentally...Anonymous, faceless; dim white phantoms equipped with light weapons and a square of chocolate (chocolate is a treat even for those who court death, but it must not be eaten straightaway, however annoying it can be to die before eating it...). A tram driver from Rostov-on-Don—Rostov, that had been burned to the ground; a tractor mechanic from the country outside Voronezh—the bombed, the ransacked Voronezh; a schoolteacher from Chernikov—occupied, ransomed Chernikov, inhabited by the hanged; a cattle farmer from the steppes of the lower Volga—a Muslim or perhaps a Buddhist, and the war was almost there; a young wine grower from the green and russet hills of Kakhetia—its hamlets emptied of young men; a printer from Moscow—wounded, famished, blacked-out Moscow...What will they achieve tonight, what will become of them, these peaceful men who believe in the future? Six, seven men counting the lieutenant, twenty-five bereavements suspended in their wake, en route to the torture of cold, darkness, fire, murder, and unknowable death...

They know it all, Daria thought, they are plunging tranquilly into an abyss, they are monstrously aware. If their souls could explode, broadcasting their lamentation to the world, all wars would end, how simple it would be! Simply impossible. The Ukrainian, Tziulik, asked the commissar for a glass of vodka. "Wiseass! You know how to exploit the situation," said the commissar. "Pass the bottle around to the others, schoolteacher." "If I don't come back, you'll be sure to write to my wife?" "I promise, but you'll be writing to her yourself, lucky bastard." The voices of these men were fraternal. The commissar put on a satisfied expression. "As for me, if one of these days I don't make it back from the middle of nowhere, there won't be anyone writing to anybody...I don't have anyone left. A bird in the air with no nest!" Tziulik clapped him heartily on the back. "You're a lucky bastard too." Move! Daria was seeing men moving out for the first time in her life. She realized that such sorties had been taking place for years now, a hundred, a thousand times a day or night, along thousands of miles of battlefronts, on both sides of the lines, for the others are like us—the same dread, the same obedience. A hundred thousand times already these men had moved out never to return, but always they were replaced by fresh men sprung from the depths of the earth and the wombs of women, from the depths of the weeping and gnashing of teeth, from the depths of rotting cadavers and of love. Pure madness.

The commando unit moved off down a winding lane through the snow dune. It was instantly swallowed up by sepulchral whiteness. The twilit land was beginning to merge with empty space, and space into darkness. On the other side of a half-invisible sloping bank, pale as death, the presence of the river was palpable under its crust of ice and snow, an expanse of camouflaged pitfalls crisscrossed by hidden threats. The woods, that by day gave every horizon a bluish tinge, were now invisible, and there was nothing left but the absolute silence of uninhabited expanses. Distant explosions and quick-fading flashes in the sky did not interrupt so much as magnify the silence and the vastness. This site of immobility evoked only feelings from beyond despair: total extinction, uselessness, the biting cold. The landscapes of dead planets must look like this. "From here, Daria Nikiforovna, you can see a long way into enemy positions, but take care not to go past the salient, they have it under observation... We've had men killed there." But there was nothing to be seen, neither there nor here, the two dead men had left no trace. And yet numberless eyes were on the lookout, trained through lenses; sound detectors were listening; radar beams were searching through space; field telephones were active from station to station; patrols were crawling over the ice... This is what man has become, this murderous worm! Machines for riddling puny human bodies, smashing holes into concrete, pulverizing the earth, whipping snow into squalls, drowning the night under torrents of fire, orchestrating screams of agony, drinking the blood of sacrifice, all these latent machines were crouched expectant on the brink of fury. The earth was as primed with violence as the air was with cold, the sky with snow, and the human spirit with that resigned anguish which journalists have distilled into "Bravery."

At the command post, men were playing cards with a pack reduced to tatters. Noncoms were on the line to other hidden dens, swiftly writing down the hour, the minute, the response, "all quiet, all quiet." Vosskov had dropped off with his elbows on the map, a wax dummy. Time flowed like invisibly falling snow, the time of the last certainty, charged like all else with the inevitability of catastrophes moving closer and closer. A devouring second toward what, yet another second toward what? Who will ever understand?

"It's starting," whispered the chubby-cheeked telephonist.

"Right," Vosskov said, shaking himself out of his torpor, "pass me the receiver."

The voice at the other end launched into an algebraic report, the pencil traced a curve on the map as though impelled by a will of its own. "I see, good, very good..." This meant: disastrous. Major Vosskov was no longer listening, but he could hear through the silence. Patkin's six stumble into hell one hour before the projected time. Bad. They will be destroyed because of that timing. First a volley of machine-gun fire rips through the emptiness, instantly followed by tracer bullets striping the night with low arcs, like maddened colored stars. Now a planet ignites in the sky and spreads a colossal glare over the white desert it conjures into being. Ice and snow become peopled with shadows, obscure forms drawing bursts of projectiles from automatic weapons; most of these shadows turn out to be illusory. Everything dies down suddenly in a panicked silence, a darkness of inexistence. And then it all begins again, the rising and sinking of northern lights, the whistling upward blast of a torpedo...Major Vosskov rose to his feet and put on his shroud, imitated by several men and by Daria. Outside, at first, they saw nothing. Even the snow was black. But there are different kinds of nothingness, and this one was a sham. Sure enough, less than a mile away a searchlight skimmed the snows like a small, jerky snake. Were the seven men headed back across the river already? Was that possible? Downstream bright planets leaped, the facing shore thundered chaotically, silence fell, and the river arched its back in an eruption of black water and fire. "They're breaking up the ice, the vicious bastards!" Vosskov hesitated. Should we start firing, to create a diversion? His orders were to operate discreetly and husband the ammunition. The enemy would fire back, which could hamper the return of the commando unit and entail the loss of a few men... Things might escalate into an artillery duel, prompting the division to hold an inquiry into the waste of munitions occasioned by his recklessness... Then should he do nothing? Like an anxious schoolboy, Vosskov imagined the general shouting: "And you simply sat back? Where did your duty lie?" A note would appear in his file: "Lacks initiative." Where did his duty lie? Our bank was silent, or nearly. Ring through to post 4 with instructions to open fire? Patience, I shall be patient as death. "Find out," he told the liaison officer in a steady voice, for the leader must display exemplary calm. "What have they seen? Have they spotted them?" Under a rigid posture, he was squirming. "No, sir." A cone of pink light had stabilized out there, boiling on the spot with each regular explosion. At last the riposte was under way. Vosskov was delighted to see that the order had been given by someone else (one less responsibility). Dark white sprays spurted up beyond the Neva, a thick cloud blurred the left flank of the luminous cone. "Ten to one the survivors are through safe... Did you understand the operation?" he asked Daria. "I think so..." It was hideously beautiful. "You there, Rodion, run back and check the casualty figures. If our people are inside the sector, increase firing for another five minutes..." He stooped to light his pipe under a soldier's coat. "I reckon they've taken more losses than we have... That big strike you saw, it must have hit a blockhouse..." His pipe had gone out immediately; he was inhaling imaginary smoke and expelling it through protruded lips. "All right, the night has had its little epileptic fit. Home we go." The battle was tapering off into ever-shorter spasms of brilliance and noise. Darkness reclaimed the snow, dappled at first, then total.

Nothing had happened. "Reporting sporadic incoming fire, lo-cation, time..." Propped over the map, Vosskov was dozing again, a wax statue. One hundred and four hours on duty and so little sleep! All he wanted was sleep. He would lie down in piles of warm fresh straw, he would sleep on stoves in peasant kitchens, sleep in meadows of grass, rest against the wall of a shelter, col-lapse wherever he could! The miracle of sleep began to steal over him, there was a lively country fair, children singing... "Right," he groaned, his blissful expression morphing into a scowl, "hand me the receiver..." Colonel Fontov was on the line. "No, Com-rade Colonel, no sign of them yet... Nothing to report..." Time crept onward, malign and inconceivable. Daria was prowling back and forth between the claustrophobic shelter, the trench, and the eternity of darkness beyond. There she ran into the colonel. During the incident, he had given himself one of those injections against physiological depression. (Humiliating to know how much we depend on our glands!) "Ah, it's you! Enjoying a breath of northern air? Bracing, isn't it? Did you like our little party? It went off very well. My plan executed to the letter. Our men are coming back..." She was still lost for a reply when he turned and ambled off, spry despite the stick, trailing a fan of shadows. Daria wrung her hands in the emptiness.

Four men returned, bringing one prisoner. Patkin reported the death of Tziulik, the Ukrainian. "I crawled up to him, I felt his head, my fingers went into his brains. A minute later the ice turned over under him. Sidorov" (the tractor mechanic from Voronezh, who had made no physical impression) "took several bullets in the back, the stretcher bearers picked him up... Leifert, dead for sure, he was a real brick, he drew the enemy fire so we could get through...I think he was in the way of that torpedo..." Killed several times over, then, the printing worker of German descent. "We've brought you one NCO, the other drowned." "Congratulations, Patkin!" the colonel said loudly (his face was like a Chinese mask with bad teeth). "Go get some rest. Have them bring in the prisoner..." The basic mission had been accomplished. The colonel's rheumatic knee, the right, was aching.

The prisoner marched in with a certain assurance. Stripped of his white shroud and the fur coat of Tziulik the Ukrainian, he appeared in a faded Wehrmacht uniform, with the insignia of a subaltern. Wrists lashed together, age about twenty-five, fair hair, domed forehead, pale clipped mustache, fluttering eyes.

"No weapons on him? Untie his hands!" the colonel ordered.

Two lamps placed at either end of the desk illuminated the captive from below. He snapped to attention. Vosskov stood behind him. Daria sat to one side with a notebook on her lap, ready to interpret. Colonel Fontov began: "Surname, first name, rank, specialty, unit!"

The prisoner, calm, answered with unhurried precision.

"How long has your unit held this position on the Neva?"

Daria noticed that the prisoner was swaying very slightly on the spot. As she translated, he looked oddly at her, blinking his eyes, and leaned toward the colonel to murmur something.

"What's that, Sublieutenant? Repeat please."

He repeated, in a low, strangled voice, "Why this playacting? I know where I am."

"What? What are you talking about?"

"Forgive me..."

He waggled his head feebly.

The colonel demanded: "Are you feeling well? Are you sick?"

"I am feeling quite well, Inspector, thank you."

He raised his eyes to the damp log beams above them, gleaming with icicles. A smile half formed on his face; the blue gaze was erratic and veiled, as if by smoke. His elbows twitched, so violently that Vosskov and the Mongolian soldier both jumped, ready to grab him... The colonel banged the flat of his hand on the table.

"Ask him if he's frightened and if so, of what. Tell him we treat prisoners fairly here, in compliance with the rules of war..."

Daria went right up to the young man to look him in the face, and it was she who felt a touch of fear. The blue eyes were transparent, intoxicated. He was grimacing.

"Repeat, woman," he said with an effort. "My head hurts... No, I am not frightened. Of anything. Why are you trying to deceive me? Why are you talking this foreign language? It is not worthy of you. I was expecting to be arrested. I have committed a serious offense before the Party and the Führer and I am ready to admit it."

He threw back his head, making the Adam's apple bulge against the rim of his collar, begging for the cutthroat's invisible knife... Major Vosskov flung a glass of cold water into his face. It had an immediate effect. He wiped his face with his knuckles, and said, "I am obliged to you, sir. Ah! That's better!"

"Are you a Nazi?"

(Almost all of them deny it...)

"Ja, Herr Offizier. *Heil* Hitler!"

He gave the raised-arm salute, impeccably smart.

"Ask him whether he understands his situation?"

"I understand. Tell the Military Police Inspector that I don't expect clemency. The culprits are Klaus Heimann, Heinrich Sittner, Werner Biederman..."

Daria wrote down the names as fast as she could. "Units?" She translated in some perplexity as the prisoner went on,

"Klaus Heimann brought the enemy radio broadcasts back from Stettin. Sittner copied them on the regimental typewriter... Biederman gave me four pages that I hid in my kit so as to give them to the authorities... I've done my duty, and if I deserve to be punished I..."

Vosskov punched him hard between the shoulder blades. The prisoner rounded on him furiously, but was grappled back. He said, "Water, quick, please..." He took a face full of water without blinking, he was laughing out loud.

The colonel cocked his revolver and put it on the table.

"Tell him that if he doesn't put an end to this pointless masquerade, I will blow his brains out."

The prisoner was laughing, not listening. They allowed him to bend his head over to stare at the revolver. "Not mine," he announced. Daria confronted him. "Listen here, prisoner of war. Look at me! Can you see me clearly? Now look at the colonel..." The word colonel brought him down to earth. He regarded Fontov with set chin, calmly. "The colonel has warned you..." The prisoner responded calmly enough, but his mouth grew unsteady.

"Kill me? But I'm innocent...You've no right...I've made amends. I await your orders, Colonel! Sir!"

His forehead wrinkled as he remembered something. "Prisoners of war? I don't know..." A telephone call alerted them to some focused artillery fire against eastern positions, in such-and-such a sector...In case it were the prelude to an attack, the battalion urgently requested instructions and ammunition. Division wanted an evaluation of the raid's success, with the number and quality of prisoners taken...Bits of ice and grit rained onto the table as the ground, shaken by an explosion, vibrated violently. Vosskov knocked over the nearest lamp as he dived for the shelter door; the light went down by half and shadows rebounded. All Colonel Fontov saw was the cherubic telephonist, going, "Post 7 is out, the line must be down, post 7 is out, the line..." "Will you please shut up!" scolded the colonel, his face sickly tense in the gloom, his beard blending with the mobile darkness. "Where's Sitkin?" he asked, too loudly (Sitkin was the chief of staff). No one answered. The prisoner said, "Sittner was arrested last night."

Daria translated without thinking.

"What?" asked Fontov who was assessing the strength of the threatened battalion, the quantity of available munitions, the ominous silence of post 7, and the wrath of the division. "What's that, Sitkin arrested?" "No, no, Sittner." "Who's Sittner?" The floor rumbled again; there followed a gaping silence. Fontov caught sight of his revolver and the smoke-blind eyes of the prisoner, who was smiling, held by the arms. Daria translated: "Tell the colonel I am immortal. Immortal, it's appalling... I am very sorry..."

"He is mad," Daria whispered, her face white.

The colonel was not feeling very sane himself. "Make him shut up," he said, shoving the gun back into its holster. "If he's playacting, he's damn good. But for pity's sake, shut the bastard up." The prisoner was gabbling in German, staccato. A blanket was thrown over his head; muffled yells came from beneath the hood. It took several men to restrain him, momentarily turning the shelter into a grotesque wrestling ring. Finally the prisoner was hustled away, bound with straps, to be thrown into the snow. "Sitkin is badly wounded... Allow me to replace him for the time being." Major Vosskov's day-old stubble was brilliant with ice crystals, as were his eyelashes and the hairs in his nose. "Good," the colonel said. "Send the lunatic to division..." "What lunatic?" The earth trembled, lifted on a swell. Fontov shrugged. Daria heard him answer, "No, do not open fire until I give the order..." She groped her way out of the shelter, the cold earth vibrating against her hands. It was like emerging from a grave. Suddenly, as night faded, gray snow was slowly swirling.... It was like entering a vast tomb.

■

The officers' club was nothing but a small, uncomfortable room, but it was heated and ornamented with pine branches and red banners. The busts of the Leaders lined up on the mantelpiece contributed no more than a pale plaster presence. Next to them, but smaller, stood a bust of the perfect poet: Pushkin, daubed with blacking, did more to inspire reverie. Officers who were hard up came here to play checkers and listen to bombs falling on the city... Daria took a magazine from the table, most likely *The New World*, *October*, or *The Star*; its cover was missing but it made no difference. The format, the paper, the crabbed grayish print, the content, all were the same from journal to journal, with as much variation as you'd discover within a regiment on the march. At first the ranks seem composed only of faded uniforms, but on closer inspection you start to notice the uniqueness of faces, you realize that humanity endures here, that man survives in solitude, perhaps, at the core of the multiple being, under his serial number, and that he may well be what gives it strength...Man, the atom of military power.

For this war, we need a mobilized, disciplined soul, the collective soul of a patient army. So let the imagination of poets and novelists put on a uniform and obey orders—but let each retain his gnarled or stony visage, as each wages war in his own way. The population of a rational society in danger must necessarily concentrate on the moment's task. Not everything can be indulged at all times, not everything has to be expressed...If hypnosis is a weapon, another means of fortifying our resolve, of winning, then let hypnosis serve our ends! The ideal would be a hypnotic literature of endurance, willpower, obedience, sacrifice, of determination to survive beyond sacrifice. In modern warfare, the writer plays the part of the tribe's witch doctor who praises the courage of warriors, conveys auspicious oracles, unleashes the communal visionary trance to the hoarse, hollow beating of the drums...The great brain that is the State assigns to the writer the duty of preparing souls for the ordeal, whether it be retreat or attack, and the writer sits down at his typewriter as though before a magic apparatus...

Daria could not conceive of literature as anything but an organized service, attuned to the needs of psychological strategy, military administration, resupply, the care of the wounded, and the reeducation of the mutilated. It was obvious that there had to be at least one decent novel and several slim volumes of verse on the topic of ambulances, triage centers, hospitals, and the nurses' duty. A story by a lady writer dwelled on the enemy's unspeakable cruelty and the edifying grandeur of our hate; then finding within herself extraordinary resources of love, she made stricken readers shed tears over the pages in which a wife worships her amputated and disfigured war hero, as a hundred cannon and a hundred searchlights turn Moscow's skies into a cosmic extravaganza of victory. Lovingly she kisses the crushed face, and whispers, "You are the one who has achieved this, my darling! It is for you the hundred cannon boom in triumph! For you, the savior of us all!" A story that provided a much-needed support to the morale of amputees' wives. Daria felt able to become such a wife, she almost wished it, and the image of a blinded Klim, shattered features seamed with pink welts, hobbling along on crutches, drifted before her mind's eye and sickened her. Better for him to be killed outright! Better a grave on which to plant a young fir tree; better to brood over a grave, or before a horizon without a grave, than that! For love of you, Klim!

Feeling let down, as much by herself as by the lady writer, Daria was turning through the pages. She came across a dramatic piece whose title should really have been *The Heroic Children*; she remembered a play she'd seen in Paris about naughty ones, *Les Enfants terribles*. The characters were a couple of selfish, twisted little monsters, and there was a sequel, *Les Parents terribles*, about the same characters in middle age when they had become even more selfish and twisted, but rendered cowardly by what they called "experience." And didn't I once read a novel deserving of the title *The Spoiled Children*? Our managed literature is superior to the other, its children are more wholesome... The play was well written, full of poetic verve. One child, twelve-year-old Zina, has chestnut pigtails and toils away at her homework in a bombed-out house. Zina is passionately keen to become class leader, "because my big brother's fighting the invaders, and this, Mother, is my way of fighting!" The siren wails, Zina shuts her exercise books and stuffs them under the floorboards, into the dirt, to preserve them from the flames, before contending with a classmate for another privilege—the job of helping the spotters out under the death-dealing sky. "It's not fair, Irina, your class has already lost three pupils, and ours is still whole!" Daria began to chafe with annoyance, and skipped the rest of Act One. Around the middle of Act Two, here was little Vanya telling how he was tortured by the Nazis. He didn't cry once, he scorned them, he hated them, he drew strength from hatred, he swore he would live to destroy them, he solemnly vowed as much to the Leader of the Fatherland, "and I didn't tell them anything, I ran away!" "Me too, me too," chirps Zoë, thirteen, "they beat me and burned my lips, look at the scars, and I didn't tell them anything...The village was on fire, the sky was on fire and so was I..." In unison the children sing "The Fatherland loves us, now let us love the Fatherland." Tossia declares she wants to be a schoolteacher, because there are millions of people to teach who are thirsty for knowledge...

Daria flung the magazine down on the straw. The lamp gave off a feeble glow, the earthen walls were animated by trickles of water. Some of the men were asleep, rolled up in their furs. The bearded telephonist said softly, "Careful with that paper, Comrade. It mustn't get wet, it's all there is to smoke." Daria retrieved the magazine and put it on the stool next to the lamp. "Do you have any children?" she asked. "Three," he said in his singsong brogue, "three little cherubs. Hah, what's become of them..." "I didn't mean to remind you," Daria apologized. The bearded man said, "Makes no difference if I talk about it or I don't, God will protect them if that is His will..."

Whoever wrote this play? Who was this author, who apparently had never met a child? Our children are heroic, or some of them are, but not like that. Funny how real heroes never talk the way they do in plays. What's wrong with the genuine article, why fabricate a travesty when we are up to our eyes in authentic heroism, through no choice of our own? The author's name was Anna Lobanova.

Daria's memory of her was precise. In her mid-fifties, with beautiful white hair and a sad, square-jawed kind of pluck, Lobanova had been living in Moscow at a Writers' Union house; she used to speak her mind quite freely, and once was arrested for several days. Her reputation rested on a powerful novel about the

Yakuti penal colonies—those of the former regime, of course. However gritty and sincere the story, it was set in 1907: the old dodge of escaping into the past. Could she possibly be as sincere now, with this turgid rehash of official heroics? Daria asked around. The woman lived in the besieged city, that was something, it gave her the right to speak of courage... So many others had evacuated to Alma-Ata, to the very frontiers of China! Under orders, to be sure; you just have to pull a few strings to get your orders. Out there you can write great war scenarios while watching the apple trees blossom in peace...

On her way home to Klim, she stopped by an old mansion house in what used to be Basseynaya Street, a writers' hive since the time of Dostoyevsky. A little girl who was brushing snow and excrement in the square courtyard directed her to staircase C, "third floor on the right, yes she's there, she nearly never goes out..." Daria offered a dry biscuit, receiving a startled glance in exchange. The child stuffed the prize into her clothes. Daria edged through a half-open door into a hallway lined with bookshelves. Dusty volumes were piled one on top of the other, abandoned, sprawling, and, she guessed, decimated by the needs of the stove. A pale man with a cough pointed her to a door. The apartment smelled of manure, but the hum of a sewing machine could be heard and a gas ring with a saucepan on top was alight in a recess of the passage. Daria knocked at the left-hand door. "Come in?" The ceiling was tarred by smoke. Good pieces of mahogany furniture from the time of mad, murdered Czar Paul were buried under rancid clothes, broken-backed books, crumbs of food. The writer Anna Lobanova, looking paler and more creased than she remembered her—altogether a shriveled old woman—lay on the bed under a rug, holding a bound book between hands encased in gray wool. "Oh! Who are you?"

Daria said, "You might remember me, we met, years ago... Permit me to give you these."

The white hair had lost its sheen but the eyes lit with childish avidity. The visitor pushed vials, ashtray, and candle stump aside to make room on the bedside table for some biscuits, a pack of cigarettes, and a jar of American vitamins.

"Thank you very much," Anna Lobanova said with a broad smile. "It's my legs, you know, what with no food—first-degree malnourishment—and the cold... You in the army? Can't quite place you."

"Think back. We met several times at Illarionov's in Moscow; I was with..."

Daria stopped short in discomfiture, with a name on the tip of her tongue that must on no account ever be pronounced, a presence-absence that did not exist. It had been crossed from the record of the living and the dead: D. "Indeed," the writer filled in quickly, lashes fluttering with the same embarrassment, "perhaps, perhaps... Hardly knew Illarionov, of course..."

Daria adopted a casual tone to say, "I've not read anything of his for ages. I have so little time for reading! I did like his style... An extraordinary stylist, don't you agree? Any idea of what he's up to, these days?"

The old lady's face hardened with hostility and alarm. Her gaze became clouded and at the same time more piercing. The effect was so incongruous that Daria understood: Illarionov was now beyond the pale as well. Anna Lobanova said, "Oh, I've heard nothing of him for years... Never interested me. It's wrong of you to like his style, it was mannered and reactionary... Yes, I don't mind calling it what it was. Counter-revolutionary."

Silence divided them. Daria was taking it in—no more Illarionov. The man, the work, both gone: the name, to be erased from memory. Should she make her excuses and go? Leaving the other sick with foreboding...

"I read your play at the front. *The Heroic Children*."

"It's not by me."

"Sorry, I meant *A Tale of Red Children*..."

The writer would not be drawn out. Her silence seemed to shout: Clear off! You've nothing to say to me, why should I trust you! Daria lied: "I thought it was rather powerful..."

The old lady stared straight ahead. The skin around her mouth was pursed into wrinkles; the aquiline nose remained plump, but only because of the unhealthy puffiness of the flesh. The mouth looked like a stitched wound. It added up to a noble profile, made ugly by sourness and morose affliction. Anna Lobanova pulled off a glove, fished under the rug for a cigarette, lit it, and blew smoke through her nostrils. At last, unwillingly, she spoke.

"I disagree with you there. *A Tale of Red Children* is terrible, a complete disgrace. Who ever saw children like those!"

"Surely," mumbled Daria, "the main episodes were true to life..."

"Documentary authenticity has nothing to do with literary creation. Didn't you read the reviews in the *Literary Gazette*? Bochkin pulled it to pieces and Pimen-Pashkov wiped the floor with them. So there we are. Nor did you read my open letter to the editor, I take it. In which I said that Bochkin and Pimen-Pashkov were justified in their opinion and that it was a piece of agitprop garbage. Subjectively honorable, objectively detestable."

Daria wanted to laugh, but felt inhibited by Lobanova's prickly solemnity.

"A writer is a craftsman who must be able to recognize a botched job."

"And what are you working on now?" Daria asked, in order to change the subject.

"Not very easy to write, with these clumsy gloves and swollen joints... I'm working on a novel about Berezina in 1812... I don't understand the youngsters of today. Mine grew up in another era."

"How are they?" (She felt idiotic saying this.)

"My son was killed at Smolensk. No news of my daughter or the grandchildren..."

A small voice shrilled behind the door: "Auntie Aniushka! The soup's boiling!" "Then turn off the gas!" the writer called back tartly. Daria offered: "Shall I bring you your meal? I'd like to do something..."

"Nothing for you to do. I'm very well where I am."

"I work for one of the staff services...I could get you evacuated, perhaps a kinder climate..."

"No. I'm not leaving this city, or my books and papers."

"I understand."

"No you don't. You can't." Lobanova relented a fraction. "You're too young."

There was nothing to say. This room embodied the utter extinction of all things. Lobanova chewed emptiness between her soft gums and said, "I never read the papers anymore. They annoy me. Think we have a chance?"

"Haven't you heard, we're saved? They'll never take Leningrad..."

As Daria talked on, Lobanova listened with inquisitorial attention. Don't even think of lying to me. I know so much. I smell out falsehood and I despise it. I need no consoling pieties to help me either die or live. I need good reason, at its just measure! She must have been satisfied, because she nodded approvingly once or twice.

"May God hear you!" she concluded, with a wry grimace. "You're no airhead, I'll give you that. Women have come on a great deal since the revolution...Now leave me alone, I'm tired."

Daria stood up, buttoning her sheepskin uniform cloak. "So there's nothing that you need? Or that I can do?" "No, nothing. But thanks for your visit! A bad play earning me a good visit...That's nice...And after, there will be room for great literature, real literature."

After us...

Daria asked affectionately, "How old are you?"

"Sixty-two...But I plan to go on working for at least five years. We writers receive good rations. And so we should. Someone has to defend the brain..."

Out of the blue, Daria thought back to Illarionov, whose name could not be spoken, to D (in a small tan café in Paris), to some of the dead. Killed: worse than dead.

"Real literature," she echoed, "without fear or lies..."

The aged, exhausted face blanched with something like fright. In a different voice, as though speaking in public, Lobanova pronounced: "In my opinion, the wartime labor of the Writers' Union has been exemplary...Always inspired by the directives of the Party and the Party's Leader."

Daria nodded vigorously at this. She managed a diffident smile. "May I come and see you again?"

"If you like. There's no need. I'm sure you have better things to do. Tell that child out there to bring me my soup."

■

That morning, she'd had a curious interview with Major Makhmudov. This fat man with an ivory-pink cranium addressed her politely, coolly, not unaffably but with authority: "Are you married?" "De facto, yes." "So I've discovered. It is not in your dossier. I should reprimand you. The personnel in this service are expected to apply for a marriage license, and to inform me of any changes to their civil status...However, your husband is a very highly regarded element among the subaltern cadres. I wish you both the best. Have you told him of your past?" "No." "I see..." He surveyed her heavily. "I needn't remind you of the rules of discipline..." "No, Comrade Major." Daria looked squarely back at him. This is how things stand. "Very good, dismissed..."

She spent the day in the office. Some shells landed not far away. At dusk she set off home via a long detour, feeling obscurely anxious but telling herself it was nothing. The frozen Neva appeared wider than usual. People followed paths over the ice like columns of slow, dull, plodding ants. The snow turned dark beneath their footfalls. Everything was sluggish, low, muted, dingy, and white. The sporadic explosions likewise. The tall gilt spires of the old imperial fortress, built level with the white river, had lost their shine. Women clustered lethargically here and there around holes in the ice; some were staggering away under buckets and jerry cans of green water strewn with floating frost needles. The sky was bluish-yellow above these open stretches. Daria realized she barely had strength enough to think, that her ideas were unraveling into wisps the color of this sky and that some of them were oppressive, to be pushed back...So Illarionov is dead. A despicable character, though he had tremendous gifts...Sacha used to say: "As a human being he's a nonentity, with next to no inner life, he's heavy, he's common: a bank account and a digestive tract. As a writer he might well be great, the remarkable parasite on vegetative man...Prisoner of the man, the writer tries his utmost to be a coward—he would like to specialize in novels written to order, fitting the ideological requisites of the season. And he writes them superbly, but here's where the real plot thickens. The parasite writer is far more intelligent and less groveling than the vegetative host; he is even prone to bursts of bold, sentimental, convoluted genius, and likes to imagine that the authorities don't really understand what he's doing. Even his most official works contain a subtle undercurrent of vitality, making them suggestive of something other than their apparently orthodox line...The bureaucrats at the Literature Office tear at their hair over them. They implore our Illarionov to change twenty-seven passages, and he does, goddamn it—by getting totally drunk! And there are still bits that get away, overlooked by the censors...The censors are afraid of him. He's undermined the careers of some of their top men. Illarionov is trembling as well, he drinks to reassure himself, but then in his cups he says things that could get him deported for life. After the hangover he'll dash off a raft of mean, vacuous articles against all and sundry: colleagues whom he accuses of lukewarm ideological commitment, or blindness to the times we live in, or not admiring him enough. His friends no longer know whether they should shake his hand or not; but being the champion of political orthodoxy, it's not a good idea to fall out with him. 'You sure come off as some strange kind of bastard!' I once told him fondly at the end of a gala dinner. Illarionov began whining, with tears in his eyes, that the essence of the old man is the old bastard...We were both drunk."

Daria tried in vain to piece together a rounded picture of Illarionov. All she could recall was a boorish face, a conical forehead, a portly presence that looked at women as though they were for sale... But he did dress well. Unhealthy to remember the dead, they are all connected, they call out to one another, they congregate inside you, they are too many, too alive. There's no getting rid of them once they have got possession of your soul, instead it's they that banish sleep, derail the train of thought, lead you where you have no wish to go. Some of them would have known better how to defend this city, our land, our blood, our idea than many who are alive today... They defend us still. Their soul is present. Every one of our promises for the future was seeded by them...

"Am I still thinking within the materialist truth of history?" In wrestling with this question, Daria recalled with pleasure this phrase from Marx: "The tradition of dead generations weighs like a bad dream on the minds of the living..." It was from *The Eighteenth Brumaire*... While tradition is a nightmarish dead weight, it can also illuminate like a shaft of healing clarity: witness the Marxian tradition itself. Such is the mystery of consciousness... What did Sacha say about that, in our tan-upholstered café in Paris?

Our millions of dead are lost, a third of the city's living are half dead, the Klims are lost, and yet we are saved, the stagnant war is beginning to turn our way, with the Nazis running out of steam, the American engine revving up—but how shall we be saved? As a luminous force or a persistent nightmare? The very question is treason, but how can I avoid asking it? Anguish is a betrayal of life only if it cries quits, anguish is a sacred warning: Beware the chasm, beware of what you may become! We alone know the nightmare we are trapped in, the ugly underside of our debilitated strength, and that our only hope lies in a resurrection from among the dead: from among defunct ideas and murdered ideologues... That's why people talk so little nowadays. Klim hardly talks. Lobanova talks, the better to perfect her silence. Makhmudov never talks. Colonel Fontov talks to himself. Captain Potapov talks only to teach, as rarely as possible ... To talk is to work on behalf of hope. People at the brink of exhaustion know the futility of this work, last hopes don't need it. Where there is anguish and hunger, silence is more eloquent. It wastes less breath and it's safer.

Climbing the stairs, Daria strained toward Klim. Klim whose muscles and sinews knew all that was amiss and made it all right, without a word ... A thickset form was blocking the landing, dressed in black, surmounted by a black fur hat whose folded flaps exposed a white wool lining. Moving from foot to foot, the man cleared his throat and said, "I recognize you ... It is you, isn't it? Klim sent me."

What had happened? Sick? Killed? (Bombs were falling to the west, earlier...) Arrested? Gone? In any case, say nothing. Daria was calm as she always was in the face of misfortune. She did not doubt that misfortune had struck.

"So," she said. "What?"

"He won't be back tonight ... Nor the coming nights either."

"When, then?"

"He doesn't know... maybe two months, if all goes well."

The darkened landing was like the bottom of a pit.

"Is it orders?"

The soldier hesitated.

"Put it this way... we're always under orders ..."

"How dangerous is it?"

"No more than usual ..."

"He didn't give you any message? Nothing for me?"

"He's not allowed. He'll try to write ... sometime soon ... He'll never forget you."

"But nothing bad has happened to him?"

"Oh no, nothing. That's all."

Everything is kept secret. The death of a fighter in action, so as not to reveal our losses and not alarm the rear guard—which is alarmed enough by the secrecy. Arrest, so as not to alarm those already haunted by the expectation of arrest. Execution, because to conceal it is humane, and to divulge it too often, impolitic. War work, any combat mission, because enemy eyes and ears surround us and the enemy is also within, in each potential failure of nerve. Thought, because it is an indomitable force that never knows where it is going or what it will demand, may suddenly find itself mired in a maze of doubts, scruples, questions, inventions, and dreams. We want efficient, disciplined thinking, technical thinking—but how is that to be separated from the other, which is anarchic, ungovernable, obsessive, and unpredictable? How to silence the mischievous twin beneath a cloak of reproof and secrecy? If only I could, once and for all! He was right, the poet who advised:

> Keep quiet, dissemble, make secret
> Your feelings and your thoughts...

He lived under a despotism. We...

Klim will never come back, because if he does I will no longer be here. It's even more likely that he, that we will no longer exist. The same water never passes between the same banks twice, said Heraclitus... Heraclitus...

Daria flung herself down on the mattress in the storeroom, now stripped of life. The grimy walls were dismal like those of a cell. Tomorrow she would move to the barracks. The ceiling seemed covered with algebraic signs and masculine shapes. She felt repulsed by the cold little stove and the brown bread hardening on the trunk they'd used for a table. She felt a horror of the days to come. They would be as flat as a track beaten through the snow and dirtied here and there by smears of blood. Decoding messages, annotating documents, dictating reports for Captain Potapov, drawing abstract images of war for a largely useless bureaucratic exercise, translating at interrogations... Some of the prisoners were garrulous and cooperative, so eager to help it was sickening. The more slippery ones endeavored to mislead but failed, in most cases, caught out by basic cross-checks. Too bad for them. Others were ludicrous, rigid with a sense of duty yet twisted by fear into knots; they might have elicited grudging respect were they not hateful to the core, the type to torture our prisoners and set villages on fire, young thugs in gleaming boots who looked on as droves of Jewish women and tearful children were herded toward mass graves... The first kind betrayed their army in a bestial, abject gurgle bubbling from the gut: these were human. The second feigned consent to treachery, so as to betray the grain of trust they hoped to inspire. The third group, loyal to their murderous cause, were traitors to human nature... That's what the men of this century have been turned into. We are better than they are. Really? Are we? Stop thinking, Daria! Klim: Klim is better. She opened her arms to the glacial air. Tears welled at the corners of her eyes without falling and grew cold on the rim of her lids.

Night fell and the cold became torture. It did not completely snuff out organic vitality, but condensed it into sharp, sleep-inducing suffering. Curled into a ball, Daria was hungry. She felt the blood cooling in her veins, her limbs going to sleep, and it was as though the slightest movement could make the blanket of cold settling slowly over her change to a hard sheet of ice. Her body merged into the vast wintriness of the city, the river, the battle-fields. Her last sparks of lucidity were like explosions of boreal brilliance over horizons of splendid, soft, deadly snow. Black water flowed toward the sea, icy river seeking icy ocean beneath the crust of ice. The ice is like a magnifying glass, I see someone walking on it through the phosphorescent night. It's me, what am I doing so weightless and disembodied on the ice? And this little girl who comes to meet me opening eyes of black water and saying: I drowned, you did too didn't you? Daria extended her disembodied hands, they clasped the drowned girl's hands, she saw the hands join hands but had no sensation of it. We will never feel anything again. Child, dearest child, we will never be warm again ...A brilliance surged up into the sky and against this silvery backdrop the spires of St. Peter and Paul's were outlined, and the massive dome of St. Isaac's, and an ancient crenellated tower somewhere near the Rambla de las Flores in Barcelona, no, no, it was a miniature Kazakh mosque in the desert ... Where are we, child, do you know? We are everywhere and everywhere we are cold ... "Listen, listen! We'll not be cold soon!" The silver-white brilliance had won, it had girdled the universe with numberless beams of pale fire overlapping at the zenith, to the rhythmic crashing of cannon ... "The war is finished, child, we've won, we've won, can it be true?" "No doubt about it, Daria my love," it was Klim speaking, and heat broke through her at the touch of his bare chest ... But, Klim, where is the child? The child who thought herself drowned when I was feeling robbed of myself, after walking on the ice for so long? Klim was laughing. What child? Our child, Dacha? They were blissfully warm and she was laughing too. Our child! The gigantic water, the water black beneath the ice creaked and moaned, full of menace ...

"Were you asleep? So sorry to disturb you, Comrade, but ..."

Dacha opened her eyes. A candle flame hovered in the emptiness of the storage room. A child, her head wrapped in old woolens, was bending over her. The drowned child with eyes of black frozen water was an aging woman. But who?

Daria felt for the revolver and was restored to reality by its touch.

"What is it? Who are you?"

"Pardon me ... I'm your neighbor, Trofimova, Elena Trofimova ... from the Budayev factory ... Oh, I am sorry ..."

"What do you want?"

"It's my sister, she's in a terribly bad way, oh, please come and see ..."

Muffled thunderclaps punctuated the night, they were falling over Ligovo, at a guess.

"Hush, no need to apologize, I'm coming. Is she sick?"

"Yes! No ... more like worn out, but she's gutsy ... top of her brigade ..."

The next-door room was like a mine shaft, littered with dark and vaguely glistening objects. The candlelight brought forth a young, drawn face, gray lips stretched into a weak smile. "She won't answer anything I say," panted Elena Trofimova, "it's as if she was dead, but her heart's still going, oh God oh God what shall I do?" Daria warmed her hands over the flame before slipping them under the layers of clothing, to explore a skeletal rib cage with two flaps of skin for breasts. The heart was beating, just, to an irregular rhythm. "It's all right, she's only fainted!" Daria said nervously. A few more swoons of that sort and she'll never come to, she'll be walking disembodied on the ice toward the aurora borealis . . .

"Can you make a little fire?"

"We have no more wood . . . But I made her some hot flour gruel earlier, with a bit of glucose, I was telling her she mustn't work so hard, take off sick for a couple of days! I was telling her . . . Oooh, Mitrofanov, he might have some hot water, I could ask him, if he's got a drop left, oh God oh God!"

"Pull yourself together! From Mitrofanov or from the devil, just get us some hot water!"

"So she's not dying then? Not yet this time? Oh God!"

Daria looked stonily into her face, into her eyes of unbearable black water.

"No, not this time. I know what I'm talking about. Stop talking! Bring hot water."

She went back to her room and searched it blindly for the last of the vodka, the vitamin bottle, the tin of fish in brine, and the half-eaten bar of stale chocolate—all that she had. How terrified people are by death! How desperate to live another day! Why? Because it's our strength, our human strength, though there's nothing specifically human about it . . . We're not afraid of death, yet we long to live a few more days in spite of death . . .

Next door was pitch black. Daria parted the cold lips and unresisting jaws with her fingers, lodged the neck of the vodka bottle between the teeth and carefully upended it. The throat jerked in a hiccup. She dribbled alcohol into her palms and rubbed the bony chest with its pathetic pouches of skin. The pulse beat more firmly. The swollen stomach became warmer. The kneaded flesh grew oily beneath her hand, in a melting of sweat and grime.

Elena Trofimova reappeared with the candle and an inch of hot water at the bottom of a tin. "What can I do?" she whispered submissively. "Die in your turn," Daria said to herself, "but not yet." "Oh thank you, thank you," said the submissive voice, "she's coming to, oh my God!" These invocations grated on Daria's nerves. She shook the rest of the vodka into the warm water and said to the woman: "Drink a bit of this."

"Hey, what about me, don't I need spoiling too?" came a gruff, somewhat wheedling voice, and Daria saw the broad stooped figure of a man somewhere in his forties, though he might have been sixty. He had come in unnoticed, wearing a fur hat and a shapeless greatcoat cut out of heavy embroidered curtains. He was shivering; his eyes glittered in a face blackened up to the cheekbones by two days' growth of stubble. Trofimova introduced him: "This is Mitrofanov, the head mechanic at the shoe plant...a Hero of Labor..."

"Hero my foot," Mitrofanov growled, bending over the sick woman, "what I say is, if your sister keeps on with her heroics much longer she's gonna die, and what good would that do? You explain to them, it's all about holding on. The victory will be won by the living, not the dead."

He spoke tenderly to the recumbent form: "C'mon, Tamarka, Tamarochka, open your peepers, don't cha recognize me?"

The sick girl moved restively.

"It's you, Anisim Savich, I feel better now...What's the matter? Am I going to be late? I'm on the third shift..."

"Forget the third shift," said Mitrofanov somberly. "They know you there; you're not getting out of bed, and you're staying put. You have nothing to fear."

Daria was opening the canned fish. "Feed her this, all of it, please! And give her these pills, six times a day. Is that clear?" She spoke with all the authority she could muster, because four greedy eyes had locked onto the pale fatty piece of fish. "You know what, I think I'll feed her myself." "Safer bet by far," drawled Mitrofanov. "Sit up, Tamarka, open wide..." The young girl obeyed, but was unable to swallow very much. "No more, I feel sick..." "Right then, split the rest between you," Daria ordered. She wormed a flake of chocolate between the girl's teeth. "No thanks, couldn't possibly," Mitrofanov said, and sniggered.

"It's only exhaustion?" asked Daria, smiling at the patient.

"What do you think?" said Mitrofanov with an odd look of satisfaction. "This whole town's like that. Where've you dropped in from, Citizen?"

"From Kazakhstan," Daria said, immediately regretting a spontaneity against regulations.

"Sand, snakes, and camels... Wish I was there now."

He was an odd mixture of malice and cordiality, with the shrewdness of a woodland bandit. "Not bad at all, that army fish... Had a whole tin to myself on Revolution day." One sensed in him the canny old working man who knows how to steal and get away with it, how to make the most of a piece of metal or leather, how to trade a switchblade or stiletto in the marketplace among flocks of soldiers; a hero nonetheless, on whom productivity could rely. He stopped Daria in the shadowy passageway.

"They're a pair of hopeless ninnies," he told her. "I don't give 'em two months if they don't learn, and soon. The little one's a sainted team leader, never misses a day, volunteers her time off to be one up on the quotas and what have you! The eldest, now, she's in better shape, being as useless with her hands as with her head. But she don't get as much to eat, her, except when she's mopping the kitchen and makes off with the scrapings of the scrapings ... Tell them to put the brakes on, that's my advice as a Labor Hero... We got to work ourselves to death for the defense effort, but not stone dead. If we all kill ourselves dead, all at the same time, who's left to win the war? Tactics and strategy, see! Right or wrong, Citizen?"

Ashamed of being healthy and well-fed herself, Daria murmured, "Right, of course. But how to go about it?"

"Oh, there's no end of tricks," Mitrofanov said. "The proletariat knows them backward and forward. If there weren't such tricks we'd have been done for years ago, take it from me, there'd be precious little left of the proletariat by now... Well, got seventy minutes left for my beauty sleep. Good night, Citizen."

Back home, Daria lifted the sacks covering the little window. It was just before dawn, though the night gave no sign of it. This spiral suction deep inside is hunger—spreading like frost through the entrails. And this stabbing emptiness in the depth of my being, that's loneliness. Hunger and loneliness, two tentacles of death. I too am beginning to die, almost painlessly, with no bitterness, in a house full of industrious lives ebbing toward death. No other kind of abode exists in this besieged, half-perished city. The awesome might of the half perished! If there is to be a victory some day, it will belong to them... The Mitrofanovs will have pulled through yet again. They will be vengeful, they will be barbaric, they will be cruelly, bafflingly tender, full of breathtaking sagacity... They will deploy an instant flair in the fight for life, not dissimilar perhaps to the instincts of Ice Age primitives. What's more, they will have the enterprising brains of civilized men who have been cured of refinements. They will have the great yearning for warmth and fraternity of disaster survivors, in the knowledge that primal heroism is redemptive only when it is underpinned by communal egoism. What will we make of this peerless energy, for ourselves and for the world? A lever, or an ax for splitting skulls?

This question was tied to the shadow of Sacha. The thought of being back in the office the next day among military men who ate their fill, strutted their medals, computed the precise amount of shed blood, projected foreseeable casualties from hunger, cold, and fire, making this work into a rather placid profession, never uttering a living word, filled Daria with revulsion. Because I belong to the generation of those who were shot, the unadaptable generation! she said bitterly. What if I applied for an intelligence assignment with one of the partisan units operating behind enemy lines, in the snow-blanketed forest? Farewell, Klim. After the war, Klim. After death, Klim.

And Klim appeared to her under formless trees thickly veiled in purest white. "Come with me," he said, "I'll light us a big fire. Come and be happy... Tomorrow we'll begin killing, because we love the earth, mankind, and life. Come, I love you..." "You mustn't love me," Daria answered through gathering mists of sleep, "I am a half-dead woman. I mean yes, you must love me... I'm a half-dead woman." A wolf cub with a gallant plume of a tail and strangely understanding little eyes watched her from behind a screen of green-needled pine boughs, the kind that are placed on coffins with red ribbons.

III.

Brigitte, Lightning, Lilacs

And still the habit of believing
more in the earth than in the grave...

IF THERE ever had been, if there ever were, somewhere in the world, another reality, it now remained in human memory as no more than a recollection, tinged more by doubt and sadness than by nostalgia. The past marked the older people most deeply, and some of them needed no prompting to talk about it, harping ad nauseam on the good old days. It was understandable that they could not avoid being intoxicated by the past, and that it pained them even more than it pained the people who wished they would shut up. In their chatter, periods and wars got mixed up: Let's see, was that before the first war or the second? Was that under the Kaiser, the Revolution, Weimar, Versailles, under Brüning or the Führer? Explain yourself! How many wars have there been, sir? The revolution was also a war, you must realize that! The clearest answers—coming from people who seemed to have lived through so many events in the half century that they were probably exaggerating—remained obscure; and the price of a good dinner or the comfort of a railway journey came to sound like preposterous yarns or, more exactly, the gibberish of half-wits. So when Frau Krammerz, down in the bomb shelter below Kellerman's Rathskeller under vaults glistening with saltpeter, took to reminiscing about how life used to be—the Sundays in the country, the exquisite pastries one could order from the cake shop, the party for Gertrude's first communion—some of the adults looked at her with hatred; and they were delighted when a little girl took her grubby fingers out of her mouth to declare, with withering finality: "S'not true." "Quiet, you snot-nose little guttersnipe..." The child went on with her irresistible "s'not true." Nobody got up to

173

give her a smack, in part because the ground was shaking (bombs were raining down on the other side of the canal, there being nothing left to flatten on this side, the connoisseurs explained, so it would be murderous bad luck if...), but mostly because she was, quite obviously, right. Frau Krammerz suddenly realized it herself. Her face, more wrinkled than an empty bottle, skin crudely decorated by primitives, crumpled as she brushed away her tears and admitted, with a pitiable attempt at a laugh, "No, it's not true, *mein Gott*!"

Thunderclaps sent huge waves through the earth; crackling outbursts transmuted into great surges of heat, as though invisible ripples of fire were pulsing outward from a fiery oven, somewhere nearby, to one side, deep underground. "We're going to be baked like potatoes in ashes," an old man calmly remarked. Fits of helpless whimpering started up in the children's corner. "Can't the little snots get used to it? Pipe down, it's over, stop bawling and wipe your noses!" Brigitte made her way across the cellar toward the children, holding a cloth-wrapped object. It was her find of the morning, the reward of hours spent picking through the fresh rubble, and aroused much excitement among the small-fry. There was barely any light to see by, as the electric bulbs had just died and the shelter had fallen back on candles, but their eyes, accustomed to the dark, discerned everything in rich detail. Brigitte unrolled a doll wearing an old-fashioned military outfit, with a tall bearskin calpac, a green tunic, a white plastron and buckled gaiters, a soldier of Frederick the Great's at Rossbach—that's a glorious piece of History, the Seven Years' War! Whereas these days, it feels more like the Thirty Years' War... "For me, for me! Here, Brigitte!" chorused high voices which a string of massive but distant impacts could not drown out. ("You see, they're going away now... all gone ... finished ...") "Not for you and not for you either," said the young woman. "We'll hold a draw."

"S'not real."

"Not real, what do you mean, you silly minx?"

"Yes it is real, look, I'm playing with it..."

"Listen all to the song of glory!" proclaimed the amiable, if strident, voice of the disabled veteran, for the sirens were sounding the all clear. That sardonic voice always brought peculiar results: now one of the lightbulbs went back on, spreading sepulchral cheer. The invalid was crutching his way over to the stairway, humming to himself. "I'm off for a breath of air..." he called. "Excellent for the health. A poetic night, my friends. I'll try to bring back some water for the sick..." The water can jangled against the complicated prostheses whose manufacturer, according to him, deserved to be summarily hanged. He had lost his left foot and right arm in some insignificant battle on the eastern front, but he managed nimbly enough on one foot, two contraptions, and a stick salvaged from the rubble that did excellent duty as a crutch, just the right length and burned to a convenient lightness. He even attended sessions at the Vocational Rehabilitation Center, charming but compulsory charades... The sick no longer left the basement shelter. They groaned for a moment, then fell quiet. During the bombing they remained silent, except for chattering teeth; the minute it was over they fell to tossing, spitting, coughing, pissing, and wanting a modicum of attention—but not for long. The disciplined character of the average man who knows there's nothing to be done about it soon reasserted itself. Besides, this beer cellar made an agreeable shelter with its tapestried walls and elegant furniture, and there were sheets on the mattresses.

Franz, the disabled vet known as "Minus-Two," hauled himself up the stairs, limped along a narrow corridor, skirted a bulwark of sandbags, struck the high notes of a piano keyboard with his prosthesis as he went by, making it blurt out a cracked lament, listened to this fragment of *lied* fade away, and continued on, with a little apprehension now because there was always a risk that the entrance to the underground system might be blocked by fresh debris. It wasn't: silvery clouds opened against a dusting of stars. Minus-Two whistled between his teeth the triumphal march of King Frederick's fifes. A steel-sharp sickle of moon illuminated the becalmed street, that is to say the line of building façades behind

whose gaping windows lay a deepening void, some mounds of collapsed masonry like fossilized monsters, and the dark black outline of a tall, thin slice of building still standing around the axis of
its chimney. The four jag-toothed floors of this tilted saw leaned
fifteen or twenty degrees south by southwest; if they ever collapsed, they would fall on the uninhabitable rubble of the White
Hunter Inn. If the collapse were gentle enough, someone might
be able to grab that fine gold-knobbed metal bedstead clinging to
the parquet of the fourth floor; as for the oval mirror framed with
brass bows on which rays of sunlight sometimes played, there'd
be nothing left of it but the frame, and in a sorry state at that.
Broken mirror, bad omen! We can expect yet another bad omen
... For now, the mirror up there was merely the augury of a bad
omen. Minus-Two pondered how nothing changed: order.

Out of idle curiosity he cocked an ear to the noises of the city.
A few searchlights were still crisscrossing the sky. Keep searching,
keep searching, my friends, for something that leaves no trace, according to Solomon's proverb: a fish in the sea, a man in a woman,
a plane in the sky. They're far away now. From somewhere a final,
bad-tempered burst of antiaircraft fire spat out it's flak flak flak
drak drak drak. "Stupid idiots!" muttered the crippled vet. He
heard ambulance sirens and motorcycle engines yapping brokenly,
way over in the new part of town, where the no-go underground
factories and the model workers' housing and the railway junc-
tions were; there can't be much left of all that, at least not above
ground; below, they can still hold out. Under the ground or otherwise, the Third Reich will hold out to the end of the millennium,
that's certain.

Minus-Two halted before a stretch of wall that had been
cleanly sheared off as though there had never been anything above
it; new grass was sprouting on top of the neatly raked rubble of
Billingen's Pharmacy! He practiced writing with his left hand in
the moonlight, tracing each word in block letters with a piece of
chalk: "One Führer, One *Volk*, One Tomb! *Heil* Death!" (This to

enrage Herr Blasch.) He judged his calligraphy to be improving; faster too, I'm making progress... If only I had a cigarette butt left! Whose head would I most gladly give for a butt? There was no shortage of choices. In his book, the number-one hateful head still belonged to a tank captain he'd run into around Poznan, a rattlesnake head—monocled, helmeted, shaved, and powdered with gray, rapping out completely unfulfillable orders like: "Take out that machine-gun nest with silver tweezers for me, no getting your fingers dirty, then goose-step across that river for me, keeping dry on the tiptoes of your boots; the valiant soldier scorns all obstacles or I'll have him court-martialed!" The Russians must have already ground that head into head cheese for the worms long ago... It's sweet to amuse oneself with private jokes, isn't it, Captain? Me Minus-Two, you Zero-Minus-a-Thousand, honorable Captain-Baron-Minus-Head, Minus-Balls, Minus-Joke, Minus-Everything! But if I ever learned that you didn't get blown away by a 177 shell up your ass, I'd have to conclude that not even the shadow of one-eyed justice remains here below...

"But that's impossible!" cried Minus-Two into the soft transparent night.

So whose head could he offer up to the Great God of Universal War so as to ensure finding tomorrow a juicy stub of genuine tobacco, the kind your Party higher-ups sometimes throw away? Crescent moon, inspire me! The head of Herr Blasch, sergeant of the elite corps' home guard, in charge of security of recovered dwellings, Führer of the neighborhood lout patrol... Tac-tac-trac-tac, the music of machine-gun fire rang out in the distance among the fresh or refreshed ruins. Herr Blasch and his henchmen—on orders from above—were busy liquidating the seriously wounded, or looters caught red-handed, or some crazed old granny who started mouthing off... I'm a lucky bugger to have only two limbs left, thought Minus-Two.

And for a little shot of schnapps, what would you give for that, Franz? For a cheery draught of Pomeranian brandy? Your Iron

Cross? Oh la la! I'll throw in the colossal Stone Cross they'll be raising over the tomb of the German people, and the columns of the imperial chancellery for good measure...

"What's impossible?" From behind came a voice as bubbly as a lovely brook running through green grass—if there still were such things as brooks, grass, cows, pearly green horizons.

"Princess!" Minus-Two exclaimed as he swung around. "You're incredible."

"It's true," said Brigitte.

She came closer, belted into her white coat, her curls blond in daylight, now the shade of metallic ash, her neck slender, her gaze unfocused. She was always looking elsewhere or beyond, so that Minus-Two had come to conceive of her eyes on the model of classical statuary. He leaned conveniently against a tidy stack of bricks made by the Schools Reconstruction Organization (thanks to Strength through Joy, of course).

"Come here, closer, white fairy." Brigitte came. With his living arm he pulled her toward him, heatedly. "When this war is over, Brigitte, I'm going to marry a rich woman, a very rich woman. We won't have kids. Because of the next war, d'you see. My wife will look like you."

"I am rich," Brigitte said gently, "but I won't get married."

The crippled vet's horsey head, with its hairy nostrils and soft angry mouth, was calling. They kissed, mouth to mouth until they ran out of breath, their breath returning as one single breath.

"Why won't you get married, Brigitte?"

"Because of love. It would be too hard to explain. I don't really understand it myself. I'm going home. Good night, Franz."

"I'll go get some water for the sick, see you later," the man said, or didn't say, perhaps only thinking the words, suddenly knocked down by exhaustion, like a human animal concussed in the vicinity of an exploding mine. It erases you in an instant and you come to dazed, drained, unable to grasp that life is continuing, or yours is at least, with a frenzied carillon of blood booming in your temples, your rib cage, your limbs, your skull scoured by a wind of

fire... With the metal pincer of his right hand, he held the can
under the spigot while pumping energetically with his left, it
worked, hallelujah! Good old pump, it was holding up better under the circumstances than the western front, the eastern front,
the Italian, the oceanic, and the home fronts! The water of this
well seemed to have remained pure, even though twenty feet away
the sewers were vomiting up stinking slime through a large crack
in the asphalt. Some rats scurried up and began lapping at the
puddles around the pump; they grew strangely thirsty after each
bombardment. Drink your fill, nasty animals, brother rats, you
are like us, we are like you.

■

If there had ever existed, if there still were, some other place, another reality, the children had no way of knowing it. They grew,
they played, they died (in large numbers, with even larger numbers surviving, the scientists couldn't understand it) in a ghostly
city bristling with the skeletons of churches lashed by sky, wind,
rain, and fire. Oases of habitation robbed the destruction of a few
torn, eerie patches of domesticity... Wherever life could take
hold, whether in basements or in bedrooms carefully refurbished
in the very heart of chaos, some on higher floors propped up by
what looked like concrete stilts, households restored a sense of intimacy: pictures and portraits on the wall, doilies on broken-
legged furniture, makeshift brick ovens standing on the buckling
parquet, access ladders with rope handholds, trunks and bed
linen, maxims embroidered by an aged aunt, since evacuated: "Do
Good and Thy Soul Shall Leap for Joy."

The earth shuddered, smoke crept across it, people dwelt in a
volcanic realm of sudden explosions, smoldering dormant fires,
smoky eddies of soot, dust clouds, the stench of reeking corpses,
charred and splintered trees that persisted in budding and even
put out, here and there, tender pale-green leaves as though nothing were amiss. Squads of women or schoolboys cleared the

ghostly path of streets where no street remained, restoring empty grids like the layout of an archaeological excavation, shoveling human debris from under a mangle of timbers to be borne away on dirty stretchers toward tumbrels disinfected by men in face masks... The children could not have dreamed that another urban landscape was possible, and they found this one simple: terrifying by night, terrifying by day when the routine horrors occurred, pleasant and packed with surprises at other times... On sunny mornings the children emerged in their clean clothes like baby scorpions scuttling out from under a stone to bask in the heat; out came the children to roll marbles, throw balls, skip rope, and play war. They played at escaped prisoners, who were chased, caught, and solemnly shot, yet despite the inevitability of this outcome they all wanted to be the prisoner... Their playground encompassed the deep rubbly crater that yawned behind the little olive-and-yellow house, almost intact, that belonged to the post office subdirector, and a mountainous redoubt they called the Sierra, a mysteriously vast domain where apartment blocks owned by the Patria Life Insurance Company used to stand. The treasure hunters struck out into the Sierra, careless of the official ban, to climb the Himalayas and Chimborazos of destruction; they posted a lookout in the Mount Rose hidey-hole to watch out for the little policemen in the green uniform or the more formidable guard with the white armband; a discreet birdcall was enough to make the energetic heads of girls and boys duck down behind the spurs of Kazbek or Popocatepetl... Because Professor Schiff, skipping the chapters on cosmology and basic physical geography, lectured his pupils passionately on the geological cataclysms that gave birth to mountain chains, on subterranean fire, on earthquakes, on the submersion of entire continents beneath the seas: for example Atlantis, mentioned by the divine Plato, northern Laurentia, Gondwanaland to the southeast... The earth was replete with lost continents.

Schiff was a very old man. He wore a frock coat singed rusty from the time his house caught fire; the atlases he brought to class were singed around the edges like old books from a corsair's booty; during breaks darkened by rain (or when he felt like it), Herr Schiff told stories about the end of the world, the Flood and Noah's ark, the San Francisco earthquake, the annihilation of Saint-Pierre de la Martinique under sulfurous clouds that melted the very bronze of the church bells, so imagine what it did to soft human flesh, *meine liebe Kinder*, my dear children! They were beautiful tales and easy to understand. "Remember when the dike broke, sir, it was like Atlantis in the shelters around there, wasn't it? Like a flood! And three families got away in an ark, sir, people saw them!" The teacher suspected that the boy who had spoken with such aptness was a Jew hidden by a Catholic family, and felt a combination of pitiful sympathy and insurmountable repugnance toward him but reacted benevolently in appreciation of the boy's correct understanding. "You have a point," he said, inclining his head to rest it against his open palm, "but of course the end of Atlantis was the end of an entire world. All the towns, all the fields, even the high mountains, and all the people of twenty tribes . . . It's rather hard to imagine." He was a splendid teacher of drawing, writing, and discipline, who greeted his classes of ten- to fourteen-year-olds with martially outstretched arm and a resounding *Heil Hitler*! that could compete with the great rallies in Nuremberg. As a result his classes performed the smartest, proudest salute of any school in town. It was common knowledge that his two sons had died like heroes, one in the Libyan desert, the other in the forests of Courland, and hence every pupil was familiar with the location of these important countries, justly conquered . . . Schiff interrupted the writing lesson to demand in stentorian tones: "Hans Büttel! What is the one and only immortal power?" Hans stood up obediently to recite a formula no one quite understood, inspiring hilarious parodies by wise guys, but which brought a look of peace onto the master's fraught countenance. "Sir, each of us is merely mortal, but the Aryan Race, is im-mor-tal!" Instructed by his mother, wan little Claudius plunked himself in front of Professor Schiff's desk, between the color poster of cereals and the portrait of the Leader-of-the-Party-and-the-People-who-is-guiding-us-to-Victory, and asked, "My mother wanted to know, sir, is victory near?" "My dear boy, fetch your pencil and write." Professor Schiff dictated: "Our victory does not reside in earthly space or time, but in the deathless principle of the Race." Frau Sonnecker framed these lines in gold paper and hung them above her son's bed ... It was a pleasant schoolroom, lacking only one corner of the roof; the hole had been patched with corrugated iron. Six gilt chairs from the confectioner's shop added a touch of glamour, but they were not to be sat on, the school will return them to Frau Deinecke when that lady comes back, after the war.

The master turned a blind eye to his pupils' expeditions, and, when they brought him books, gravely acknowledged the gift. The warrior-explorers, Argonauts, Conquistadors, Knights of the Round Table, or Teutonic heroes, as the fancy took them, unearthed all sorts of trophies in the volcano zone ... The great trick was to detect a cave, unblock the entrance, and worm your way inside ... And if, at the edge of the dark emptiness, you suddenly spied a convulsed hand or some grayish hair clinging to a bleached skull, you closed the lair and continued your explorations. Bad luck! Sometimes you penetrated into a kitchen or a bathroom, or the corner of a bedroom where the most extraordinary objects preserved a virginity appropriate to treasure troves. There might be a bag of potatoes, an umbrella, some books, a photograph album, a pretty fan decorated in faded watercolors (Charlotte and Werther...), a slightly crushed camera, repairable and salable, clothing holed by bits of metal but still usable ... Needless to say you had to watch out for the owners, real or pretend, the latter being the more vindictive; they materialized without warning, able to spot "their stuff" at twenty yards, they snatched the treasure, boxed your ears, and stormed off to complain to the parents or Herr Schiff! They were nicknamed the Winged Vampires. Fortunately, three-quarters of the Winged Vampires had disappeared. On the flank of Chimborazo a precisely printed sign proclaimed LOOTING IS PUNISHABLE BY DEATH, *Todestrafe*, but that applied chiefly to inferior races, the escaped Poles, Russians, and Serbs who were rumored to be living deep underground, well below the level of cellars and shelters, creeping forth at night under cover of the bombs to attack the SS and people in uniform and to steal marmalade. The twelve-year-old explorer felt rather proud to be braving the *Todestrafe*, DEATH PENALTY.

◼

If in truth a different world had ever existed, Brigitte would have retained a more convincing memory of it. Nonetheless, she did not doubt that the city had once been completely different, disoriented though she was by the changes being wrought by wave upon wave of destruction. Last week, the flat half-moon edifice of the chamber of commerce was still in its place, at the bottom of Grand Elector Plaza. The carcass of a bus sat rusting next to the kiosk that provided sweets, cigarettes, newspapers, and a washroom. The bronze Grand Elector lay on his back on the lawn, his comical paunch swelling upward; the female figure from the pedestal had also fallen over and was sleeping on her side with her eyes open; she was holding a laurel branch and the Grand Elector, a book; they lay back to back is if they were quarreling. The main shopping artery still paraded its wounded façades and signboards over its vanished businesses. After last night's hurricane, the artery was buried under a desert of scorched, blackened rubble, dusted with a powder as fine and light as mineral dew. The recumbent statues, the shell of the bus, the friendly news-and-chocolates building, the chamber of commerce itself were nowhere to be found: the whole square had slid sideways before being erased. Brigitte found herself wandering through an unfamiliar neighborhood where the downstairs of redbrick houses were still inhabited and some men in uniform were assembled in a conclave outside the door of a tavern, *Bierstube*. Someone shouted, "Hurry up there, Fraülein, the cleanup squad..." She nodded, yes, yes, and walked on. Soon she came to a mobile kitchen handing out soup to about a hundred people, several of whom were elegantly dressed. Humiliated at losing her way, Brigitte asked for directions. "Go right as far as Westphalia, then third left, that's Marie-Louise Strasse." But there was no left or right, no way of identifying Westphalia Strasse; *Volkssturm* roadblocks were inexplicably set up across steep dunes of rubble. A haze of gray smoke rose toward the noonday sun. Instinct led Brigitte back to her familiar territory.

So inexorably did the present annul the past, so simply, so mercilessly did this present perpetuate itself, that no room was left for the anticipation of any other future. The linear direction of time was scrambled, the calendar lost its meaning, the everyday milestones of existence were gradually effaced. Of the past Brigitte retained nothing but a handful of images, devoid of substance, as implausible and yet tenacious as those of recurring dreams. Reality commenced this side of a frontier defined by glowing summer evenings which weren't prewar, but already wartime, since He was dead. The sirens started howling after midnight...Brigitte got up without any fear. What was there to be afraid of, now that He had ceased to exist, He who may never have existed but in His letters and the wonderful slumber that came before reality? A spreading sound of hurried steps told of the tenants making for the shelters. "Order, order...!" The sirens stopped and an absolute hush fell, like the cradling of the world. Brigitte took the little suitcase containing His letters, underwear, and money, but instead of going downstairs she went up...Ascend, she thought; that's what you should do, poor souls, ascend toward the stars, (ascend toward Him); the neighbors she tried to tell this to pushed roughly past her muttering *Was? Was?* What? What? She climbed the ladder to the roof and went to lean her back against a chimney. All the constellations were glittering at once, even the faint Northern Crown was clearly visible, and surrounding them, beyond them, the deep pure blue of celestial space, grander still for containing secret constellations that could be discerned only by the most powerful telescopes...And the dark earth, blossoming all of a sudden into an immense flashing star emitting rays, spears, scimitars, and fans of light. The whiteness wove a tissue of radiance around the city, around the entire planet: the planet in her wedding dress. A bright cupola rose above Brigitte's rapt, thrown-back head. She wished for cricket song: the crickets sang. Trac-tac-tac, tractac-tac-tac, trrraac, their song grew louder, the crickets all died in a millionth of a second and a deafening buzz of elytrons blew the shredded sails of great maddened ships in every direction of the compass as they plied the rocking firmament. "Good God, great God, Lord God!" stammered Brigitte, alone at the apex of a city turned into a dark, petrified gulf (daughter of a social-democrat academic, she was not a believer, but since His death she thought she half believed, not in the *words* of the faith but in the inexpressible intuition the words tried vainly to express...). A white-hot symphony of steel struck up. A thousand motors droned in the cold incandescent furnace of the sky. Brigitte glimpsed dull fragments and even a metal fuselage briefly captured in the searchlights: the fragments and fuselage got away... No light, however murderous, is a prison! At the foot of the electric beams garishly colored firebirds soared and fell in triangles of night... The thunders crashed. Was there a beginning? Did they all crash together? Was it a single bouquet of lightning bolts multiplying through space? The black prostrate city did not cry out, despite the continuous shaking of the ground and the unendurable flashing of yellow-and-gold bursts over by the freight yards. The cathedral spire glittered darkly like a piercing scream. Geysers of green water spurted from the disemboweled river, Brigitte could see them clearly. "My God, if only the bridge... Oh, surely there is no more bridge, no quays, no river ...All the water sprites have faded into radiant death... Why weren't you one of them, Brigitte!" Now black waves arose. The lightning struck closer, but strangely in the opposite direction, with long, crackling reverberations, but nothing was visible, over there lay White Queen Park, populated by bronze antelopes and musicians' busts... From there, oppressive clouds of black yet sulfurous smoke twisted into the air, spreading as they rose. Brigitte breathed in warm air full of nauseous odors... The bouquets of this demented dawn broke apart, some falling to earth, crashing in dark fields. Holes appeared in the sky where the calm sand grains of constellations were insanely still. The Northern Crown was shining again. "Lord God, hear me! Let us all die, all of us, down to the last innocent babe in its loving mother's arms!" So Brigitte prayed, rigid yet calm, her eyes still dazzled by the inhuman revelry of glimmers and flashes, now convulsing spasmodically, now abating, on the verge of expiring, and bursting back to life like a firebox short of fuel... The thundering symphony stopped all at once. Stray searchlights swiped the air with wounded wings and flickered out. The darkness spread in stony waves over the gulf of the city, but clouds were crawling like wild beasts over the rail yards and the industrial district emitting dull roars and nauseating smells... Sirens proclaimed the all clear...

As Brigitte returned downstairs, she met Frau Hoffberger coming up—a courageous woman, widowed during the first war, who liked to talk. "So where on earth were you, Brigitte? I was horribly worried about you. But it wasn't too bad, was it? Did you hear our artillery! Herr Flatt, who was in the other war with my late husband, says we were attacked by a hundred planes, and they were all shot down or chased away, it's a marvelous victory and our city can be proud, Brigitte, what a headache I have, and Frau Sachs, she fainted away as soon as our big guns opened up! And she'd brought her poodle down with her, I do think pets should be absolutely forbidden in shelters, I mean, I know animals are also at risk and they're family for some people, but there's hygiene and morale to be considered... Oh well, it's all blown over, I don't mind telling you I'm relieved, they won't be back in a hurry after the hiding we gave them. You'll see tomorrow, I'm sure those firecrackers of theirs did far more harm than noise" (Frau Hoffberger meant this the other way around), "Herr Flatt says the Americans are the most incompetent flyers, they get a search beam in their eyes and down they go... Herr Jochsl didn't agree, he was so jumpy I had to tug him by the sleeve and tell him, discreetly, don't go on like that, Herr Jochsl, someone might turn you in, of course

I know what a patriot you are, but . . . He was teary eyed as a girl, and a veteran too! They say he's a Social Democrat! The electricity's out, by the way, but it's sure to be fixed tomorrow. Oh dear, how am I going to get through my day tomorrow, I've lost at least two hours' sleep . . ."

"Good night, Frau Hoffberger," said Brigitte. "Go right to bed."

In her own room, Brigitte ran her hands over her face several times, as though to remove an invisible veil and firm up her shaky features . . . The candle burned in the middle of its porcelain flower. How many flowers would be needed for this night's graves, how many flowers? One enormous flower of light and fire, and of calm, for the city, for us all, Lord! For the world! She opened the old iron-filigreed casket containing His letters, in chronological order and tied with a ribbon. Some of these missives, delivered by the military postal service, contained only expressions of love, but there were others—so overwhelming and she could hardly read them—which had arrived after the notice of His Death on the Field of Honor for Folk and Fatherland: there were also photostats of the official report and the divisional order of His citation, and a photo of His Iron Cross, all forwarded to the fiancée by the fiancé's parents.

Moments overlap, time is no longer continuous, but it was sometime later—which is to say, after the death notice but before the first heavy bombardment—that an olive-green private on furlough turned up, a shy, grim-looking young man who would only identify himself as Günther. He placed a parcel on the table and said, "Here are His letters. I have read them, at His request. The whole of Germany should read them. Good day, Fraülein." "But you can't just leave!" cried Brigitte despairingly. The crumpled forage cap came off again.

He had a receding hairline, pale sparse eyebrows, the face of a young athlete recovering from an illness. Overcoming his embarrassment he began, "Pardon me, Fraülein, I only . . ."

"You were his friend?"

"Yes."

"You know how it happened?"

"Yes."

"I want to know everything. I have the right to know everything."

Maybe he was measuring her strength, and the anxiety at the bottom of the little strength he saw. *Frauenkind*, a child-woman; there are also *Männerkinder*, child-men, you see them on the firing line, despite their fear, because combat and unknown horrors frighten them less than the idea of letting their weakness show; they make good soldiers and excellent corpses (but not very good wounded: they tend to weep and moan and their misery aggravates their pain . . .). Brigitte understood that he was going to hurt her, badly, unsparingly, out of a kind of pitiless kindness. She begged him: "Go on, tell me, I'm not afraid of anything . . ."

"He didn't suffer . . . He died at once. A dozen bullets, chest, belly . . . They were experienced marksmen, shooting at almost point-blank range . . ."

Chest, belly—carnal words, they lacked for Brigitte their full human density. "I'm glad," she said, "that his face was spared . . ." And she saw he was going to hurt her again, but what more could there be?

"On his face there was nothing but great astonishment."

Brigitte smiled, as though half released. The astonishment of ceasing to be, mystery and mystery's end, she too wanted that. Unintelligible words broke in on her. "What? What did you say? I didn't quite . . ."

"I said he was killed by our own men, he and the rest of his tank crew."

"Our own men? What men?"

"The others!" the soldier said with hatred. "The killers. Oh yes. They exist. Maybe they have to . . . That tank crew was noted for its bad attitude, do you understand? Well, I didn't understand, but I did afterward. They'd been sacrificed; they weren't supposed to come back. But they did come back, that sometimes happens. So an elite squad shot them down between the lines . . ."

These words burned slowly and unforgettably into Brigitte's mind. There was no astonishment.

"Fraülein, it's even happened to generals..." "Yes, yes, I understand, and I am very grateful you told me the truth...The truth..." Our own men, the others, the killers...

■

Time is in shreds and the soldier's letters were in shreds. Brigitte could reread only some torn fragments.

"...We were working back through villages burned out during the retreat. As though the land had been killed off. A few people were still living in cellars, they were afraid of us and kept their raped women hidden, but sometimes they'd come out and scrounge for food; and creatures who once were women were still offering themselves. S said we ought to put them out of their misery, but he threw them some bread...The bread fell into the mud, where they scrabbled for it. A desert is what we have made—that may not be the truth, but that's what I saw. M explained the strategy behind the retreat. He's the only one who thinks and speaks; he tells us that next we're going to beat America, now that the Führer's goals have been met in Russia...And how are we going to beat America, I ask? He's counting on secret weapons, scientific warfare. He talks about the stratosphere without knowing what it is—as though it were some sort of magical immensity set aside for the most devastating weapons. He's obstinate and brave, with an unformed intelligence inside a rather noble skull. No experience upsets him. The Führer knows what he's doing, and thus our defeats become transmuted into brilliant feints. M is aware of my 'doubts' and said to me: I hope you will be killed for the Fatherland because I respect you.

"...Once my tank ran over some living men. They were hiding under the snow, lying in wait for us perhaps, the machine swerved as it accelerated and they screamed like mice being crushed. Our treads were clogged with bleeding flesh and we left a red trail on the snow. I had to see it all, since I'm the observer. I've seen them finish off wounded men—our men—for lack of stretchers to take them away. The important thing was that they shouldn't be able to disclose anything about our units' movements. In any case, that's how M explained it, approving orders he deems harsh but wise. 'War,' he said, 'lifts man above himself.' 'Would you like such an end for yourself?' I asked. 'And why not,' he replied, 'better than falling into the hands of Jews and Jew lovers . . .' He means it too. I respect him; I think I hate him. I've seen prisoners lined up to be shot one by one by a *Feldwebel* because they wouldn't tell what they could not know about enemy plans. Some of them got down on their knees and talked, making things up. M said laughing: 'We'll liquidate these liars a little later . . .' He loves to remind us that the Russians never signed the Geneva convention regarding POWs, too bad for them. Then what about our prisoners? M has an answer for that too: I've no pity to waste on cowards, I have pity only for the unlucky ones, but they must face up to the law of nature: Vae victis! The powerful races will only triumph by accomplishing nature's law. His logic is seamless, like a paranoiac's.

". . . We directed a concentrated barrage on a small infantry tank whose motor had conked out forty yards away. It was a pitiful box of cardboard and steel with three men inside, one of them waving a dirty white rag. The sublieutenant was beside himself because we'd had a terrible attack of jitters as we were pulling back, one of those uncontrollable panics that comes over even the best soldiers now and then, like an electric shock to the nerves. G was yelling, 'Ha, so they surrender do they, the dirty dogs, the cowardly curs!' He wouldn't listen to me, he looked completely out of his mind; normally, he's a decent fellow, a flower gardener by trade. He ordered us to fire and we watched the tin can burn, the magazine blow up, I watched a blond twenty-year-old burning, half out of the turret. I told myself: Look at what you're doing, you must look without blinking, you're not allowed to close your eyes. I watched the flames leap to his blond hair, I watched his face twist like a paper mask tossed onto a bonfire. And I said to myself, When I've been killed, I want my pure Brigitte to meet this youth—because he will live again—and to love him for love of me...

"...I was thinking that there's no natural law for mankind, whose natural law is human law. The tiger and the termite obey their natures; we must be true to ours, which is divine, that is to say a thinking, merciful nature...

"...The bodies of hanged men were dangling from telegraph poles, there were more swinging from the porch of the church. There were too many, they no longer frightened anyone. Fear results from a surprise inflicted on the imagination. Once the surprise has worn off, a hanged man seems perfectly simple, getting hanged becomes quite natural, you realize it's only a few painful moments and that there are worse ways to die. We were talking about a rabbi. 'He was lucky to swing so soon,' says M, who is not personally cruel but accepts that others should be, so as to surmount their instinctive cowardice and face up to responsibility. The average man, in his view, has gone soft, domesticated by an ailing civilization, and will benefit from being trained to cruelty. (M does not consider himself an average man; he regards himself, so he told me, as a normal Aryan.) I questioned this, playfully, just to rile him a little—evoking the Aryans of India, who profess detachment from material things and nonviolence even toward animals. M broke out laughing: 'If that's what they teach you at the university, then the universities are overdue for disinfection, and the professors of Aryanism belong in Buchenwald, cleaning the latrines.' That was mostly to annoy me back, I think, for then he was patient, explaining how the decadence of the Aryan races, weakened by Semitic infiltration, was the root cause of all historical calamities. The Aryan renaissance began with the Party. The more I talk with him, the more I have the impression of a dialogue with a systematic psychopath, and yet I have a humiliating compulsion to converse with him. Of the dozen men who constitute my circle of hell, he's the only one who talks; I don't know whether he thinks or merely repeats a series of memorized formulas. I am obsessed by the awful possibility of our souls being imprinted with a whole system of notions designed to prevent us from becoming conscious, smothering thought beneath ersatz thought.

"... There were more children than adults, probably as a result of earlier waves of deportation. The little girls were carrying their dolls, pitiful dolls. In the pathos of their silence and the pathos of their wailing lamentation these Jews exhibited two contradictory characteristics. I remained very calm, I wanted only to understand the victims. To understand means to identify. To understand rather than surrender to suffering, which amounts to no more than a carnal, emotional communion. I sought a communion of the spirit. At first, the silence seemed to me to be nobler than the wailing. Women tearing at their hair, old men chanting their prayers and pulling their white beards... I observed that the blows of rifle butts did not interrupt the rhythm of their lamentation. I understood that this was the rhythm of a lamentation echoing down through the centuries; that it is a community's song of consent. I saw myself: a calm, rigid onlooker, like a disciplined lunatic. They were being herded into the boxcars. M assures me they will be destroyed in the most painless way possible, with cyanide gas, and recalls the Gospel's injunction to separate the wheat from the chaff. Then he moves on to eugenics and human selection, look how stunted, sniveling, anemic, and infirm they are, how weepy the old men, how ugly the women! At this point F and W broke in, talking about the beautiful girls in Serbia and Holland... I'll never forget the asphyxiated howls that came from inside the boxcars... The troops were in a good mood because a ration of brandy had been distributed. Many men felt that it was necessary to evacuate the populations of these little towns to make room for the folks from our bombed-out cities.

"... Brigitte, I only have tonight to write you the truth of my soul. I know I am hurting you, but I have no one else in the world with whom to share the bitterness of a cup I must drink to the dregs. And since you are my wife in spirit, you must find the courage to drink this cup with me, even if your reason is shaken, as mine often is. The single absolute duty of those alive today is to drain the bitter cup to the last drop, overcoming our shaking limbs and minds, perhaps in order to be able to say afterward: Everything is accomplished. Here I am.

"...I can't tell you all of it, it's impossible to tell it all, even more to see it all and to understand it all. We are moving through the banality of chaos and I can only recall minor, episodic things, poor simple things that sometimes enlighten me. I am a man without grandeur, a humble man unable to take in big events... But don't doubt me, Brigitte, I am a very good soldier who fulfills his duty at every moment, conscientiously, as if I had no conscience. They're going to put me up for another decoration, which would mean a few days' special leave to see you, and then they'll make me a noncommissioned officer. I'm not especially eager, having no wish for personal responsibility, but do I have the right to abandon it to others? If I'm chosen, I will obey. My body and my will obey, my spirit remains free and refuses. What more can I do? If it weren't for you, I would consent to be shot. Through you, I perceive a living world for whose sake the survivors must live. They alone will know, will reflect unceasingly upon what must never happen again, upon that which must be excised from mankind. I live in remorse and apprehension because I dread betraying our people's cause in my thoughts, but I also fear to betray the universal principle of which our people is just one moment, one face. Maybe that's the truly unpardonable war: between a people and its universal homeland...

"...Was it necessary to unleash hell on earth, did we have to do what we are doing? I have no right to stand apart from anyone, not from the Jews and not from M, who desires the death of the Jews; I've no right to consider myself superior to anyone. The only thing I'm certain of is that this crime is the crime of all men. We were the victims of tremendous historical injustices, but every country can say the same, and we've inflicted injustices on others —it goes around and around. Were we really so stifled by the Treaty of Versailles? I don't know anymore. I do know that the world is far more stifled today, and we're the ones who beckoned to the avalanches and told them: Fall! If the unparalleled energy we devoted in central Europe to a reenactment of the conquests of Sargon and Ramses had been used to build a new, just, dignified nation at the service of the Universal, what an ideal victory we should have won! All the wrongs would be put to rights on a higher plane than that of borders, and what border would not dissolve before the mere presence of a superior humanity?

"... Now the whole world is against us and we are alone. I wonder whether the Seer, in whom so many of the disheartened believed so as to escape from their small despairs, may not be mad. However many gallons of blood we shed, our own or that of others—for human blood is a single substance—we'll never reach New York, or Tobolsk, or San Francisco, or Baghdad, and that being so we will never gain victory, or peace, or pride (for those who feel compensated by pride), or forgiveness. Our pitiable armies are on the run, our pitiable dead remain as sole occupiers of the conquered lands, sole fraternizers with the dead of other peoples. The Seer should have foreseen it, the Seer was blind! The murder and destruction we have dealt out are turning around to devour us. We should never have followed the Seer! We should have kept our reason, but had we any other choice? I could have let myself be sent to Dachau—I thought about it. Can I be more useful there? I asked myself. Now I see that I might have been more upright, more faithful there. But how could I have known then what I know now? There are plenty of sleepwalkers in our ranks, but almost all of them are beginning to feel, deep down in their hearts, however confusedly, something of what I write here. We are prisoners, all of us. We condemn ourselves...

"... The death of another man is my own death. A man who kills may not know it, but in reality he is killing himself. The frenzy of certain warriors—even more that of the exterminators, whose baseness places them a thousand million leagues below the warriors—is a suicidal frenzy...

"... But is it still permissible to believe in mankind? If our side alone were to blame, it would fill me with relief, it would help me to regain my trust. But I've seen too much to believe that... Is it all the fault of the system? Systems are such heavy chains that they exonerate the infinitesimal individual, the thinking reed, the trampled reed. What would Pascal or Spinoza have done in Dachau? Or at the front, under a helmet? The reed stops thinking, becomes malleable matter, identifies with its chains. The system is the work of men, after all, men who are made by it as much as they were makers of it. And not all of them are deranged, clearly; most aspire simply to live off it in peace, killing with the calculated, businesslike temperance of their mentors. I am wrestling with these problems, but, *I am and I do not consent*! Since I said these salutary words to myself, weak as I am, groping in darkness, I felt I was at the dawn of deliverance. And you'll know that if I fall, the end will have been the lighter for it. Proof exists that a man need not necessarily consent to what he does. Obey and disobey. Submit to earthly solidarity—or to the crushing weight of the chain—while salvaging something more essential. If I woke up the men who are lying asleep around me in this derelict schoolroom and asked each one (even the incredibly brutal elite soldiers, prey to regressive neuroses): What do you wish for the most? they would all answer: The end! Some would unconsciously be including their own end in that of the nightmare. Of course, one out of three would turn me in, and I'd be shot before the day was out. A curse on the blind Seer, a curse on ourselves!

"... We have been defeated. Even the fanatics can't help but see it. Someone was saying that we should hold up to the whole world our refusal to capitulate by committing mass suicide. I managed not to ask the question that was on the tip of my tongue: Have the whole people commit suicide? The Race? (For that matter, didn't we begin the suicide? Not only ours, but Europe's?) A single word can become deadly dangerous. I've learned of a secret order for the immediate execution of suspects. Too little, too late, according to M. He feels that the elimination of two million Germans during the early days of the regime would have made the regime more exemplary, more homogeneous, and might even have avoided a war by scaring the daylights out of international Jewry ...I pointed out that a lot more than two million Germans have died as it is. He was so caught up by his reasoning that he stared at me pensively through those stony blue eyes without losing his temper. He then produced a theory—I believe that disaster stimulates his brain. The trick, he said, would be to select death itself, a selection that would be the apotheosis of eugenics...

"...Brigitte, my pure Brigitte, you must prepare your heart for a new love, since life must be continued and it seems that I, like so many others, am destined to fail in that duty. See how guilty we are, how we have failed to honor a supreme commandment, a rule so exalted that it defies formulation. My premonition is that I shall not return. I read the truth of my fate a long time ago, as one reads an equation, advancing toward the Russian flamethrowers through a wood full of frantic animals. All of us in the condemned armies are men who will never recover anything, never resume what was once dear to us. Prepare yourself, I am ready. Be calm, be strong, and forgive me. By forgiving me, you will be forgiving millions of others...Our people will survive like a desperately wounded man, maimed in his very soul; but we will not find forgiveness, since we have lost and history forgives only the strong. We, the dead and the survivors, will be the unforgiven people, we who revealed in their blackest depths the frailty and blindness of human energy. I envision this future without bitterness, because only then, having touched the bottom of the abyss, shall we be able to rise again toward an integral consciousness, in a century...And if that day should ever come to pass, blessed be defeat!"

The handwriting was regular, rank upon rank of firm, slanting downstrokes. Brigitte knew that to understand, she had to penetrate beyond the words. This time, with the light of the great white fires in the sky still glowing inside her, she thought, dry-eyed, that she had truly understood. She decided to forget His name. "The soul of the millions was in him and he was nothing but that soul. All the names are his, and almost all the faces..."

She burned his photographs. She wept at burning them, repeating his name all the while. Abruptly her eyes dried and her wish was granted: she no longer knew the name.

"Brigitte, are you crying?" inquired Frau Hoffberger through the door.

Brigitte opened the door, laughing and disheveled.

"Not at all, just look at me!"

"Here's some herb tea, my girl, it'll do you good."

Brigitte accepted the tepid infusion, yellow as urine, maybe poisoned, who could tell? Frau Hoffberger is a kind soul, but does she know her own poisons? The hands of kindness are steeped in poison. She opened the window and flung the tisane into the poisonous smoke of the night. Then she returned the cup to her neighbor: "Thank you so much, you are kind...Have you had some yourself?" "Yes, I drink one every night before bed..." Brigitte's pupils dilated with a strange suspicion. "Is there something wrong, my dear?" "No, nothing, sleep well..."

Arms folded behind her head, Brigitte lay peacefully waiting for the sun to come up, though now and then a tremor went through her body and she let it, for it was the trembling of the universe.

■

Next morning, the street looked the same as always. This encouraged a feeling of immutable normality, despite the rumors. People said that fifteen thousand had perished in the industrial suburbs, which were now cordoned off by the police. So much heat had swept the city in wave upon wave that the air remained acrid. Under the low clouds fires were struggling upward, spawning clouds of their own from rising black columns...The bishop toured the periphery of destruction, places that had emerged relatively unscathed but where many people had gone insane. Herr Blasch, the Party's right-hand man, performed a solemn walkabout through the streets under his control (nothing had happened there). He was wearing a combat uniform, an Iron Cross, several other important insignia, a silver swastika, a thick brown leather belt, a peaked cap as tall as a general's, and a skull badge... Stiff necked, all black and silver, vigilant yet benevolent, conversing with women, inquiring after the children's health as he walked by, finding plausible explanations for everything. The underground factories, he could report, had escaped destruction thanks to the foresight of our strategic engineers... Other damage was more apparent than real, forty killer bombers had been shot down, the enemy airmen would be court-martialed—but the verdict was in no doubt—for having violated every law of warfare... Herr Blasch added that this was nothing—less than nothing I assure you— compared to the punishment London had been taking for weeks, London where our automatic rockets, our Secret Weapon of Vengeance Number One, were razing entire neighborhoods so thoroughly that any rescue or clearance efforts were a waste of time ... Oh yes, it was raining over London all right, raining meteors night and day, and volcanoes were spouting, eruption upon eruption! And this was only a modest beginning: the second and third Secret Weapons were lined up ready to obliterate whole chunks of England, the soil would be laid waste for years, not a blade of grass would grow back. "Then they will surrender. The Führer knows what he's doing. They played right into his hands when he let them disembark in France, you wait and see. Let cowards and cretins doubt him, they'll pay the price!" Herr Blasch's jet-and-silver uniform was cut from the cloth of confidence itself. The population received an extra ration of foodstuffs that made an excellent impression in the districts which had been spared.

That night, that morning of the time of origins, marked for Brigitte the border between reality and a peaceful, now unimaginable world, which may never have been real at all.

■

There were daylight raids, nighttime raids, twilight raids, dawn raids, and errors in the warning system, which announced a bombing raid when it had already begun and sounded the all clear as it was starting over again...The city was simultaneously subsisting and disappearing, yet its new, protean physiognomy imposed itself so perfectly that the old was obliterated forever: the cruel curves of twisted rafters appeared more natural than a stupefying, pristine mailbox that had been left untouched by the arcane physics of two deflagrations canceling each other out over precisely that spot. Had the city's inhabitants possessed the leisure or the inclination to found a philosophy, it would have been a philosophy of the End of the World and personal survival (albeit painful and provisional)—survival barely explicable without evoking the activity of completely irrational good genies or the instinct of self-preservation combined with luck, as well as black markets, esoteric frauds, providential larcenies, influential patrons, the connivance of all and sundry, and a handful of good-luck charms. Each explosion was like a throw of the dice, and people grew accustomed to winning, since the losers never got a chance to voice their disappointment. Everybody clung to their precious little suitcase containing their last riches and dressed as smartly as possible, as though every day were Sunday, to avoid—by having their prettiest dress or best topcoat on them all the time—being robbed during a panic; as a result, there was a certain air of elegance and good taste on the breadline and some of the men even still looked dapper. Everyone had survived several times over by now, and they were all beginning to believe (or ended up believing) in their lucky star, though this did not cure them of worrying. Two voices dueled deep inside, one said: You will die without knowing how, killed like all the rest who hoped against hope as you are doing; the other: You will live, since you are yourself, the living person par excellence—if not, why are you still here, condemned to life? Such people exist, after all, men, women, and children condemned to life, before whom the speeding bullet fractionally alters course, and the pestilent miasmas of stricken cities recede...

Professor Schiff was developing a theory around this topic, based on the great fourteenth-century epidemics of the Black

Death, during a period when neither hygiene nor antiseptics existed. The plague came to Altstadt and carried off two-thirds of the population; modern knowledge would lead us to expect all of the population to have succumbed, for the known natural causes are all working in that direction with the inflexibility of a celestial clockworks. But Bishop Othon had known better, as it turned out: the scourge was turned away by prayers and penance, and the final third of the population was saved. This carpet bombing, however meticulously planned by the most expert—to do them justice—high commands, could scarcely be more effective than a medieval plague! Here the good professor's interlocutor demurred, in view of the mathematical perfection of modern inventions... We'll soon see! Some attacks were rather entertaining, like the plucky little airplane that would zoom in one morning, drop a few bombs, incendiaries it was thought, and hightail it away with a distant mosquito whine... Pierced by sky and breeze, the wonderfully tenacious spire of the cathedral ascended into the blue, much more sharply visible than it was a moment ago, for the last of the historic old quarter had just crumbled around its feet, raising billows of dust that had quickly blown away. If one ventured closer, pink tongues of flame could be seen to palpitate under a low, stagnant lid of grayish smoke. Nothing else had changed.

Brigitte's roost defied every calamity. Now that the hurricanes of war had blurred the calendar, jammed the sclerotic clockworks of the administration, and filled the world with horribly banal horrors, Frau Hoffberger had left. All that remained of the building where that lady had occupied a third-floor apartment overlooking the street was a rack of window frames standing about fifteen yards high at the corner, between two eerily empty spaces, one of which contained an unexploded bomb. *ACHTUNG!* CAUTION! Curious passersby, sidling up gingerly to inspect the tip of a green fin, took this opportunity to launch into a rant against the Security Service—too busy with its special rations of Spam to bother about a bomb stuck between the school and the single local water pump, and in the middle of a hundred middle-class dwellings! Brigitte was living in a nearby building, which, though badly damaged, was listed as forty-seven percent habitable. Why not forty-six or forty-eight percent?—No one would ever know. The upper stories swayed gently at the slightest impact to the ground, whether at night from a convoy rumbling past or by day from a collapsing wall (walls, peculiarly enough, only fell during the day, usually under the caress of the sun's warmth). The way to Brigitte's second-story room was via a ladder, for the stairwell had been gutted by fire and any remaining planks had gone to feed the neighbors' hearths. "The enchanted roost of the fairy," as Franz Minus-Two referred to it with a snicker. "Why are you making fun of me?" asked Brigitte, startled. "But I swear to God, you are a fairy, Fraülein, and your roost is enchanted or it would have vanished long ago, and you with it ... But maybe fairies are immortal?" This was his way of joking by acting the delicate suitor. Brigitte's face fell. Immortal? Me? What a frightful curse! Mortal, mortal, I'll prove it. Die? She was as scared of immortality as she was of death, except that her fear of death was nothing but a small fear of the flesh mingled with a great longing, whereas the other fear was becoming a vague, insurmountable dread. "Why must you always say such mean things to me, Franz?" He was genuinely stung.

"Mean things? Me?"

"Oh, you don't understand. Such a lovely morning, and you've spoiled it for me. I'm going out, I have to get my food card stamped."

A bony young girl strode up to them. Braids coiled over ears, short rubber boots, satchel on hip, armband—she must have been fifteen or sixteen, and she surveyed Minus-Two with equal measures of respect and pitying condescension. A hero; a sad reject of a man whom no one could love, unable to fertilize a woman for the virile perpetuation of the Race. On second thought ... The tall young girl's pale, sharp face grew pink. She said, "*Heil* Hitler! Civil Defense Evacuation and Reinscription Control and Verification Service for the ... " (et cetera).

Minus-Two answered jovially, "*Heil Heil!* Bugles and kettle-drums! Glory!"

"Checking the papers of all non-evacuees by reason of special dispensation or overriding circumstances to be specified..."

Her pencil between her teeth, she consulted a typed list of names. To Brigitte, "Your name, Comrade of the People?"

"Brigitte."

That was the only name Brigitte could remember, unique, inseparable from herself, like a tiny blue candle burning in the depths of a vast darkness. Franz filled in discreetly. "Very well," said the girl. "Fraülein, you missed the third evacuation column, illness or reason unknown. You've failed to report to the Recovered Auxiliaries Workshop... You're not in order."

Minus-Two rounded on her. "What! Young Comrade of the People! I think I know rather better than you do who's in order and who isn't around here. Talking about the third evacuation column, what about Counterorder Number Two Amended? As for your precious workshop for the ugly, the maimed, the skewed, and the screwed, that went up in smoke, like the boxes of matches we so lack these days. And the directress took off, or didn't you know? Brush up on the facts before throwing your rules and regulations around... Mistress Fairy here is a registered C-category exemption on grounds of nervous illness, curable, with care and respect. Brigitte, show her your papers. And you, adorable zealot, make a note of it. There's no mistake. D'you realize who's talking to you? Iron Cross, three citations, seriously wounded, that's who. I'll answer for everything."

To himself, he added, gaily, "Because I don't answer for anything, you skinny little goose on stilts! I'd like to know who does answer for something anymore! One less limb and I'd have been given a merciful injection and right now I'd be rotting underground, or a pinch of ashes in a one-mark urn, and even then those goddamn idiots would put the wrong name on the urn, and I wouldn't be able to give a damn..."

"Very well," said the teenager, somewhat worried to see that the hero displayed no Party insignia, "I have confidence in you. Your papers, Herr Noncommissioned Officer?"

And splendid papers they were too, covered with emblems, seals, stamps, and signatures...Up to date. Civil Defense Volunteer, specially enrolled by virtue of paragraph G of ordinance number..."Not that one," said Minus-Two carelessly. "Secret."

The girl shifted into conspiratorial mode. Her eyes, amusingly blue, seemed to glow red. Franz felt like asking her whether she still liked to play with dolls, or if she already knew how to make love. With a jerk of the chin she indicated a building some distance away, hollowed out but with one gable still standing. "It seems there's a nest of dangerous elements in there, enemies of the people perhaps. Have you noticed anything, Herr Noncommissioned Officer?" "Dangerous as a litter of white rabbits. I know this neighborhood." In the most depopulated section, to the west, gangs of outlaws crept out after dark from beneath the earth and its tombs...The quieter stretches of every night were interrupted by bursts of gunfire and brief, inconsequential explosions. The special security forces combed through the ruins neighborhood by neighborhood, shooting Russian, Polish, Mongolian, or Yugoslav refugees on the spot, along with army deserters and unidentified strangers who might be enemy parachutists...Other fugitives, not so easily disposed of—Frenchmen, Dutchmen, Czechs—were marched away under heavy escort, probably to be shot the next day. Minus-Two reflected on this. "All the same, don't go there, Comrade of the People. Or I'd better go with you."

"Oh, I've no intention. The Special Troops had planned to raid it tonight, but they won't get to it till tomorrow, there's so much to be done around the cathedral!"

"I can imagine," said Minus-Two, and he contemplated the low cloud, darker now, that crawled under the flayed spire.

There was lots of horizon. The city was full of horizons.

■

Brigitte stood engrossed in the play of light and shade. The city was dappled with it, as though covered by a fantastic lacy veil. Sunbeams shining through rows of high windows projected a brilliant checkerboard on the white dust of streets and cleared rubble. The shredded, gaping masonry threw down the queerest shadows whose contours spoke of mythic monsters, Eastern temples, works of art no artist could ever imagine, born of the amorous fray between a tangle of bared rafters and the sun. Schoolboys and People's Defense teams were working to reinstall the telephone lines and other cables lying on the ground, sometimes marked with warnings: *ACHTUNG!* HAZARD. LETHAL DANGER. They've got to be kidding, just another little lethal danger! Day after day these diligent spiders rewove the torn web, and now they were mounting a loudspeaker against what was left of the beer hall ... Soon the news will be broadcast, sibylline communiqués on lost battles in the east, the west, the south, and every other point of the compass, reports on the destruction of London which weren't of much comfort (and "How are we going to pay for that?"), along with marches and fanfares (apparently good for morale) and occasional snippets of grand opera: *The Twilight of the Gods* ...

Brigitte climbed the ladder to her roost and spread out some gritty bread, a sausage, a dollop of sweet fruit paste, and some wrinkled prunes on the white tabletop. A childish order reigned over this room, hanging over several voids: she was fond of it. The fancy stores downstairs had been burned out; then the side walls, brought slithering down by furious thunderbolts, had blocked up the shop spaces, warping the parquet here above and spearing it through the middle with the end of a beam. There were corpses in the last stages of decomposition in the cellars giving off, through the cracks in the floor, sudden whiffs of sickly, fetid odor, more marshy than human, but corpses are everywhere, and there's so little difference between them and us! They don't bother anybody anymore, no longer provoke embarrassing pity, they are there, we are here, we're all together, the least we can do is try to feel homey at home, or no more uncomfortable than we have to be. The stench didn't linger in Brigitte's room because the cracks in the walls allowed for good ventilation and insured a permanent connection with the great outdoors, the rain, the wind, as if under a golden tent in the middle of a verdant meadow. The daffodil-yellow muslin curtains at the window framed a picturesque field of rubble in shades of rose, white, and black. The next-door house, painted pink, had crumbled into the little garden, the flames had smudged the broken walls with charcoal and half consumed a young oak tree, whose other half was turning green; a square of wallpaper still cheered the eye, turquoise sprigged with gladioli. "My garden the air," thought Brigitte... Her possessions included a sturdy virginal bedstead, a round iron table scavenged from the garden, and a little rusty mirror, strangely cracked in a way that unsettled her. In it she looked quite unlike herself. Can this be me, this girl with a livid, greenish complexion, lips swollen with dark blood, cavernous cheeks, bulging eyes too deeply ensconced in their dark-shadowed sockets, dilated pupils half open onto the night within? The planes of this face had slipped out of line, the smile itself was crooked, the left side remaining stern as the right softened. Only the hair, in tight tresses rolled into a low bun on the nape, seemed not to have changed or been betrayed... "Lying mirror, shame on you!" It had been a present, hadn't it, but from whom? Given when? Brigitte's forehead crinkled in a helpless effort to remember. She saw herself fleeing through a tempest of ashes with the mirror under her arm, afraid of tripping, it would break if she fell. There was only one thought in her head: save it. Now what should she do with it, break it? You don't break a mirror. There were women in the market square who'd gladly pay for it. It was worth, said Franz, "at least four slices of pressed horse, dog, rat, or other novelty meats..." Should she perhaps give the lying thing away? That would be wrong. "Some night I'll have to bury it," she decided, "deep enough so that neither the children nor the cleanup squad can uncover it." Suddenly the mirror brightened, Brigitte recognized herself and pealed with laughter, unreasonable joy bubbling from her heart into her throat, what in heaven's name came over me? Laughing to herself, she searched through the drawer for her embroidered blouse, hummed a tune as she made herself up with lipstick and powder; some artistes put golden glitter on their eyelids, now that would look lovely on you, Brigitte... She ate quickly, holding an intimate, sparkling conversation with herself throughout the meal. Then she sat straight-backed upon the bed, her face upturned, her eyes half shut, picturing the notes of a score, while her lively hands played a keyboard of air and the charm of a Mozart concerto vibrated softly through her, bathed in silence; the strains of music drowning the thunders reverberating throughout the world. Brigitte's eyes opened again, her hands sank to rest on her knees, her shoulders drooped forward as though with lassitude. A stealthy tremor was starting up at the base of her being, like the buzzing of malevolent insects in the gloom, like the approach of a solitary bomber in the sky. It was only the approach of the nameless terror, senseless, bottomless, lightless, lifeless and deathless, unspeakable, unendurable, ungraspable, imponderable; a wave rising from the very depths of darkness... Brigitte was tearing something to pieces, trying to rip the smallest shreds between sore fingers until her nails were tearing at one another. What more to destroy, how to sleep, where to disappear? She began reeling about the narrow room in short, crazed lunges.

Night fell. There was a tap at the door.

"Who is it?"

The terror was ebbing away. A man's voice said, "It's me... Günther."

Brigitte opened the door. The penumbras of inside and out coalesced over a helmeted figure erect on the ladder, tall and braced, yet seeming to sway.

"Oh, so it's you," she said without surprise. "At last."

A flurry of gunshots rang out and died into the unknown. A screech, nipped off like that of a slaughtered animal, fell into the emptiness.

"Who are you? What do you want?" she said in a sharp voice.

Was he real, did he have eyes under that helmet? With a careful forefinger, she touched his chest. She thought she discerned a reflection in the shape of a skull.

"Ah, it is you..." she said dreamily. "I've been waiting so long. Come in."

He stepped up and over, lifted by the emptiness beyond; lithe, solid, remote.

"Is there no light in here, Fraülein?"

"Light? You know very well there's no more light. No sun, no electricity." (She giggled.) "You mean the candle?"

And by the light of the candle, she recognized him: a tank corpsman, sunburned, with a scar across his jaw and unruly, fire-flecked hair. He was holding his helmet between large coppery hands.

"I'm the one who brought you the letters from..."

"What letters? There's no one to write to me anymore."

He repeated uneasily, "Well, I...it was me."

"Of course it was. I was waiting for you. Sit down."

The only place to sit was this schoolgirl bed. He hesitated.

"You are Fraülein Brigitte W——?"

"Leave me alone. I don't know. I'm Brigitte."

He nodded slowly. Strident whistles slashed the darkness around them.

"I was his friend," he said in a muffled voice. "He was my only friend."

"Who was?"

He showed a flash of strong teeth. His breath felt good.

"I beg your pardon. I'll go. Please excuse me for..."

"Don't be silly," said Brigitte, and gripped his arm. "Stay. I was waiting. I haven't changed. I've been so frightened, if only you knew...Sit down, I say. Are you hungry?"

Bed and floor sagged under the visitor's weight. Brigitte, thin, her blouse splashed with embroidered flowers like flowers of blood, smiled at him serenely. "Listen to me, Fraülein. I was his friend. I came back to this city, from the eastern front to the western front . . . if fronts still exist . . . I looked for you. The house has gone, but they directed me here . . ."

"It's all gone," Brigitte said. "And no wonder. Do I exist? Do you?"

He hung his head.

"I didn't know where to go . . . Our company disbanded. The barracks burned down. Did you know they're fighting very close to here? The city's about to fall . . ."

"Fall where?"

Those peculiar queries—"Do I exist? Do you?"—had broken slowly through the man's fatigue and he registered them. He peered around the room in desperation. There was no safety in here. Outside were the patrols, bent on making examples of all and sundry. What good are examples? It's total madness. They're all stark staring mad at the rear. I must get out. Spend the night in a hole somewhere. Tomorrow will be worse than yesterday. The death throes. All our tanks wiped out. "Please try to understand, Brigitte. I have to leave. Goodbye."

His hand was on the doorknob when a small noise grated the silence. The sound a famished rat would make, gnawing rabidly on a bone. He turned. Brigitte's teeth were chattering. She was shaking from head to foot. "Don't leave me again, I've waited so long. I always knew that you existed. I know your letters by heart. I'm scared." He pulled her toward him. A heavy arm cradled Brigitte's shoulders, warm breath enfolded her. "Shush, it's all right. Nothing to be afraid of . . . We've no more to fear." Ecstatically she repeated, "No more to fear . . ." The noise of a rat in a tomb stopped. "You're warming me," Brigitte murmured, "down to my soul. It's my soul that was shivering . . ." She quieted, with both hands laid against the man's chest and her cheek pressed against her hands. Like a fluid, fear seeped from her into him. Günther gazed without blinking at the tremulous flame of the candle. Such a tiny fire! Was it really fire at all? Real fire is what erupts from the ravaged earth in black, blinding spouts. It vaporizes the men, the trees, it reduces the machine to a mass of twisted metal...

(It happened like this: the torpedo made a noise like a hurricane—earsplitting—the men threw themselves flat on the ground; a fat beetle was zigzagging down the road, its back striped green and gray...The torpedo must have blown up within a few yards of the car; by the time the men ran through a hot, buffeting windstorm, puffs of steam were gathering above the chassis of the overturned machine...Not a trace left of windows or tires or the three officers they had just encountered. It was such a puzzle that a squad was detailed to sift through the ground, pounded into chalky dust...Death disappeared: no more danse macabre! The crater was a great oval wound gouged into the field, and no living thing subsisted in this earth cleansed by fire; not a worm, not a root, not a blade of grass...Günther tried to remember the general's face: a tight-ass engineer in a high collar, insignia, splendid kepi...The troops feared him, for he was a stickler in hopeless situations. His gloveless hand was like a hook: the inexorable claw of a ghoul dragging whole regiments to counterattack in retreat, and on down to the underworld of butchered armies and peoples... The general's remains would be sorely missed by the disciplined multitudes in limbo...Günther did not think all of this, but he relived it in the stillness of the moment. "There are no warriors anymore: only poor bastards facing exploding volcanoes. The cosmos has gone berserk...THIS CAN NEVER STOP...")

Strange to have a silent young woman against one's chest as if asleep. And this carcass of a city, barer even than Warsaw, laid out dead in the first warmth of spring! He, Günther, was alive, living under the cold light of a huge, dark, sulfurous star: the sun of destruction.

"Talk to me," whispered Brigitte cajolingly. "You're alive."

"Apparently," he snickered to himself. Wasn't the calm night going to explode? If it didn't explode, it wouldn't make sense.

"You're real. You're not a hallucination, are you? Sometimes I thought I was going mad."

He answered, lying eagerly, "No, I'm not a hallucination," because not one of those seconds was really real to him. What double of himself was speaking?

"Brigitte. I feel great tenderness for you."

"I know. Tell me again."

He could not say the words again. He could not make a move or the spell would be broken. Indestructible, this immobility, more joyful perhaps than fearful. But NOTHING IS INDESTRUCTIBLE, EVERYTHING WILL BE DESTROYED. Günther asked, "Do you feel better now?"

"I feel fine."

He was thinking: I'm nearly as disoriented as this young woman, me, the strong, rational one. Strong, what a laughable idea. You wish you were made of bronze, cast by Krupp! You end up foolishly believing that you are, in spite of your melting innards and your foggy brain...

"Brigitte, you ought to rest."

"I'm yours, don't you see, why do you talk to me like a stranger?"

The young woman's fragility eventually communicated to him an animal thirst with which he was all too familiar. All soldiers know it. Slacking off or overworked, their sole virtues are those of beasts. Where was it? A shapely pair of female legs, frozen in an upside-down dance step, tipped with high-heeled patent pumps, poking out from beneath a fall of rocks; they were only just beginning to turn blue. The gang made dirty jokes. It occurred to me that this would make a good photograph to hang beside the one of the carbonized head, still imperiously erect, that I saw on a burned-out turret. The diptych could be called *A Match Made in Heaven.* He felt hot, thirsty, he wanted the woman, he wanted sleep more than anything. I really should kill you, out of kindness. The only forgivable murder, and the hardest to commit. Brigitte, do you know that the odious time of rape has arrived? All rutting armies fall upon all women cornered in vacated cities, roofless barns, woods sheared by fire. The peasant women of Poland,

Russia, or Serbia know it, they run from the armed man, but only a little way; then they stop, turned in on themselves, with watchful, frightened eyes, and quickly lift the skirts under which they keep only their bodies; they glance about for the couch of dead leaves, grass, straw, stones, any good place to get it over with quickly, to pay for their lives. They know all about the bloodthirsty brutes who strangle or eviscerate you afterward—the young women talk about it when they sit up late, after reading love letters from the front to each other; they also know that the stranglers and slashers are a minority, whereas plenty of soldiers reward you with a cigarette, a piece of chocolate, a tin of Spam, a few small coins, a stolen trinket if you're lucky. Most don't give a woman anything, but sneer contemptuously when they're through, or cringe in sudden, stupid shame. And it may be that some of those who kill do it to kill the shame. Do you suppose, poor mad Brigitte, that I'm any different from the others? Elementarily, we're all the same. And you're like every other female caught up in the banality of destruction. And the victors who will be storming in next week, if not before, they're the same. They will shove your legs open and fall roughly on top of you. A resurgence of our primate ancestors. Wouldn't I truly be doing better if I put my hands around your neck and squeezed a little, a little harder, like this? Next I could kill myself, and you would have delivered me . . . Not that way, the world will deal with me, I want to see it through, the strong one. Usually, you don't see anything or know anything or feel anything . . . Enough.

Brigitte said, "It feels so good, your hands on my throat . . . Hold tighter."

The man's grip slackened. The only thing in the world I care for now is sleep, a deep sleep in warm grass under a white apple tree. Postcard poetry. What am I doing? What if she's sick, as if it mattered? She's insane. Shock, schizophrenia? Whole continents have gone insane, civilization is a form of schizophrenia. The sky will blow up and there'll be nothing left of us, or of this absurd room at the top of a ladder surrounded by the corpses of houses, or of this candle watching over our corpses. The female saints were like you, Brigitte, and they martyred those saints, such was the imperial law of the times. Latin civilization. Cicero. I've got to make my brain shut up. We'll be happy like animals in a hole, ten minutes before they're smoked out or crushed to death...War is an incredible carnage of innocent creatures...Blessed are the simple-minded, for they shall inherit the kingdom of heaven... Goddammit! How to make my brain shut up? We are still alive, tomorrow it'll all be over. Nothing will be over...

"I'm thirsty, Brigitte."

"There's some disinfected water."

She poured cloudy liquid into a monogrammed glass. "Are those your initials?" "Yes," she said, though they were N's intertwined below a crown ... From force of habit, he placed his loaded pistol and his dagger within instant, instinctive reach of his hand, and adjusted the elastic bandage around the scar on his left calf. His underwear was dirty and he removed it all, happy to go naked to bed, something he had not done for weeks. A man is freer in the nude, he enjoys the relief of disarming himself. To take off a filthy uniform is to strip oneself of power and obedience, to cease being a dangerous quasi-robot harassed by fears and cunning, the petty fear of hassles and the overwhelming fear of... Distractedly, he watched Brigitte put on a silky white nightgown. The cool touch of the silk exhilarated him more than that of the long, feeble body, fevered and yet cold, that sought refuge against his. The flesh was pitiful, the silk, luxurious. Rats began or resumed their noisy business beneath the floorboards. Millions of rats proliferate among these ruins. Their kind will outlive ours. Günther, on his back, let Brigitte snuggle up with her head on his shoulder. She had put on perfume...The silk, the skin, the verbena tea, the rats, the pungency of the snuffed candle, the glint of night through the crack in the wall that ran up to a triangular hole beneath the ceiling...He wanted to desire this woman but he felt leaden, paralyzed by the weight of a hopeless inertia. In the present world, the only natural coupling is a rape in the barn of some smoldering farm. That skinny black-haired Slovene, the way she'd hidden under a pile of old sacks, what a childish ploy! She opened her mouth to scream, but didn't because others were already screaming below us...But I hardly looked like a murderer, I was afraid of myself, I only wanted to feel myself alive, quench my thirst, and escape the inner presence of death, I was afraid of hurting the lass...He brushed Brigitte's nipples with his fingers. Her breasts were wrinkled and baggy, like the Slovene's, like the teats of wandering bitches...Packs of stray dogs run wild through the wrecks of cities, and idiots in armbands are sent out to shoot them...The bitches are quick to recognize the armbands, and bolt at full speed, like the children of the Jews, whenever they see one ...The idiots in armbands also shoot the children of the Jews...

A crackling volley of small-arms fire dwindled into the distance. The night patrols were shooting down men-dogs-bitches-rats.

And Günther completely remembered the Brigitte to whom he had brought the letters, in a prosperous town: the drive lined with chestnut trees, the lawn before the house, the mullioned casements fringed with creeper, the piano, the young woman with the tentative smile, her lightness among things, the Brigitte whom he had recognized, whom he already knew from his friend's confidences. "I'm here for one who is no longer anywhere, Brigitte..." And so he was restored to innocence, virility, and the desire for a tender grind.

Light stole into the room. He was dressed by the time Brigitte opened her eyes, shivering.

"I was cold suddenly...You're leaving already?"

Furtively, he touched her forehead with his lips.

"I'll be back. Go back to sleep."

"Oh yes, I'll go back to sleep. Make sure the door's closed. Come back."

Hours later, Brigitte no longer knew whether she'd lived or dreamed that night. Still she thought, "Maybe I'm going to have his child..."

Franz Minus-Two had a ground-floor room which had acquired a marked resemblance to the corner of a stable. It was handy, though, for reaching the air-raid cellar in under a minute. To get in and out he had to negotiate the Schulzes' pigsty, the whole family snoring in a heap. He roughly prodded his "Baltic mare," Ilse by name. "Help me change my clothes, precious..." They weren't hampered by the dark, you get used to it, like moles... He put on an overcoat and a workingman's cloth cap, picked up the flashlight he used stintingly (no more spare batteries), but left the pistol: you could have your throat cut for one of those... "I'm off for a healthy breath of air, all right, sausage?" "Yes, Franz, and don't forget your scarf..." Her solicitude pleased him; he rummaged his good hand through Ilse's short, untidy hair by way of a caress: good-quality horsehair, that. He levered himself ponderously over the windowsill. No need to keep the Schulzes informed of his lunar wanderings. The "Baltic mare" slumped back into sleep.

"We've both been lucky," Franz thought to himself. "Me for picking her up, she for being on my way." Had it not been for him, Ilse would now be on the roads of Mecklenburg or someplace among the scum of the drifting crowds, little more than a straw mattress open to panicked soldiers caught between disorderly retreat and desertion, emaciated foreign workers, disreputable marauders; or perhaps the SS, rating her on sight as "clap-ridden and incurably demoralized," would have put her out of her misery for good, so as to improve by a millionth the chances of the Race, already shelled to smithereens! That's how they are, the guys in the last Special Security squads with their sharp uniforms, spit and polish as if the days of parades were not over, equipped with orders, motorbikes, revolvers, syringes, ideology, and inflexibility, in short admirable men! (Some of the more far-sighted ones sneaked into civvies, had themselves listed as casualties of the previous night's skirmish, and resurfaced miles away, bearing the papers of an ordinary citizen; the perfectionists among them could even

produce from their right pocket a release form stamped Teufel-
bronn Work and Protection Camp...) Ilse's story was enough to
break your heart, at a time, that is, when hearts were a run-of-the-
mill, breakable commodity—not made of stone blocks designed
to withstand missiles and high temperatures. 1. A husband gloriously buried at Mozdok, below the Caucasian peaks. 2. An un-
grateful lover, a French prisoner who ran away—after all they did
to keep him fed! 3. The parents, the last horse, and the two toddlers lost between the Oder and the Elbe, behind Russian lines. 4.
The experience of serving in an auxiliary service not recognized in
infantry regulations...All the tears in her body having dried up
long ago by the fireless bivouacs of a motorized company without
motors, Ilse maintained the sturdy taciturnity of a mare, the hygiene of a peasant woman inured to the icy waters of the Spirding-
See, the silence taught by the pine forests, and the fatalism dinned
into Mazurian serfs by the thirteenth-century sword-bearers—a
submission to destiny wisely maintained, nearer our times, on the
baron's potato acres. A good girl, was she more stupid than stolid,
or more stolid than stupid? "Blockhead, Jenny-ass!" jeered Franz
when she was clumsy in helping him to dress. An expression of sly,
or perhaps merely fearful, subservience would come over Ilse's
round, ruddy face but she never felt offended, perhaps finding in
the man's gruff ways some confirmation of her right as a woman.
This had initially been a problem for Minus-Two: How can I ever
mount a female with these stumps and prostheses? And which of
them'd want me, apart from a few specialized old nags? Ilse, submitting, was all motherly tenderness and he even suspected the
woman's eyes were moist. "Cut it out!" he spat. "Don't you get
mawkish with me, or you'll be feeling the back of my hand like
you won't forget in a hurry!" She, who spoke so rarely, answered,
"Oh no, no pity for you!" (She'd used the word pity... "If not,
why not?" wondered the cripple, exasperated.)

Franz set off down Foundling Strasse, that is, down a track
tamped into the rough brick dust. There was no moon, and the
stars were overrun by clouds which moved forward like invaders

across a map. The earth has a phosphorescence all its own. The crutch, the cane, and the iron tip of the prosthesis added nothing to the scattered sounds of solitude. Stones fell of their own accord. The nocturnal rustlings of the city were like those of a forest: they filled the silence with a minute tremor that was the very substance of silence. The vibration of a spring night in the Black Forest orchestrates the beating of wings, the cries of animals seeking one another out or simply expressing their joy to be alive, the pricking of deer hooves along paths known only to them, the fall of dead branches, the hum of the wind...And there can be no doubt that the respiration of leaves, the radiance of the stars, the thrust of roots through the soil, the rising saps must chime in with subtle, essential descants on this enchanted frequency. What's got into you, Minus-Two, dreaming of the Black Forest as you haul yourself, gasping, over the rubble? Fairly stinks around here, sure enough there's a family of refugees asleep in that cavity underneath, if you can call it sleeping, rotting's more like it...An arresting clash of odors made him stop and sniff the air. He was in a bulldozed clearing where the Fraüleins Hahn-Simmelholz had once presided over their drugstore, the Scented Herb. One of these ladies might still be alive, if she could live without her sister, her Siamese cats, her potted plants, her window display; the other was last seen as a pool of guts caramelized by acids, essences, medicinal potions, and Lord knows what else. All of the esoteric liquids stored in the basement had run or burned or melted, hissing and fizzing through everything in their path, including Fraülein Mitzi's plump chaste tummy. Around the tidied rubble (for it had happened in the far-off days when there were still enough sweepers to meet the demand, who were even paid a meager wage) blew cloying, faintly heady fumes. The old biddies had kept quite a respectable stock hidden under their hats, "to save for a rainy day, hooray" tooted Franz cruelly, and he gave a laugh, balanced on a chaotic tumulus that rose seven feet above this extravagant landscape. He laughed because he was remembering a lecture on the redistribution of stocks in wartime, which he'd heard at his advanced course in Work Reinsertion Training for the Maimed in Action. This was a compulsory sprint through economic geopolitics or geopolitical economics, otherwise known as the art of selling a moon of green cheese by promising world domination to a bunch of cripples at the very moment when our invincible army, instead of taking Suez, was taking it on the chin at El Alamein ... Behold the theory:

Grandparents save. Parents save. "In saving lies the strength of nations," says the Great Economist. The Fraüleins Hahn-Simmelholz save. An elite division is goose-stepping by; the Fraüleins Hahn-Simmelholz, throwing thrift to the winds for the sake of patriotism, ply the boys of the division with sandwiches and pretty gifts; the next day, there are a few pfennigs added to the price of the perfumes the factory girls buy before going to bed with their boyfriends, home on convalescent leave ... This young soldier was in fact decorated for destroying a boutique identical to the one run by the Misses Hahnkowski-Simmelkowski—in Warsaw. And down comes a bomblet straight from the United States: adieu savings, thrifty sisters, declared inventory, hidden inventory! From out of his tall silk hat, the professorial magician pulls a hilarious monster with a death's-head and seven flaccid limbs and introduces him to the audience: Herr Geopolitik! Wild clapping from the audience, which continues to save ...

Franz, still chuckling to himself, started to applaud, but you need two hands for that. He smote his cane against the ground with contained fury. Men are insane, Franz! Their destructiveness will not be sated while anything exists, since the magician-professor is probably still teaching his course, people are still alive in the cellars, I am still here to watch the show. The horizon was quieter now, the fighting had moved elsewhere. Not yet the end, goddammit!

He clearly saw a big human bat drop silently between two walls, as though fallen from the stars. A quadruped that was part bear, part pig, part jackal, and part outlaw slunk close to the ground, paused to test the air with its snout, wiggled its rump grotesquely, and disappeared ... "Ha ha! Geopolitik, my friend, geopolitics! I know where you're headed: toward a bullet in the ass. I'd give something to know where you crawled out of: Bosnia, the Volga, Normandy, Zeeland, or Neukölln, like me? Fugitive, looter, deserter, parachutist, Black Front, dead white all over, d-d-death penalty, my good friend. Same goes for me if I don't report you. If I do report you, your pals will take care of me instead. If we happen to bump into each other ten minutes from now, it could go either way..." Franz did not quite know what he was doing. But then what's the use of knowing that?

Before following the animal shadow, he let himself be distracted listening again to Altstadt breathe. Pieces of cornice broke off and skittered down with a noise like tiny landslides. A door was banging emptily. A tinkle of shattered glass, a cock crowed. Somewhere a tank column was rumbling along on metal treads. Two muffled whistle blasts chased each other from one constellation to another and were gobbled up by a fat fish of cloud. A child started crying, where? Franz pressed his eye to a crack in a wall and saw a white-haired woman stretched out, reading a book bound in black, the New Testament presumably. What light was she using to read by, the witch? He put his lips against the slit in the brickwork and lowed, spectrally: "The good Lord protect us!" He looked again. The old lady was beaming and nodding, their eyes met but she could not have seen him, she must have thought the voice had been sent from heaven above, the end was nigh! Franz considered following up with a ripe rosary of imprecations, before deciding it was too much trouble.

The manhole through which his four-legged quarry had just vanished made him hesitate. The ladder was twisted, and he would never be able to crutch his way down without being heard. But the warren below probably connected with the old brasserie cellars; some, considered inaccessible, were probably inhabited. Franz found the way in. He moved along as nimbly as a spider. He dragged himself over the sharp stones of a tunnel, making only surreptitious use of his torch. The tongue of light licked at a seething of white maggots in a viscous, purplish slick. He was glad not to have stuck his hand in it, even with his canvas glove on. Just what you'd see if your personal idea of fun was crawling beneath a graveyard. As he was about to turn back, thinking he was lost, the murmuring of voices reached him. He had only to raise his head in order to see. The cellar was open to the sky: a jagged hole in the vault let in the unreal glow of the cloudy heavens. There were human shapes down there, talking low, each in turn, holding council; a poised female voice said something in a language he couldn't identify—Czech, Russian, Serbian, Polish? He was watching from above, through an oblong hole the size of his hand. If he'd had his revolver on him, it would have been easy to knock down those four opaque forms and collect the four rewards, not to mention a Civil Defense Merit Badge, yes sir. He trained two fingers on the sitting, thinking ducks, one by one, click-clack, your worries would be over my dears. The game amused him. And it was a good job he'd left that gun behind, because the temptation would have been strong: the ingrained habit of killing, the urge to do the right thing, the spirit of fraternity! The incentive of the reward: human motivation is nothing if not complex. Down below, the woman struck a match over a sheet of paper. Franz had a glimpse of slender fingers, an oval face, chestnut-ash hair above the brow. The match went out, but the vision of that stern countenance, youthful yet aging, had imprinted itself so well upon the cripple's retina that he seemed still to see it in the darkness. Gleefully he prepared his throat for his spectral voice, waited for a silence, and pronounced: "Lady, gentlemen..."

The four shapes scattered into the blackest depths of the vaults. Franz could feel them below him, tense, crouched, unsheathing knives, intently scanning the recesses of the walls, the hole to the sky... Not a flicker of movement. He paced his phrasing, to bring out the humor.

"Honorable fodder for the gallows and the stake! An unknown well-wisher, who doesn't actually give a fart about anything, advises you to decamp without delay... The neighborhood is getting dangerous."

Feeling better now, graveyard rats? Franz believed he was feeling in his own breast the beating of four terrified hearts calmed by the balm of such an improbable reprieve. Taking a deep breath, he concluded: "Reasons of State. Good night."

A man's deep voice rose from the cavern and said, in good German, "Thank you. Good night. Beat it."

A pause ensued, like a rising tide of silence slowly sealing off the underground world. And the woman's voice added, from farther away, "Brotherhood."

Franz lost his temper. In the light of day, this woman would be repelled by him, his crutch, his stick, his rubberized extension, the hook in place of a hand, the sourness etched into his zero-hero kisser. "Which one's the glass eye?" she'd wonder, and, "Tell me, are your balls synthetic too?" He loathed her. There's precious little brotherhood to spare for the armless and the legless, except in official speeches . . . He answered violently, "And a bucket of flaming shit to you too!"

Laughter melted his anger.

You see, there's only one brotherhood these days, and that's in the pit, the common pit, where the same fraternal lime is shoveled over Slavs and Aryans, Negroes and Jews! They're all the same when they've twitched and defecated their last, all equally stinking, putrid, impotent, pacified, delivered . . . All the drowned look alike, salt water or fresh, and corpses are the truest brothers, the only ones you can trust: they neither murder nor betray . . . Just as the devastated cities are sisters, Stalingrad, Warsaw, Coventry, London, Lübeck, and this city too: they could all be mistaken for one another in a photograph. Brotherhood.

He was still feeling jubilant, carried away by his speeches to himself, when a security patrol hailed him at the corner of an erstwhile street. It was nearly sunrise. The corporal recognized him.

"Out prowling, Franz?"

The cripple produced an engraved silver goblet he had just found, undamaged, in a thicket of scrap iron.

"It was shining like a cat's eye!"

"Anything suspicious back there?" "Everything, you name it. A ballet of ghosts. What's the news?" The corporal edged a step away from his men, mobilized civilians who looked like the defeated insurgents they could never be. "It seems the elite division was crushed to a pulp this morning... The general's killed himself..." "White of him," murmured Franz hypocritically. "Does that mean the city is surrounded?" "Only halfway," said the corporal, a perfect vessel in which official lies were preserved forever fresh. "An army of shock troops is poised to break through their exposed flank, but not for a few days..." "Only a few days?" marveled Minus-Two, reaching for a smirk of gratification, and rounding it off with a wink. His amputated hand was beginning to throb, it must be the damp. He raised his other hand in a parade-ground salute: "*Sieg Heil!*"

Back at home he removed his clothes by himself, in an agony of pain. His amputated limbs felt as though they were bleeding, severed raw, gnawed by the icy cold. "Warm me, Ilse." At such times the Pomeranian woman would stretch out on top of him so as to clasp both of his stumps, and the prostheses would cut into her; but a saving warmth crept from her body into his. He began to doze off to the vision of a flaring match which threw light onto a hand and thence onto a face strangely framed by rays intermingled with ash-brown locks. Three human shapes, molded in opacity, were worshipping or menacing that hand, that brow... So he made haste, pointing his machine gun at the hand, the brow, the three crouching forms: fire, fire, fire! I killed all. Duty. Franz let out a groan, his head struck the partition, flakes of plaster rained down on his face. Ilse still sprawled hotly on top of him, suffocating him. "Ha, strangle me would you, vermin!" He shook her off in one convulsive jerk. Ilse knew these nightmares, when he joined battle with things unseen and often hit or abused her, without waking. She made herself passive, as if she didn't exist, and waited for the storm of the blood to spend itself through his clenched body.

"What is it? An alert?" he asked in a childish voice.

A submachine gun, great strangling pincers, white maggots in the gruesome sludge, tetanus, a vault punctured by the sky; and the sound of the Schulzes snoring in the next room, like in a stable. "Ilse," he said plaintively...

"Try to sleep, my man," she answered roughly. "It'll be light soon."

■

Nurse Erna Laub's dossier had of course been "carefully reviewed" by the appropriate offices... Her father was an agronomical engineer, Oscar-Julius Laub, a card-carrying National Socialist and vice president of a national association abroad, entrusted with the most delicate assignments, awarded top marks, last heard of in 1941 at a civilian prisoners' camp in the north Obi, Eastern Siberia (there was no more on Oscar-Julius). Erna was his only child, unmarried, a nurse with a Red Cross diploma from Riga; fluent Russian from infancy, smattering of Spanish for having accompanied her father on a six-month journey to Peru, competent French after several visits to Paris; slight Slavonic accent in German. The data regarding her character could be summarized as follows: highly patriotic, member of the National Women's Association, diligent, conscientious, of below-average intelligence (underlined). Doesn't speak up at meetings, but ardent in her applause. Generous with donations. Not especially gregarious, strict morals, no offspring (underlined, a black mark). War record: crossed Lithuanian lines with a group of escapees from Russian prisons, which made a twenty-four-hour stand against the Sokolin gang. Slightly wounded in the shoulder, excellent morale, exerted a positive influence upon companions. Personal acquaintance of Standartenführer F. M. B., former Communist, sterling Party member, killed at... and of Lieutenant Colonel H. W. W., a boyhood friend of her father's. Political acumen: nil. Physical appearance: forty years of age, appears younger, medium height, well built, sober of dress, extremely proper in demeanor. Chestnut hair, pulled back from the forehead and gathered into a low bun, sprinkled with gray strands; blue-gray eyes, and a set to the lips expressing severity.

Discreetly accompanied by the confidential papers that drew this rather accurate portrait of her, Nurse (First Class) Erna Laub, usually well provided with money, looked for jobs just behind the front lines—the sort of posting her colleagues did their best to evade with the help of their connections (in violation of a draconian rule) and even of their amorous liaisons. Laub's only known liaison occurred in Breslau, with a twenty-six-year-old flying ace who was distinguishing himself on the eastern front. After his sorties over the Red Army munitions depots, this handsome Siegfried, an occasional drug-taker, easily obtained a twenty-four-hour leave from his chiefs in order to attend a concert with Erna and end the night in the arms of this yielding statue. He only tore himself away, still ravished by that embrace, to meet a somewhat unaccountable bullet during a nighttime rumpus in the city itself. Suspicion fell on some Polish workers, who were executed without fuss. A few days later, the deceased's elite squadron was destroyed in its magnificently camouflaged and isolated hangars by Russian bombs of breathtaking precision. Placing fatherland above friendship, Nurse Erna Laub wrote to denounce the careless talk of a certain officer who drank too much, slept with the first women who came along, and talked about his exploits to all and sundry, neglecting, in short, the most elementary precautions. In view of his service record, the culprit was merely demoted and transferred from the air force to a disciplinary infantry unit, where the soldiers lasted an average of forty-five days. Such a courageous show of patriotism on the part of Erna Laub further bolstered the trust in which she was held, and soon after she was appointed head nurse to Army General von G, recovering from a serious fracture to the skull. This task she fulfilled with "matchless devotion," though the patient died from rampant septicemia four days after beginning his convalescence...It happened at the spa town of Bad Schanden, in Erzgebirge. The view of lofty ranges and white mists framed by the window was so restful, so invigorating, that General von G felt he was coming back to life. The nurses offered him the first cup of some hot, delicious coffee—a gift from the field marshal—while he talked to them innocently about his mountain-climbing youth, his explorations in Anatolia, his fallen sons, and the execution of a pack of Jews at Tarnopol, carried out by those nasty little bandits of the Reprisals Brigade, the worst soldiers in the world! He explained that the Slavs' very name had derived in ancient times from the Latin *slavus*, slave—proof of the immemorially servile nature of these tribes from the Asian steppes. Leavening erudition with wit, the general went on to discuss the alternative etymologies peddled by philosophers with more imagination than sense. These would have "Slav" derive from *slovo*, the Slavonic for verb; or *slava*, glory, also in Slavonic—for to cap it all, the slaves aspire to the word, they lay claim to glory! Erna Laub implored him several times not to overtax himself by talking; as dusk fell, she injected him with a sedative. "He is saved," she repeated, "this great man of war! And such a dazzling conversationalist!" The fever attacked the next morning. The head nurse offered herself for a transfusion, but she was not of the same blood group... The bereaved family sent a miserly one hundred marks to the nursing staff.

Two American parachutists isolated at the top of the Fourth Field Hospital developed a hatred of Erna Laub, marching in and out of their garret several times a day. Privately they called her Old Lace, after the play *Arsenic and Old Lace*. Torn between hope and fear, they listened to the throb of battle beyond the horizon. The abrupt silence of the guns plunged them into such despondency that Old Lace, noting the rise in their temperatures, fixed them with a gimlet eye straight out of the Last Judgment. She was standing by the door, thin in starchy white, and to them she looked like a Prussian death's-head. The latch clicked into place behind her. "Our number is up," said the young man from Arkansas to the young man from Illinois, without specifying whether he meant them personally, the nearby fighting, or global war. "See that poison look on her face?" Old Lace returned to administer some tablets. Bending toward the ear of the young man from Arkansas, she asked, in English, "Speak French?" The parachutist bit back an expletive, and said, "I understand a bit, *un peu.*" Old Poison Lace was whispering, unbelievably, "*Courage,* you have won, *gagné la bataille.* Elite division *kaput, comprenez?*" "*Ja,*" stammered the prisoner, he thought he was dreaming, and gaped admiringly at the austere visage that now looked nothing like a death's-head. The nurse put a finger to her lips.

"Not possible," protested the young man from Illinois, "you must be nuts..." But he'd seen the finger on the lips. "She's great, amazing, what a woman! What chumps we've been!" Their temperatures returned to normal. Meanwhile, in the mess, Captain Gerhard Koppel and Heiderman the medical officer were debating the prisoners' fate with Erna Laub. "I vote we get rid of them quietly," said Dr. Heiderman. "There's a circular that gives us the right...You know that if Altstadt falls, there's not enough transport for all of our wounded..." Captain Koppel objected that the circular had been overruled by a subsequent order from the divisional chief, in the interests of intelligence. Erna Laub proved to have some political acumen after all: "Besides, precisely if the town falls, such captives will indirectly serve to protect the population..." She backed this up, tactfully, with: "Anyway, you can always decide at the last moment. It'll only take two minutes." If there is a last moment, even lasting two minutes, and anyone around to decide anything at all...

The thought of the last moment passed through their three minds, stirring up unconfessable anxieties and expectations. Koppel admitted that the local situation was getting worse, but that the general situation would improve, despite appearances. You never knew with this model officer whether he believed what he was saying or if he said what must be believed. "Berlin stands fast, and the enemy's plans will be foiled in time; the outlying bits of territory we are losing are as insignificant as the bomb damage, which is really a golden opportunity to rebuild...Between ourselves, let's face it, many of our venerable old piles were crying out to be demolished long ago. The justifiable respect in which they were held were a brake on modern urban development... And what we shall erect in their place will be equally historic..." He gave the final tug to his glove with a little laugh. Straight and supple, agreeably blond, he might have been a life-sized cutout, soul included, from a military fashion magazine. Was he as genuinely steeped in high official stupidity as he appeared? Or did he put on his stupidity in the morning after his cold shower, along with his uniform, well brushed by an orderly? Was it part and parcel of his contempt for others, did it afford him a secret pleasure in deriding the cowardly? Koppel continued: "We only need a few weeks more to perfect a new technology of warfare... England will be destroyed when she least expects it. In future the real war will be a war of scientific inventions..."

The nervous, anemic Dr. Heiderman nodded eagerly in approval, having no other course. But he was sick with foreboding, and it showed; Koppel's gaze slid over him with polite disdain. "Erna will address herself to me concerning the two parachutists as soon as the evacuation order has been given." "And if you should be absent, Captain?" The nurse put just enough stress on the word absent to imbue it with the notion of death. A good officer never knows when he may be putting on his gloves for the last time. If you happen to be killed tonight, Captain? Koppel deemed it a reasonable, if distasteful, query; he affected to ignore the doctor. "In that case you yourself will be the judge, Erna, do whatever you think best." Dr. Heiderman's trim mustache quivered pitifully, and Koppel saw chaos begin. What connection is there between the muffled buzz of a bell, a cravenly quivering upper lip, and the immense disorder closing over one's head? The futility of it all was blinding, especially the futility of refusing to look things squarely in the face. Koppel, old chap, you'll be killed one of these evenings, sooner rather than later, and it'll be for nothing. Your resolve not to be taken alive serves no purpose whatsoever. The scientific inventions will come afterward, if at all; too late for you, too late for everything. As he was leaving, Koppel turned once, intending to say, "Execute the prisoners!"—and let a few more of those who will kill me meet their end before I do! But the disorder was already taking effect. Koppel shrank from letting a woman perceive the clouding he felt at the back of his own eyes. He did not say the words he wanted to say. Dr. Heiderman let out a sigh. "Asthmatic, are we?" the captain said insultingly, with the unspoken thought: "You'll be killed too, you repulsive coward!" That's defeat all over: you feel it as the tooth feels the cavity, it poisons your very breath. The monstrous disorder was rising, drowning out the sounds of water faucets, bells, motors in the courtyard, injured men groaning, and ideas as sonorous as the smash of a boxer's fist. Koppel pulled off his gloves, just for the sake of pulling off his gloves, made the nurse and the doctor sit down again, and listened to himself speak.

"I'm waiting on the miracle of our technical genius. We may shortly be in a position to blow up half the planet. From what I hear, the tests are proceeding with considerable success..."

A door banged, a furious voice shouted, "Erna! For God's sake get over here, are you deaf? You too, Doctor, on the double." The bell was still vibrating. When all is lost, a mindless bell will keep on ringing through whitewashed basements, and glasses will stand empty on tables long after our mouths have rotted...Quick march! Tonight Koppel was expected to lead a special unit, reduced to a third of its strength, into the breach opened by the sacrifice of the elite division. Away he strode like a energetic sleepwalker. Under the arch at the entrance of the former tourist hotel, he saluted the last batch of mangled bodies from the division. Blood-soaked men were stretched out against the embankment of the road as if it were a litter. Repulsive stretchers moved hurriedly back and forth carried by medics with dark rings under their eyes. The workers of the last day! In the center of the courtyard, like a hatless white-maned puppet stuffed with the sawdust of dignity, the chief medical officer was directing the traffic in person. "Immediate surgery, I'll be there in five minutes, this one to the barn, nothing doing, this one simple: amputation—don't give me a hard time; this one's a problem, check him later, get a move on Loschek, no not him, the other one! You there, phone the auxiliary hospital and say I refuse—I refuse—to take the sixty they want to send! No! What are you saying? Idiot! To the cemetery, that's right. Short of bandages, are you? Anesthetics? I don't give a...Tell Herr Brückmeister from me, if he hasn't supplied them by six o'clock, I'll have him court-martialed...Watch out, gently. Immediate double amputation, Yes, Doctor...Blithering idiots! Can't you see he's dead! Not my line of business!" With sarcasm: "Forgotten the difference between fainting and death, have you, young man? What do you mean, no Herr Brückmeister? He's deserted? The dog, the stinking dog!"

This was neither the place nor the job for a chief medical officer, and he was courting reproof from his superiors. To the colonel approaching through the crush of stretchers and bearers, he addressed a lugubrious salute and looked away. The colonel's crimson head, squat on his shoulders, suggested the onset of apoplexy. If you want to establish order here, honorable Colonel, try not to burst like a skin full of beer and shit. As for your reproofs, your dressing-downs, your orders, I wipe my a...with them. The colonel was speaking to him confidentially; the doctor caught sight of a gaping, mud-smeared thigh, a pearly gleam of femur deep inside... "No. I'm the boss here. A written order, in writing please! Bring on the badly wounded ones, over there! Idiots! Wake up, man, keep 'em moving...I'll see you in the operating room..." The red-faced colonel was gazing glassily at another, green-faced colonel being stretchered past. "What's wrong with him?" "The colonel has been eviscerated, Colonel..." "Quite so, quite so. Keep up the good work." Above the milling of vertical and horizontal bodies stood huge white clouds. The chief medic ran to the courtyard entrance and with one glance took in the clouds, the banks of the road lined with pale beeches, and the multitude of the wounded emitting what sounded like a harmonious chorus of pain. The white coat and white mane were seen to charge, flailing, at a truck: "Go to blazes! You can't unload them here! No more! Full up!" A hum was floating on the air: Planes, planes! Hurry up!

Nurse Erna contemplated the chaos from an upstairs window in the officers' wing. There was Koppel disappearing around the corner with small reluctant steps, on the way to his destruction, no doubt about it! The red-faced colonel was climbing back into his tiny green car, with a boa constrictor painted in yellowish gray on it; swallowed by a boa. A truck blocked his path, the colonel emerged from the boa's stomach waving a stubby arm: no one saw or heard him. The muffled noise of the alert continued to crackle obstinately through the halls because a plane suddenly appeared, skimming the treetops. Erna picked up the internal telephone: "Turn off that stupid racket, you morons! It's useless." She recognized the enemy insignia on the monster's underwing. It ground sinisterly over their heads, ignoring the Fourth Hospital, but seconds later a slow explosion made the remaining windowpanes vibrate loudly (the less glass there is, the more noise it makes). The heavenly thunderbolt had scored a bull's-eye on the motor fleet reserved for their evacuation. She looked at her watch. It was time for the kid's dressing.

The blinded boy endured his darkness fairly well, but he still had a suppurating wound in the groin, threaded with catheters which were torture to replace. "Is that you, Erna?" he asked in an imposingly quiet voice. "It's not just for show out there, right? Talk to me. I can hear all the sounds. I feel so much better, you know. I was thinking about you. What's going on?" "Nothing new, Tony...Here, drink this." The scarred and voided sockets no longer tortured him. Without the bandage, his head was hideously alluring: thick chestnut locks swept the domed forehead, the nose was straight, the mouth full and serious, but the outsize hollows of the eyes, pale as gold in places, devastated a face condemned to the night. "If only I could believe in God!" she thought. She would give the blind boy a final, pacifying injection, as soon as she could arrange it. "Let Tony sleep, let him sleep for good." If she still loved anyone in this world it was him, this big kid lost in the dark between nothingness and the bitter drink of life to come . . . His file, penned by someone with a twisted sense of humor, read: "twenty-two years old . . . draftsman . . . outstanding performance in the field."

Once they had conversed as follows: "Do you trust me, Tony?" "Yes." "How do you imagine me?" (Erna avoided any references to sight.) He reflected for a moment, his features bizarrely illuminated by a smile in which the eyes played no part. "Young, very young . . ." (Erna felt herself aging; thank you, blind man!) "And tall and slim . . . with long soft tresses, all gathered up. Loyal and understanding. Straightforward." (Erna's frizzy hair was turning gray. Loyal, that was true, mortally so, and yet the word was like a slap. Understanding, indeed, knowing that the deepest grief is to understand. Straightforward, yes, as a string of infernal knots . . .) "You're a little off the mark, Tony. No tresses, not soft hair . . ." But let him think that I'm young! "May I touch you?" he said, moving a translucent hand toward her. She clasped it between her own. "And I'm tough." "One's got to be," the invalid said, with conviction. "So be tough, Tony, and answer me, your friend. Do you want to live—or—" (warming these words with her voice) "would you prefer not to?" She saw the almost imperceptible tightening of his nostrils, his lips, the premature lines around his mouth. "But do you think I can live, Erna?" (No reprieve from lies and treachery!) "Yes, I do." "Then I want to live." And pity, which is the last form of love, must also be betrayed. The nurse knew she was lying again. "And so you will, I know you will." She forced a tinkling laugh (the sound of laughter a lie) and added, "I've never been wrong before . . ." The ward doctor was taking a twenty-four-hour leave, she could do it then. She was sorry she'd put it off.

Tony ground his teeth while she removed the antiseptic dressings and replaced the catheters. A testicle was turning blue beneath the shrunken member. "I hope I didn't hurt you too much, Tony?" He smiled, beads of sweat under his nostrils. "Not too much. Just a little . . . You're so good! I get the feeling you're pleased, too. Are you?"

If only he didn't ask why!

"I am, it's true. Rest now. I'll drop in later."

Footsteps were running up the stairs. Someone was whimpering wretchedly. "Erna, come quickly to the operating room..." Pleased by the breakdown, the demise of an entire world, pleased! You should never say the word "good" again, Tony, it's a meaningless word, a blind word... The old rafters of the operating room were black. White-shrouded forms were stooping and shifting around prostrate forms. The lamps created a mist of asphyxiating brightness surrounded by visceral penumbras. Scissors could be heard snipping through cloth and leather to expose wounds. Three surgeons, their faces partly masked, stoked with Benzedrine to keep them awake, worked amid raw flesh, pus, gangrene, dying flesh, hallucination. Their shining steel instruments, wondrously pure and cruel, preserved an impenetrable yet intelligent disorder from one torture to the next. Basins filled up with reddened cotton swabs mixed with scraps of flesh. In the bucket by the door, a pink, bristly male ear was resting on dark and light tufts of hair, beside some severed fingers. Rubber tubes and electric cables curved gracefully through the foggy glare... Erna, at a sign, clamped a man's head between both hands. His throat was an open wound, and she immediately felt the death tremors through her palms. Dr. Felix put down the scalpel, gazed hypnotically into the gray face, and clicked his tongue: "Done for. Take him away..." And he turned aside wearily. On the neighboring table a colossus with an uncovered belly, starred with wounds, had fallen into an incoherently euphoric delirium: "Ha ha, ha ha, La Chênaie... four thousand... three thousand six hundred marks... Snapdragons! Mama..." A long bout of groaning, then he launched into a verse from the Ninth Symphony: "We enter, drunk with joy, Thy bright sanctuary... Drunk with joy." Gently Erna fitted the anesthetic mask onto a feverish head like a ball of roots pulled out of the soil.

The day staff usually partied through the night, for life is short, death easy (in a certain sense), and joy fleeting, so

> the boy he's for the girl,
> and the girl she's for the boy!

The demolished city was preparing for sleep. Patrols were following perilous itineraries which intersected with those of lucky pass
holders who were out looking for a good time. Muted singing
could be heard deep in the charred ruins, in alcoves like the dens
of shipwreckers, around daintily embroidered tablecloths, with
plentiful quaffing of that delectable scotch someone swiped after
an American retreat, or the last of the champagne from the plun-
der of France, or the sweet Rhineland wine they call *liebsfrau-
milch*, Milk of the Beloved Woman, or the chiefs' coffee filched
from the storeroom; and every bottle, if its story could be known,
would relate a gory melodrama full of episodes of the last days of a
civilization. "The trophies most prized by victorious armies,"
Conrad once remarked, "are the ones they treasure up to the very
last minute of their own defeats, are the bottles..." The heroic
survivors of slaughtered units organized group-sex parties, for lack
of privacy and anyway the proud but not-too-proud depravity of
warriors is more fun. Couples entwined wherever they could,
mingling lips, breasts, hips, and groins, bursts of laughter and
tears, rage and joy. All together now, softly, allegretto:

> Let's make love
> On top of the grave,
> The common grave
> That is our fate!
> You'll be my grave,
> Adelina!
> The worms will have to wait till after,
> After, after, after, after, after!
> Come Herminia, Adelina!

Or suddenly switching to a mode of lyrical lamentation so
touching that the eyes of the Adelinas became moist and it

took five men to prevent a pilot from emptying his revolver on everyone:

> Sweet young maiden, fair of breath,
> Marlene with hips to die for,
> What do you wait for 'neath the crescent moon?
> Nevermore will he return!
>   O Marlene Marleeeene!

"I find myself wondering," confessed a grenadier of the Battalion of Death, "whether I shall ever again be able to sleep with a woman in private and without beating her; I actually tried it the other day, with a classy, good-looking one—between clean sheets if you can imagine that—and I couldn't get it up! Me!" Someone shot back gaily, "You won't have that problem much longer!" Indeed (*in aparte*):

> Long live endless war!
> Empire of the World,
> End of the World,
> Great universal grave!

Sung to the tune of a lively march, the words were Conrad's, disseminated thanks to the Secret Service, which was hell-bent on arresting the author. Under cover of such fraternal orgies of boozing and brawling (after which the corpse, thrown into the street, would be attributed to Polish outlaws), Erna met with Conrad, a volunteer on the night security shift with perforated lungs; skinny, properly helmeted and shined, the young man looked shy—and resolute. People imagined that they enjoyed having their pleasure in the open air, pressed up against derelict walls like homeless animals, and this was the subject of a good deal of joking speculation.

"Well?" Erna questioned anxiously, when Conrad had come for her and they were standing outside under the portico of a bank that still lorded over the surrounding devastation.

"The committee has found a new meeting place," he said.

"And the voice, do we know who?"

"No, but I suspect an amputee who ran into Corporal Boehm's patrol about twenty minutes later. I'll find out. Come along. Careful. There are six steps down, then a gap to hop over, it's got water in it. Hold on to my arm, we can't use the light."

Conrad did not switch on his flashlight until they were crawling over a rubble of cement dust and burned paper. The candlelit vault was genuinely pleasant and clean, though chill as the grave. Erna shook hands with Bartek the Polish delegate, Alain from France, and the Spaniard Ignacio before glancing around her. There were separate piles of weapons, canned food, and clothes. More surprising was the presence of a pair of massive strongboxes, tilted toward each other, intact.

"How about it, we've infiltrated the very foundations of capitalism," said Conrad, the German delegate. "Now for the superstructure!"

He went straight on to the technical specifications.

"The volume of air and the seriously inadequate ventilation limit us to a maximum of ten people staying here. There's a risk of flooding if bombed. Extremely unlikely to be detected, though, save through our own carelessness. The two schoolboys who found it have been evacuated to Thuringia. They used it for hiding potatoes..."

Bartek the shoemaker, based on his experience as a staff officer, predicted that the Americans would capture the city within the week; much given to making solemn prognostications, his rate of accuracy was as high as fifty percent, if he said so himself—a not dishonorable record for a tactician trained by ignoramuses who understood nothing of warfare...Apart from two groups of armaments workers, his Polish contingent was proving hard to discipline. They got into fights every night: yesterday, seven were shot! Alain reported the formation of a tolerable resistance committee within the most privileged—that is, the most corrupt—French commando. Alain was afraid of gangsters, informers, anti-

Semitism, the radio, dirty deals. He asked for two guys with guts, dressed as petty bourgeois, to carry out a delicate assignment. "Got them for you," Ignacio said. "Myself and a Trotskyite from Madrid I know..." Erna shot him an arch look. "You heard right, dear lady," Ignacio said teasingly. "Right," said Alain.

Conrad briefed them on the latest developments. The elite division—it was discussed all over the town—had melted away under a storm of sulfurous bombs and the like, ground into pulp by the Shermans, the last survivors machine-gunned from the air by well-targeted fire, for lack of air cover. Formed of veterans and recently drafted young replacements, half fanatics and the other half chickenshits, marching toward the firing line like condemned men to the scaffold, encouraged by summary executions. The division was not at its full complement, either. "So which half were chicken?" Bartek wanted to know, moved by a professional interest in the behavior of fighters under pressure. "Both," smiled Conrad. As for the population, it was on its knees. "The petty bourgeois is skidding on the vomit of its own abjectness..." "Ugh!" Ignacio winced. "Nobly put!" "Factual. They've always been that way." The *Volkssturm* was thoroughly demoralized, save for one ravening company of Young Wolves packed with the teenage scions of Nazi families. "So anyone who hasn't deserted already will be chopped into little pieces, which is fine by me. Good riddance. Seventeen-year-old brain matter is so damn malleable, it's enough to put one off youth forever..." A surprisingly healthy black market, *Gott sei Dank*!, kept supplied by the quartermaster general. Prices for civilian clothing rising, identity papers, ration cards, and certificates declining: the colossal demand stimulated wholesale production, and the supply of forgeries nearly outstripped the demand. The Party was on its last legs. The hard-line faction was contemplating suicide or possible resistance from mountain redoubts ("That's a laugh!" said Bartek). There was some acknowledgment of ideological and political blunders; the military caste ought to have been purged long ago. The hard-liners, though numerically insignificant, might still pull off some desperate coup. The bulk of the

Party, stupefied and discouraged; but there's no shortage of smart thinkers discreetly getting rid of their Führer portraits, calf-bound *Mein Kampfs*, uniforms, and armbands, which means we can get hold of some. Those rats think only about leaving the ship, the trouble is they have a deadly fear of salt water! As for the old working class, all but a handful of true stalwarts have become disoriented by the bitterness they feel. "You can see their point. Two wars, a revolution, waves of inflation, crises, persecutions, unemployment, demagogy, anti-Bolshevism, pact with Bolshevism, war on Bolshevism, a whirlwind of traumatic events, all in one generation! The worst of it is, these used to be men with sound heads on their shoulders..." "Come to the point," said Alain. "Right. The Communists are more active than the Social Democrats, the Social Democrats more reliable..."

Erna cut in, her voice level: "In the interests of unity, best to abstain from political psychologizing. Broadly, what do people think?"

"They think they're in hell, that tomorrow will be worse than today, that there's nothing left to believe in or to hope for, but still, they'd rather not all be wiped out just yet..."

Ignacio remarked fliply, "They do display a healthy philosophy of nature. Lacking a political psychology they have a zoological mentality... And I couldn't agree with you more, Erna, providing we could forget an awful lot of things... I'm all for unity, no one keener, but I won't hide from you that if I were in the east and the CP took over, I would adopt a few personal precautions pronto: *Underground zwei*, number two!"

Bartek concurred, with a pained grimace. Alain shrugged grumpily. The Pole distracted the committee by tiptoeing up to one of the safes and gluing his ear to the side. "Something is up," he said. "I have had eighteen long hours to study the hard heart of these financial idols, and I've found it reacts to the great emotions of the earth. My reading is, major artillery offensive west by northwest..."

Conrad led Erna out by the other exit: a good meeting place

must have two exits. The pair of them emerged on what used to be a commercial thoroughfare, strangely well preserved and animated. Large clumps of splintered buildings remained upright around their blacked-out display windows and vacant interiors; this architecture was vaguely reminiscent of the badlands of Colorado or Afghanistan as seen in geography books: vertical mountains chiseled into castles...A procession of trucks straggled down the cleared roadway like a giant snake of black vehicles, hissing and growling, guided onward by obscure glimmers of light. A youth tightly belted into leathers checked Erna's pass and Conrad's registration card, zealous enough to play his flashlight over their faces. "Where have you come from?"

"Bed," answered Erna, smiling. "Does that tempt you?"

"No thanks, Fraülein, move along. No loitering in this zone."

The last motorized infantry were crammed into the squat personnel carriers—a conglomeration of heads massed together with slim barrels. All of a sudden, one hundred yards ahead, a white star was born in the inky sky releasing an unbearable brilliance floating to the ground among the convulsed buildings, highlighting the marquee of a cinema...The fez, thick mustache, and smoke rings of Khedive cigarettes loomed over the startled convoy from the center of this inhuman glare.

"Precise targeting," muttered Conrad. "Let's hurry."

The star faded, having broken the silence of the sky where now a hum of engines could be heard far above. The star flared once more in the form of a scream, a sudden demented howl that rippled heavily over the convoy, echoing through a thousand thunderstruck spines. The human mass smothered the cry beneath its weight as one smothers remorse, as one would want to smother fear...

Conrad slipped his arm around Erna's waist for appearances, for invisible eyes were watching.

"Sometimes I feel I could let rip like that madman...That madman who had already been killed, I think. I'm disciplined enough to stop myself, but which is the crazier, I wonder, to be disciplined or to scream? You, Erna, you put up a great show of being the woman with nerves of steel, but you're as bad as I am. And all those poor bastards riding off to the slaughterhouse without a peep, how they'd love to howl their guts out. It would be an overwhelming relief, the convoy would stop, the Special Troops would go wild, then join in three minutes late: AAAAGGHH! The battle would be over before it began. The victors would quake to enter such a madhouse. It could mean the return of sanity..."

"Shut up," Erna said stiffly. "Shut up or I'll scream."

The first deep thumps of an artillery barrage resounded somewhere. The ruins shook. Immense veils were ripped asunder in the night. There was silence among men.

■

The importance that explosives have acquired in people's lives is equal only to that of papers. With barely a glance at the man, the robot on guard before some trapdoor peruses "your papers," *die Dokumenten*; his decision is the result of a series of dates, rubber stamps, and itemized rules interlocking like cogwheels in his head at roughly an inch below the helmet. The robot pronounces: "Not in order, come this way." This may be the beginning of the end of one's own small but cherished world, within the larger end of the world...Alain naturally attempted to argue with the robot; he very nearly groveled. "*Mein Kamerad, sehen Sie doch!* Just look!" I'm *almost* in order, surely, hardly out at all, look, lovely blue card, pink card, travel permit (expired), crucial other paper here...! The man-robot of the final hour, pumped up with a zeal that would make as much difference as the flight of a gnat in a cordite explosion, was impervious to argument. He had the build for the job—a big brute with watery eyes. The well-worn record spun in his larynx to produce the stock response under every clime, still changeless amid pan-destruction: "Tell it to the sergeant." But where was the robot sergeant? A hundred marks might have nuanced his sense of responsibility, oiled the rusty wheels of his mental clockwork—after all, banknotes are also made of paper, that's why the magic sometimes works . . . Alain started playing his own record, stuck on a single word: "Shit shit shit shit shit!" What could be more infuriating than to be shot by mistake or misplaced zeal on the eve of deliverance, to be the last casualty of a lost war, minutes before the cease-fire? But until this happens there's always the luck factor, you never know. If you made a list of the ways luck has shepherded you—defenseless, trembling, and alive—through a global massacre, there'd be no choice but to accept the complete randomness of the universe, its sovereign absurdity, the existence of an unimaginably insane God.

Alain continued his meditation in a prison that looked like nothing known, while being essentially the same as every other prison. Comforting sunshine, pouring like warm water over his dirty, aching body, warmed the rear playground of this shattered school, whose ground floor and basement had been converted into a holding pen for prisoners. Rumor had it that Altstadt's jail, symbolically spared by the fires of heaven and earth, was full to bursting with enemies of the people, traitors, suspects, and for-eigners; one privileged wing—with rations of meat and dried fruits—was reserved for unworthy Party members, or perhaps not so unworthy, who could say? They may have sold army tires and provisions, changed their names, burned their uniforms, denied the Race and the Führer, yet no sooner did they feel the robot's iron grip on their scruffs than repentance gushed touchingly forth, the faith returned, the selfless service of the past was brought to bear so earnestly that it was hard to know what to do with them, despite the implacable orders from above . . . Especially as the judges themselves . . . Here, barbed wire enclosed a makeshift jail as provisional as life itself; from a catwalk of rickety planks, with a sentry box on top, the guard could see down into the yards, the doorways, the windows, and the latrines dug here and there behind broken-down walls.

Alain lay on his belly under the sun, watching the man with the submachine gun trudge back and forth on his aerial gangway;

from behind he looked massive in his forest-green cloak, but on turning he showed the fretful face of a convalescent. The Italian was stretched out opposite the Frenchman. The Croat, lounging against the wall of the pisshouse, had stuck his legs out wide apart, trousers rolled above the knee to expose his shins and naked feet to the sunshine. His feet were mottled, swollen, blackened lumps that seemed to be going rotten beneath the skin. The Croat: a hirsute giant built for strength, now sucked dry, sunk in a permanent stupor. The Italian—short, with bright eyes and hands that seemed agile even at rest—said, "Only four soldiers, and at least seventy of us."

The Frenchman looked skeptical.

"The wire is pretty well laid out. If they rained a few more bombs over this corpse of a town, I might have an idea."

"Can't count on that," the Italian said glumly. He winked in the direction of the bushy-haired Croat. "A goner, that one. Don't worry, he only understands his own lingo and a few words of Hun, especially *Schwein*! Did you see the soles of his feet, the veins on his calves? He took a beating last night, he was hollering like ten stuck pigs. It was in the store cupboard to the right, with the iron-trellis window. They'll bump him off tonight or tomorrow when they have the time or the inclination, you know how they are. There's no gallows so they can't hang him. There's no ammo, no firing squad, they'll just dish him a bullet or two in the gut so he can watch himself die... The executioner is Henschel, the fat one who looks like Göring with fangs. Eunuch voice, eyes drowned in blubber, chestful of decorations he must have stolen... He's off duty this morning."

"And you?" asked Alain without curiosity.

"Might be down for the same treatment. I was caught crossing over the lines, my job was pouring concrete for the artillery. I might just have a chance."

"Fascio?"

"Barely. My ass was in it, but I kept my head cool."

The sickly guard's gaze wandered reproachfully in their direction. Grinning, the Frenchman raised his hand in a cordial wave, laughing *Heil*! The man with the submachine gun jumped, thrust the weapon aggressively forward, answered *Schweigen*! Silence! like an automaton, and resumed his pacing. The prisoners had a clear view of his pinched face—a child sapped by a tapeworm.

"Don't know what he's been marinating in," Alain said, "but if it wasn't his superiors' latrine, then it must have been in a pus-filled hospital."

The Italian sniggered, showing a mouthful of broken teeth.

"I reckon we're in T section: condemned to death, probably. Henschel came around and gave me a funny look from over the wall. I'd never forgive myself for getting knocked off during the last three days of the Great Reich."

"Me neither."

The guard was walking over again, without looking at them, head down. The Frenchman uttered softly: "*Blut und Tod!*" The guard stopped short and they heard him cock his weapon. "Don't move!" whispered the Frenchman to the Italian. The Croat flexed his feet in the sun. Suddenly, piteously, he bellowed over and over: "*Nein! Nein! Nein!*" Above them the guard was shaking in a fury, or a nervous fit. Nothing happened. The Croat relapsed into lethargy. Then a small man in a big peaked cap appeared in a gap in the wall and stood staring. He looked like a sun-dazzled owl. The guard trudged along the gangway. The Owl vanished, then reappeared through the pale wooden door of the yard. He hopped toward the Croat and looked him over impassively. A short length of something hard bounced repeatedly off the prisoner's bushy head, making a thick, deadened sound. The prisoner turned on his side with a groan and lay doubled up in an odd position. Black rivulets of blood trickled down his forehead. The man in the high kepi decorated by a silver eagle turned toward the other two in the yard. His boots creaked, he was trim and elegant, cinched by a black leather belt. Slope-shouldered. The Italian turned the other way and played dead. The Frenchman, without rising, executed a crisp military salute. The Owl was swinging a piece of iron pipe at the end of his fist. The moment darkened. The Owl turned on his heel. They heard him lock the door.

"Phew!" said Alain.

The Italian opened his tunic a fraction to reveal the handle of a tool.

"I had this, but we were fucked. Now shut up. There's nothing to do but stick it to them between the shoulder blades from behind, round midnight. Only snag is, we'd need to be outside."

The sun shone mildly. Now every time the guard passed by them, he slowed down. He seemed hypnotized by the expanding puddle of the Croat's blood. Alain was biting his lips. He began speaking under his breath, as if to himself, offering the back of his head to the submachine gun: "*Blut, Blut, Blut, Tod, Tod, und Tod*! Blood, blood, blood, death, death, and death!"

"Shut the fuck up, you'll get us killed!" the Italian hissed.

"Possibly," said Alain.

The obsessive litany ticked on: Blood, blood, blood, and death, death, blood and death, blood . . .

The forest-green cape halted above them, dark against an azure sky in the full glare of noon. In a low, personal voice, imitating the Frenchman's, he ordered: "*Schweigen*! Silence!"

The Frenchman merely lowered his own voice further, and it was still audible, an obedient muttering: "Blood, blood, blood, death, death, and death, blood, blood, blood . . ."

It went on for seconds or minutes, in a sluggish interval that clotted like blood. The blackish puddle spread outward. The guard walked jerkily on, boards squeaking under his weight. The incantation continued. The squeaking stopped. There was an abrupt thump, followed by a sun-drowned stillness. The guard had collapsed at the foot of the sentry box; his helmet had come off, and the childish head with its shaven skull was lolling against the boards.

"Got him," breathed Alain, his forehead dripping. "I knew it."

A whistle blew in another sentry post, rapid footsteps thudded along the boards. Some figures bustled around the fallen guard before bumping him down the ladder like a sack of potatoes. A beardless youth in a policeman's cap, with bunches of grenades attached to his belt, paced the catwalk nervously.

"Now we're fucked," the Italian said.

"Yes," said Alain.

The chain of events progressed in broad daylight as though in a madman's nightmare. The new guard looked at the coagulating pool under the Croat's thatch of hair. Alain struck up his muted litany once more: Blood, blood, blood, death. The boy in the policeman's cap burst out laughing. His laughter was answered from the remote horizon by great rumbling, like air coming out of a tire, deepening into a hurricane roar, the distant sabbath of the big guns. The laughter of the grenade-belted boy broke off in a kind of hiccup. Two important commanders were coming into the main yard; Alain could see them through the gap in the wall. The Italian rolled over onto his back, arms flung out, laughing with all of his broken teeth, all of his arched spine, his eyelids fluttering against the sun. His head lay close to the black puddle, so that in laughing he, too, seemed to bleed. The litany of blood continued, the distant booming of the sabbath continued, the placid sunshine continued, guttural commands raked the air.

The Italian and the Frenchman appeared together before the two commanders, in a spotless office with potted geraniums flowering on the windowsills. They performed the ritual salute in style. The chief of the subdivision for guest workers attached to the Extraordinary Security Service of the (et cetera), Fauckel by name, questioned the Frenchman at the same time as Gutapfel, the joint subdirector of Civil Defense under the Department for Emergency Mobilization of the Counterespionage Corps of the State Secret Police (or whatever it was) questioned the Italian—thus expediting the proceedings. Fauckel had stiff, brush-cut hair and appeared to be chewing gum, but it was only a facial tic. Gutapfel had slicked-down hair, a starched collar, a bulging tunic, and a blunt nose, like a pig's snout. The eyes of the first were tiny, creased, and watery, the eyes of the second bulged dully. Neither trusted the other. "Listen to that," said Fauckel into Gutapfel's ear, "they're going at it hammer and tongs to the north." "The north, you think so?" In the direction of our one single decent supply or evacuation route? Are we to being sacrificed like lambs, or will the evacuation orders come through in time? It's all very well to hold out and die standing fast, but who will save the nation then? We are the flower of the nation, after all. The gauleiter's last remarks were inspired by the field marshal's "Order of the Day"—as if this were a time for epic literature!

The red-eyed Owl thrust his kepi—peaked like the crest of a silver cock—between their heads; as he whispered, the two commanders stared at the two prisoners. "Very good," Gutapfel said to the Owl, "I approve!" From the next room came the exhausted sobs of a woman punctuated by cries of "I won't! I won't!" A male voice rapped "Silence, whores!" just as the artillery salvos appeared to be moving closer. "Those are our big guns," Fauckel hoped, sweaty browed. After reaming out his nostrils with a pudgy finger, Gutapfel assumed the impassivity of a younger Hindenburg. Next door the weeping ceased for a moment, then broke out afresh. "I'm the wife of an unimpeachable Party member! You have no right!" The callow and pomaded Hindenburg turned into a bull-dog about to bite. "Silence those hysterical females! Not another sound!" "Straightaway, Commander." Clicked heels and ramrod shoulders, even if they were only the Owl's, provided a heartening reminder of the existence of discipline. The cannon to the north emitted a prolonged hoo-hoo-hoo that was crushed flat by a baoom-rrh at the very instant at which the wailing—next door—was cut off. "Explain yourself!" Fauckel demanded of the Frenchman. "Pitelli, deserted to the enemy," Gutapfel read out in quiet voice. "Do you admit the charges?" The accusation—death penalty—had become so commonplace that it impressed him no more than the theft of a can of beans, red-handed pillaging, unpatriotic talk, or the fornication of a refugee's daughter with some Polish worker; if the laws were actually to be enforced in our demolished cities it would require execution squads working around the clock (when the manpower is badly needed elsewhere) and a limitless concentration camp. Fauckel listened as Alain, standing at attention, recited a string of explanations that formed an irrefutable argument like a madman's closed system. Fauckel studied this dirty, determined, reasonable young man with grudging interest, for the French were beginning to regain, in his esteem, something of the prestige of the victors of 1918. He well remembered the occupation of the Rhineland, and de Gaulle was undeniably a character to be reckoned with. Alain was breezing through a faultless enumeration of the blown-up bridges, obstructed railway lines, barred roads, and broken-down trains, the orders from one checkpoint and counterorders from the next that all together had combined to make his progress so tortuous; he did not omit to relate what he had seen at the third checkpoint—sergeants hacked to pieces in a tiny guardroom drenched from ceiling to floor in blood. *Blut, Blut, Blut* everywhere, it was terrifying, and the corpses were minus their heads! "That's quite enough," Fauckel interrupted. Due to these contretemps, the honest truth was that while Altstadt was not perhaps on the prescribed route for this prisoner-of-war-cum-voluntary-worker-on-sick-leave, he simply could not have gone anywhere else, given his firm and loyal undertaking never to infringe regulations. For some time now, Fauckel had been unable to tolerate the sight, the very idea, of blood, "our blood." He returned the Frenchman's papers, supplemented with a new violet card on which he stamped his stamp. "You will report to Workforce Center at headquarters..." Alain's heart leaped. Was there still a Workforce Center at headquarters? You've got a bad case of the runs, Commandant.

A smartly dressed housewife had already pushed past him to the desk, invoking the authority of some *Oberleutnant* and waving a paper that was not in her name but in that of a dead woman. Distracted by the pounding cannon fire, Fauckel struggled to grasp that she had been signing in the deceased's name in order to obtain her rations. "It was my sister-in-law, I've taken in her daughter, Grete, her husband's disappeared and the *Oberleutnant* assured me that..."

"Of what did he assure you, the *Oberleutnant*? That I can resurrect a sister-in-law?" He continued: "And that a forgery is not a forgery?"

His fit of bluster subsided into throat-clearing, because the paper he was reading had caught his attention.

"So your husband is in the Party, an army chauffeur?"

He most certainly is, and very well regarded, ask anyone in the twelfth sector...When evacuation orders are imminently expected, it's sound policy to do favors for the drivers, especially those of the twelfth sector. "Very good, you're free to go while inquiries proceed. Send your husband to see me..."

The Italian, Giacomo Pitelli, was explaining to Commander Gutapfel that he'd momentarily lost his head under the bombardment; his chiefs and supervisors had vanished, and there was only one way to get out, in the direction of the enemy as it happens, but he didn't realize, he thought he was catching up with what was left of the company. "Couldn't you see where the firing was issuing from?" "Apparently from the sky, sir, I swear, all hell was crashing down on top of us..." "That's enough," said Gutapfel, energetically scratching his thigh. "Court-martial, transfer him..." The Owl did not dare to mention that there was nowhere to transfer him to, and that the courts-martial were no longer functioning... After eighty minutes of business the commanders called it a day. Standing by their motorcycles, they conferred, stiff with mutual mistrust. "Not very promising," Fauckel said. "Should I evacuate the archives on my own initiative?" "Your archives are your responsibility...I'm against evacuation." Gutapfel shrugged a padded shoulder. "I'm staying, unless ordered personally." The small vial of poison, hanging from a cord against the fleece of his chest, steeled him while burning a hole in his heart. (He was counting on receiving that personal order...) What titans were about to fall! Germany would never recover. But having served in an extermination camp for Jewish vermin in Poland, he did not greatly rate his chances of "crossing over" in the event of a capitulation. This abject colleague was the last person he could tell of his decision not to be hanged by a cabal of New York Jews, now that everything was hopeless. "What about you people?" he inquired unpleasantly. "The pullback of our offices has been postponed for the moment, in view of the imminent counteroffensive, I understand." "Oh?" Fauckel had evoked this counteroffensive merely to infuriate the fanatical dullard before him, the kind of maniac who would like nothing better than to drag a whole people to suicide. "But your department is hardly essential to the front line!" Gutapfel objected, in a derogatory tone which Fauckel chose to overlook, edging closer to speak privately—for there were other motorcyclists nearby, who might have read derision or defeatism into a perfectly reasonable remark: "Whatever may lie in store, I have faith in the genius of the Führer." (If that's of any consolation to you, my friend!) "Don't we all!" cried Gutapfel angrily. You fraud, he thought, if you haven't already wangled yourself an Alsatian passport, I've lost my nose for cowards and quitters. They parted with a exchange of rigid salutes.

■

The Frenchman was wandering through the ruins. He would go up to policemen, waving his violet card and asking for the new address of the Workforce Center for Foreign Defense Workers, apparently no longer at the address marked. They answered him politely, with dazed incomprehension. Panic was rising. He drank a cup of potato-flour broth. He was hungry. His fountain pen and half of his cash had been retained by the Owl, that was inevitable. To unstitch his jacket collar and remove a banknote, he would need some privacy. Breaking in somewhere and stealing things he could sell on the black market seemed simpler and, above all, more attractive. On pain of death, of course, but then the *Todestrafe* stared you in the face every hundred yards in the form of laughable notices, treacherous holes in the road, collapsing walls, dangling power lines, uniforms of every stripe, informers without uniforms, marauders on the prowl—and it could also drop on you by the purest of chance, like a meteor. Best to not be entirely innocent, you'll feel less of a fool when you get caught.

Toward the end of the afternoon Alain's attention was caught by the shuttered prow of a house in a badly damaged neighborhood; the tradesmen's entrance was masked by a pair of tall thin walls, leaning toward each other like parodies of the Tower of Pisa, the sparse bricks sagging until the tops nearly touched, a truly comic sight . . . No imagination, however wild or drunk, could ever conceive the wealth of fantastical architectural effects to be found in bombed-out cities. Kids growing up in them may someday, as these visions mature within them, create a new art that will be neither realistic nor surrealistic, for destruction nurtures a special reality basically close to the unreal. The bogus reality of civilization reverted back to first principles, violent death, the dissolution of beings and works, the anxious persistence of a life force free of justification . . . Paintings of individual psychological terrors would seem ridiculous here. Start expressing the Great Authentic Terror, or buzz off . . . You're still busy thinking, my boy, as though it were of any use, as though there were avant-guard journals to . . .

Anyway, let's go inside! Alain tapped with sly insistence at a the obviously locked door. What if someone were taking a nap inside? I'd say, "Please excuse me, madame, sir, or would you rather I crushed your larynx and jugular with these fingers here?" Silence. The kitchen shutter was easily prized off. Alain stepped over sacks, mattresses, and broken glass to reach a small room furnished in light-colored wood, presumably occupied, for it was as cluttered with odds and ends as a fairground cart. Shiny tins ranged on a shelf contained some sourdough and bitter herbal tea. "How little it takes to reawaken my good intentions! If my unknown host turns up, I'll be all apologies. I was terribly hungry, madame or sir, and it's time you knew you've lost the war . . . Whereas I am winning it, so, though I may not look much like a conqueror, allow me to offer my protection . . ." All the same he picked up the meat cleaver, an excellent means of persuasion. If they come back in a group of two or three, I'm done for. Death is the penalty, my friend. A coin tossed in the air for the hundred-thousandth time. You can't win every time, but maybe the hundred-thousand-and-first time. Let's win!

He was winning! Bottles, poorly hidden under the couch behind books and boxes, their sealed necks protruding. Wonderful, stupendous, incredible! To be shot after getting wasted, at least that would be a worthy end. Alain popped a cork (with one blow of the cleaver) and greedily drank the Moselle, a pert little vintage ripened beneath the tender rays of peacetime which brightened your mind, revived your optimism, and reburnished the shine of your lucky star... He must have drunk too much, for fatigue began to sway in him, leaden and yet weightless. It would be risky to sleep here. The alarm clock marked five, and night would be a long time coming. The clock ticked away like all the timepieces in the world, indifferent to the colicky burpings of the cannon. They don't bother me either, my plucky little robot, so tell me, what do you have to say about the flow of time? Imbecile, you count the minutes without knowing what they are, the miser counts his pennies, the general counts his bombs, the refugee counts his fleas, the executioner counts his victims, no one knows what it is...

> One more little glass of wine
> A glass to get us feeling fine...

Good song, that! Alain smashed the neck of another bottle and drank.

> Clock! Sinister, dread, impassive God...
> Remember! *Souviens-toi*! Squanderer! *Esto memor*...

Off the mark, Baudelaire! Better not to remember. *Esto memor*, pain of death. I'm good, that is to say drunk, wine is good. *The Solitary's Wine, The Murderer's Wine.* We're all solitaries and murderers, old boy. I'm as drunk as a drunken mule. I'll piss on the carpet, can't expect me to go hunting for a nonexistent toilet.

Carpets, *lieber Herr, gnädige Frau*, are made to be pissed on the day of victory and if today isn't the day of victory, I'll piss as though it were the day of victory. And if you don't like it, landlord, I'll smash your face in, drink more of your wine, and piss again if I please.

The cleaver gleamed, last weapon of the last fighter of the last hour of the last battle of the last city... And the drunken man's eyes widened, the scenery changed. Life is continuity, death is rupture, and between the two lies w-w-war—the whoosh of shells, the towers of mounting smoke, the mushrooms of clouds, the stupefaction of finding myself intact, in one piece, little me, in my own home on the rue de Fleurus. The proof? All I need is to put out my hand—really must wash my hands, so tired, I have the hands of a road worker!—and reach over to the bookshelf, like so, and pull out my Botticelli, here it is, and open it...

Good Lord, or is it Lucifer, I no longer believed it possible. Mathilde will have a fit when she sees me here. "Get those muddy shoes off the sofa!" she'll scold. "You're priceless, Tilde..." He opened a large, coffered book. Botticellian figures of long-necked women with candid eyes, wreathed in leaves and flowers, were coming toward him. Look, Tilde! What a draftsman... that loving vigor in every stroke, that clear-eyed vision elevated to the highest degree of purity. Real vision, ideally superior to reality, just as the essential and the eternal are superior to contingency. Is it Lionello Venturi's book, or Jacques Mesnil's? Both those writers understood him. It would have taken your sad-day pencil, Botticelli, to do the portrait of a Jacques Mensil... Mesnil is dead, Sandro. Alessandro di Mariano Filipepi, Botticelli, a name like a beautiful line of poetry. His power was not to express dreams but to achieve the synthesis of a golden-age dream and a purified reality: thus he encountered the marvel of truth. Faces tend to fulfill an archetype bequeathed by the millennia which themselves refined our human features. Material faces, asserting themselves in space, pick up all the bruises, deformations, blemishes, and blurrings that our flesh of clay is prone to, and every expression of misery adheres to them. They are more carnal, more social, than truthful. Sandro restores them to an eternally adolescent oval, youth knowing neither regret nor repression, with eyes slightly enlarged for the right visual effect, because Sandro is aware of the infirmity of our eyes which he heals. Learn to see in this way, love the healer of our eyes! The eyes of Botticelli's figures bring peace—like the charm of flowers. His slim women remind us of tall young trees, pushing upward under the caress of sun and wind. No trickery here: Sandro draws his eyes by the rules, much more accurate than sight; he withdraws it from the flesh and from the abstract, this geometric magician! He puts true freshness into them, but rinsed off; he washes out your eyes from inside. Their expression is limpid, direct, they have the courage to live, they have the firmness of crystal and also a crystalline anxiety, for they have seen the mists of falsehood dispersed. They smile gravely, with darkness hidden beneath their clarity; they can look upon the tragic without blinking because spring lives inside them, their eyes untroubled by the tragedy they reflect. The fear that has been overcome but still lingers at the back of their pupils comes from knowledge and secrecy mastered by innocence.

Where's my *Etruscan Art*? In God's name what have they done with my *Etruscan Art*? I forbade these books to be lent, because who'd be fool enough to return them! He foraged among the spines, irritated, with stumbling fingers. Here was Kandinsky's book, *Abstract Art*. Kandinsky begins by lifting from reality its colors, lights, and volumes, its essential substance, and that is doubtless a process of abstraction—but it's even more a process of reduction to a concrete, rather than abstract, symbol, resulting in a densely simplified landscape. Pushing this procedure to the limit, Kandinsky arrives at a purely mental sign, as conventional as the algebraic X, which might with no loss of meaning be replaced by a triangle, an asterisk, or a dot, yes, a dot, the perfect unknown reduced to a minimum of visible existence. Abstraction, destruction. Straining to see beyond the visible, the artist is left with nothing at his disposal but a set of signs, no longer images or symbols, on their way to becoming number; hold it there, friend, you're turning away from the earth, the lovely, living earth, you're squandering the gifts of form, you're betraying the real, you're losing the eyes which Sandro had healed ... Abstraction culminates in the black-on-white grids of Mondrian: straight lines, right angles, ingenious variations on the prison-bar theme. Then poor old Mondrian remembers about color, and fills in a corner of his jail with a minute square of wash, better than nothing, to be sure; but after that, how gorgeous, how unforgettable a red blouse looks or a richly patterned scarf! All that remains of art is an imprisoned whiteness. You'll say it's powerful, and I won't deny it. Very powerful and very dead.

Prison for prison, allow me to prefer that painting by Raphael, the martyrdom of ... who was it now? Here we go, this good wine is mixing up my martyrdoms and my deliverances, much the same thing as it may be, doesn't martyrdom begin again after deliverance? That's it, *The Deliverance of Saint Peter*, in the Vatican apartments—if the Vatican has not been bombed to smithereens in a hail of deliverance ... In the foreground, the bars, the only part Mondrian would have thought worth keeping! Behind the bars, the group of warriors, jailers, and the angel, the source of celestial radiance, and old man Peter in chains, drooping, not understanding that deliverance is at hand; or understanding that it is darker than martyrdom in prison ...

Where's that bottle? There were still a few dregs from the source in it. I drink to the source, to the archangel, to the breeze beating the bushes, and no more bars, oops someone's coming. A woman, Mathilde, not Mathilde, it can't be, I hear her stepping down from a leafy grove by Botticelli ...

He shouted, "Who's there?"

He grabbed the meat cleaver. The kitchen door was opening ... "It's me, Brigitte ... Is Gertrude out? Who are you?" Alain put down the bottle, empty, saw the art books lying open, the matt blade in his hand. Waves pulsed through his head. "What? Who? Let's see, Alain. I saw you at my show, at Fortuné's, right?"

The intruder, in narrow jacket and white beret, slender-necked, was in truth Botticellian—but that poor lopsided face, those enormous twelve-year-old's eyes seared by the fires of hell, you're ill, tell me. You look crazy, that's natural, it will happen or it won't happen, keep drinking, there's more left. Alain smashed the neck of another bottle and held it out to Brigitte, golden bubbles splashing onto the books and foaming all over his hand, my hands are incredibly filthy, I'm going to disgust you, Mademoiselle. Don't drink it all, I'm thirsty too. The intruder asked, "Did Gertrude go out?"

"Out with her lover, by Jove!... Have a seat, you're charming. Not feeling so well? Make yourself comfy and tell me all about it. You can trust me, you know. My head hurts, but that's what a fine wine will do..."

"Who are you?" the intruder repeated in so penetrating a tone that she found her answer. "You're French, aren't you? An artist? But what is that for?" She was pointing at the meat cleaver. He cried out in a low voice, "Touch that and I'll..." It almost sobered him. Damn the whole pack of you, don't think I won't put up a fight! Brigitte said, "You're drunk. You can't stay here. Come to my house, where you can sleep. Come on, get up."

He smiled, beatifically compliant. Young, clear-featured, staggering with tiredness. "Your word is my command, Empress. You're superb. Have another swig to please me, and I'll finish the bottle..." Brigitte took a few swallows of the cheerful wine.

"Give me your arm. No one will ask any questions. Minus-Two knows me."

"Minus what?"

(The algebraic X, the dot, the reduction to the abstract, to nonexistence. Minus times minus equals plus...)

"Franz. He lost a leg and an arm, so we call him Minus-Two. He's a very good man."

"What if I finished him off? Then he'd be minus everything. Zero. The ideal point."

Alain spun the cleaver into the air and caught it like a juggler, nearly falling over in his exuberance.

"But there's no ideal point," she said mournfully, "and nothing is ever finished."

He stuffed the cleaver into his clothing and took the Botticelli book under his arm. Under the arch of a bridge, blown there by the wind perhaps, he searched for a glimpse of water. There was none. Brigitte helped him up a ladder. "Lie down. Go to sleep." Alain dropped onto the bed, opened the art book. The book fell from his hands. How good it is to fall asleep at last, how...

■

Every morning Herr Schiff the schoolmaster paid a visit to his lilac bushes. Neither the heat of the fires nor the cement dust in the air had deterred them from flowering. The force of simple vegetal vitality. His shrubs enjoyed more space and light, now that there were no houses around. Schiff pruned a few deviant spears, for the plant will be hardier if it concentrates its sap in a few well-proportioned branches. Then he noticed the silence. A blissful silence. Suspiciously so. What did it mean? The gravel crunched under the uneven step of Franz the cripple.

"Good day, Herr Professor. How are your lilacs doing? You're a happy man, Herr Professor, to have such splendid blooms... *Donnerwetter*! Always so pleasant in your domain."

The little garden measured less than eight yards square. Its wrought-iron railings, uprooted in some places, ballooned like a metallic sail in others. The neatly raked walk was the more enticing for the fact that it led nowhere: intimacy without issue. The diabolical stone lacework all around was kept at bay by this smooth path with its reminder that humble toil, order, and perseverance existed, and might still (albeit exceptionally) claim their reward from the very jaws of pan-destruction. To build and rebuild without tiring, without end, was that not man's mission? Or not so much his mission as his chore. How many times was Rome rebuilt? Some nod of providential approval, Herr Schiff was sure of it, had spared this tiny corner of the world for the benefit of three lilac bushes, one of them stunted...A bomb could so easily have fallen here; flames had licked at the bushes, the smoke could have suffocated them, but Schiff, his gravel, his flowers, and his gardening shears had pulled off a gentle and astounding victory.

"My congratulations, Herr Professor," said Franz.

The amputee was looking white and chapped, as though his skin were encrusted with lime scale. His voice sarcastic, slightly breathless. The hook where his hand used to be gleamed like the part of some bizarre machine. Herr Schiff felt vaguely uneasy.

"To what do I owe this compliment, Herr Noncommissioned Officer?"

"To your lilacs. Are there still any birds about, Herr Professor?"

"Yes. Look up there, a new swallows' nest, up in the corner of the third window of Herr Kettelgruber's apartment."

Of course, neither Herr Kettelgruber nor his apartment existed, but the nest was there among the ruddy stones. With swallows dashing in and out, veering through the wide bays filled with sky.

"Marvelous," said Franz.

"Indeed it is! Divine nature! What is new, Herr Noncommissioned Officer? Those swallows have returned from Egypt."

"A lot of our boys won't be returning from Egypt."

Old Herr Schiff's head wobbled erratically, as if about to lose its balance and fall off a neck which had been sliced through long ago.

"It's the end, Herr Professor, and the beginning, for as I've heard you say, an end is always a beginning...Only one never knows if the new beginning won't be worse than the end...The Americans, the British, the New Zealanders, the Kaffirs, and the Patagonians are in the city. Another hour or so and you'll be able to show them your lilacs, assuming they are fond of flowers."

"What? What? Ah yes, I understand."

But Schiff did not understand. He groped for his stick with a doddering hand. Unable to find it, he leaned against the contorted fence.

"It was only to be expected," he said after a few seconds.

"Germany is finished for the next fifty years... Fifty years, I tell you, Herr Noncommissioned Officer!"

"As little as that? And when the fifty years are up, our grand-children will pick up the noble dance right where we left off, I suppose!"

Seeing the papery old face turn haggard with bewilderment and dismay, Franz toned down his teasing.

"You are a peaceful citizen, Herr Professor. I suggest that you hang a white rag out the window. Then call your pupils together. Keep them from hanging about anywhere near the tanks. Very inconsiderate, tanks, they crush things and spit bullets just like that, for the hell of it."

"You're right, Herr Franz. I am a peaceful citizen, I have been so all my life. The true human ideal is one of orderly concord... No, I swear that Germany will never initiate another war, never... There will be no revenge, there will never be a just revenge... I say to you: Enough!"

He was rambling. He was thinking. An old schoolteacher who couldn't prevent himself from rambling when he thought he was thinking.

"How about a sprig of lilac," Franz said, "for my buttonhole?"

Lilac does not suit a buttonhole, but the unfortunate cripple is a bit touched in the head, it's common knowledge. The teacher selected a good thick spray. "Here you are, my friend. A dreadful day lies ahead..."

"Thank you. And no, not half as bad a day as some others... Good day, Professor. Lots to attend to. I fancy killing someone to round off my war... Can't decide who."

"Oh, Herr Franz, don't whatever you do shoot at the Americans! Innocent hostages would pay the price... I beg you!"

As he hobbled away, the cripple with the flowered breast threw back: "First: those innocents of yours might be the worst kind of culprits. Second: I don't mean the Americans, I mean the intolerable scum..."

"Ah yes," babbled Schiff, "I understand"—for he less and less understood.

Schiff went back into the house, took from the linen cupboard a worn-out pillowcase, tied it to a school ruler, and went outside to hang the white flag above his door. Already white rags were flocking across the ruins, some floating with the gay flutter of doves. As far as the eye could see, the whole city was covering itself with white birds, captives who would never take wing. The dead birds were born out of a humming silence, in whose depths you could make out the breathing of death throes. The teacher cupped a hand to his ear and listened: convoys on the march, here and there loud cries diminished by distance to the point of insignificance, sounds of weeping, of singing, of sharp gunshots like pinholes in space... This neighborhood seemed completely quiet. The cripple's wife, Ilse, came along with her bucket, heading for the pump. Schiff whistled like a blackbird. Ilse put down the bucket and tramped over to the window, rested her forearms on the sill in front of the professor.

"Are you not frightened, Ilse?"

"No, Herr Schiff. What should I be afraid of?"

"Are you upset?"

"No, Herr Schiff. Why be upset?"

Schiff recognized the same dusty film over the young woman's homely face and ugly yellow hair tied with a blue ribbon—a think layer of limestone dust that was probably coating every face at present, even the faces of portraits in their frames. Ilse's meaty, thick-veined fists. Her discolored nails, cut too short, exposing the animal pads of her fingertips.

"You know the city has fallen, Ilse?"

"Yes, Herr Schiff. So the war's over for us. And not a day too soon, Herr Schiff."

"Aren't you sorry at all, then, that the war has been lost?"

"Everything has been lost for ages, Herr Schiff."

So many white doves in the broken window frames of the

city...Ilse could see the lilacs beyond the professor's old white petit-point waistcoat; she spoke to them rather than to him.

"The SS are still holding out in the underground factories... They raped the female workers last night, since today they'd be dead or prisoners, they were saying...Lennchen was roughed up. Those poor men...The Poles killed several officers...Frau Hinck says they're committing suicide, lots of suicides everywhere, the Party leaders are all killing themselves...Frau Hinck says it's very grand of them, but I'm not sure. Why kill yourself? If someone else kills you, that's their business, but you yourself?...And Brigitte is dead. She spent the night before with a French prisoner...Then this soldier came last night and strangled her. She can't hardly have suffered, such a thin little neck she had...So she's at peace now, Herr Schiff."

Schiff started. "What's that you say? Strangled?" The white stitches of his waistcoat formed diamonds, the lilacs shimmered and Ilse smiled stupidly at them. The sun enveloped her shoulders in warmth.

"She's like a happy little girl on her cot. Give me some lilacs for her, Herr Schiff, lots of lilacs. It's for Brigitte."

Schiff had lost his fear of war, doubtless a great crime; but a crime in a neighboring house made him shudder. And no more policemen!

"You are out of your mind, Ilse, you don't know what you're saying!"

Ilse ignored the rebuke, she looked away, and insisted without raising her voice—her thick fingers were unpleasant to look at, as if they had the power in them to strangle.

"Give me the lilacs, Herr Schiff, or I'll have to help myself: quick, so I can fetch my water and take the lilacs to Brigitte's bedside. I'm glad for her. I really must get on now, Herr Schiff, there's the soup to cook, seeing as there's no food distribution today because of the Americans." (All at once, in the middle of her chatter, an inflexible note.) "The flowers, Herr Schiff, they're for Brigitte, and you don't need them anymore!"

"In truth, I don't," thought the schoolmaster, enlightened by an unaccustomed lucidity. "I don't need them anymore. Do I need anything, anymore?" "Right away, Ilse." He drew his reading glasses from their case and with great slashes of scissors cut a sumptuous armful of blossoms. Ilse went off, vanishing like a heavy apparition carrying off the last flowers on earth. If anything can still stir up some pride in an ossified old brain stuffed with cliché and vaporized by the heat of events, it's rhetoric. Schiff looked at his devastated bushes and told himself that he had offered up their flowers for the ravaged Fatherland. "But how did that female know I no longer needed them, when I didn't know it myself?" So many suicides, so many deaths, as simple as that! Frau Hinck is right about the greatness of the vanquished. What is greatness? Tonight, yes, tonight . . . Finish the day. Which of the Stoics said, "The sage finishes his day without complaining about the gods"? "Each seed falls at its appointed time," that was Marcus Aurelius. With a serene heart like Marcus Aurelius, Schiff sat in his study before a volume of *The History of War*, by the great German scholar Hans Delbrück. Lately, it was true, the sense of most of what he read escaped him; but being incapable of inattention, the mechanical act of reading acted upon him like a sedative. His cheek cupped in his hand, he reread the works he admired out of duty. Out of duty he slept, or tried to sleep, or thought he was asleep. Was he falling short of his duty at this time? He would not call the schoolchildren together. Goodbye, children. The murky swirling of the end of a world perceived through the end of a life filled him with dismal reveries on which he brooded in a state of bearable affliction, even contentment. Tonight, thirty barbiturate pills . . .

■

A tank moved rapidly over the paths of solitude. Hidden eyes were watching. The enemy. White signals fluttered to meet it, lifted on the breeze. The tank detoured around the fallen granite blocks of the bank, and plunged out of sight into a colossal brush pile of steel girders. The emptiness in its wake merely condensed an unknown expectancy. Then a jeep approached, moving slowly. You could see it coming from afar, then it vanished behind some stumps of dead houses, reappeared in the vicinity of Schiff's lilac bushes, and advanced toward the pump. Suddenly there were children running to meet it, waving white flags . . . They were overcome with curiosity, avid anticipation of violence and handouts. The enemy was not scary close up. The enemy was distinguishable only by small differences in the color of his equipment and the shape of his helmet; under a coating of chalky dust, such differences were less noticeable. The jeep driver's ugly face looked comical and fierce, but he was laughing. The jeep pulled up by the pump. A fat man got out and splashed water on his hands and face. Another fat man, platinum-blond hair surmounted by an undersize overseas cap, stood squarely, legs spread, hands on hips, surveying his surroundings. His was wearing beautiful boots and green sunglasses. No one had ever seen a big bushy mustache like the one he sported. Probably some big shot. The driver was busy with his motor.

Ilse came out of her room, lugging her pail again. At the sight of the newcomers she caught her breath, hesitated for a quarter of a second, and walked up to the pump. "*Guten Morgen*," she said, fixing the enemy with a long frosty stare. The driver rolled his shoulders. "*Guten Tag*," he replied caustically from beneath his helmet. He was holding a shiny metal wrench in his fist. Ilse wondered whether he might not crack her on the back of head with it as she bent over the tap. She reckoned it wouldn't be enough to kill her, but then there was the cooking and the housework . . . The sound of Franz's crutch making pebbles fly was audible close by as he labored up a low rampart of rubble. He surged into view in front of a bearded officer, who lowered his revolver when he saw him. "Okay!"* greeted Franz cordially. "Hello!" said the bearded officer, sounding perplexed. Instead of looking at the conquerors, Franz turned his attention to their machine, making small clucks

---

* The following exchange is conducted in English in original French text.

of appreciation through pursed lips. "Well, well," he coughed, in a bid to get maximum mileage from his ten words of English. With his good hand, he took the liberty of prodding one of the tires. Superb piece of manufacturing! Synthetic? The guy with the beard offered him a cigarette. "Thank you." "Speak English?" "No." The crippled vet's face split into an friendly grin. Herr Schiff was approaching with measured step, leaning on the antler handle of his cane. The Schulzes all emerged from their lair together, the wife, the children, the man in his cap and sweater. Other people were appearing across the ruins like larvae emerging from the soil—and they were indistinguishable, on the whole, from the inhabitants of Chicago's slums or any other poverty-stricken corner of the world. A rather elegant woman, wearing a Red Cross armband on her jacket sleeve, climbed down from a sort of chicken coop stuck to the side of a blasted building. A thin, hairy young man, lost in an outsize tramp's overcoat on which he had pinned a red, white, and blue ribbon, jumped off the ladder and loped unsteadily toward the jeep. His wild eyes and big, gesticulating hands would have made him quite frightening, had this been the time for fear. Everyone stared at him. On his way, he knocked over a little Schulze, pushed Ilse aside, blurted "French war prisoner!"* in a voice from the other side of the grave, and opened his arms wide ... One of the Americans punched him lightly in the ribs, made him stagger, caught him in a bear hug, and the two men clung to each other as though wrestling, about to collapse in a heap. "Christ almighty!" gasped Alain. "I don't believe it!" Someone was slapping him on the back hard enough to dislodge his lungs. Someone else stuck a cigarette between his chattering teeth. There were friendly faces in broad daylight, USA insignia, a genuine jeep, white rags snapping in the sunshine as far as you could see, an emaciated Brigitte smiling for eternity on her schoolgirl bed, with something of Botticelli about the hardened oval of her chin; there was a hail of luminous stones falling overhead, each stone an idea,

* In English.

an unbreakable reality, an incredible certainty, a grenade of rapture which could never explode . . . We're alive, rescued, delivered, how hollow the words sounded! Victorious, does that make me a victor? Shivering, gripped by a burning chill, Alain chewed on his cigarette. "Speak French,* anybody? Quick! *Schnell, schnell!*" The fat important one with the green sunglasses said, "*Je parle français* . . . Journalist. Paris." Alain drew himself up before him like a marionette, like remorse itself, crying in a low voice, "The hell with Paris! The guys in jail . . . Did you think about the jail?" "It's bound to be occupied by now," said the journalist, who had no idea. Alain's vehemence was spent. The nurse took his arm. "We thought of that too," she said gently. "Oh, you did . . ." Alain tensed again. We the impotent, we the moles under the ground, we the less than nothings! "You're special, Erna," he said, spitting shreds of tobacco. The green sunglasses turned to Erna Laub with amusement. Heavily powdered, her lips rouged, the nurse looked almost insolent, as if wearing a Prussian mask. Make mental note of this vignette. "Health service, Fräulein?" "Underground," the woman replied. "What?" "You understood me perfectly, I hope."

There was a growing circle of people around the jeep. Here, as elsewhere, the vanquished were behaving with curious familiarity. The kids, fairly well dressed, however did they manage? The women, worn to a shadow . . . The journalist chose Herr Schiff, an average elderly German, former officer and civil servant by the looks of him; he beckoned him to come over. Schiff, fulminating against the universe, didn't budge. The journalist moved toward him. The children, interested, stepped out of the way. The journalist introduced himself in passable German. He mentioned his press agency, whose name meant less to Herr Schiff than the canals on Mars. The old man introduced himself in turn: "Professor Herman-Helmut Schiff." "If you'll allow me," the reporter said, scrawling a few shorthand signs into his notebook.

"Now then, what do you think about the Americans?"

* In English.

A didactic question could never catch the professor off guard, for he was constantly putting them to himself, and supplying interminable answers in the form of monologues upon eugenics, the world conceived as a representation, the genius of race, or the political errors of Julius Caesar and Wilhelm II.

"A very great people, the Americans...The United States is presently the foremost industrial power in the world, and superior at waging war...On the other hand, there is a certain lack of social cohesion and spiritual tradition..."

"You think so?"

"Beyond a doubt," Schiff declaimed, getting into his lecturer's stride. "You will realize that in fifty years."

"Phew, we got time to turn around then."

A swift pencil and shorthand pad recorded the schoolmaster's extravagant ramblings for the benefit of countless newspaper readers.

"Do you people feel guilty?"

If there was one emotion which had never been experienced by Herr Schiff (at least not since his adolescent religious crises) in his half century of diligent service, that emotion was guilt. It is healthy to live one's life in the meticulous fulfillment of duty. The schoolteacher cocked his head obligingly. "Pardon me. I didn't quite catch...?"

"Guilty for the war?"

Schiff's gaze swept the horizon of the broken city, strewn with the dead doves of humiliation. The grander generalizations existed for him on a different plane from everyday reality. The Second World War was already down as a great historical tragedy—a quasi-mythological one—which neither Mommsen, Hans Delbrück, Gobineau, Houston Stewart Chamberlain, Oswald Spengler, or *Mein Kampf* could elucidate entirely...The sons immolated themselves upon the altar of blind gods. A new, unholy war, unworthy of human nobility, had begun with the destruction of Altstadt; and this war alone existed in reality.

"Guilty?" Herr Schiff said in flinty tones, with the air of a livid turkey-cock. "Guilty of that?" (And he bobbed his head at the surrounding devastation.)

"No," the reporter said patiently, not quite grasping the response, "guilty for the war."

"And you," Herr Schiff retorted, "do you feel guilty for this?"

Franz could not contain his delight. He slapped his thigh uproariously. "*Wunderbar*! Wonderful old idiot!" Alain's hairy face expressed furious disgust.

"My dear Professor," the journalist began, striving for an offensive politeness, "you started this war... You bombed Coventry."

"I?" said Schiff, in frank astonishment. "I?"

Several women were following the exchange from the sidelines, noting the green glasses and heavy mustache of the American and Herr Schiff's upstanding attitude. They were too discreet to come close enough to hear properly, but it seemed certain that important matters for the neighborhood were being discussed. Franz butted in unceremoniously: "Well, I fought in the war, as perhaps you can tell by looking at me. I give you my faithful, one hundred percent amputee's word of honor that I didn't start it."

"Herr Professor," whispered a daring old lady in a black lace cap, "do ask them whether the soup kitchens will be allowed to continue? Or do the American gentlemen intend to feed the city?" She spoke the last three words more loudly, to make sure that the authority would hear them. The reporter's eyes popped with outrage behind his shades. No shame, no guilt, not a shred! These folks seem to think we come over, leaving a hundred thousand of our boys underground along the way, just to sort out their next meal! He turned on the old lady.

"Madam, have you ever heard of a place called Dachau?"

Intimidated by his tone, but happy to help out, she quavered enthusiastically: "Oh yes, it's a pretty little town in Bavaria, where they held interesting popular festivals in the old days... "

"That's all?"

"Yes, sir... " (The old lady blanched at the covert fury of the question.)

"What about the concentration camp?"

"Ooh, that may be, I can't tell you about that, I'm afraid . . . I so seldom read the newspapers."

Franz was grinning maniacally. Alain's face too was that of a madman, a dangerous one. The old lady felt inexplicable tears wetting the corners of her eyes. She murmured, very humbly, "I beg the gentleman to excuse me if I offended him," for these were clearly military persons of influence. Schiff was aware that his height, his age, and tonight's thirty barbiturate pills gave him the edge over the other man, whose exasperation was patent. "I bid you good day, mister journalist!" he stated with pointed courtesy, and turned his back.

"They don't look like bad men," a woman was saying. Schiff paused, looking sternly down his nose at this housewife. "The Americans are not bad men," he informed her sententiously. "No more than are the Chinese, dear Madame. But we have been defeated, Madame, and you must never forget it." "Certainly not, Herr Professor."

The burly officer with the round beard, like a sailor in an old-fashioned illustration, hailed the reporter. "We're leaving, old man! Happy with your little interview?" "They are staggeringly unconscious of everything," the journalist said, climbing back into the jeep. "Well, if you're looking for consciousness from bombed-out towns . . ."

Ilse carried her full bucket inside. Franz inhaled the fragrance of a cigarette from across the seas, incontestably superior to the Party cadres' special-issue reserve rolled with the last of the Bulgarian tobacco. "They take good care of themselves, these victors. Victors always do," he said to himself, feeling queerly elated and at the same time inert. An exquisite satisfaction weighted his whole body down with languor, as though he had just made love well, his arms and legs intact, with a vigorous, clean-smelling woman. It was only an hour ago that Herr Blasch, vicious dog of the Special Surveillance Unit, was getting ready to mount his bicycle, knapsack on back, swaddled in musette bags, pockets bursting with banknotes and forged documents, when suddenly he saw the barrel of a revolver appear between his eyes at the same time as he heard the cripple say, "Have a nice trip, Herr Blasch!" amplified by the trumpet blast of the Last Judgment . . . The ants were presently taking care of this turd of officialdom. "I sure fixed him!" thought Franz sarcastically. "My war's over. The sun's out."

■

Stupendous lawn! The thick grass was pampered as men nowhere are! Mowed to the perfect length, watered every day, and doubtless nourished with vitamin-rich chemical fertilizers . . . The lawn sloped down to the river, on the far side of which more gardens rose toward their villas. I'll be damned! Some people were living the good life right up until yesterday. People for whom "the Great Reich in danger" was more than a hollow phrase!

In every war there is a rear that holds better than the front, a rear fat with noble sentiments, creature comforts, and lucrative deals; this rear, which balances the front, makes the insanity total . . . The beaches of California still exhibit, in season, a full complement of pretty women with smiling thighs: such is the natural order of things. After all, there's philosophical solace to be found in the fact that some still live while others die, an obvious improvement on everyone dying . . . But it is no longer possible to embark upon a coherent line of reasoning without falling into absurdity. Thinking this way, Alain felt indulgence, tinged with temptation, toward those pretty Californians. What had they to do with these people, this upper crust of profiteering slavers? He floundered in contradictions. The villa next door belonged to a Standartenführer (to be killed, no discussion!) whose two daughters were said to be charming . . . Innocent, you think? Innocent? He dimly hoped they would fall into the hands of the most brutal convicts . . . Have I become a brute myself?

Alain, after waking between fresh sheets, had just shaved. He was "swimming" inside his new clothes, but the fabric was luxurious and the trouser pleats ironed...This manicured landscape, twenty miles outside the corpselike city, carpets over the parquet flooring, all the faultless appointments of a civilized gentleman's home...A bastard, in any case, the civilized gentleman: the worthy pastor, a Lutheran and a Nazi for good measure, a fat Christian, blesser of executioners, is probably trudging along the highways of defeat right now, among the uniforms at last marked out for a just destruction...Alain stood before a crucifix, his face blurred by sadness. "He made a proper fool out of you, Nazarene, didn't he, this pastor of your flock of bastards?"

The night before, Alain and his companions, having entered the picture-perfect little town like a gang of scary tramps, were shocked at the sight of prosperous homes with well-tended parterres of flowers and windows nestling in ivy. It was such a strange spectacle that they had to force themselves to enter a garden and knock on a door. As soon as their fists touched this door, they wanted to smash it in. A white-haired woman opened it. "*Was wünschen Sie, meine Herren?* What do the gentlemen wish? The reverend is out..." Now they were "gentlemen," now they could have "wishes"! The old housekeeper recognized a Dutch laborer among the group, who began shouting hysterically at her: "Out, you bet he's out, and he won't be coming back neither, the old swine!" A torrent of abuse followed. Fortunately, having heard nothing but seemly language during her forty years in service, Frau Hermenegilda failed to comprehend the epithets directed at her. She was deafened by bursts of shrill, stallion laughter. Hairy paws were almost on her, like in one of those horror films. Images of rape and murder flashed through her crafty child's brain. Must push the door, slam it shut! *Mein Gott!* Several beggars shoved past her. The Frenchman said in a voice you didn't argue with: "Get out, Madame. Take your clothes, your guts, and go. I give you ten minutes to vanish, you old tittle-tattle. This house is requisitioned, understand?" Requisitioned is a word everyone understands immediately, and here the hairy young man's rough German was as plain as day. But "old tittle-tattle"? What did that mean? Was it very rude? Frau Hermenegilda, backed against the wall, clutching the silver crucifix on her bosom, drew courage from the fact that requisitions are legal procedures—the reverend himself drove a requisitioned automobile... "Might I see a warrant, sir?" This reasonable query opened the floodgates. A gorilla in rags lurched into the drawing room and, grabbing a valuable bronze, hurled it against the family portrait. The noise of splintering glass was followed by that of imprecations and a scuffle, as the others fought to overpower the vandal. A demonic mouth was snarling into the old retainer's ear, "*Raus*! Get out! Clear off, you sawdust fart, you old boiled tarantula! If you weren't so puckered up I'd ... Beat it or I'll kick your ass inside out! *Raus!*" What godless bandits were these? Frau Hermenegilda shrieked for help, but she lost her voice and all that came out was a plaintive meow. A flat blow, as one beats a carpet, silenced her; when she came to her senses her cheek was swelling, the doors of neighboring villas were being kicked in and the Frenchman was leading her to the kitchen, saying, "Put a wet towel on your face, there's nothing to fear, Madame, just get your things and scram, that's all we ask." He cuffed the Dutchman in passing. "Leave the prune alone, Petersen, we're not that desperate..."

Frau Hermenegilda showed proof of character. "So the war is over. And not an American policemen in sight! My God!" She donned her mistress's best remaining coat and took nothing with her except a jewelry box overlooked by the reverend, and him such a careful man as a rule. He won't see his baubles again, thought Frau Hermenegilda severely, serve him right for leaving me in the lurch. She ran away across the lawn, a little black crocheted hat squashed over her white hair. When she reached the hedge along the river, she spotted, through the branches, a switch of ginger hair that could only belong to Paulina, Doctor-at-Law Freidrich Ochsen's junior housemaid. "Paulina!" Frau Hermenegilda cried. "Come here quick, girl, the most disgraceful things are going on!" Where had the little redhead got to? The old servant was sure they'd be safer, the two of them, hidden under the hedge. And then, suddenly, for an unforgettable instant, all she could see was the open mouth and staring eyes of Paulina, her hair spread out on the grass. A man was arched over her, Paulina was gasping. Frau Hermenegilda ran away down the river path. "Jesus and Mary, Jesus and Mary!"

Unimaginable house! The victorious prisoners saw themselves in a picture-book setting—ready to burn the fucking thing down! The semicircular drawing room, the organ, the framed photographs, the books in their glass cases, the pure-white kitchen that made one want to spit all over it, the bedrooms... Petersen crawled into the marital bed, boots and all, chortling with satisfaction. But when he spied a photo of the newlyweds on the wall— the handsome officer, the bride in white—he jumped out of bed for the pleasure of grinding it under both heels.

Alain chose for himself a girl's bedroom on the second floor, whence an unexpected view of the wide green lawn brought him down to earth like a billy club to the kidneys. A short redhead, her fists screwed into her eyes, burst from the bushes and began stumbling across the grass. A black figure came after her, joined her, pulled her back toward the hedge. The little redhead didn't struggle... "Fine time for a marital squabble!" thought Alain. Then, as he understood, he shrugged his shoulders. He sat down on the bed, elbows on knees, head in hands, concentrating on the blue cornflowers of the pitcher on the washstand. Drunken giants' footfalls reverberated on the stairs. A door was broken down in the attic. His buddies made as if to enter more than once, but each time Alain turned toward the door, looking like a crazed invalid, and in a mechanical voice said, "Leave me alone, huh!" He only knew one thing, something he could not articulate even to himself. It's all over. Finished. What is finished? Dry-eyed, he wept. He wept in spasms, his whole body trembling.

That was yesterday. Today he was washed clean, replete with half a chicken brought in by scavengers, and draped in an excellent suit that was baggy at the armholes but too short in the sleeve and leg (the pastor must have been slightly obese): Alain was becoming himself again, like the others. The atmosphere of this wealthy suburb spared by the bombers gave him a bitter feeling of well-being. The Croat's blood spread into a puddle on the cement. Brigitte's throat bore the shadow of petals pressed there by a strangler's fingers. The ruins stank, the ruins snickered. And all the time this lawn was basking, gilding itself in the sun, and the reverend and his missus were being served lunch in the dining room. A little worried to be sure, but not for reasons of remorse... The world was in its death throes, we were dying like flies, these people were dining in their customary way, official, overweight, at ease, accomplices in everything... No one will ever understand it!

Alain was beginning to own things again: the Botticelli book lay open among the covers of his bed. Would you understand it, pure eyes, unveiled by Sandro? The very silence of those eyes seemed to say: Peace, be at rest, we see the other side of the world, think about what we see! And little by little, silence actually overcame the tumult. Alain roamed from room to room. He let his fingers idle over the organ keys, releasing an invisible treasure of colors and tears. Church music, the tango, Rachmaninoff, Debussy, they still exist somewhere! The idea was oddly funny and painful enough to make your head spin. Alain contemplated the flowers, he stopped to admire those of the carpet, he bent to touch them. He took men's shirts with starched fronts out of the drawers, he felt like slashing them, but they would find buyers on the black market, got to be practical. Someone had already made off with the silver from the sideboard, but the glassware remained, useless transparence, limpid transparence; when Alain raised them carefully to the light, tiny leaves etched into the crystal sprang alive with rainbows... There were Bibles, theological tracts, books of canon law—canon law, tell me if that isn't splendid! Burn them, burn the lot! But he couldn't summon the energy to do it.

In the study he took the pastor's chair, tinkered with a pencil, opened a leather folder and found blank sheets of headed consistory paper. His hand, unprompted, began to draw. The elongated body of a woman, hanging, with a thick rope around her neck and a smile of ecstasy upon her face. A rough-hatched sketch of the Arc de Triomphe at the top of the Champs-Élysées. Ruins and helmets. A skull, frontal view, superimposed. In one of the sockets a clear pale eye, a Botticelli eye, a gaze of sad innocence, a gaze of forgiveness...

He stood up, eyes moist, teeth chattering, shouting, "There is no forgiveness! There will never be forgiveness! Not for them, not for us, not for anyone!"

Alain tore the sketch into tiny pieces, flung the pencil out of the window, and ran to put his head under the faucet.

■

It was on the path along the river's edge, reminiscent of a path along the banks of the Seine, that he recovered his peace of mind. An extraordinary woman was strolling toward him under the yews and willows. She arrived on an old-fashioned tram. Erna, not pretty, better than pretty. "I was looking for you. How are you feeling, Alain?"

"Magnificent. How about you?" He kissed her. "You know, I've just made my first drawing. It's years since I held a pencil. A madman's drawing, naturally...I was shouting with fury over it. But it wasn't bad..." He was exultant. "How lovely it is around here... The war's over."

"Nearly," Erna said. "And the consequences are about to begin."

"What consequences? What do you mean?"

Thus began a long, digressive exchange between them which resembled the sparring of masked antagonists who were deeply fond, deeply mistrustful of each other and delighted by every sudden chance to face each other, for a moment, with their guard down. "Erna, you're worth several men," said Alain. "I see through you, more than you think. You are strong and full of faith." ("Less than you imagine," thought Erna.)

Alain, lying against a tree stump, looked up to where she sat, sharp-kneed, too preoccupied to reassure him.

"Don't think too much, Erna, it drives you off the track. It becomes unlivable. The good thing about war is that it leaves no time for thinking. All you care about is not getting killed, finding something to eat, killing someone else, destroying something, and holding out another day. It puts your consciousness at ease, by suppressing it. The misfortune of prisoners is that they have time . . . I've just spent two extraordinary days, Erna, windows flying open inside my skull, my skull was like the ruins, with empty casements gaping on all sides, the sky pouring in, and the winds, the memories, the future, all this in the form of ideas without form. I couldn't sleep, nor could I make any order out of the mess in my mind. I let it go, I thought: Either I hang myself tomorrow, singing 'Why do you tarry under the moon, Marlene, Marlene?' or else the mess will settle, I'll see things more clearly, decisions will have been made . . . It's now been proved, Erna; I'm not destined to hang myself. I've decided."

The nurse found him childish.

"And what have you decided?"

"I'm changing my life, changing my soul. I've realized that everything in this world is geared to destroying mankind, to destroying me, among others. Everything: even the faith I once had. The Party, the triumphant revolution, I used to believe in all that. Deep down I still believe in it, but only as one believes in a dream after waking . . . I am on my own. I have the right to want to live, even through the decline of Europe. The right to defend myself and to run away. From now on I only want to serve life—my own to start with, the only one I've got."

"But your life will no longer be of any use," Erna objected.

"Say rather that it will no longer be of any use even to me? That I won't be able to forget and that I'll be a mere ectoplasm in the ruins or join the rodent band of schemers and survivors? I was afraid of that. But no. I am alive. I am the proof that some such remain! I take things in my hands and I work and I make something exist that didn't before. I'm nothing, you might say? I take destruction, suicide, folly, grief, and joy and I create something new and meaningful out of them, I restore meaning to the corpses of men, cities, and ideas, to the thistles growing over them, to the stars that rise in the sky despite everything, to the lovers who walk over the earth or lie decomposing beneath it... From all this I knead an unknown substance which is my gift to all eyes, or to some eyes..."

"Art?"

"Yes, art, though I think I despise that word. I know too much about its impotence. I've witnessed the exhibitionism of those greater or lesser swindlers who are more con than artist, I know all about the scams of dealers and merchants, the publicity circus and the snobs in New York or elsewhere who gush—whether it's a piece of shit, a bloody marvel, or a dark conundrum—'Too too fantastic, darling!' Art be damned, if that's all it is! But who is to bring the first hint of order to chaos, of light to the caverns, of hope to the graveyards, of balm to the wounds, who is to place a love incarnate among broken beings, an irrefutable reason beneath the cataracts of absurdity? Who else but the artist? Tell me who!"

Erna answered feebly: "The revolutionary."

"Oh, really? Show me one, give me one name—a living one, mind you, because we could make up a dazzling catalogue of dead ones. I've been through the east, between escapes and arrests, I went over the lines with some German refugees. I was robbed, beaten up, and what have you by the comrades, I don't hold that against them. I know what they've suffered and are still suffering, and I know what man is now. I sought among them men of faith, men of ideas, men of justice. At first my fresh illusions were protected by an elephant's skin of ideology. Then I found the men I was looking for. They were all convicts. Every machine rolled over them. Little lieutenants who were big brutes would blow their brains out as an example, to scare the rest. I remember one of these killers shouting: 'I need to speed up the pace here, work faster!' I watched the road crews hacking away, nothing but women, children, old men, and I don't know what else, not to speak of enemy prisoners. I saw them bogged down, squelching half starved through the Lithuanian mud, first-class mud it was too. It was easy for them to escape by burrowing into the mud, at the risk of getting buried and of getting your companions shot for it . . . I was working there too. One day on a slippery, disintegrating embankment I met an ex-sailor who spoke French, knew Marseille, who had just returned from the penal colony at Kamchatka and was nostalgic for the fisheries there. 'So how many of you are behind the great Fatherland's barbed-wire fences?' I asked him. 'Millions,' he answered, without appearing to say anything sensational. This made me furious. 'You're lying! Someone should have perforated your counter-revolutionary brain long ago!' 'You have a point there,' he said seriously. 'I don't know why I'm still trying to hang on . . . They promise us pardons and bonuses . . . But listen to me, brother, before you condemn me out of ignorance.' We spent an hour together in the rain working out the rough statistics, by social class and by region across Eurasia . . . He'd been expelled from the Party, a militant from 1920 who had heard Lenin speak in the factories . . . A patriot and a socialist in spite of it all! Tell me it isn't true!"

"It's true," said Erna. "I know it better than you."

Alain seemed sadly satisfied.

"Once I knew a man who was authentic. A man who served. Who probably carried out his fair share of dirty work as well. A man of knowledge and will. He was strong. I believed in him. And I believed he betrayed us. I would happily have killed him. Now I understand. The traitor was myself, who understood nothing. There's a truth about man and a truth for man, don't you see?"

"Quite so," said Erna dryly. "Who was he?"

He told the story as though he were sketching successive images on a pad. Erna saw a familiar face come together in the silky river dappled with leaf fronds and patches of sky. It was exactly the feeling she had experienced, in another universe, when writing the rigorous, nebulous text of a private diary whose every line was surrounded with blank spaces, silences, shadows, secret lights. She tasted sand on her lips. There is no escape from oneself or from numbers. Numbers are what give rise to chance, and this can be a prodigiously significant flash of light: the thing that counts.

By breaking the rule of secrecy, Erna unconsciously made a decision without which she could never have pronounced the syllable formed by a single initial.

"D," she said. "I knew him too."

Alain felt no surprise. The nature of his astonishments had changed. An exploding bomb would have startled him, but only out of instinct . . . But that there should be virginal grass, a simple possible future, this troubled and confused him.

"Well," he said simply, "then you know what kind of man he was.

"Peace must be declared to the world, and at long last all the victims must be told that it's over, over for good. That we will reconstruct with justice, after a ruthless cleansing, without forgetting that it's the most wretched who have the greatest need of justice . . . Proclaim freedom, even in the midst of abysmal poverty. They hardly go together, true freedom and miserable poverty amid the rubble and tombstones; you don't need much Marxism to see that. But the match is necessary if moral poverty is not to be added to the other kind. How can the survivor be consoled, how can he regain hope and courage if he's not allowed to have his say—and if he stammers, that's his right!—and to shoot his mouth off if he feels the urge? It's a relief to mouth off when you're backed into a corner. How can we reconstruct without first constructing a new chaos, but a chaos this time of ideas, utopias, vengeance, and generosity, an unheard-of freedom—which would be quite simple in reality?"

"Yes, but how?" wondered Erna.

Alain continued slowly, as though groping for something in the dark.

"But where are the men? Where are the grand ideas? Perhaps ideas are nothing but ephemeral stars. They point the way while they last, and then they go out, and other stars should flare up . . . But they haven't yet. And everything has been done to stamp out the light of minds. The old revolution is dead, I say. We need another, completely different revolution, and I don't see it anywhere. Are you angry with me?"

Erna felt more nauseous than she ever had in the field hospital's operating room.

"No," she said, "go on."

It was a superhuman effort not to implore him to stop. "*You must* hear this voice, Erna. *You must.*

"It's a great thing to have won, but victory is hollow if it isn't the beginning of something else . . . Wild beasts have always known how to vanquish. What will victory bring us? A tiny drop of equity, a tiny extra drop of humanity in an ocean clogged with dead bodies? Or the most highly mechanized secret and visible police forces?

"What about you, Erna, what will you do?" Erna was taking stock of her problem. Return to the great land of mute suffering? Already, while writing her latest report, she had felt uncertain about what political orientation to adapt to. Once the official line was established, this ignorance might become suspect in itself. She wished she could say, "Just let me go back to Ak-Aul, let me be a desert recluse again, writing my notebooks and burning them afterward." Unthinkable words. Her one glimmer of a chance lay in feigning mindless zeal. Get an interview with the chief of the service, seduce him not so much by her devotion as by her willingness, quickly accept an assignment in Paris, Rome, or Trieste and resume her clandestine activities. During wartime, it was facts about the enemy that were wanted, the stark truth about resources, risks, losses, hopes. And there was no ambiguity as to the enemy's identity or the necessity of destroying him, no doubt about the action to be undertaken which—transcending crime—became the saving exploit. Now, already, the smokescreens of doubt and deceit were spreading irresistibly. H, the liaison officer, had told her: "Your memorandum must stress what people think about us: the populations, the women, the Jews, the Americans, the prisoners, don't leave anyone out . . . That's essential . . ." Essential, ha! But how to say it? How to report the rumors of terror seeping from the liberated countries, the comments upon the rumors, the despair of so many comrades? It would be criminal not to record the truth. To record it would be worse...H also said, "For us, esteemed Comrade, the war continues...Indeed who knows if... Can two such different worlds coexist? We are the stronger by virtue of planning, realism, and discipline, and we have hidden allies all over the world...Our opponents enjoy technological superiority, for the time being, and wealth. But technology can be learned and wealth can be conquered. There are no clear boundaries between war and peace nowadays...Wars may be waged almost invisibly. Be very careful." Wisely feigning to agree, Erna had stocked up on dollars and was close to obtaining an excellent passport...Years passed, wars passed, crushing millions of innocents, cities crumbled, a civilization was dying, and the same problems were rearing their heads...The river shimmered.

"It's four o'clock," said Erna. "I must be off. Will you go back to Paris?"

"Straight through the Porte de Bagnolet, the fastest way...But you, come on, you're not going to remain in these graveyards, are you? Save yourself. We've every right to put life first, when what reigns is death."

These words revolted her. (We have no life beyond working for a great common destiny. And what work is that, Alain might retort—is it humane and decent, is it liberating? By saving ourselves, we attempt to save what little we can save...)

"So this is where we've come to," she said.

"Where? You look like you're talking to yourself. Your face is all twisted. What's the matter?"

"Nothing in particular. Goodbye."

She thought: Farewell.

IV.

Journey's End

And let fall the smoking rains
over the cerebral forest!
So many funeral masks
lie preserved in the earth
that nothing yet is lost.

THE PASSENGERS on the first ship to leave port the day after the end of a cataclysm in no way resemble the passengers escaping on the last ship . . . The refugees of the recent past carried the mark of defeat but also the joy of surviving in the middle of the storm. Some of them escaped with nothing but a shirt and a few papers, enriched—as well as ravaged—by ideas. Of another breed altogether were the two dozen passengers of the Swedish freighter *Morgenstern* (*Morning Star*). Outwardly, they belonged to a vanished or vanishing world, to a stable world impervious to apocalypses in which bank accounts, business deals, government ministries, compliant women, expensive liquors sufficed to make human existence bearable. A mix of businessmen and envoys, of women, middle-aged and younger—many of the latter sporting rank in various armies. One guessed the women had lovers doubly influential—in the bureaucracy and in semi-legal businesses . . . The gentlemen, frequently drunk, bandied stories about their times in Cairo, Bombay, Moscow, São Paulo, Ottawa, Tunis, or Sidney as though the globe of the earth were a ball for them to play with. They paid court to a chestnut-haired woman dressed in vibrant colors, who had been parachuted into Lombardy . . . Now the parachutist exhibited a coarse laugh, a worn-out voice, an athletic bust, and the inability to stand alone at the rail or suffer more than three minutes of conversation if it did not include open allusions to her femininity or valor.

Very different, this crowd, from the people at the front—or for that matter at the rear in the hospitals and shelters, in the railway stations and on the roads. As different as show dogs are different from the cringing, abandoned curs of blasted cities; as different as stallions on a stud farm from the sturdy ponies with matted coats and penetrating eyes patiently pulling an ambulance cart through the mud of the Ukraine under gray lowering clouds. "Domestic animals," Daria reflected, "also participate in our sociology of iniquity, but they have no choice..." She was thinking too that the organization of today's world has attained a perfection singularly hostile to men who suffer as well as to better men. The glaciers of the Himalayas, the jungles, deserts, and oceans have been conquered by motors more magical than any flying carpet; but this has not made escape, or the fulfillment of dreams, in any way easier. In order to cross borders, however fluid, you need to possess the mystic bureaucratic passwords of secret services and government stamps—those ridiculous, often sinister talismans; this magic can only be countered by the science of connections and checkbooks. Ordinary people—people, simply—can no longer move from one continent to another, as nineteenth-century emigrants used to do; neither flight nor discovery is open to them, neither enterprise nor mission. The pioneer life is denied them, although half the earth's surface is waiting to be cleared...If Europeans were permitted to colonize the poles, Uganda, Rhodesia, the Ubanghi, the Matto Grosso, millions of eager daredevils would sign up with a fierce acquiescence—of which perhaps three-quarters would perish; still in a hundred years, the poles and the equator would be rich in scientists, philosophers, and artists, richer than golden-age Greece (which was an age of slavery). A cynical mystification presides over the captivity of peoples and individuals. The barriers against mobility are counterproductive, patently designed to be outwitted by their proper targets. These nets trap none but the anonymous irregular, the stateless refugee, the veteran of selfless struggles (for what could be more suspect than the generosity of idealists?), the fugitive from persecution whose papers were lost somewhere between a lake of blood and a penal colony, the good European thrilling to the call of distant lands, the Jew unnailed from his unimaginable cross. After the barracks of torture and humiliation, who wouldn't appreciate a vista of palm trees over blue water? It should be an inalienable right . . . But the pillagers of the wrecks that were once sovereign states, the painted-over citizens of the sham democracies, the traffickers entrusted with profitable economic missions, the spies and the disinformation merchants, these by contrast know all the rules of the game. They fly at whim across the oceans as though the laws of mechanics and the strategic map of the world were theirs by rights (which they probably are). In this still-mysterious mutation of a civilization, it may be that such hybrid beings, their vitality all the more exacerbated in its final upsurge, will prevail for some time . . .

The freighter was making its way through the unstable element, cleaving the green seas. How many similar freighters and handsome steel submarines lay at the bottom? No one seemed to care . . . Daria was traveling on her last passport, her last money; outside every law, very possibly pursued, free, free!—but distraught. The last passport, as authentic as it was fake, delivered by her liaison officer, would within weeks be transformed (if it were not already) into a pass into deadly traps. The last dollars were barely sufficient to cover the expenses of this complicated journey, and would run out in three months. If she failed to locate D on the other side of the Atlantic, there was one final resort: a painless injection. Reassuring thought. Because, you see, there's the philosophical "why live" and the concrete why (and how to) live; there's the hunted individual, his unfailing will to live, his goals, infinitely greater than himself, his impasse at the end of a barren wasteland, his solitude there, the impossibility of scraping a hundred dollars together . . . Though not afraid of nothingness in itself, Daria felt unsettled by its approach, for she was delighting in being alive ever since the high seas had filled her lungs with bracing salt air and her senses and mind with an immense, intelligible poem. Suicide is often an act of vitality, and even—if it is not the result of neurosis—the act of a person who is powerfully attached to life. Eminent psychologists might dispute this, but only because they know nothing of the scientific experience of their colleagues who committed suicide in the ghettos . . . Daria clung to this argument, because she felt attached to too many things.

In a word, she was happy. The frenzied weeks of preparation, the lies she was forced to sow around her, the masks she had to wear, the sleepless nights, the crises of conscience in which true conscience played no part—usurped as it was by fear and a childish docility—all this was blown away by the sea air. She couldn't stop smiling. Mr. Winifred, a businessman from Oslo, complimented her on her eyes: "They have the very hue of water at the crest of a wave . . ." "You're being rather poetical," she replied inanely, with a pointless laugh that made her look fifteen years younger—younger by one shipwrecked revolution, several descents into hell, and a universal war. Mr. Winifred said there was a poetry of destiny in business; that he had begun to write a play when he was twenty, that he would visit the Museum of Modern Art in New York. "Was it Shakespearian, your early drama?" "No . . . Closer to Ibsen." He relished the opportunity to pronounce, for the benefit of the traveler with the eyes (that was it! Ibsen eyes!), a roster of potent names: Brancusi, Archipenko, Chagall, Henry Moore—the very latest in ultramodern moderns, and you'll never guess the sums they go for! Mr. Winifred confided that, thanks to the war, art was acquiring new value. "I dare say it is," exclaimed Daria warmly, "a profound value of creation and reconciliation . . ." Mr. Winifred listened distractedly to things said by women. He was listening to himself. Pillaging had given rise to a black market of minor masterpieces; under the auspices of this trade, the production of forgeries registered an unexpected increase; and some forgeries are themselves masterpieces! The Latin American market lapped up everything indiscriminately, for newly acquired or expanded wealth appreciates old masters and dependable moderns. Mr. Winifred, a specialist in the minerals trade, was expanding for pleasure his collection of mostly religious works from Eastern Europe. Under the Nazi occupation, old families were forced to sell their heirlooms, while representatives of the Great Reich conducted a roaring trade in the spoils of confiscation. Knowledgeable dealers combed the terrain from the mouth of the Danube to the Baltic, swiping the aristocracy's every precious icon, seventeenth-century portrait, landscape, and battle scene. The treasures of the old worlds are being carried away in the deluge, to the profit of the quick-witted denizens of the new world—a thought that made Mr. Winifred smile slyly, for he was of the new world, and nothing if not quick-witted.

Mr. Ostrowieczki joined them from the bar, and the three of them leaned their elbows on the iron rail over the heavy, lava-slow seas. Mr. Ostrowieczki, an engineer on a government mission, had a broad, pale, fleshy face, a shaved scalp in the Russian style, a taciturn disposition, and pearl-gray irises so pale that they sometimes seemed white. Daria disliked him and he ignored her, preferring to flirt (like a bear in a tweed jacket) with a member of the Women's Corps of an army that had covered itself in glory. The notion of the wealth of the old and new worlds merging under the pressure of merciless events provoked in him laughter more sarcastic than porcine. His tiny pearly pupils contemplated the waves as he said—congenially, for he too was half drunk— "Ha! Ha! Lots of artworks will be drowned, not that it matters to me. It's only old art perishing..." Daria felt a secret jolt. "What do you mean?" she demanded point-blank. "Old feudal art, old religious art, old bourgeois art... I am an engineer, Madame, and for me there's nothing more beautiful than a turbine." Daria threw him a sharp look which unsettled him. "The wind is coming up," he went on, "how about something to warm us up, below?" Daria acquiesced. The technocrat's bare, high cranium preoccupied her. She was all too familiar with this summary ideology, these doctrines set in polished stone—invented during the age of Einsteinean relativity! Mr. Ostrowieczki avoided speaking to her again, wisely, for she would have found him out. In the mess, they played gramophone records while the sunset glowed through the window frames like a memory of horizons set on fire.

How easy it had become not to question herself about anything without blaming herself for egotism! The vastness of the waves filled the terrestrial half of space; the rocking of the world lulled the soul into a sleepy sense of liberation ... Daria mingled sociably, to the point where a lady drew her aside and prayed to be allowed to divine the secrets of her palm. Its lines spelled a shattered destiny (hardly difficult to read, in the palms of our time!). "Ah, my dear! If only you would dare speak to me openly! And you could, I assure you, for I understand every sin, every crime ..."

"Do you see many crimes in my hand?" Daria asked curiously.

"Heavens, no! I didn't say that! I didn't say anything of the sort, now did I?"

The lady was a young fifty, reading a Charlotte Brontë novel; she was petite, carefully made up, decorated with several ribbons of merit; she was on her way to join her husband, a civil servant posted in the West Indies. (There are dozens of islands in the West Indies, however the lady didn't name hers.)

"Yes, you did, you were talking about crimes."

"Oh dear, I didn't really mean that at all ... You're so nice, so reserved, so silent ..."

"Are those the marks of criminality? Or of capital sins?"

"Perhaps," the lady replied. "To each his marks ... Look at that black bird, there, following the ship ... Isn't it romantic?"

A solitary bird alone in the middle of the ocean was "romantic" indeed. For the second time, Daria felt pangs of foreboding; but then dismissed them, charmed by the gentle rocking of the waves and rediscovering through it a love for all things, a deliverance. Daria pushed her anxieties aside. "We'll see when we arrive." Everything was simple, in reality; the little social menagerie on board, elementary; Daria did not think she was being followed.

■

She had to keep moving to economize her dollars. The American cities she glimpsed might well have struck her with awe, had she not settled into a contented torpor, with no other lucidity than the practical—tensed toward the goal...This giant civilization, these vertical cities where the pedestrian feels insignificant, sees himself numberless, suddenly realizes that the real world is his and that nothing is his since he himself is nothing...An atom is all and nothing in the universe; these crowds, so well dressed, so busy, so cheerful, so callous...Atoms are unaware of themselves and unaware of each other, even in the densest steel...Daria kept moving. Mr. Winifred said hello to her on Broadway; hours later, Mr. Ostrowieczki was standing ten feet from her in the subway, though he did not see her. These chance collisions of atoms were enough to make her tremble. The traveler took obsessive precautions, vanished into elevators, fled, alone, quickstep down corridors on sixtieth floors and at one point looked down on the prodigious stalagmite city from a rooftop terrace: this was the wide gateway to a continent into which all of unfortunate Europe would pour if it could...The sky and the sea were as gray as tears. If the shaved head of Mr. Ostrowieczki had chosen that moment to appear on her crag of reinforced concrete, Daria would have vaulted the parapet and dropped into the vast human emptiness. Alone among the rain-swept pedestrians, she felt herself buoyed by an enthusiasm that was stronger than despair. The power of mankind rivaled that of the ocean. All that was needed was to heal mankind...

She saw plains, the empire of wheat; at the smallest bus terminals, the restrooms were luxuriously clean; the newspapers ran to forty pages, offering comfort-enhancing gadgets at bargain prices (sums which elsewhere would represent years of toil or self-denial), the opulence of standardized apparel, the hum of classified ads alongside detailed reports on the famines and massacres which were the dreary staple of other continents...That this could appear normal, acceptable to one who had just changed hemispheres, was disconcerting; but no more mysterious, perhaps, than the physical well-being of a people emerging from the home where someone very dear, someone very great, someone irreplaceable has just died after a long and painful agony...Or was it evidence of total absurdity? Of the irreparable disequilibrium of our souls thirsty for justice, fairness, kindness—concepts alien to the gyrations of oceans and planets? But would there be oceans and planets without equilibrium, necessary rhythm, and musical harmony? What would intelligence, what would pity be, divorced from the quest for a luminous equilibrium expressed by the stars themselves, the structure of molecules, the graceful proportions of a bridge flung over a river? Several times, on buses racing along sleek highways, laundry flapping from the upper stories of tenements, Daria had to hold herself in to keep from laughing and crying, inconceivably happy, suppressing her angry distress, and finding within herself only a childish answer: "They're alive! Alive! It's splendid how millions of people are alive while..."

All she had to pin her hopes on were two addresses in the United States. If both of these spider threads broke, what then? Then nothing! Having preserved them in her mind for years, she now fretted over the accuracy of her recall until one morning her memory was a blank. It was only to tease herself, for they were also written down: in code in a notebook and plain but scrambled in the double sole of a shoe. The first, in Brooklyn, had already been ruled out—a wisp of smoke long since dispelled into the steaming plumes of New York. She was all the more happy, if the state of tragic, spellbound euphoria in which she moved could be called happiness. "I consent to my disappearance..." No one needs me over here, I very nearly no longer need myself. To disappear in a world where nothing could disappear, where a suicide's gunshot was equal in insignificance to the striking of a match, to disappear into this outpouring of plethoric energy might be a bitter outcome, yet not altogether desperate.

None of this slowed her down. The second address led Daria to a small town in Virginia and to a white colonnaded porch that reminded her of the dachas of small Russian landowners in the old days, in Chekhov's time. She pressed the bell as blithely as a gambler throwing the dice for the last time, nearly certain of losing, having lost everything. A colored butler let her into a vestibule which was overbright, overdecorated, apparently purposeless. The thread is about to break, everything is meaningless. Daria inquired after a certain lady, but instead of answering her: "Nothing left for you but suicide, Ma'am, in approximately four weeks..." the black man inquired, "Are you expected, Ma'am? Whom shall I announce?"

I'm completely unexpected and don't announce anyone! "Just a minute," Daria said. She got out her notebook, wrote "D sent me," and slipped the page into an envelope. "Please give this to the lady of the house..." Good domestics never betray surprise. A woman with over-dyed red hair received her immediately in a small sitting room cluttered with cushions and floral arrangements. Visibly flustered, she was crumpling Daria's note in one hand while the other plucked nervously at the blue beads of her necklace. Her pupils were enlarged by as if by fright.

"What do you want from me? Who are you?"

"Please forgive my turning up like this... There's no danger."

"And who is this D? I don't know any D."

What a stupid lie, Daria nearly said aloud. You must know several names beginning with D... Just stupidity. "You're my prisoner," Daria thought spitefully, for she hated the cushions, the bouquets, the showy lampshade... The woman tore up the envelope and its contents, brushing the pieces into an ashtray. "You'd be wiser to burn them," Daria advised hypocritically. Her hostess was pink and blowsy, a shapely little gourmande.

"If you didn't know D, you wouldn't have invited me in. There's nothing to fear, at least not from me... You've got his instructions. All I need is his address."

"This is ridiculous! It's a mistake! Who are you?"

Daria, as if looking for something, opened the leather-bound book she held pressed against her bag: *Leaves of Grass*.

"Ah," her hostess said, her face clearing, "you're reading Whitman?"

Never, perhaps nowhere, did the poet of "Salut au Monde!" ever dispel such dark suspicions as he did then. The two women looked at each other simply. "Actually, I've been out of touch with him for years..." said the red-haired lady. "Take this down. He's in Mexico...Throw the address away when you've memorized it..."

The spider's thread had held against the storms of earth and history! "I don't have to write it down," said Daria, "my memory is good." She tried to spark a contact. "So is yours, I dare say..."—meaning, we are alike somewhere, we know what no one can know or understand without having ventured down certain dark pathways...

"Are you going to join him?" asked the auburn lady, confidentially.

"Yes." "For the same reasons?" "Could there be others?" The two women felt that the passing years diminished the reasons for assassination. The red-haired woman took Daria's dry hands between her satiny palms. A current of intimacy shot between them. The woman began to speak in a low, feverish voice: "How terrible the world is...I used to believe with all my heart and soul... Don't mention me to him, I'm of no interest now. Do you need funds? Are you sure? Really and truly? Are you sure you haven't been followed by...by anyone?" "As sure as I can be..." "Well, if ever...you'll say you only know me from Paris, from the Sorbonne. I'm so scared...!"

"Scared of what?" Daria said casually, not really asking. She shrugged her shoulders, suddenly withdrawn, overcome with distaste for the expensive comfort of the room, the heavy drapes, the Skye terrier that trotted in twitching its ears. What would be so scary if you lost your cozy decorations, your husband or lover or both, if even you found yourself in jail, Madame? The contact was broken. The woman saw Daria to the door. Outside, cars slid over the damp pavement. Tall yellow trees arched elegantly over the avenue; politely inclining their branches, natural conformists, they appeared to following the autumn fashion; the homes spaced at intervals amid shrubberies looked as blandly identical as the different guests at a dinner party.

At the corner of the drive, a young woman was leaning against the door of her car. Had Daria done more than register her without seeing her, she might have detected in this American girl's eyes the impassioned gaze of her own twentieth year. But Daria only noticed a gray suede jacket, the cut of which she appreciated. The thing we least recognize in the eyes of others is the flame of our own youth...

■

The white floor of clouds ripped open like magic disclosing sun-gilded hills, the whole living map tilted beneath the plane, a city spread around pink cathedrals, marooned in the arid land—a city like nowhere else on earth, drowsy with sunset, flushed as the sunset, fringed by the desert, abandoned to the sweetness of existence...Donkeys laden with heavy baskets stepped delicately down streets of earth between pastel-washed walls. Windows framed by wrought iron, awnings sloping over narrow sidewalks ...Old cobblestones, and every door gave onto another sculpted door, holding back a mass of greenery. Enchanted city. The meat displayed on the counter at the back of a shadowy butcher's shop exuded a charm of dark blood: the butcher's shop was called the Flower of Paradise. A small black-haired boy was carrying Daria's suitcase on his shoulder. He might have been a dark angel, an unwashed cherub with tough little muscles and a little heart that was very violent, very pure...Humble and proud: so must the angels be, who walk on earth as Indian children.

The large rectangular plaza was strung with white bulbs, spangling the blue translucence as though for a fete of long ago. Stately trees loomed over it, and above them rose the old towers of the cathedral, bathed in a fading radiance that would never wholly fade, it was so pure, so richly infused with the expiring colors of the sky. A chattering broke out as legions of wings, excited by some infinitesimal disturbance, described an aerial arc from one canopy to the next...Cheap bars turned on a rainbow of lights which did not clash with the sunset. Brown heads floated aureoled in wide pale sombreros, black hair cascaded over young girls' shoulders. Barrows of fruits and sweets trundled by, like displays of massive gems formed by the genius of color itself for caressing the eye...In front of a rudimentary grill heaped with dark organ meats glistening with grease, three hatless men stood in a row. All three curiously shapeless; the first olive-faced, the second lemon-faced, and the last with a solemn death's-head perched on his neck; violet glints fell as three pairs of sticks flew up and down the wooden keyboard of the marimba and crystalline music poured out. The little dark angel glanced longingly at the marimba. Daria signaled him to stop. They listened for a moment, the visitor from another world of cruelty and the Indio child caked up to the eyes in dirt—to wide eyes as dark as agate, as expressionless as polished agate. The music cradled a canoe floating invisible among festoons of creepers, long ghostly lizards lay in wait beneath tepid waters in darkness... "What's your name?" Daria asked the dirty angel, to break the spell. "Jesús Sánchez Olivares, at your service." She heard only his first name of Jesús. Listen to the music of innocence, Jesús, if you can...The boy added in dignified tones, "You may call me Chucho, Señora"—that being the diminutive of Jesús. When the music stopped, Chucho produced a copper coin from a pocket of his torn pants and put it into a musician's hand.

Daria avoided the tourist hotel, repulsed perhaps by the frigid glance of a blond traveler who stood smoking at the entrance, his Leica dangling on his chest... "Not these creatures, no no no..." "Well then," proposed Chucho, "I can take you to Don Saturnino's hostelry..." Where better to spend one's first night in Mexico than under the roof of Don Saturnino? "It's clean, and much cheaper," the boy told her. "So you're not an American?" "No, I'm not"—but she didn't say what she was.

The majestic door of the Casa de Huéspedes opened onto a little blue alley which wandered off toward a mountainscape resembling a cloud-covered sea. The lighted patio was nothing less than a green fairyland of tall plants. A fountain whispered. Under the mysterious seclusion of archways, a bare bulb lit what must have been the laundry area: two dark-skinned girls were slowly moving about there, one dressed in beetle-wing green with a glint of red, the other in nuptial white. They appeared as the sacred spirits of this place, but they were simple servants, busy with the ironing.

The voyager found herself face-to-face with an idol standing out against a background of huge green leaves; it was surely very old, made of a gray porous volcanic stone. The hero or god was squatting on his heels, hands on knees, forgetful of movement. Its head was girded by an intricate diadem. The massive face, as large as the torso, was stark, attentive, abstract. "The god of silence," Daria decided, "the only one of the ancient gods we should think about resurrecting…" The god seemed to answer her: "You are welcome here, Señora." It was the guttural voice of Don Saturnino, who indeed looked very like the god but with a clipped white mustache, earthy wrinkled skin, two gold teeth, and a short white jacket stitched with green arabesques. He was totally incurious about her. The names and papers of his guests concerned him no more than their itineraries. He sprinkled his laconic remarks with a *bueno, bueno* that implied nothing in particular; mentally continuing his game of dominoes with Don Gorgono, he quickly sized up this undemanding pilgrim, not rolling in dollars, harmless, one of those forlorn ladies who often retire to a pueblo, to collect the local pottery and write—or not—a book…He showed her to a spacious room covered in tiles, opening directly onto the patio. "The shower is here, Señora." A tiny light was burning beneath a votive picture of the Virgin in glory. The air was cooled by a breeze like a clear pond.

Daria had her broth, chicken, and rice served to her beside a spindly bush, some of whose leaves were green and others bright red…Don Saturnino ambled over for a smoke. He had the head of a marvelously human, friendly chimpanzee, penetrated with a peculiar intelligence. His straight white hair was cut short. He looked at the voyager with eyes both sunny and remote, as though to say: I have nothing to say to you, but your presence pleases me; I see many things in you that do not concern me. Pleasant cool of the evening! Daria spoke first.

"Your country is very beautiful," she said.

"*Verdad*? It's a magnificent country, Señora, an opulent country..." (Don Saturnino made no attempt to conceal his pride.) "And yet so backward! A country of much poverty, as you will see... Are you planning to visit the Lagoon?"

"I am," Daria said, startled.

"From here you can only go to the Lagoon, and no farther than San Blas..."

Daria repressed a shudder: San Blas was her goal (just beyond San Blas).

"Are there many ruins around here?" (She knew from the guidebook that there were.)

"We live on top of ruins, Señora. But there are not so many in these parts. The pyramids of Isla Verde, you can reach them by boat from El Águila... And up in the sierra behind San Blas there is Las Calaveras, the Skulls, an ancient altar of sacrifice. Many thousands of years old."

(According to the books, these Aztec, or Toltec, or other ruins were at most a thousand years old. But here, in the everyday strangeness of this courtyard, exact chronologies—always a chimera—counted for very little. One was closer to the time scheme of rocks, of plants, than to historical time calculated by learned men...)

"Thousands of years," Daria echoed, entranced.

Don Saturnino liked a woman who was attracted by the centuries. He remembered his youth, and his eyelids crinkled. He said, "I fought for the revolution here, in my country. We made a good stand at Isla Verde, on top of the pyramids..."

"So, you fought for the revolution too," went vaguely through her mind.

"*Bueno, bueno,*" went on Don Saturnino. "There's a tourist at the Hotel Gloria, he's traveling in a very fine car... a Mr. Brown. Perhaps you could arrange with him? Our buses are so poor, Señora."

"What tourist? Do you know him? Where is he going?"

The genial brown face dimmed. "He is an American. I saw him in the plaza. He has a fine car...I like horses better, horses are intelligent..." Daria explained that she wished to travel alone, at her own speed. "I understand. *Bueno*...Good night, Señora..." Don Saturnino went to lock the outside door with a big, old-fashioned key. Some of the bush's leaves were a beautiful red, the color of fresh blood, of dark blood, of pink blood. It was a *nochebuena*, "Tree of the Blessed Night."

Even on a good map, San Blas figured as nothing more than an insignificant circle marked on an ocher stain between the shore of the lake and the hatching of the sierra; no roads passed through, no trace of an Indian settlement. The lake spread out among wooded hills, but here was only rock and sky. The end of the world—in this part of the world. The automobile road ran along the Laguna, passed through the mountain village of Pozo Viejo—Old Well—descended toward San Blas, then cut at right angles away from it. The dotted line of a track seemed to follow the shoreline farther, petering out after a few miles...Bruno and Noémi Battisti were probably living at that spot. From the city to San Blas it was a good five hours by bus. The guidebook discouraged expeditions in that direction: there were no first-class hotels, no unusual fiestas, no famous landmarks, no indigenous crafts to speak of, nothing but harsh mountains, the Indian earth, the ancient race, unembellished...The map brought a smile of reminiscence to Daria's lips. Far north of the Trans-Siberian, beyond Lake Baikal, the maps would look much like this one, highways bordering desert lands, and the guidebook, if there was one, would inform of another Isla Verde: "On Green Island stands a tumulus attributed to the Reindeer Civilization..." There, too, the years are counted in the thousands. Under a wan Nordic sun, the solitude might be broken by a sinister encounter with a penitentiary work brigade...Special travel permits would be required...Even more essential, a special armor for the heart, to guard against pity. No Trees of the Blessed Night, only dour, rugged conifers, planted along the slopes like a mounting crowd, an austere motionless army, endlessly measuring the harsh grandeur of existence... Earth, our mother, your deserts are sisters.

On the roads around Samarkand you would ride buses much like this one. Now discolored by dirt, scratches, and dents, it had once been blue. The skins of the men and women who traveled in it were bronzed, burned, golden, coppery, ashen, mirroring the hues of sun-soaked boulders and composted earth, revealing the mix of bloods. The taciturn watchfulness of their eyes, the power of their muscles, their human indigence approached the animal— as did their natural nobility. Their antique Asian faces were pleasant—more closed than pleasant. Silver crosses on strands of coral beads hung over white embroidered blouses (loose blouses, similar to the smocks worn by Komi women in the upper Volga...). The driver was a frizzy-headed, negroid athlete dressed in a pink shirt; an image of the Virgin and a profusion of ex-votos composed of nuts and miniature revolvers filled most of his visual field. Instead of forty passengers, the heroic rattletrap took on seventy, plus their hens, turkeys, cats, and a fighting cock. A brown child slept in Daria's lap; beside her the mother suckling an infant, her swollen breasts as matt as sunbaked clay; she must have been about fifteen, and crossed herself at every pothole like an old woman. So much sweaty flesh, soiled whiteness, patient breathing, and resignation filled the bus that Daria saw little of the ruddy incandescence of the countryside... "San Blas!" The frizzy-haired driver helped two passengers down, a centenarian native woman and the foreigner. The engine hiccupped once and the bus was gone. Balancing her baskets, the old Indian woman was already climbing the slope, following an invisible path between outcrops singed with rust; her bare feet gripping the stones like a faun's. She plodded steadily on, bent double, toward a bare, gray summit under the reddening sky. When she vanished between the boulders, the solitude was for a moment total.

"Journey's end," thought Daria.

She also thought of snakes: of the graceful snakes that must lie coiled everywhere unseen in the rocky wilderness, of the huge stylized serpents of these people's ancient art, of serpents of fire, serpents of night.

All of a sudden two dark children dressed in white rags materialized in front of her. They pounced on her suitcase. One said, "To Don Gamelindo's," since clearly the stranger could be going nowhere else along this stony path, indiscernible at first, then lined with wild nopals, bristling with thorns, pathetically twisted . . . The path forked toward tumbledown walls. And Don Gamelindo's store appeared in the corner of a small rustic plaza: arcades, tall trees outlined against the sunset, baroque church set apart on a crest overlooking the lake . . . Daria had no time to appreciate all of it, so quickly did the night come down. An electric bulb cast a desiccated glare across the store. The counter, the ropes, the candles, the piles of shoes, the rolls of cloth, the bottles were immersed in emptiness and silence . . . The dark eyes of a thin-necked nocturnal child peered out from beneath tangled hair but said nothing. They seemed to be the eyes of motionless things. Don Gamelindo appeared at Daria's back, seemingly from nowhere. He moved without making a sound. "*Buenas noches*, what do you want?" Thickset, unshaven, in shirtsleeves and waistcoat, with a paunch sagging over his belt and a holster on his hip. His complexion was pale, his small greenish eyes shifted watchfully between puffy lids. Daria explained that she was looking for the plantation of Don Bruno Battisti. Even as she spoke, she felt a sensation of total uselessness. Nothing could exist for her here: no past, no present, no continuity and no tomorrow, no questions and no answers. She herself would cease to exist in the eyes of anything that might be knowable. She nearly said, dreamily, "Where are the snakes?" A hostile land, sharp rocks, aggressive plants, oppressive silence, a night for a disappearance. Don Gamelindo answered, "Yes, La Huerta."

As he studied her—if indeed he was taking the trouble to study her—he seemed to be waiting for the silence to complete its work of destruction.

"But you can't go to La Huerta tonight. You must spend the night in San Blas."

"Where?"

"At my place."

He barricaded the street door. A raw smell of tanned hides filled the air. Don Gamelindo's hairy pink hand protected a candle from the dead breeze. They crossed a large, dark courtyard under a ceiling of stars. "In there." Daria obeyed, like a prisoner. She ducked into a whitewashed room containing a prisoner's pallet, a stool, an earthenware jug, and an altar to the Virgin where he placed the candle. The door of disjointed planks was secured only by a hook and a nail. The candle shed an amazing light.

"No danger at my house," said Don Gamelindo. "Sleep well. God protect you."

As he left, he added, ceremoniously: "Don Bruno is my friend. I'll take you to him tomorrow."

His friend? Sacha, the man of ardent ideals—what a strange friend for him to have! "Thank you," said Daria. "Good night."

She was not offered anything to eat. She drank some cool water from the jug and walked around the yard. The ocean of constellations sparkled sharply. Shooting stars darted between immobile stars. The Milky Way lay like a blurred serpent across the heavens. A murmur rose from the lake, the croaking of toads grew louder, coyotes howled intermittently in the distance. The complaint of silence. Suddenly Daria was faced with a shadowy beast—hairy, bulky, humble. A tiny speck of light, like a fixed star of infinitesimal size, pinpointed the mule's eye. Comforting presence . . . Daria rubbed her fist over its warm withers.

"Well, well," she said to herself, "here we are, saved; here we are, completely lost . . ."

Almost the same silence as in Kazakhstan, and almost the same firmament; but Daria recognized none of the constellations.

"All the pages of life are torn out..." The fullness of the night remained.

■

Out early into the yard, Daria renewed contact with a splendidly simple world. Purple sprays of bougainvillea poured over the broken walls. A thicket of menacing nopals—fleshy green—bristled vehemently, and they bore bulbous flowers of a delicate red. A yellow campanile rose above its surround of tall trees, hairy with creepers trailing from every branch. The brightness of the morning was expanding into a vivid symphony of color that promised to intensify almost beyond endurance after this hour of exquisite softness. A monumental joy—not of living, more primordial than that; of existing—conjoined earth and sky in the embrace of the light. Naked toddlers with bulging bellies scattered at the sight of the foreigner brushing her hair at the door of her room.

Don Gamelindo was a different man by day. "Can you ride a horse?" "Oh yes..." Now he seemed reduced to a pair of stumpy legs supporting a disproportionate stomach, with the aid of a belt pulled up from his crotch to his hips. On his holster was incised the round face of the Aztec sun god, with forked tongue stuck out. On his head was a tall white conical hat worn horizontally just over his eyes. His small features, modeled out of the rosy clay of his flesh, were marred by countless small pockmarks. He was laughing to himself, exposing rotten teeth; a friendly effusiveness animated his sly green eyes without relaxing their vigilance. Daria realized that he found her attractive, as had Don Saturnino. "¡*Gracias a Dios todopoderoso*! Thanks to God Almighty!" he said, thanking the Creator for this morning's welcome distraction.

Once or twice a year, female American tourists drove up to San Blas in their heavy motorcars, flounced into the store, asked for Coca-Cola, refused to drink from glasses that had been washed in the pure water of the well, drank out of silly paper cups. How stuck-up those fair-haired women were, like their well-groomed dogs who warily sniffed our half-coyote mongrels—so reliable in dangerous situations—from a cautious distance. Don Gamelindo quadrupled his prices. The tourists snapped their cameras at the church, the naked children, the view over the lake . . . The women's tight slacks flattered their rumps indecently, so that the village elders were of two minds about allowing these women dressed as men into the church. A wise man carried the day (in favor, there being dollars at stake) with the argument that "since trousers on a woman is the Devil's doing, let it be the Devil's business to roast her in the next world." (All the same, the equestrian statue of St. James the Sword-bearer was kept covered up in the presence of slacks, for he is easily piqued and quite capable of retaliating with a wave of drought or smallpox . . .) How different was this woman, in her sandals, plain black skirt, white top, and broad-brimmed Indian hat; how different her muscular arms and erect carriage, her face, still young but aging already; the calm severity of that face! Don Gamelindo guessed that she was unlikely to believe in God (may He forgive her), was not especially rich, and had known many men without becoming soiled; some women are like that, like horses caked in lather and the dust of the road, who emerge from the lake cleansed, so noble of form, so glowing with sunshine that you feel proud of them and proud of yourself.

The horses trotted down a narrow lane of emerald green. It could have been the entrance to a labyrinth of vegetation. On both sides tall, rigid cacti raised airy walls traversed by light and breeze, bristling on every side with nasty spines . . . Planted this way, these *órgano* cacti were used to fence-in yards. The stony soil was red as rust. There was to be no labyrinth; the countryside opened out, or rather the desert, surrounded in the distance by a broken line of glinting arid peaks . . . Makeshift crosses leaned here and there by the side of the track. Don Gamelindo remarked, "Our 'little dead.' All in the prime of youth. Quick little bullet, quick little death. Youth must have its day, *verdad*?"

The graves took up very little space under the brilliance of the morning sun. To their left shone the Lagoon, like a sheet of quick-silver.

"It's not like this in your country, Señorita?" inquired Don Gamelindo, easy and heavy in the saddle, barely remembering back to when he was young himself, lying in wait at sundown be-hind these rocks to settle family scores with the Menéndezes... He was a better shot than any of them, shooting only when he was sober, whereas they would drink before an ambush, boasting that mezcal sharpened their eyesight. Big mistake. "May God forgive them!" The tombs of the three Menéndezes—Felipe, Blas, and Tranquilino—had long since disappeared, and in the mind of their now-respectable assassin the memory of those treacherous Sunday evening gunfights had become depersonalized into a tale of manly murder among others... Folks nowadays are going soft, there are too many laws, the slightest brawl makes headline news because reporters—*¡Hijos de puta!*—need to earn their tortillas and greasy refried beans... Don Gamelindo jogged along, lively yet unhappy to be growing old in an aging world... In some far-away land, for a woman like this—and young!—a few skulls must lie buried by the side of the road... This thought made him swivel gracefully in the saddle toward the woman riding behind him.

"In my country," Daria answered, "there was the war... And if, in my country, we were to plant little crosses by the wayside for every murder victim, they would spread over the immensity of the continent to the horizons, to the pole..." Even at this image, Daria remained smiling, because her joy—trotting through these spaces of pure barrenness, pure sunlight—was stronger than all else, was pure.

Don Gamelindo encouraged his mount with a soft cluck of the tongue.

"I heard about that," he said. "The war between the Jews and the Nazis. War is impious. God preserve us from wars and revolu-tions, eh, Señorita?"

By luck, Daria's horse made a bound forward, so she didn't have to answer him.

■

The sierra was becoming more and more torrid; the lake gleamed like molten metal in a crucible. They rode through the fiery monotony without talking, without thinking, without dreaming, with no sensation other than the furnace above them. The plantation came into view, an oasis of green. They entered the enclosure, a wall of rough stones. They saw a man in white standing under a cluster of big, smooth-barked trees nearly bare of leaves but sprouting white flowers. Hands on hips, he was overseeing the work of two half-naked Indians as they shoveled earth from a trench. From behind Daria's eyes floated the memory of an illustration from a childhood book or perhaps a propaganda manual: "The Planter and His Slaves." The planter turned toward them. He raised a hand in greeting. A floppy palm-fiber hat obscured much of his face. Not until they were three steps apart did Sacha and Daria recognize each other, and the look they exchanged was so fraught with apprehension that they had to feign joy at seeing each other, force themselves to smile while shaking hands as though they had parted the day before. The presence of Don Gamelindo, far from being an encumbrance, made it easier for both of them to put the right face on things.

Bruno Battisti's first thoughts were: Why is she here? To kill me? Unlikely after all these years. I sank into obscurity, I kept quiet. To escape herself? Then she's probably being followed. Women are never rational enough about covering their tracks. It's her they'll be after, but they'll throw us in for free. Nothing could be easier, in this place...Accustomed to ordinary, everyday dangers, but long out of the habit of those mysteriously organized threats that close in out of nowhere to ensnare you, he shuddered. "Is it really you?" he said to Daria. "What a happy surprise..." "Sacha, I've run away," Daria whispered, aware of his fears, yet ecstatic—as if a cup of joy, downed in one draft, was going to her head. "Don't look at me like that, there's nothing to be afraid of..." (Not that assurances made any difference!) His gray eyes brightened the way they used to. He shrugged his shoulders; older, stronger, sunburned.

"That's magnificent, my friend. Here you'll be safe. Life. The desert. See how beautiful it is."

From the height of his velvet-and-silver-decorated saddle, Don Gamelindo, framed in sunlight and by looming green shrubbery, smiled down at them like a grinning Chinese mask. To Daria, back in her picture book, he was the image of their master: "The Foreigner, the Planter, and the Great Cacique." Banana trees bent their fronds over tumescent fruit. Coffee bushes climbed the slopes. At the end of the avenue of greenery appeared a plain white house surrounded by slender palms. "Please, don't say anything upsetting in front of Noémi. She's very vulnerable," said Bruno Battisti.

"Please dismount, Don Gamelindo, and come see my improvements! We're piping water in, and building a reservoir..." All that could be seen of the two men digging the trench was their bronze backs, gleaming with perspiration. Spadefuls of ferrous earth, as if tinged with blood, landed noiselessly at the horses' feet. Daria, in her sad ecstasy, thought of a grave. An Indian led the horses away. Don Gamelindo was saying, "You should finish that reservoir. The rains are coming and the earth is parched. There were clouds over El Águila just now...A good sign."

He crushed tender coffee leaves between his fingers and smelled them, raising a connoisseur's eyebrow.

"Healthy plant, that, and the right species of Uruapan...Did you hear, Don Bruno, about what happened at Pozo Viejo the other week? Basilio Tronco killed young Alejo Reyes...That's more trouble in the making. The Troncos have sent a calf to the chairman of the town council."

"Ah," said Bruno simply.

"And in San Blas, the youngest Álvarez girl has got engaged to the son of the lawyer Carbajo. You're invited to the fiesta."

"Please thank them for me. I'll do my best to attend."

Don Gamelindo took a moment to reflect on what further news was worth sharing.

"Yes... Sunday's cockfight, you know old Tigre, well he killed the other one in seven minutes flat. I was eleven pesos the richer for it! I knew to bet on the old bruiser, even if he's only got one eye. He's crafty, that's what it is. Not a cock to match him in the country. The loser was Dorado, Don Arnulfo's little strutter. Evil-tempered, I always said so, but no good at pacing himself, too impetuous on the attack... You've got to be able to tell if a young cock's got the brains, haven't you, same as with a growing lad, true or not true?"

"True."

"The fountain's dried up in the square. People are fetching water from the lake, and there's sickness about. At least I've got my well, though it cost me an arm and a leg."

"Of course."

All the news having been told, they fell silent. Great big black-and-yellow butterflies were flying in pairs through the warm air.

Noémi came toward them on the terrace. She had hardly changed: calm, the eyes perhaps a little larger, the sockets deeper; wearing a white embroidered Indian shift. She gave Daria a hug.

"I knew you'd come. Bruno didn't believe me, he never does."

"How could you have known, my love?"

"Through Doña Luz. She knows secrets. I don't trust anyone else... We should be afraid right now, because she is, I can tell... I'm always afraid and I'm happy, would you believe it?"

■

The question was hanging so obviously in the air between them that Bruno Battisti gave voice to it himself: "So, what has become of me?" His eyes narrowed. He raised his hand and pointed to the contours of the lake and of the mountain. He began: "Listen to me, my friend. The plantation lives by the rhythm of seasons different from those of Europe. Our one earth has many faces. Here life is ruled by two primordial divinities: Fire and Water, Sun and Rain. They are the true mother-deities. The ancient brown race once adored them with a robust sense of reality. The Indios still bow to the maize on entering the field they are about to harvest, and I know they sometimes fertilize the soil with human semen. In the past, they used to regale the gods with their own flesh, their own blood, something which made unimpeachable sense: one nourishment for another, and all nourishment is terrestrial... They drowned small children in this lake so that the god of the water would allow for a plentiful crop. They tore out the hearts of prisoners and offered them up, still beating, so that a fortified sun would be sure to prevail over the darkness. You'll note that the Nahua were not terribly confident of the power of the sun, whereas they lived in awe of the destructive forces, harboring an exaggerated respect for them rather like ours in some ways... They lived in an unstable cosmos, as we live in an unstable humanity armed with cosmic powers... I subscribe to a modern meteorological service whose bulletins are useless, for they always arrive too late. My real weatherman is Lame Pánfilo, a fellow who can read the path of storms and predict the coming of the rains... When he's too drunk, I patiently await what no one can change.

"There's the dry season, when the highlands become a yellow desert. During that time, only the cactuses survive, thanks to their bitter energy and what scarce moisture is condensed by the night ... Proof that a humble, resistant victory is nearly always possible, even if it amounts to little more than holding out. There's the rainy season, when huge clouds gathered over the Pacific suddenly burst open, raining tempests and lightning down over the thirsty land, fertilizing it with magnificent violence. Torrents spill gleaming down the mountain, the lake overflows its banks, life begins to ferment in the soil—where it was only suspended—and in the rocks themselves, if you believe your eyes. The storms calmed and the downpours spent, the green season arrives. From here to the farthest peaks, the country is nothing but an empire of rising sap. Every bit of basalt has its crown of greenery and flowers sprung from lifeless aridity. It's the miracle of resurrection, like when the snows melt in our cold countries... For months there was nothing to see but a dried-up desert; who could guess that beneath the calcined ground, millions of invincible seeds were concealed, ready to germinate. We observe that the true power is not that of darkness, of barrenness, but of life. All that exists cries, whispers, or sings that we must never despair, for true death does not exist.

"The fire in the sky first blesses the sap, the loves of insects and birds, the euphoria of the herds, the darting quickness of tadpoles in the ponds . . . Then the fire in the sky turns to a burning hardness, as though the gods were reminding creation that no euphoria can last and that existence is not just the exultation of being; existence is also ordeal, courage, blind tenacity, hidden resourcefulness. The heavens' severity becomes an outburst of angry luminescence, a vast fierce rapture insensible to being, destructive of beings, sufficient to itself, blazing, mindless, and superb.

"The herds graze the last yellowed grasses, which rasp their throats . . . Here at the plantation, the perennial problem is water. I drilled a well. The streams dry up . . . When all else fails I have to get water from the lake, an exhausting job for my peons. You see, the earth is dying of thirst at the water's edge. And yet we've accomplished the miracle of rescuing this small piece of it. After the coffee is picked, I climb into my old Ford and go into town. I make just enough to live on and to order a few books from New York . . . I could easily get rich, like others do, lending to the poor against the next harvest and stockpiling maize and sugarcane against the inevitable rise in prices. The idea made me ashamed, and I chose instead to pass for a fool. Living among wolves, it would be reasonable to learn how to howl and bite like the wolves, but I preferred another fate, a more dangerous one I suppose because here as everywhere, a kind of sentence weighs upon the man who tries to be a bit more human than the general lot . . . I won't pretend I wasn't tempted to overcome this repugnance and make money so as to return to Europe when Europe is once again the continent of the most amazing germinations. These must come after the desert seasons. We shall see ideas, forces, men, and works sprouting up from the graveyards, no matter the rot and decay . . .

Well, either I'll never go back, or I'll go back penniless and old, which is worse, to end in the midst of beginnings.

"Tropical countries are full of aging men who still remember having followed dreams, wanting to become artists, scientists, discoverers, revolutionaries, reformers, sages! But one day they said to themselves: Let's make some money first, otherwise we're powerless. And it was all the easier because it was diving into another powerlessness. They became wealthy; disillusioned with themselves and hence with everything, they frittered their lives away in gilding their cages, while a cynical bitterness grew within them. The best of them keep up subscriptions to high-minded journals of literature or theosophy, as a reminder of extinguished passions . . . They play bridge and continue to speculate in real estate and commodity values, largely out of habit . . . I know some of these men. We've smoked sad cigars together in good restaurants, pontificating about the war—not without flashes of insight. I've stopped seeing them, because some of them stupidly admire a dead revolution. They depend on it like an injection to prolong their final breathing.

"I work my peons and pay them well; they steal from me well too, but within reason; they're aware that I know about it, but not that I judge them to be in the right. If I paid them any more, they'd lose motivation and the local powers would brand me a public menace . . . I'm up at sunrise, the dawns here are as fresh as the first day of creation. I supervise all the work . . . In the evening I lie in my hammock with a few books and newspapers, the papers several days old but it makes no difference, filled as they are with layers of lies and nonsense . . . In books, though, you may still encounter living men. I don't much care for the literary fabrications in vogue today: they too often feed on baseness, cultivating a false despair. Genuine despair would disdain royalties. Why write, why read, if not to offer, to find, a larger image of life, an image of man as deep as the problems that make up his greatness? I prefer reading scientific works, they have more imagination, they induce in me a sense of dizzying precision.

"I miss everything and that's another form of captivity, the only one I consent to, the only one that is a healthy part of our nature. I am the owner of this plantation, lush and overgrown as a patch of jungle, and despite this, sterile for me. I tend it with a kind of love. And thus I fulfill an instinctive duty toward the earth, the dead, and the defeats which are great temporary deaths...Thanks to this, I don't have much time for conscious regret; the other is always present. Sometimes I feel overwhelmed by the enchantment of plants, but animals are for me more eloquent. I see a big amber scorpion go by, and I think of him as a sort of ancestor to so many creatures in this world, a survivor of Paleozoic ages. The wild ducks come down in droves; as they skid onto the lake, I see an Indio marksman hiding behind the calabash stalks; the birds take off as soon as they see him—a war of ruses between them and the hunter; but they don't mind me, they know I'm unarmed. I fling a stone at them, they laugh at men: Learn that men are bad!...Or perhaps I'm reading, and a rattlesnake slips over for a look. He rears his fine stylized head, flicks a tongue like a living black needle, shakes his tail, which rings agreeably, decides that I'm a creature like him, a solitary, no worse than he is, sketches a little dance, and goes coolly on his way. He is very beautiful, the rattlesnake...I know the hours when the hummingbird comes flitting among the flowers like a butterfly. The frailest of birds, tiny, dark, and iridescent, with a life experience limited to searching for pollen, making love, and fleeing before huge, incomprehensible dangers from which its tininess protects it; this tiny spark of intelligence has enabled it to weather more than one geological upheaval...I watch for the ungainly flight of the pelican, a bird which seems to me ugly because it belongs to an aesthetic of nature from very ancient times...Such are my daily encounters, full of meaning.

"People are somewhat more dangerous. Crescenciano, the blacksmith, has taken a few shots at me—from a safe distance it must be said, and with no intent to harm. We are on cordial terms, so I assume he was high at the time, maybe on something other than alcohol. It's so tempting to hold someone else's life at the end of a barrel, to play with it a bit, it makes you feel powerful, you might even feel good. Crescenciano is a good man, because I'm still alive. A mournful man and a contemplative one—if contemplating is what he's doing when he squats under the moonlight in his sarape and doesn't budge for hours. Then he resembles the small black vultures you see all over like perpetually famished monks. His wife assures me he meant no offense and was in fact distressed at the possibility of hitting me, unless it happened to be God's will (and how to know whether it is His will or not except by pulling the trigger?). All he wanted was to play a good joke on me, shoot a hole in my hat brim. I went over to Crescenciano one night during fiesta; we hung our best hats on stakes in the ground and shot at them, laughing uproariously (that is to say soundlessly). It was one of my ideas; after that, I felt a little safer...I treat the children's illnesses. Pancho's have amoebas, Isidro's suffer from glands. I administer light doses of sulfa and so am reckoned to be a bit of a sorcerer, even if nothing prevents them from buying the stuff themselves at Don Gamelindo's...The real sorceress, Doña Luz, knows I haven't a clue about the secret arts; just as the friendly rattlesnake knows that I have no venom whereas he does. I treat young Ponce when he falls down dead drunk. He also gets epileptic fits, which Doña Luz cures better than me—by letting them run their course, not without burning herbs and powdered bone...Her medicine beats mine by a few centuries, for she is the repository of a knowledge that goes back to Neolithic cultures. Doña Luz has cured me of fevers I couldn't even identify. She is very good for Noémi.

"You know Noémi's transparent eyes, their ephemeral, indecisive attentiveness, their luminous panic...Noémi is calm; she pretends, especially to herself, to have forgotten everything, not to know about the war; she pretends she has overcome the fear of fear. She reads the same books over and over, line by line, and I believe she's not so much reading as abandoning herself to the reveries engendered in her by the words on the page. She does the housework singing to herself. Sometimes she doesn't recognize me anymore or thinks I'm someone else. She laughs like a child: 'You think you're fooling me! You play him very well! I don't hold it against you...' I think I do play my characters very well indeed, and that no one should hold it against me. Then she changes, and sees me again. 'Ah, there you are again, I'm happy!' But there is a note of resentment in her tone. I believe Doña Luz keeps a double of me, a magic doll, and does to it whatever is required to bring me back from the most mysterious journeys.

"Noémi can sense the approach of earthquakes, which are frequent and harmless. She says, 'My bones are cold, the earth is going to shiver...' She wakes me in the night and says, 'Listen...' I light the candle, we look at each other and smile, alert as one body to the trembling of the mountain and the whispers of the lake. Her eyes are seldom as beautiful as at these times, and these are precious moments between us...If the earth begins to roll and pitch more, we go out into the garden, stumbling against each other; because I don't really trust this old roof and the open air is safer. Out under the great stars, we have the sensation of walking on floating ground. Branches whip to and fro, and the birds, alarmed, fill the air with wingbeats and cries. I think of the rattlesnake, who like me must have ventured from his lair, like me reassured to observe that while the firmament seems a little wobbly, the pattern of its brilliant specks remains the same. The great comet we expect in our heart of hearts does not appear. Noémi leans her head against my shoulder...Once she said afterward that the planet must twinkle beautifully in the sky when it shakes like that. In any case, it's a poetic thought...

"A psychiatrist would say that Noémi is schizophrenic, or that she suffers from manic depression, loss of touch with reality, personality breakdown, and the rest. Yet my feeling is that she's made contact with a reality she finds more acceptable than the version of it commonly held. And as there's no psychiatrist within a thousand miles, she has nothing to fear from superfluous diagnoses..."

Bruno seemed glad to be talking. Daria guessed he was releasing himself from a very long silence. Bitterness flooded up to Daria's brain. She was restraining herself from crying out: "So that's how you lived while...while...! Doing nothing for anyone else in the world! And you didn't even take your part in..." Bruno Battisti looked at her with the knowing eyes of the old days: "I know what you're thinking. I confess that I suffered over it. That was unfair and useless. Come have supper."

He asked her no questions. Whenever she brought up the war, he appeared to be listening merely out of friendship, as though he already knew everything. She was starting to tell him about the bombing of Altstadt; while listening, he led her over to a banana tree and pointed out its violet turgescence, the intense sexuality of the ripening fruits. "Beautiful, isn't it?" The terrible events and their train of anxious thoughts began to lose their sharpness. After a few days, Daria succumbed to a lucid somnolence. "We'll speak of all this again," Bruno Battisti said, "when you are delivered. But for now, look at the mountains. Look at the baby chicks..."

"Thought must be delivered," Daria assented suddenly.

"If it's possible."

■

Solitude shrouded the world in a light yet impenetrable veil. The excess of luminosity became blinding, erasing whatever was not this dazzle of sunlight, this reverberation of sunlight, this burning sunlight on the platinum lake, this humid jungle warmth under the tall sweet-smelling foliage of the eucalyptus trees. Noémi's white silhouette appeared crossing an avenue of trees or crossing the terrace, present-absent, real-unreal. A cat sprang after a lizard. Doña Luz was glimpsed prowling among the coffee plants, a black silhouette with abundant white hair tumbling over the shoulders of a little girl—who might be a hundred—with bright eyes... Wide-brimmed hats appeared and disappeared atop heads of burned clay whose eyebrows, mustaches, and eyes were intensely black; white rags floating over brown bodies...Fishermen called out from one dugout canoe to another across the glassy lake—a call, a response—and that single voice seemed to reverberate through the stillness long after it died out. The fruit on the mango trees was being impregnated by the sun. Other enormous fruits were ripening inside hard spiny casings. Beautiful black spiders, their abdomens adorned with a scarlet symbol, hung suspended in the architecture of their shining threads. Under the shadow of the trees, orchids revealed their delicate, fleshy complexions. There was no imaginable finality to any of this: only a riotous disorder, stable yet changing, a mayhem of primeval voluptuousness and innocent cruelty, which, swelled by the surging of sap and blood, spilled over exultantly into the plantation and lay surrounded by the desert. No human notions retained their customary meanings.

"So there's really nobody, nobody to talk to?" Daria asked one evening, as they sat on after supper in the low-ceilinged dining room, watching the cat play with her kittens.

Noémi raised her pale irises whose pupils were always too large. "Talk, what for, Dachenka?"

"Nobody," Bruno Battisti said placidly. "We are alone. Like stones being stones. The thing is to wait."

"What do stones wait for?" Daria thought.

"You're bored," said Bruno. "Would you like to play a game of chess? Harris is probably coming over tomorrow."

■

Harris came over two or three times a week. This young American lived in a solitude even greater and more parched than their own, a good hour's trek from the plantation, in the heart of the forest, where he occupied a big, tumbledown adobe dwelling hemmed in by ferocious, resplendent agaves. "As far away from two-legged creatures as I can get," he'd say. Harris was generally a man of few words, but when in a philosophical mood he might explain: "Man, attempting to change his fate, has come up with only one liberating invention: scotch whiskey!" This gave rise to commentaries verging on the profound, allowing one to recall that the ancient barbarian civilizations, in this land so close to the present, made their liquor by fermenting the milk of the agave plant. "Scotch is better," Harris declared, "but if that's the only proof of the white man's superiority, it's a feeble one..." Harris was a steady drinker who never lost his self-control. But until he was loaded with "the right dose of gunpowder," all you saw of him was a big brute with ruddy-brown hair—a rather mournful, listless lout who yawned a lot and sometimes bit his nails. Having been a sailor, he nursed a grudge against the sea, like an old betrayed lover. "A big wet desert, right? The most inhuman place in the world, along with factories. And every ship's a floating prison or a floating cathouse. Or else a floating fortress, packed with poor dumb suckers. And not easy to sink!" Their being hard to sink seemed to have left him with malevolent regrets. He had fought "honorably" in the Pacific Islands, but whether he had come home with medals or a warrant for his arrest, he did not say. "The sea and the war: two big piles of shit..." You could easily imagine him, with his hard, fleshy face, his round boxer's shoulders, his cynical expression and clouded eyes, in some mobsters' dive, as ruthless as the worst of them and as snappy a dresser, with that slightly louche elegance; then later dressed like them in a striped suit breaking up rocks on a chain gang. All purely imaginary, of course, since flipping a coin would be the best way to decide whether his past was ordinary or adventurous... He read nothing but hard-boiled thrillers, the kind with lots of killing, where at the end they're going to hang the seductive heroine who for three hundred pages seemed to be the most mysterious, the most desirable, the most tantalizing young woman in distress... But on page 287, when her wickedness has emerged beyond any reasonable doubt, the detective gives in and kisses her on the lips, gently takes her hands—and brings out the handcuffs... She's been had, the vixen, and so have you, dear reader, since only then did you understand that the roots of crime lay here, in this melting gaze, this soft disarming flesh... Harris reveled at the idea of the pleasure he would have kicking in the teeth of that detective or of the author, that dirty "son of a bitch!"* When he was finished reading, Harris would toss the book onto the little heap of paperbacks, each offering a detective puzzle to be deciphered for twenty-five cents. This library gathered dust in a corner; the hens pecked around it sometimes, attracted by—what? What could these birds find to peck at in or under all these nasty stories? Harris poured himself a shot of tequila. Harris called out: "Monica! Mon-i-ca!"

Monica showed herself in the doorway, framed between the radiant space without and the shadows within; a beautiful tall girl with a long pleated skirt down to her toes, hair piled on the back of her neck, a Polynesian face with open, level brown eyes. She was scrubbing an earthenware vessel with sand. "¿Qué quieres? What do you want?" In Spanish, the verb querer means both to want and to love, with no possible confusion between them, so that a man might as easily answer "Te quiero" as "Bring me a glass of water." But Harris often answered nothing at all and simply gazed pleasurably at her, thinking something wordless like: "You're an adorable creature, Monica, but my god, what real difference is there between you and the jungle flowers who open their crimson vulvas?" In Monica's eyes he was ugly, as the male ought to be: ugly, brawny, serious, never too drunk, and never violent toward her, with never more than a passing glance for the other girls from the few hovels scattered around here...And rich, because there was never a shortage of maize. To ensure his lasting love, Monica spiked his tequila with pinches of a white powder that was a specialty of Doña Luz. It seemed to do the trick! Harris undressed her when the heat went down (it didn't take long, she wore only a loose blouse, a loose skirt) and made a charcoal sketch which he soon crumpled and threw into the corner of the "son-of-a-bitch's library." Then he was upon her in two short bounds, the naked amber girl as she stood against a slit of window with the mountainside still blazing beyond. He was more magnificently ugly

* Phrase appears in English in the original text.

then than at any other time, this laughing, furious white man with the muzzle of a sorrowful beast. Almost all men were like that, according to the girls of San Blas, but none of the local men were acquainted with the drawing ritual, which must therefore have a hidden meaning. Was it an appeal for vigor, for sweetness? For joy? Monica questioned Doña Luz, and she, from the height of her sixty years of experience, handed down an incomprehensible but favorable judgment: "Your man is an *artista*, my child." "What's an *artista*, Doña Luz, *madrecita*, little mother?" "I know many secrets, child, but not that one. I can't be expected to know everything. An *artista* is an unbeliever, but he is not usually a bad man. Better than most gringos, God have mercy!" Harris had a way of kissing and caressing that the men around here don't know; it must be another custom of his country, an easy thing to submit to and not a sin to emulate, for you see, Virgin of Wonders, Holy Queen of Heaven, Our Lady of the Lake, you see that he is my man and that I love him! He possessed her on the hard mat with a long, leisurely passion. While they were tangled up in lovemaking, a distracted hen might wander in, or Nacho, the gleaming purple turkey-cock, whose hard, coral-ringed eye made Monica uncomfortable. Rising above the fire of blessed fever within her, she would call out, "Nacho! Nacho! Shame on you! Scram!" The wicked old bird would mince off with the utmost dignity, swinging his purple crop as though he didn't understand, but he'd be back, the sneak...And when Monica reappeared in the yard he would spread his cartwheel of a tail at her, lifting his feet in a little jig... "Yes, Nacho, you're beautiful, you are..." she crooned, still smiling at the sweet giddiness inside her. Harris had paid the price of a fine horse to Monica's parents; he had laid on a fiesta for the whole community, a memorable event enlivened by ten bottles of pulque and two hundred firecrackers; the padre of San Blas, Don Maclovio himself, had been good enough to attend.

Harris was no artist, if truth be told, for all that most artists are frauds. He drew like a schoolboy, for the enjoyment of tracing the shape of a woman or the lines of a landscape; for the humiliation of failure, for the pleasure of destroying what he had made and of making it expressly to destroy. The earth behaves no differently: it makes plants and sentient beings and destroys them, only to start all over again, right? He drew when he was slightly drunk and destroyed when he was sober, pained by the limits of his own lucidity. He hunted hares, quail, wild ducks; if luck was on his side he might kill an iguana, that big blunt-nosed lizard with a sumptuously green skin, which Monica turned into a feast, dressed with hot spices. "In my country," Harris told her, "there are people who never saw a hare take off from under the rocks, can you understand that?" "Poor people!" said Monica, eyes shining with pleasure because he was talking to her. "They buy their hares ready-skinned in big stores which sell hundreds at a time..." "Hundreds!" Monica repeated, incredulous. "Stores as big as that?" "And the people are bastards, most of them!" Harris concluded, in opaque laughter.

Equipped like an Indian with a machete to clear the way, wearing sandals with thick rubber soles cut from tires and a conical sombrero, Harris would set off along the mountain trail that led to the plantation. It took him past the abandoned gold mine, a bald hump topped by a single candelabra cactus which might be one or more centuries old, nearly forty feet tall, raising its phallic spars above a monstrous trunk in two tones of green: silvery olive and midnight emerald. "You feed off the seams, eh, *candelero*! But it's hard to live like that, you get as thirsty as the next guy and you're even uglier." Wandering prospectors had tried to chop the monster down so as to delve between its roots, but they soon gave up, leaving the trunk deformed around the base. Some gold mine! A mine of schemes! By dynamiting the rock and sluicing through the sand and clay and god knows what else, you might get a thimbleful of gold dust worth twenty crates of scotch, *si caballero*! Unless you happened to land plumb on the jolly seam that's mocking us six inches under this track here. You might just as well send away to Mexico City for lottery tickets, after consulting Doña Luz on the numbers to choose, or choose them for themselves, because the good numbers aren't necessarily the winners, this being a matter of fate, not of money—Doña Luz is surely right on that score—which means that the losers can be lucky all the same.

Harris's route now took him past Las Calaveras, the Skulls. Following the lure of the ruins, he deviated from the main track to take a look at them. Did time humanize these anguished stones, or did it dehumanize them? First you walked through a stretch of dry, prickly undergrowth, bristling with dead needles. The rock-strewn slope dipped toward a granite cliff, tinted blue or gold, according to the time of day. If you turned around you had a vista of the lake, calm as a mirror, a divine mirror of water resting on the earth. All that was left of an altar was a base of reddish-gray andesite, the color of dried blood, the appropriate color. Crudely carved skulls protrude from the earth on both sides of worn stones that once might have formed steps. Schematic skulls with clenched stripes of teeth, eye sockets that seemed still to cast a baleful stare into the horizontal sky. Harris felt his life-beat slowing. Expectant, he listened for the thud of drums in the distance, the mesmerizing, muffled tattoo of the forest. To regain his aplomb he always said the same words, aloud: "These cannibals sure knew how to choose their sites!" Twenty paces farther on, a broken column lying half hidden in the brush offered up to the face of the sky another huge face with geometric eyes contemplating the zenith indefinitely. This god of an unknown race, assumed to be Mongoloid, did not present the features of that race but features more refined, European or Malaysian, hybrid in their abstraction. His diadem was broken into pieces. Harris bowed his head, absorbed by the problem of human duration, the problem of . . . of what, man! You'll never be able to put it into words, but the problem remains. The sudden appearance of a lizard, gray with emerald spots, startled him. "Well, well," he muttered. Whistling, he continued on his way. The Battistis and the Harrises sometimes met up here for an evening picnic. Bruno, stimulated by a swallow of rum or by the proximity of the unknown god, told stories about the ruins of Central Asia, the Roof of the World, Pamir's . . . Harris would slap his thigh, booming: "Roof of the World! And on top of that, another roof?" There can't have even been a sky, if it was really the Roof of the World! He laughed even louder: "A stratospheric sleight of hand!" Monica and Noémi discussed the embroidery stitches of Los Altos and the Tarascan country. They understood each other well.

On this occasion, an amusing encounter awaited Harris at Las Calaveras. He found two Indians squatting on their heels, having a smoke. A bald gent, masked by large sunglasses that made him look like a skull himself, sportily clad in a combination of beige and brown, was measuring the unknown god's nose with a compass. "Hello there!" cried Harris. "I'll bet you're half a millimeter off!" Startled, the man jumped up—"How do you do"—and put on a toothy smile like a dog's. Harris strode nearer, swinging his machete so that the light bounced off its blade. "Who do you think you're kidding, Mister, with your little compass? The venerable god, yourself, everybody else, or mathematics?" The erudite tourist appreciated the joke. Repressing the giggles, Harris became quite sociable. "These are difficult measurements," the man said, "but take it from me, they'll be accurate..."

"Accurate?" went Harris, brimming with ironical glee. "So you're an archaeologist?"

"Oh, just in my spare time," the other said modestly. "And you, an artist?"

"Amateur, old pal, like yourself."

"Care for a drink?" proposed the amateur archaeologist.

Harris brightened. "What are you carrying in the way of bottles?" The expedition's supplies turned out to include a first-class brandy, and Harris in mounting good cheer became cordially insolent. "So you go around measuring idols' noses, and probably their backsides, in godforsaken holes like this? Funny! And where d'you come from in the first place, Mister?" "Actually, I'm from Wisconsin..." He was priceless, this archaeologist, amateur or otherwise: the panama hat with the crimson ribbon, the coffee-colored silk necktie over the khaki shirt, the pink skin, the fastidiously clipped blond mustache, those dark glasses which must be hiding the eyes of a learned rabbit... "I've been working on my book on pre-Colombian sculpture for the past eight years." Harris poured himself another brandy.

"If that means carrying around brandy this good, I guess you'll be forgiven upstairs... Just think, in those eight years you might have slept with a thousand women of all different colors, committed a whole string of crimes, at a profit or at a loss, lost and remade a dozen fortunes, spent years cooling off in Sing Sing or San Quentin or someplace—no lack of good spots! You could have gone around the world on a bicycle! Crossed the ocean in a rowboat! Got yourself killed eight hundred different ways in the war!"

"Certainly," said the archaeologist. "Except for getting yourself killed, even once, in the war, I hope you've done a fair number of those things yourself..."

"I beg your pardon! I even got myself killed in New Guinea!"

"Congratulations. Life feels so much grander after that, doesn't it? Well, in exceptional cases it does..."

"Obviously."

The archaeologist, Mr. Brown, spent every night in his car, which was parked four or five miles away. He invited Harris to partake of his cold chicken, whiskey, and wines. "I have a weakness for fine wines, Mr. Harris..." Harris agreed that fine wines were conducive to the study of old stone carvings. "Take me, for instance. Me who's never read a single book on the subject—god forbid—well, once I've enough of the noble fluid in my belly, I could tell you the authentic history of this old god and describe the dances the young Olmec girls, if there were such girls, used to dance around him on carpets of flowers and decapitated birds..."

"You're way off," answered Mr. Brown, shocked. "These monuments don't belong to the Olmec culture!"

"They don't? What do you know? Not that I give a damn."

Mr. Brown was unaware of the existence nearby of a hospitable plantation, owned by an Italian, Bruno Battisti, "a nice old fellow who's traveled all over. Now he knows the history of the Olmecs and the Tarambiretls and the rest. His wife is a charming woman too, only she's out of her mind..." Harris invited the archaeologist to go along with him. Mr. Brown was tempted, but hated to be indiscreet...The word "indiscreet" made Harris guffaw as he twirled his machete. Mr. Brown accepted the invitation.

■

Two or three times a year, the Battistis were visited by tourists on their way to take pictures of each other at Las Calaveras and under the picturesque candelabra cactus on the Cerro de Oro. They had even received copies of such snapshots in the post: sunny girls seated with grinning skulls between their knees, a young sportsman with movie-star looks. "You are a sage..." wrote the prettiest girl to Bruno, with news of her engagement...And yet he was disturbed by Mr. Brown's dusty automobile the minute he saw it drive up. Harris alighted first. Then the archaeologist appeared, removing his sunglasses and glancing about like a dazzled white rabbit.

"Where did you pick up this specimen?" growled Bruno to Harris.

"A weirdo. He was camped out by the idol, measuring its nostrils. With a hamper full of choice bottles. He's a complete idiot."

Nothing abnormal in any of this.

Mr. Brown complimented Mr. Battisti: "Sir, you live in an absolute paradise..."

Mr. Brown placed a pair of blue-tinted spectacles over his gray, anemic eyes. He admired the coffee bushes, the euphorbia, the calabash grove, the mangoes, the eucalyptus, the tall royal palms ...He had the gift of inarticulate appreciation. He brought out his field glasses to inspect Green Island, where there were pyramids, one of which was semicircular, a rare and probably very ancient design, between fifteen hundred and two thousand years old. The Cuicuilco pyramid was reputed to be older still...

"Ten thousand years!" declared Harris, all jovial.

"No! Really? I find that hard to believe..."

Harris gave him a vigorous thwack on the back, so friendly that the fellow pitched forward.

"We're not even close by five thousand years, joker!"

Mr. Brown gave the stuttering laugh of the shy man, slave to erudition, who doesn't realize he's being made fun of. Daria found him repellent. "A machine for quantifying *calaveras* and pickling their statistics in useless file cards..." His magazines, with their recent American fashions, interested Noémi. In the course of a friendly chat skillfully managed by Bruno Battisti, Mr. Brown emerged as the owner of a business in Wisconsin; raised as a Presbyterian but personally an atheist, "scientific" as he put it, though deeply respectful of religion; rather conservative but with liberal leanings. When he completed his study of Mexican antiquities, he looked forward to lengthy sojourns in Peru, where the ruins of Tiahuanaco, in particular, merited close and conscientious description as the first phase of an investigation that would embark in an entirely unprecedented direction, taking account of...Mr. Brown spent several days at the plantation, happy to sleep in a comfortable bed and to lose at chess against Daria or Bruno, in serious games which he began cleverly and usually muffed toward the end, as though some inhibition prevented him from winning. He let fall something relevant to this, one day. "I went toward science because I was intimidated being successful at business...My father was extremely wealthy. Brown and Coldman, you'll have heard the name?" "Nobody, in these mountains, has ever heard of it," said Daria maliciously.

"Really?" said Mr. Brown with the look of a marionette that sometimes came over him.

Before the evening meal, he invariably changed into a dress shirt adorned by a floppy cravat the color of dead leaves.

The air at the end of an oppressive afternoon was supercharged with electricity. A ceiling of clouds weighed down on the place.

All day, the plantation had been full of the sounds of restless animals; two peons had fought without being drunk. Flocks of low-flying birds enlivened the sunset, swarms of bats fluttered on the fringe of the night, but the immobility of the trees remained vaster than everything. For a second, outlined against the purple glow of the sunset, the tops of isolated palm trees looked like huge, black, curiously unhappy spiders... Daria and Noémi set the table with the maid, Melita, who was clumsier than usual tonight and broke two Jalisco pottery plates. Harris had left. Mr. Brown and Bruno Battisti were sprawled in deck chairs, exchanging desultory scraps of talk. Only the lightning seemed alive. It flashed and sheeted through the clouds, almost unceasing but erratic and freakish, there a stealthy glimmer, here a blinding flash, illuminating with lifeless whiteness a vast, sharply etched panorama void of color and movement. "This landscape," said Bruno, "seems to be only the memory of itself..." After requesting a repetition of that sentence, the visitor gave a passive "Ah, yes." With each crackling flash the two men glimpsed their own forms bleached white from head to foot, as though they had been turned into stone. "The storms won't break for two or three days yet, you'll see," Bruno said.

"Ah, you think so?"

"It would be best for you, Mr. Brown, to go to the pyramids at first light tomorrow and return by midafternoon, to avoid being caught in a gale over the lake. The Indian canoes are very well built, but it's a risk nonetheless..."

"Tomorrow at first light," the visitor repeated apathetically.

"It's no more than three hours' rowing," Bruno said, vexed by the groundless irritation he felt. "And one hour's walk as far as the teocalli..."

"I'm thirsty," said Mr. Brown. "Could you ask for a glass of water, please? I find this bath of electricity enervating." A splintering glare exposed his livid countenance, mouth wide open gasping for air. Don Bruno reached for the little bell made of volcanic ash, and a gay tinkle rang out. Bare feet padded quickly over the tiles, a swarthy girl was illuminated, like a dancer in the jungle, by a flash of lightning. "A glass of water, Celia, for the señor..." "Thank you," said Mr. Brown in a satisfied voice. "This tropical climate..."

"A climate of cosmic vigor," Bruno said. "When you get used to it, you love it. A climate of destruction and fertilization..."

The archaeologist attempted a laugh. "I think we're getting a darn sight more destruction than fertilization!"

"The opinion of someone who's impotent," thought Bruno, who was still beset by an old virility which sometimes tortured him and sometimes exalted him when in contact with young dusky flesh exuding a savage fragrance of sweat. "I disagree," he said with effort. He was beginning to feel an unreasonable antipathy toward this guest.

The glimmers succeeded one another noiselessly in the sky; stars were coming out, and a distant grumble of thunder was heard. "Ah," said Don Bruno. "I love this. The storms here are magnificent..." Mr. Brown lit a cigar; his austere profile shone in the yellow glow of the lighter.

It was a relief to both men when Noémi came out to announce that the table was set. Noémi had dressed up and looked ravishing in a long native dress, dark with leafy patterns. The material swished around her hips, her movements seeming to reveal her body's hidden harmony. Her eyes bathed in lightning shone blue as phosphorus. Mr. Brown took her arm. "I love storms! They terrify me..." she said. "You have a lyrical nature," he intoned, which made her laugh. "Can't you find something sillier to say?" "Not really," Mr. Brown replied, with his self-deprecating smile.

Dinner was a grand affair. Daria carved the turkey by the light of six candles ranged along the mahogany table on which little brightly colored napkins looked like square flowers. Orchids stood in amber goblets from Guadalajara. Safely away from the lightning, Mr. Brown recovered his good humor. "Allow me to fetch the last and best of my bottles..." Bruno offered to go with him. They came back from the car with a California red which was undoubtedly a treat, imitating the most alkaline and yet softly rounded of Andalusian vintages. Noémi apologized for not drinking it because Doña Luz had forbidden her. Her magnetic eyes met the benevolent eyes of Mr. Brown. "You don't know what you're missing!"

The first spoonful of soup made Mr. Brown seem almost perky. His voice rose in pitch; his hands, rather overlarge but delicate, traced tiny gestures as he complimented the ladies on everything: the needlework on the linen bought at a pueblo market, the matchless cuisine which would put the best hotels to shame, the coral necklace hung with tiny silver fish which Daria was wearing, the wonderfully barbaric string of chunky clay beads and a jade figurine which so suited Noémi; how young they both looked, and how artful the lighting of the room, positively Rembrandt! "Here we go," thought Bruno. "The marionette is on the loose." Bruno preferred silence to the inane chatter that does nothing but add a bit of noise to a bit of vanity. He was so annoyed that toward the end of the meal, lest his contempt get the better of his manners, he drained two glasses of wine in quick succession and felt better at once. Mr. Brown was explaining the many pitfalls involved in transplanting delicate European vine stocks to the New World. No laboratory has yet succeeded in unraveling the secret chemistry, or should we say the wondrous alchemy, of wine. Its components are: the quality of the plant, its health, its capacity for regeneration; the characteristics of the soil; the type of sunlight and the angle of exposure of the vines; one would also have to study the nature of solar radiation and, beyond that, the effect of radiations from the night sky, as well as the nature of the microscopic fauna and flora that assist in fermentation; then of course there is the related science of volcanism, for Mr. Brown was convinced that a thousand subtle emanations are at work above volcanic subsoils, and thus, since Burgundy, Champagne, the Rhineland, or Andalusia are geologically stable, they must benefit from a telluric environment quite different from that of California, with its proximity to the volcanic plates of Mexico... The host was becoming perceptibly moody again. He reached for a bottle. "No, enough of that one, my dear fellow," said Mr. Brown. "You must sample this other, which is by far the best." This other was not the best—rather the opposite—but Bruno allowed politely that it was excellent, because he couldn't care less.

■

Noémi was the first to retire, toward ten o'clock. Mr. Brown excused himself shortly thereafter. Daria and Bruno wandered out onto the terrace. From the horizon to the zenith the flashing ballet continued. Daria was fighting down tides of dizziness. "I drank much too much, Sacha. What a learned animal he is, of what fossilized erudition! This world mass-produces marionettes and fossils... Elsewhere they turn out automatons, with the instinct for torture and destruction loose in their mechanism... The same stars everywhere. Sacha! But where is hope?" "Everywhere," Bruno answered evasively. "Remember the beach at Feodossia?"

Myriads of insects, drawn by the light, imprisoned by the light, were lying on the stone sill around the oil lamp that had been burning all evening. "Are they all going to die, having thrown themselves at an incomprehensible light?" "No. Most survive, saved by the sunrise... The banality of daylight. Insects have a strong grip on life." "Feodossia... I'd forgotten. Do you know, I imagined in those days that I was in love with you, that's why I was always pushing you away. You couldn't understand, and I didn't want to love again, after so many necessary and needless massacres... In another sense, I didn't understand either. What have we understood since then?"

"Just what remains essential, it seems to me," said Bruno.

It almost seemed that they might easily touch on some great and simple truth together, but too many lightning flashes surrounded them, passing through brains split between excitation and torpor. "Oh, how sleepy I am!" said Daria. At the door to her room, he gave her a brotherly kiss.

Bruno slept in a spartan bedroom next to Noémi's, separated

by a glass-bead doorway. He was dreaming as he put on his paja-mas. He was young, entering a palace. There were smooth-faced soldiers and bearded soldiers, asleep on the marble staircase. He must wake them for this night's duty, the march along frozen canals, the danger at dawn. Tomorrow some of these men would look the same as they did now, except that they would be asleep forever... "We have achieved justice," Sacha told them. "We have changed one of the faces of the world, enough to make living and dying worthwhile. Let us consent to everything!" Did they hear him, understand him? They were swearing and grumbling. "We're coming, Comrade!" What happened after that? One should never consent to everything, there are always non-consentments, re-fusals to be maintained... Our failure to admit this was the great error, or one of them... What happened after that? A red fox rolling in the sunlit snow—shivering, shivering! I'm frozen to the bone—a brown fox scampering through the sand toward the ru-ins. Shivering! I'm hit bad... "N'ga! Are you sleeping?" The young Uzbek glided in, as beautiful as a girl. "The water is pure, master, you drink..." Where were the secret papers? The most secret, in the briefcase, the briefcase in the strongbox, the nightmare in the strongbox, the death warrants in the strongbox... Dead, all of them, dead, the greatest, the purest and best, the builders, the lost, the fanatics, the knowing, the unknown, the humblest, in their thousands, their millions, absurdly, iniquitously dead. Why? How did we—insurgent, united, uplifted, and victorious—bring about the opposite of what we wanted to do? Reread the texts... But what use are old texts in the afterglow of cataclysms...? A young woman who resembled N'ga sidled up to the last customer in a café on place Wagram, showed him her pretty hands; he touched her hands with a kind of panicky desire... Troubled, he asked, "Did you pour the poison—the poison into the texts?" Autumn yellowed the Bois de Boulogne, the atrophy of life, everything is lost, everything is sullied... No! No, because I still possess con-sciousness, sovereign, useless, silent consciousness, tranquil con-sciousness... Rhetoric or truth? Noémi, Noémi, the ocean...

Had he been sleeping? Feverish, belly knotted with the urge to vomit, cardiac anxiety rising, Bruno called softly: "Noémi... N'ga!" From the next room Noémi answered, "I'm all right, Sacha, are you?" "I'm fine, don't worry..." He groped for the important objects: flashlight, revolver. Hairy beasts blundered about in his head, predatory ideas with dripping muzzles..."What's happening, for godsake?" He hadn't drunk that much! He managed, unsteadily, to get outside. Lightning split the sky. Welcome, comets! Fall, comets! Bruno was trying so hard to think that his facial muscles cramped painfully. A lightning flash revealed the bougainvilleas covered with spume, and he realized he had just vomited. His bare feet dragged over the cool flagstones. "Where did we go wrong?" His heart thundered in his chest, crushing his lungs, hurting the back of his eyes at the place where the true eye lay, the eye that saw into the black chamber of the retina; how does it see without erring? "Check to the queen, checkmate! Be hard, never give in, believe, believe-know! Will! Everything will be transformed...This sick and crazy world..." A flash of relief. I vomited, that's good, I may be all right. These eternal lightning flashes...What I need is an emetic and there isn't one in the house...In a flash he understood: it was as clear as the sparkling vision of the lake in an upside-down world, with the sky below. The veins on his hands were hardening.

The door to Daria's room cracked open at a blow from his shoulder. The advantage of having worm-eaten doors! He entered, shining the flashlight in front of him. "Do you remember Feodossia?" Chestnut-and-ash hair spread around her exhausted face, her head encircled in a halo of light, Daria was smiling, a convulsive smile. There was no mistaking that smile! "Daria, are you dead?" "Yes I am, Sacha..." She was icy. Bruno took her hand; it fell back with rigid finality. With an uncertain forefinger, he eased back her eyelid, observed the motionless eyeball, its sclera yellowed with tiny dark veins. The lid closed back slowly of its own accord. A bluish glimmer of lightning lingered on Daria's forehead...Bruno's legs gave way and he sat down abruptly, head bowed, still holding the revolver and the flashlight in dangling hands. The light shone a white circle at his feet. A bug crawled aimlessly in the circle. Was it sleep or did he faint for a moment? When he came to, back from the brink, he shone the flashlight once more onto Daria's waxen face. Not a hope...He spat a thread of greenish spittle into the circle of light, stood up, and left the room. The lightning flashes were moving off, barely perceptible on the horizon. An illusion! They were all around, playing among themselves, making the gold beads of the stars vibrate, eternity's chant. Nothing but that chant remains. No more error, no more doubt, only a flickering consciousness about to be extinguished, reabsorbed into lightning, stars, and darkness...Bruno felt a rush of exasperation. Ah! That murderous marionette with his fine wines, not such a marionette after all, not such a learned fossil, Mr. so-called Brown, it's the end of you, you little bastard, if I have ten more minutes to live...Which I have, because I threw up, I might be saved! The sonorous gongs beating in his heart answered: No.

A ray of light filtered under Mr. Brown's bedroom door. Good old worm-eaten doors! This one too gave way at the first shove. The guest, clad in a stylish dressing gown, started up from the pillows, one hand under the sheet where his weapon must be. "I say, you gave me a turn, Don Bruno! You don't look so well...What's wrong?"

"Nothing wrong with you, I'm sure!" Bruno spat back at him between bared teeth, his mouth foamy. "But I threw up, I'm going to be all right."

For all his anger, which seemed to him completely lucid, Bruno was growing weaker. Black flashes spiraled around him. Why did I come here? Why did I bring this revolver? Who is this? What is happening?

"Daria's dead."

"You think so? That can't be possible..."

Mr. Brown made as if to rise. "Calm yourself, my friend, it'll pass, have some water..." He felt for the carafe with a hand outlined in green; his lower jaw trembled, his colorless lips fluttered. "You rotten death's-head!" Bruno spoke firmly through his black lightning flashes, his burning temples and the blue flame in his cerebellum, where the bullet enters when they execute you. "Don't move or I'll..." He raised the revolver. "You see I'm saved. I vomited. I vomited you up, you piece of shit, I vomited you all up..."

Mr. Brown—facing the end of a short, black, steel barrel shakily following the movements of his head—lay back into the pillows.

"That's good news," he said. "An organic reaction has taken place...But tell me, Don Bruno, how many glasses did you drink?"

"Three..."

Mr. Brown pouted with regret.

"In that case, my friend, I hate to say it, but there's nothing more to do for you. Shoot me now, then be patient, it won't take long..."

The marionette was fading, leaving behind a hard head of washed-out bones, distress, tension. "Shoot quickly," Mr. Brown insisted, "because in a few moments you won't be able to..." In his face, Bruno recognized faces from long ago. He lowered the gun and sat on the edge of the bed, brows knitted, struggling against asphyxiation. Each word germinated slowly within him before his pasty mouth was able to deliver it. He conceived of himself as opaque, colossal, disembodied, eternal, annihilated, infinitesimal...The stars were falling into the ocean, consciousness was falling into nothingness. Rhymes. Nothing rhymes with nothing. He closed his eyes, the better to think of himself as dead, and was surprised to hear himself speak from a long way off, from the beyond. He opened his eyes with a decisive effort. Mr. Brown was delicately prizing the revolver from his hand. No more revolver, of no importance, I'm not an executioner. A thing to be proud of in an age of executioners, even if it's the last thing! Bruno asked, "Are you...from...from the Party?"

"Naturally," Mr. Brown replied. "I acted under orders, please believe me."

Bruno shrugged his shoulders. Heavy, heavy shoulders, what were they still carrying? The burning in the marrow of his bones was past endurance, the hammer blows in his chest were slowing, no less violent but widely spaced; between one beat and the next a crack opened—an abyss—these are the last...Noémi sleeping, the ocean, the ocean...He slowly slumped sideways, mouth gaping, fringed with specks of froth.

It was really heavy, this big body, made for a long and regrettable life. Mr. Brown moved over to make room for Bruno, pushed him a little, helped him to lie flat, arms outstretched, watched him sink into oblivion, eyes wide open. Mr. Brown was trembling in every limb. He swallowed some pills and went out to breathe the electric night air. Panting, he dragged the big body onto the terrace and laid it out, still warm, under the dulling glimmers of the sky...After this, Mr. Brown washed his hands with eau de cologne.

■

Although Mr. Brown—who had become Mr. Brown only for the purposes of this short journey to the ends of obedience—had played his part in certain events, assisted in the destruction of many men, and adopted more than one unsavory disguise before now, he really was not cut out for this kind of assignment, better described as a dangerously reckless adventure, however refined its methods and means. The greatest danger is that which one creates oneself, through an excess of nervous tension; the malignities of chance are thus compounded by an adverse factor which should never be underestimated. While Mr. Brown was personally acquainted with bloodshed thanks to his experiences in another hemisphere, notably under the favorable conditions of Spain and the Balkans, he had been tempted to forget this fact ever since his professional duties had begun to coincide with his personal inclinations. His natural temperament, belatedly brought to the surface by contact with bourgeois society, disposed him to appreciate creature comforts, regular habits, hobnobbing with intellectuals and academics, taking trips through the best-organized country in modern society...As a fake U.S. citizen, he had involuntary assimilationist tendencies; a few years more in this undercover persona and he would become an almost-real U.S. citizen, which would be something of a problem. His abilities equipped him to be of genuine service in two related areas: the collection of hard, indeed scientific, information, and the exercise of a profoundly political influence upon Protestant intellectuals. To risk such gains for the sake of this particular mission could prove a grave misjudgment, should anything happen to him. Putting these reasons squarely before Mr. Ostrowieczki did no more than to reinforce a cast-iron decision that had been taken at the highest level. Ostrowieczki replied that no one was irreplaceable, not in a well-organized service. "In former times, esteemed Comrade, in Sofia..." Thus certifying his comprehensive knowledge of the other man's history, Ostrowieczki moved smoothly on to the technicalities. "According to our sources, the local circumstances are extremely propitious...Nothing can or will happen to you, provided you carry out your instructions to the letter. The scheme includes a number of possible variations...Unfortunately, personnel is rather limited at present." This might be true; it could also be the case that Mr. Brown (whose alias was something else at the time of the interview) was considered due for a test, to make sure he was not sliding into the complacency of taking his Americanization too much for granted...Mr. Ostrowieczki calculated lavish travel expenses. "The call we are making upon your dedication represents the highest honor." Mr. Brown had no choice but to manifest his gratitude.

The plan had gone without a hitch. The bottles lay at the bottom of the lake, while in the kitchen stood a couple of perfectly innocent substitutes. The poisons were recent and obscure, prepared in laboratories that were yet more obscure and would elude the average toxicologist (even if the autopsy were conducted at once). Mr. Brown's identity was proof against two months' investigation, and should any inquiry eventually spell trouble for the real Mr. Brown, presently in Honolulu, that was too bad; he would never know the truth . . . Now what, start the motor and slip away before sunup? Mr. Brown entertained this thought for a second. It would look suspicious, and besides, Mr. Ostrowieczki had stressed the desirability of postmortem pictures for the archives (newspaper clippings would do in the case of having fallen back upon plans A or B). Lastly, the old man—or rather the authentically young man—awakening in Mr. Brown's soul enjoined him to "face the music," which was the most sensible course of action and easier to carry off than he had anticipated, in view of the nervous hysteria that overwhelmed him without clouding his judgment.

He paced his room like a caged animal, like certain condemned men as they wait out their last hours. Sweat drenched his body; next his flesh felt so desiccated that he seemed to be burning up. Waves of nausea came, and he was glad to disgorge what had been an overrich meal. A diabolical doubt now took hold: Had he perhaps drunk something of the extra-special vintage? Blood draining from his face, he went back over his recollections of the dinner. Impossible. But what if . . . But there'd be no problem, if . . . Confounded America, overcivilized despite its brutalities, how it spoils one for the rough life of our times! This appalling malaise could only be caused by nervous shock which, although humiliating, was useful. Mr. Brown ripped the lining of his dressing gown with satisfaction. He took two potent sleeping pills, checked the mess of the room, assuring himself of his discipline and willpower. The drug was already working its divinely sedative effect when he remembered the revolver he had taken from Bruno Battisti. (So who could he really be, this "Bruno Battisti"? Oh well, none of my business . . .) He managed to wipe the gun carefully and carry it out into the middle of the coffee fields. But he was unable to shut the door on his return and collapsed, snoring already, onto the cool hard mat at the foot of his bed.

When Mr. Brown regained his senses, it was broad daylight. The room had been cleaned up. A native serving girl was changing the cold compress on his forehead. "*Gracias!*" he said. "Where am I?" The bewilderment was not entirely feigned, because on sinking deep into slumber he had genuinely thought he was dying, dying happily, it was fantastically great to die while falling asleep... Harris's ruddy snout rose before him like the moon—or like one of those huge gangster faces on a movie poster. Terribly severe, with a jaw like a hanging judge and eyes like an executioner! He was saying, "There's only one good medicine in my book. Take a drink, old man!" The voice was full of tenderness. Mr. Brown made no objection and swallowed a shot of whiskey, which happened to be just the right medicine. "Thank you!" he said, stretching. He pretended total amazement. "What's happening? What are you doing here, Harris? What time is it?"

"Congratulations, pal!" said Harris. "You've come back from a long way off. Bring him some hot broth, quick," he ordered the maid. "And tell Don Gamelindo he's OK... The lousiest day of a lousy world, my friend. But at least for you it's the first day again, and all is well..."

Harris turned around, rubbing his hands together, flushed with relief.

Don Gamelindo's huge sombrero loomed in the doorway silhouetted against the light. Mr. Brown turned pale with thoughts of the police, his fingers fluttered nervously against his throat. Harris said impatiently, "Buzz off, Don Gamelindo, he's over it ...Don't come in...Take care of the padre."

"All's for the best in the best of all worlds..." sang like a jolly jig at the back of Mr. Brown's head, in the most remote convolutions of his gray matter. If the priest is here, that means immediate burial! The salty broth the servant brought in tasted wonderful, especially when compared to the broth of the drowned. "Let me take your pulse," Harris was saying. "You know I studied medicine in New Guinea..."

"How was that?" asked Mr. Brown foolishly.

"A tale too long to tell. Your heart's fine, archaeologist. Too bad. You'll still be able to go on measuring idols' assholes..."

"That's enough," said Mr. Brown, suddenly sitting up. "Now tell me what all this is about? I overslept, and then what?"

He pretended to try to get out of bed, a movement promptly checked by Harris's robust hand.

"Hey, not so fast. You're supposed to take it easy... Dr. Harris's orders... You've had a brief illness which might have been pretty serious, and was, in fact, more than serious for some people... Do you understand?"

"No."

"Well, all in good time. Meanwhile: bed rest, stewed fruit, glass of beer... Did you hear that, Ramona? Pronto!"

There hung only one shadow over Mr. Brown's speedy recovery. He kept glancing at Harris's blunt face, admiring his features deformed by bitterness, the way he dried the welling tears before they overflowed, swelling his hairy nostrils, chewing on something with dull ferocity, all the while acting jovial, tender, fraternal. "How happy he would be to kill me," reflected Mr. Brown, tranquilly. "And he'd be right."

■

Everything is simple in this land of incandescent sunshine. Just a while ago there was drought, the suffering of a thirsty world. Then compact clouds the color of menace advanced over the Laguna, hiding the mountains... The tension is broken by a thunderclap. Warm fat raindrops begin to lash the water gently and raise a mist of dust across the fields. And then a million liquid javelins fall. This is the way things happen. Suddenly. Another time, on the road to Pozo Viejo, a courting couple dashed for shelter under the only nearby tree, a cypress half a dozen centuries old. The rain was pelting down. The lovers clung together, wrapped in the boy's serape. It might have excited their desire, but they were not to be married before the feast of San Pedro. How good it feels, they whispered laughing. A white ball of fire tore through the ancient foliage, drew the sign of the serpent in black upon the trunk, and rebounded off the couple. When the families came to collect the bodies they found them holding hands, both half burned: he the left side, she the right. They nailed two crosses to the old tree. They wrote the names: Ponciano (the rest illegible) and Cristina (the rest torn off), "Pray for their souls." They were fine, good-looking youngsters. Christians. Such is life. *Así es la vida.*

Thus the drift of Don Gamelindo's half-conscious meditation, at the end of a harrowing day. Singularly saddened, grotesquely attired in black for the occasion, satisfied at having been of great service—without charge—because somebody had to organize things. Cars had bumped along the potholed road; horses ridden by half-naked boys (happy to have been entrusted with important missions) had galloped through the sweltering noon. You see it was like this: At around seven in the morning Don Gamelindo had been awakened with the news. By eight he was on his chestnut horse trotting toward Pozo Viejo to fetch Dr. Rigoberto Merino in his gray gabardine jacket, felt hat, and maroon boots, astride his proud Arabian, a bay mare worth three thousand piasters, Señor!... Dr. Merino spent more time in consultation with the servants than on examining the remains. Ramona explained that a can of olives that had been opened for last night's dinner was at least a year old; three years ago, in her home village, several people had expired after consuming a tin of salmon, *sí* Señor! Melita—too-short skirt revealing muscular knees, sweat in the crease of her arms, wide puffy neck, small teeth pertly aligned in prominent gums—had heard of many similar cases, which she recounted. Dr. Merino interrupted her in order to take a professional look at those gums, brushing the nipple of her breasts with a hypocritical hand as he did so. He summoned her for next Sunday morning, after his regular office hours, for she was evidently suffering from a lack of certain vitamins. Melita promised to come without fail, sneaking velvety glances at him in between sniffles, dabbing her eyes and mumbling, "*Santísima Virgen, Virgen purísima...*" Before filling in the death certificate, the good doctor had the foresight to collect his hundred piasters from Don

Gamelindo. "Struck down by virulent food poisoning" et cetera, in a careful calligraphy decorated by the great flourishes of the signature. Don Tiburcio, San Blas's town chairman, who had hastened over still wearing his mechanic's overalls, countersigned the certificate without reading it—because he did not know how to read. Nonetheless, he asked the doctor: "Nothing suspicious, compadre?" The embarrassment of this little man with the noble Nahua profile laboriously tracing the letters of his signature amused Dr. Merino. "What suspicions would you like there to be, *compañero?*" he replied in a superior tone.

Don Gamelindo rode back to San Blas to purchase the coffins personally, for this task could be entrusted to none but the most dependable friend. Don Cuauhtémoc's store, The Keys to the Kingdom, made sure to stock, along with ordinary coffins, a pair of deluxe caskets, big ones because a short customer can always be accommodated, whereas there's no way around the opposite problem, is there? To each his size in this world, but once inside there, a human being's got to have the room he needs! You can deny a man his rightful space in the sun, sir, but not in the grave! Don Cuauhtémoc knew that the Reaper tends to reap by twos, if not two the same day, then it's within the fortnight, take my word for it. The twin body boxes were made of good pine lumber logged on the far side of the lake, upholstered in gray silk and embellished with brass handles. Don Cuauhtémoc and Don Gamelindo discussed the price for a leisurely quarter of an hour, taking alternate sips of tequila, for its fiery taste, and Coca-Cola, for its refreshing one; courtesy of the seller, of course. The negotiations were hard-headed but amicable. "That's genuine silk, Don Gamelindo! Do you know how much real silk is fetching these days in town? No, you do not. Those brass handles, they don't make 'em anymore! These are my last from before the war, compadre!" By the third little glass, Don Gamelindo had won a reduction of forty-two percent. Had he held out for two more glasses, he might have obtained fifty percent. But while Don Bruno was his dear departed friend, Don Cuauhtémoc had been his compadre for the past nineteen years. It was a good bargain for both of them and one from which Don Gamelindo, out of friendship, took nothing.

A mule cart driven by boys who whistled and sang and chucked small stones at one another or skimmed them over the lake, making as many as six bounces, transported the deluxe caskets under a hard, festive sun.

Padre Maclovio, who had promised to come around four, trotted over on the back of his own mule, balancing the little suitcase with his vestments against the pommel of his saddle. He complimented Doña Luz on her improvisation of a simple altar in the dining room, where the two coffins lay open on the great table, surrounded by candles and flowers; such an abundance of flowers that their savage, heady scents masked the odor of corpses. It was a beautiful funeral, something rare in this parish where many poor folk and too many children die, but rarely people of means. To be fair, the Battistis were not rich, only comfortably off. A more active owner could have made himself a fortune out of that plantation.

Thoroughly estimable people, in any case: naturalized Italians who lived (or had lived...) quietly, never wronging a soul. Padre Maclovio was well aware that they were atheists, from reading too many books—the punishment of a fallacious science; but it is just that the Holy Church triumphs in the end, and it is just that her minister should intercede for the souls of hardened sinners. Once upstairs, these can do their own explaining.

Mr. Brown, whose recovery, quite possibly miraculous, made him the object of unanimous goodwill, faced up to the trying day with authentic courage—maintained by the alcoholic beverages and delicacies Harris made him ingest at regular intervals. He took several photographs of the deceased, promising to send copies only if the roll of film were not spoiled, as he had reason to fear it might be... "He that in life was Don Bruno Battisti" (as they say in this country)—the seasoned traveler, the indefatigable worker, the educated man, *culto*, the obliging neighbor—lay there, displaying a grave countenance of pacified strength. The dome of the forehead stood out, the acute convexity of imperfectly closed eyes concealed an enigma; the closed mouth suggested a faint expression of disdain. That's what Harris thought, at any rate, during the hours he spent gazing down at the pair of them, arms folded across his chest, eyebrows knit, concentrating on the two inanimate faces. Daria was beautiful. How could a woman who was no longer young radiate such a youthful beauty, blanched by an invisible frosting of snow, modeled out of purity itself? She was smiling—just barely. It's common for dead faces to smile, nothing but a muscular contraction apparently, but that glow of deliverance within the smile, where did that come from? Harris found the fragility of it echoed in the pale face of Noémi, who often stood next to him, chin in hand, huge eyes unmoving.

Her eyelids never blinked. Nothing about this sudden denouement had taken her by surprise, as though it were merely the fulfillment of her night's dream. When Doña Luz carefully broke the news to her, she accepted it with childlike simplicity. Except that she seemed to dry up then and there, like a plant that has consumed its last sap. "It had to happen, Doña Luz, I've been expecting it for so long! But why was I left behind, why?" The old woman regarded such prescience as a gift that came naturally to the simple-minded. "You must give thanks to God, my little girl," she said. "Oh no," Noémi said harshly, with a peculiar laugh.

The burial took place during the late afternoon, in the desert cemetery where the dead of some thirty families sent into the wild lay sleeping along with several of the plantation workers' children. It was Harris who insisted that the remains should not be moved to San Blas. "If I croaked here, I'd want them to put me to earth here too...They'd agree with me, you know they would!" The priest made no objection. Our perishable remains can rest anywhere, so long as the soul has been taken care of... It was an invisible resting place halfway up to Las Calaveras. A rugged slope climbing toward the sierra. The hillside contained pockets of soil which were impossible to farm, since they were deposited at random among sharp outcroppings of naked rock. Thus, a very big cemetery for a few scattered dead. Few crosses to be seen. A merciless sun quickly burned the flowers. Cactuses pushing up here and there. After the rains the field was covered in a glorious profusion of wildflowers, submerging the tombs, for this was only intermittently a graveyard! On All Saints' Day the families who came to share the midnight meal with their dead enjoyed an incomparable seclusion; their fluttering candles seemed closer to other stellar worlds than to one another.

Don Bruno's workmen dug a single pit. Padre Maclovio, in his white surplice, spoke the prayer. The women and children of the solitudes formed a speechless group. Monica and Doña Luz were supporting Noémi, who had no need of their support but who was murmuring, amazed, "Sacha, Sacha." (At moments she imagined that none of this was real, that Sacha would turn up by and by, as he always had throughout life... Why should he be there?) Thirty clay-brown faces, tragically concentrated, were massed behind the important people: Don Gamelindo, Mr. Brown, Don Harris, and the elegant doctor in his gray gabardine coat. The rites performed, Noémi cast the first spadeful of earth—since they told her to—clumsily, between the two coffins. Doña Luz, like an ancient fairy with sharp, dark features and a silver mane, told her: "On your husband's coffin, little girl" and guided her hand for the second shovelful. The oldest friend, Don Gamelindo, came next and acquitted himself like a true gravedigger—and what gravedigger could be better than the truest friend? He grunted "ugh" and the back of his neck turned crimson as he stooped to drive a spade deep into the dry, light earth. "*Adios*, Don Bruno!" The whole circle heard his authoritative voice and the noble, machine-gun clatter of earth showering onto wood. But now Don Gamelindo realized that he did not know Daria's first name, so he stepped back and wiped his face with a red bandanna so as to inquire it very quietly from Harris. Then, voice raised, he intoned "*Adios*, Doña María!" and once again the earth fell nobly. Mr. Brown's shaky shovelfuls made a stealthy sound, while Harris's, rageful, produced a dull thud. The peons finished the job off energetically. Vultures circled low in the pink sky.

Don Gamelindo, taking his leave, said humbly to Noémi, "If the Señora is considering selling her land, there's no one who would offer her a better price than myself."

"What are you talking about?" said Noémi, vaguely frightened.

"The Señora is not selling anything," said Doña Luz, squaring her thin shoulders.

Don Gamelindo kissed both women's hands: the strange white hand, the old brown hand. He swung into the saddle, saluted the onlookers with a gallant wave of his sombrero, reared his silver-studded mount, and made off at a high-stepping trot... The land will be sold off one day or another! I have plenty of time... Life is patience, money is patience, the land is patience! *Adios*...

Mr. Brown left one hour later, at nightfall. Harris and Monica walked with him as far as the road. A thin crescent moon was rising over the transparent lake. Harris, trying to be friendly, asked, "Will you be returning to Las Calaveras, Mr. Brown? You'd be most welcome at our place... It's not as comfortable as here, but..."

"I don't think so," Mr. Brown replied in a feeble voice. "Anyhow, my work here is done."

"The main thing is to get your strength back Señor... *Adios*, Señor," said Monica with emotion.

Mr. Brown let up on the clutch. The headlights projected their objective glare over the hellish little stone piles.

Harris enclosed Monica—softly resisting—in his arms. The crescent moon shimmered twice, in the sky and in the water. "Monica," he said in a deep, unknown voice, "Monica." The young woman felt, as never before, that he loved her. A pulsing surge of joy spread throughout her being. She saw his face disfigured by suffering, and lifted her own broad, dull, massive face toward it in calm exaltation. "If you want to cry, Harris, go ahead and cry...It helps." She felt a flash of anger harden him. "Me, cry? Are you kidding?"

Mexico, 1946

OTHER NEW YORK REVIEW BOOKS CLASSICS*

* For a complete list of titles, visit www.nyrb.com or write to:
Catalog Requests, NYRB, 1755 Broadway, New York, NY 10009-3780